SKY HIGH

To the memory of Joe Horsman

SKY HIGH

The Inside Story of BSkyB

Mathew Horsman

ORION BUSINESS
BOOKS

First published in Great Britain in 1997 by
Orion Business
An imprint of The Orion Publishing Group Ltd
Orion House, 5 Upper St Martin's Lane, London WC2H 9EA

A CIP catalogue record for this book
is available from the British Library

ISBN 0-75281-196-7

Typeset by Selwood Systems, Midsomer Norton
Printed in Great Britain by
Butler & Tanner Ltd, Frome and London

CONTENTS

ACKNOWLEDGEMENTS

This book would not have been written without the co-operation of one exasperating, exhilarating, difficult and remarkable man – Sam Chisholm, the departing chief executive of BSkyB. It is highly unlikely that he will entirely approve of it, but at least I hope he believes it has been written in good faith, and with care and respect.

This is not, in other words, an 'authorised' history of the phenomenon known as BSkyB. But it has been shaped and informed by the generous time Chisholm has consecrated to the project.

I am also indebted to Rupert Murdoch, who agreed to speak on the record about his British broadcasting interests. His daughter, Elisabeth Murdoch, also agreed to grant time for an interview. David Chance, the deputy managing director, was unfailingly co-operative. And I owe a debt of gratitude to Richard Brooke, the finance director, for his patience and good humour. Many others at BSkyB, not all of whom can be mentioned, gave openly of their time, and I wish to thank them here. They include: Deanna Bates, Nick Carrington, Trevor East, Samantha Eaton, Ray Gallagher, Chris Haynes, Kevin Kinsella, Bruce McWilliam, Peter Shea, Chris Towsend, Vic Wakeling, Sue Ward, Ian West, Mark Winterbottom and Alexandria Wight. A special thanks must go to Gerry Robinson, the chairman of Granada and of BSkyB. The former chairman of BSkyB, Frank Barlow, was especially generous with his time, as was Richard Dunn, who was a witness not only in the early days but, in his role at News Corporation, to the most recent events at BSkyB. David Elstein provided key insights into BSkyB's development and British broadcasting generally. Both Dunn and Elstein graciously agreed to read the manuscript, saving me from some real howlers.

Outside BSkyB, I am indebted to many at the BBC, Carlton, Granada, Pearson, Flextech, Arsenal FC and the Football Association, whom I may not name. I am eternally grateful to John Birt, Barry Cox, Greg Dyke, Michael Grade, Michael Green, Bruce Gyngell, Janice Hughes, Roger Luard, Kelvin MacKenzie, Bob Phillis, Bill Roedy, Peter Rogers, Sir George Russell, Adam Singer, Joyce Taylor and Ward Thomas. Generous help was also provided by Roy Addison, Stephen Barden, David Cameron, Bob Doulson, Dick Emery, Bruce Fireman, Mike Gardner, Ian Hood, Nicola Howson, Janie Ironside-Wood, Denise Lewis, Catherine May, Christine Mitchell, Roger Morris, Sally Osman and Liz Roberts.

Thanks are due, as well, to Marie Dyne, who transcribed so many of the interviews on which this book is based, to the information department of Henderson Crosthwaite for critical research, and the library of the Independent Television Commission.

Over the time I spent covering the media for *The Independent* and for Henderson Crosthwaite, which has proved crucial to completing this book, I have developed a long list of debts. I wish particularly to thank Dawn Airey, Matt Baker, Geoff Brownlee, James Conway, Stephen David-son, Simon Forrest, Stuart Fraser, Chris Griffin Beale, Richard Holwood, Chris Hopson, Piers Inscape, Roger Laughton, Peter Law, Virginia Lee, David Montgomery, Steve Morrison, Nick Mearing-Smith, John Mul-holland, Ian Ritchie, Richard Saunders, David Simonson, Allison Smith, Dan Somers, Sarah Thane, Jeremy Thorpe, Gary Tongue, Peter van Gelder and Will Whitehorn.

In critical ways, Stuart Crosgrove, Brent Harman, Jim Hytner, Chris Rowlands, Malcolm Wall, Nigel Walmsley and Andrea Wonfor provided recent, important insights. A luncheon organised by *The New Statesman* in early 1997 afforded an opportunity to discuss some of what follows with Patricia Hodgson and Don Cruickshank. An intense dose of 'mediatalk' at the *Guardian* Edinburgh International Television Festival in August 1997 was highly germaine to the themes of the latter chapters of this book. My heartfelt thanks go to Charlotte Ashton.

There are many others I would dearly have loved to interview had time permitted. It is perhaps only of journalists that publishers would demand such tight deadlines.

At *The Independent*, I owe a huge debt of gratitude to Jeremy Warner, the City Editor, and to Ian Hargreaves, former editor (now editor of *The New Statesman*), and to my many colleagues, past and present, but particularly Nic Cicutti, Mary Fagan, Chris Godsmark, David Hellier, (who kindly read portions of the manuscript) Colin Hughes, David and Vicky Lennon, Andrew Marr, Andrew Marshall, Philip Robinson, David Robson, John

Shepherd, Patrick Tooher and John Willcock. At Henderson Crosthwaite Institutional Brokers, I want particularly to thank Louise Barton, the media analyst's media analyst, and Perry Crosthwaite and Brian Newman, particularly for their understanding of a writer under pressure. I owe a debt of gratitude, too, to David Potter, head of Guinness Mahony, Henderson Crosthwaite's sister company.

Among my long-suffering friends and family, who got used, finally, to missed dinners, late arrivals and lame excuses, I'd like to say sorry to David Benedict, Colette Camil, Nic Coward, Katelijne De Backer, Pierre Denieuil, John Dunton-Downer, Leslie Dunton-Downer, Georgia Glynn Smith, Brian and Angela Hall, Barbara Holloway, Cassandra Horsman, Debbie Mason, Doris Mills, John Murray, Debbie Phillips, Ashley Rountree, Jordan Rountree, David Sturgess, and Simon Waldman. Particular thanks must go to Nancy Horsman, for watching a son go quietly mad in front of a computer screen during what should have been a summer holiday.

I am grateful to my agent, Felicity Bryan, for excellent advice as always, and to Martin Liu, at Orion Publishing, for pulling off the impossible (and for commissioning the book in the first place).

All these people, in some form, are responsible for those bits of the book that entertain, inform and illuminate. For the rest, and for any errors it still contains, the fault is completely mine.

Mathew Horsman
London, October 1997

A note about sources. As this is a contemporary history, there are few published records of any description. I am grateful to my former colleagues in the media for their excellent work at *The Independent, The Independent on Sunday, The Financial Times, The Times, The Sunday Times, The Guardian, The Observer, The Daily Express, The Daily Telegraph, The Sunday Telegraph, The Economist, Campaign, New Media Markets* and *Broadcast*. Invaluable material was made available by the BBC, Ray Gallagher and all those who cannot be named who provided internal documents. The early story of BSB was written by Peter Chippindale and Suzanne Franks, *Dished! The Rise and Fall of British Satellite Broadcasting* (London: Simon & Schuster,

1991). Sam Chisholm's views on business were published as part of Martyn Lewis, *Reflections on Success* (London: Lennard Publishing Ltd, 1997). A recent book on British television is Raymond Snoddy, *Greenfinger: The Rise of Michael Green and Carlton Communications* (London: Faber & Faber, 1996). An idiosyncratic but sometimes useful book on Murdoch is William Shawcross' *Rupert Murdoch* (New York: Chatto & Windus, 1992). On the early career, there is the excellent Georg Munster, *Rupert Murdoch: A Paper Prince* (London: Penguin, 1985). Various publications of the UK government have also been useful, particularly the Office of Fair Trading, *The Director General's Review of BSkyB's Position in the Wholesale Pay TV Market* (December 1996). Andrew Neil's autobiography, *Full Disclosure* (London: Macmillan, 1996), covers the early days of Sky.

CHRONOLOGY

1978: Sky Television created.

1983: Rupert Murdoch buys Sky Television.

December 1986: licence awarded to British Satellite Broadcasting.

June 1988: Murdoch announces Sky TV in the UK.

February 1989: Sky launches.

April 1990: BSB launches.

September 1990: Sam Chisholm joins Sky after 25 years at Australia's Channel Nine.

November 1990: BSB and Sky agree to merger.

March 1991: £200 million refinancing at BSkyB.

August 1991: high-stakes talks with studios lead to lower contract fees for movies.

March 1992: BSkyB reaches operating profit for the first time.

May 1992: BSkyB signs exclusive £304 million pay-TV deal with Premier League.

December 1992: David Elstein joins BSkyB from Thames.

February 1993: Reed sells stake in BSkyB; books £40 million loss.

September 1993: multi-channel package scrambled.

December 1993: BSkyB shareholders get first pay-out.

January 1994: Kelvin MacKenzie joins BSkyB.

April 1994: BSkyB completes £500-million refinancing; owners get partially repaid.

August 1994: Kelvin MacKenzie leaves BSkyB.

August 1994: BSkyB unveils record £93 million profits.

October 1994: BSkyB signals intention to float.

December 1994: Sky float values company at £4.4 million; executives share out multi-million pound pay-out.

March 1995: cable launches campaign to rein in 'Murdoch monopoly'.

March 1995: BSkyB agrees informal undertakings with the OFT.

May 1995: subscriptions top four million.

August 1995: BSkyB profits climb to £155 million.

August 1995: Pearson announces intention to sell BSkyB stake.

September 1995: Pearson earns £492 million from BSkyB sale.

November 1995: BSkyB signs Endsleigh League TV deal worth £125 million.

December 1995: OFT announces inquiry into BSkyB's supply of cable.

December 1995: Granada and BSkyB to develop new channels.

December 1995: the great sport broadcasting debate begins.

February 1996: Elisabeth Murdoch joins BSkyB as general manager.

March 1996: four-way German alliance announced with Bertelsmann.

March 1996: 660,000 tune in for Bruno–Tyson boxing match.

June 1996: BSkyB wins new Premier League deal for £670 million.

June 1996: BSkyB reaches Twickenham deal.

July 1996: BSkyB exonerated in OFT inquiry.

July 1996: BSkyB switches to Kirch as German digital partner.

July 1996: BSkyB to add 11 new channels.

August 1996: David Elstein decamps to Channel 5.

August 1996: BSkyB profits soared to £257 million.

August 1996: BSkyB competes with Flextech to win BBC joint-venture business.

October 1996: Murdoch announces mortgage of BSkyB stake.

October 1996: cable merger unveiled: C&W CableComms to become new industry leader.

October 1996: Elisabeth Murdoch made head of programmes.

December 1996: OFT clears new rate card for cable.

December 1996: Oftel vows to ensure fair and open access in digital era.

December 1996: Chisholm tells Murdoch privately that he wants to step down.

January 1997: Granada and Carlton join BSkyB to bid for DTT licences.

March 1997: plug pulled on German digital deal.

March 1997: Oftel guidelines published.

March 1997: Flextech reaches final deal with BBC.

May 1997: BSkyB announces formation of BIB, its digital services joint venture.

June 1997: BSkyB forced out of BDB consortium, which is then awarded the DTT licences.

June 1997: BSkyB announces both Chisholm and Chance are to leave; the share price drops.

PERFORMANCE CHARTS

BSkyB: Years ending 30 June

	1991	1992	1993	1994	1995	1996	1997
Revenues	93	233	380	550	778	1,008	1,270
Profit/loss	(759)	(188)	(76)	93	155	257	314
No. subs	1.2m	2m	2.4m	3.4m	4.1m	5.5m	6.3m
Debt	2bn	1.8bn	1.4bn	1.4bn	1bn	715m	670m

BSkyB Share price since flotation

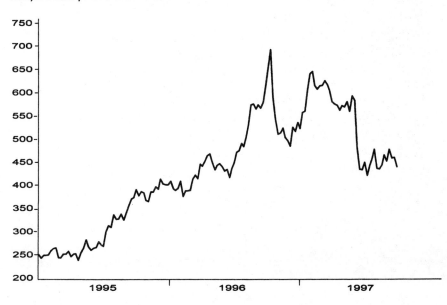

Source: DATASTREAM

CAST OF CHARACTERS

News Corporation
Rupert Murdoch, chairman
Andrew Knight, chief executive, News International
Andrew Neil, editor, *The Sunday Times*
Peter Stehrenberger, News International lawyer
Lachlan Murdoch, chief executive, News Limited, Australia
Richard Dunn, head of non-US TV interests (formerly chief executive of Thames Television)
Mark Booth, chief operating officer, JSkyB (later chief executive, BSkyB)
Bruce McWilliam, lawyer (specialising in BSkyB)

BSkyB
Sam Chisholm, chief executive
David Chance, deputy managing director
Richard Brooke, group finance director
Elisabeth Murdoch, general manager, broadcasting and head of programmes
David Elstein, head of programmes (formerly head of programmes, Thames Television; later chief executive, Channel 5)
Gary Davey, joint managing director (later head of Star TV)
Pat Mastandrea, joint managing director (until 1990)
Nick Carrington, chief financial officer
Vic Wakeling, head of sports
Trevor East, executive director of sports
Deanna Bates, legal affairs
Ray Gallagher, corporate and public affairs
Peter Shea, sales director
Ian West, director of digital and business development

Kelvin MacKenzie, managing director (later head of Mirror Group Television)

BSB (pre-merger)
Anthony Simonds-Gooding, chief executive
John Gau, head of programmes

The BSB shareholders
Frank Barlow, managing director, Pearson (and later chairman, BSkyB)
Ian Irvine, director, Reed International
Peter Davis, chief executive, Reed International
Jérôme Seydoux, chief executive, Chargeurs
Michel Crépon, executive vice-president, Chargeurs (later Pathé)
Richard Branson, chairman, Virgin
Gerry Robinson, chairman, Granada
Alex Bernstein, former chairman, Granada

TCI–Flextech
John Malone, chairman, TCI
Fred Vierra, head of UK development
Adam Singer, executive chairman, Flextech
Roger Luard, chief executive, Flextech
Brent Harman, managing director, Flextech
Joyce Taylor, director, Discovery Europe

The BBC
Sir Christopher Bland, chairman of the board of governors
John Birt, director-general
Bob Phillis, deputy director-general and head of BBC Worldwide (later chief executive, Guardian Media Group)
Jonathan Martin, head of sport
Patricia Hodgson, head of policy and planning

Channel 4
Michael Grade, chief executive

ITV
Gerry Robinson, chairman, Granada
Charles Allen, chief executive, Granada

Greg Dyke, London Weekend Television (later Pearson Television)
Ward Thomas, chairman, Yorkshire–Tyne Tees
Bruce Gyngell, managing director, Yorkshire–Tyne Tees (formerly chief
    executive, TV-Am)
Michael Green, chairman, Carlton Communications
Nigel Walmsley, director of broadcasting, Carlton Communications
Lord Hollick, chief executive, United News & Media
Barry Cox, director, ITV Association

The Regulators
Sir George Russell, former chairman, Independent Television Commission
Peter Rogers, chief executive, ITC
Sheila Cassels, finance director, ITC
Don Cruickshank, director general, Oftel

INTRODUCTION

British Sky Broadcasting (BSkyB), the UK's leading pay-TV company, rev-olutionised British media in just seven years. Thanks to its pioneering efforts, households that once selected from among the four national channels, BBC1, BBC2, ITV and Channel 4, could choose from more than 40, with news, educational programming, children's channels, travel, soaps and – crucially – sport and Hollywood movies. From losses of £14 million a week in 1990, BSkyB made more than £300 million in pre-tax profits in the financial year ending 30 June 1997, or nearly £10 a second. With revenues exceeding £1.2 billion, and with more than six million subscribers on satellite and cable, BSkyB was, by far, the country's most profitable broadcaster, and one of Britain's top 20 corporations.

In the process, BSkyB made a fortune for its shareholders, not least global media mogul Rupert Murdoch, its 40 per cent shareholder, who bet his entire empire (newspapers like *The Times* and *The Sun* in Britain, TV networks in the US and Australia, magazines around the world, even a Hollywood studio, Fox) on this one, highly risky venture. It confounded those, particularly among traditional British broadcasters, who thought it could not be done. It introduced to the UK TV sector the clever practices used by Murdoch in his other media companies, and the informed and effective marketing strategies that all broadcasters have since had to follow. It disrupted what Murdoch called 'the comfortable duopoly' of the BBC and ITV, long used to divvying up the broadcasting spoils (notably top sport) between them. The rise of BSkyB even helped force the mighty BBC, the public service broadcaster financed by a mandatory, universal licence fee paid by all TV owners, to refashion itself as a commercial player in the marketplace. The very existence of a pay-TV alternative in the UK threw into deep doubt the BBC's special claim on the leisure budget of the nation's consumers. Most fundamentally of all, the success of BSkyB proved a point that many in the industry had long believed: television in Britain was too cheap.

Murdoch himself talked openly of giving the consumer what he or she wanted, and of breaking the hold traditional, elitist broadcasting had on Britain. Says Murdoch: 'When it was suggested to have a second ITV [in the late 1970s], they went for an upmarket choice – Channel 4, and this simply extended the monopoly. This was, I believed, enormously vulnerable to attack. So all the time, I was looking for a way of giving the public an alternative.' His alternative was Sky TV (and later, after a controversial merger with its only competitor, British Satellite Broadcasting, BSkyB).

Murdoch and his executives made a success out of Sky because they were populists, trained in a newspaper culture. They came of the school that knew you had to prove yourself every day in order to ensure that people bought your product. The content had to be right, and it had to be right nearly all the time. That ethos was adopted in Australian television as well – not surprisingly, since it was that country's press barons who emerged as major owners of TV stations there.

Traditional British TV media executives did not think that way. Mainstream broadcasters were safe and serene in their individual, protected franchises, while cable operators spent more time fighting amongst themselves than co-operating to create a new market for pay-TV. Says Adam Singer, executive chairman of Flextech, the pay-TV channel operator, and one of the earliest investors in the UK cable industry, the mainstream broadcasters 'had spent the 1980s in denial about what the new media was going to be about. In exactly the same way that the British motorcycle industry saw its first Honda, [broadcasters] could not imagine that this [pay-TV] was nemesis, and because they could not believe it, they thought it was a joke'.

BSkyB also flourished because it broke the rules, or at least ignored their spirit. To the pioneer goes the title to fresh lands. In this case, those lands were outside traditional broadcasting, so much on the outskirts as to be ignored and even disdained by those living in town. BSkyB's market was brand new – £1 billion worth of spending that the mainstream broadcasters had lacked the imagination and the courage to tap. BSkyB was a trespasser, but no one had previously claimed the ground that so enriched Murdoch and his partners. Not so much a trespasser, then, but a squatter, seeing value in occupying space left vacant by those who preferred more normal digs, for which they held long-term leases. ITV rented its accommodation, with the lease all drawn up and proper; BSkyB was an owner-occupier, answerable to no landlord save itself.

The success of BSkyB made the reputation, as well, of the company's departing chief executive, the once-obscure Antipodean TV executive, Sam Chisholm, the one man, other than Murdoch himself, most closely identified with the incredible rise of Sky. Until Chisholm – short, blustering, and a television man through and through – broke with Murdoch, in a rift that speaks volumes about the attitudes and characters of both executives, they were one of the most effective shareholder–manager teams in British corporate history. By the end, with Chisholm poised to step down, the messy question of succession at BSkyB (not least the future role of Elisabeth Murdoch, the media mogul's younger daughter, and a senior employee at the company), coupled with Chisholm's whispering campaign to ensure he won proper credit for his seven years at Sky and Murdoch's own sniping about BSkyB and its prospects, began to sour what had been a close association.

The ructions of mid-1997, as a new management team prepared to take over at BSkyB, should not be allowed to obscure one of the most compelling business tales of recent decades. Without a doubt, the rise of BSkyB was Britain's corporate success story of the 1990s. How was it done? What took BSkyB from basket case to unprecedented dominance? And, in light of the tensions that came to the fore in the wake of Chisholm and Murdoch's dissonance, could it last? Critics of multi-channel television, and of Murdoch's iron grip on the pay-TV sector in the UK, point to loose regulation, compliant politicians and Murdoch's ruthless use of his extensive UK newspaper empire (ranging from the downmarket *Sun* to the broadsheet *Times* and *Sunday Times*) to promote his TV interests. Why, for instance, was Murdoch's Sky, the first full-service, UK-oriented satellite broadcaster, allowed to 'merge' with British Satellite Broadcasting (BSB), its only competition, in 1990, with barely a whimper from regulators and with what many believe was the connivance of the BBC-hating Thatcher government? Why was BSkyB allowed to dictate terms to the country's cable operators, who were forced to pay high prices to get Murdoch's film and sport channels? Others bemoan the lack of serious competition from Britain's cosseted traditional broadcasters, in particular the regional monopolies of ITV and the slow-moving, bureaucratic BBC, the country's public sector broadcaster. British home-grown television is on par with the best in the world; but the commercial instincts of the media industry were sorely under-developed. Traditional broadcasters themselves ought to have known how to develop a multi-channel, pay-TV service, using the best of British drama, comedy and current affairs to compete with the sports, film and imports schedule of mighty BSkyB. Despite some tentative steps, which might, in the end, bear fruit, none has yet done so.

Most professional media practitioners concede, however, that good (if at times ruthless) management, just as much as luck and weak regulation, helped power BSkyB's growth. The top executives, led by Sam Chisholm, proved they could second-guess the competition with amazing accuracy, routinely wrong-footing rivals. Key to Chisholm's ability was a network of friends and contacts in sport, the broadcast media and the press. He astonished his competitors with the depth of his knowledge of the marketplace, and his seemingly unerring sense of timing.

Chisholm, viewed by some as suffering the Napoleonic syndrome of small men ('a Kiwi James Cagney,' says one former Sky executive), also benefited from his ruthless reputation. Even those who had never met him feared him. That reputation proved useful time and time again to middle-ranking executives at Sky. 'When we came to an impasse in nego-tiations, we merely had to suggest that Chisholm would come to the table and the other side would often crumble,' says one insider. Chisholm was also not above using threats to get what he wanted, and was never more dangerous than when he was thwarted. Insiders recall the time that Sue Barker, then a commentator with Sky Sports, was 'lent' to the BBC for their coverage of the Wimbledon tennis championships. To Chisholm's fury, the BBC's head of sports, Jonathan Martin, convinced Barker to sign a full-time contract at the public service broadcaster, and she went on to become the BBC's 'face of tennis' and a host of *Grandstand*, the weekend sports digest. Chisholm rang Martin and warned: 'You don't cross me in this town. Everybody is afraid of me, and of what I will do.' In this case, Martin was warned he would not, under any circumstances, be able to win the broadcasting rights to Formula One motor car racing, then under negotiation. (Chisholm was a close friend of Bernie Ecclestone, the head of Formula One.) And indeed, for whatever reason, the rights went instead to ITV. 'You don't get stung by the same bee twice,' Chisholm told his colleagues about Martin's manoeuvre.

The prospect that a senior BSkyB commentator would be poached by another company came up again, in 1997, and this time, Chisholm vowed he would not be thwarted. Vic Wakeling, head of sports at BSkyB, knew that Andy Gray, the former Everton footballer and more recently the 'voice' of Premier League coverage on Sky, would heed the call to go to

Everton as manager if asked. Gray, whose best days as a player had been at Everton, was very sensitive to the charge that it was easy to make comments on television but harder actually to manage a football team on the field. Everton approached Gray in mid-1997, with a lucrative offer, considerably more than he was making at Sky. (Newspaper reports at the time suggested £200,000.) Wakeling told Chisholm about the bid, worried that he would lose his key commentator. Chisholm knew how important Gray was to the organisation, although privately, he admitted that he couldn't understand Gray's Scottish brogue half the time. Chisholm swung into action, telling Gray not to make a decision quickly. Why not wait until after his holiday, and then come to Chisholm's flat in Hyde Park for a chat? Meanwhile, Wakeling briefed Chisholm about Gray's situation at Sky. The key card BSkyB could play was loyalty: Gray would not leave his mates in the lurch. Chief among them was Andy Melvin, a producer of Sky Sports' football coverage, with whom Gray was very close. As agreed, Gray returned from a golfing holiday, and went round to Chisholm's flat. His agent was barred from attending, much to his annoyance. Chisholm offered a sharply higher financial package, although not as much as Everton had been discussing. He also talked about Gray's importance to the broadcasting world, and how he was the ultimate interpreter of what was going on out on the field. Gray was moved, and agreed he would stay. Chisholm called his lawyer, Bruce McWilliam, who was on stand-by around the corner. A contract was drawn up, and the three men witnessed the final agreement. After the fact, Gray's agent complained that he had not been consulted. Chisholm had been firm, however: 'I don't want any agents involved,' he had told Gray. Despite Chisholm's success in keeping Gray, the chief executive had been nervous. 'It was touch and go,' he told Wakeling later. 'I thought I might be losing my touch.'

Personalities did count in the extraordinary tale of BSkyB's rise. But clear-headed strategy was also key. The company, supported by Murdoch's other businesses, relentlessly promoted the sale of satellite dishes; invested in new technology for the set-top boxes needed by satellite subscribers to receive the Sky signal; marketed the channels with some of the most sophisticated campaigns yet developed for the media; built from scratch the country's best subscription management system ('Sky Television at your service,' intoned the Scottish women who answered the help line in Livingston, home to Sky's service centre dedicated to handling problems for Britain's 4.3 million satellite TV subscribers); and realised that television could be a commodity like any other. There are lessons, here, for those who can read them.

Films and football, and more particularly the Premier League of top soccer, the rights to which BSkyB first won in 1992, were the making of the company. Only top sport and Hollywood films could drive dish sales in the UK, and selling satellite receiving equipment was the crucial first step toward creating a functioning market for multi-channel television. The renegotiation of the Hollywood movie contracts following the 1990 merger of Sky and its only competitor, BSB, took more money off the US studios than anyone had ever managed to do outside a courtroom. Later, the heady weeks of negotiation leading to the exclusive Premier League deal in 1992 were complex and nerve-wracking. The contract, worth £304 million over five years, made live Premier League games available exclusively to Sky subscribers, forming the foundation on which the rest of the pay-TV service was built. The UK cable operators, still struggling after more than a decade, were obliged to buy Sky programming on onerous terms, as even they recognised that film and sport were the only proven drivers of multi-channel TV.

The football deal was the anchor to a new strategy at BSkyB, one that was to prove a veritable money spinner. The key was to 'encrypt' the whole of the Sky service, and make everybody pay a basic subscription fee to receive even the formerly 'free' channels. It took months of negotiation with outside channel operators to transform the multi-channel satellite business into a financial success.

BSkyB saw off regulators, charmed (some say hoodwinked) government ministers, and rebuffed sniping from frustrated cable operators – the only other distribution system, so far, with the capacity to compete in pay television. No one would pay £300 a year (well more than three times the mandatory, universal TV licence fee for the BBC) to watch sport and movies, the critics said. Yet by 1997, satellite and cable viewers in four million homes (those who took the full Sky package) paid that and more. People wouldn't stand for pay-per-view, they said. Who wants to pay for individual programmes on top of already high charges for subscription television? Yet 660,000 forked out £9.95 or £14.95 to watch Frank Bruno get massacred by Mike Tyson in the world heavyweight title in March 1996, and 420,000 coughed up for the follow-on match between Tyson and Holyfield, when there wasn't even a British boxer in the ring. Soon thereafter, three other pay-per-view boxing matches scored moderately well – certainly compared to the take-up rates of similar events in the US.

But then, who wouldn't have made a success of Sky, some of the company's rivals complained. Kelvin MacKenzie, the former editor of *The Sun* and for a few raucous months a senior executive at Sky, was blunt: 'Once there was a monopoly in pay-TV, a black rat could have run the show.' Like most rivals, of course, MacKenzie had an axe to grind. He left Sky to become managing director of L!veTV, the cheap and cheerful cable station that Mirror Group, its owners, hoped would grow into a national network of local city-TV affiliates. And his anger was very personal. He fought seriously with BSkyB's Sam Chisholm during the brief tenure at Sky and nursed a few wounds.

Murdoch, at any rate, had a healthy respect for Chisholm when he hired him in 1990, and (the late-stage tensions notwithstanding) certainly ensured that he was paid for his pains. Chisholm, who shared Murdoch's infamous (and calculated) disdain for the English, received at least £25 million in salaries, bonuses and shares from Murdoch in just seven years – enough to build a beach house near Sydney, to buy a ranch in Southern Australia and to fashion a *faux* Roman villa for his daughter, Caroline, a journalist in Australia.

But MacKenzie was right about one thing: BSkyB emerged as a monopoly player in a new market, able – at least until the late 1990s – to dictate terms and prices with near impunity. By buying up the rights to key programming, BSkyB in effect became the main wholesale supplier to the cable industry, and the dominant player in the direct-to-home satellite market. It appeared to have the support of the Conservative government, which resisted all efforts to rein in Sky – for instance, by imposing taxes on its super-normal profits – in the 1996 Broadcasting Act. Even the Office of Fair Trading, the competition watchdog, seemed relaxed about BSkyB's dominant position in the marketplace, leaving it free to grow and grow. Consider that no other part of Murdoch's pay-TV empire – not the US, not Asia, not South America – could match BSkyB's profitability. The combination of factors in the UK – few terrestrial channels, weak regulation, disorganised competition and a philosophically compliant government – obtained nowhere else in the Murdoch universe. Witness the trouble Murdoch had in the US, with his direct-to-home satellite aspirations. He was forced, finally to abandon plans to develop a separate direct-to-home digital TV service, called ASkyB, and accept a non-voting position in Primestar, a rival DTH system controlled by Time Warner and other cable companies – a retreat that Murdoch himself concedes was humiliating.

Murdoch well knew how conducive a philosophically compliant government could be. In 1986, a few months after he moved his newspaper titles to Wapping, in the East End of London, breaking the grip of the print unions once and for all in Britain, he was asked by Bill Cotton, a senior BBC executive, when he would do the same thing with his newspaper in New York. 'Are you crazy?,' Murdoch responded. 'Britain's the only country in the world where the police protect you in this kind of situation. In New York, they would just walk away.'

Yet despite Murdoch's undoubted success in the UK, there were already signs by 1997 that the tide might have been turning. New rivals – such as Cable & Wireless Communications, the result of a four-way cable and telephony merger – appeared on the horizon. The new Labour government, elected in May 1997, began to take a harder line. Doubts surfaced over whether the company's key programming rights to film and sport (football above all) could be secured into the digital age, as rights holders themselves woke up to the value of their franchises. The digital revolution, and its promise of hundreds of channels, interactivity and greater competition, was likely to prove a sore test for BSkyB. By late 1997, the company was girding itself against sharper regulatory scrutiny and more competition from other broadcasters and distributors, who were, it appeared, finally learning to use some of the tactics BSkyB itself had pioneered in the pay-TV market. BSkyB was facing the two Rs: rivals and regulation.

More troubling for BSkyB, the two men most closely associated with the company's phenomenal success, Sam Chisholm and his number two David Chance, were poised to quit the company, in a shock announcement in mid-1997 that helped wipe £2.5 billion off the company's stock market value. Could their successors manage the transition to digital? The announcement of Chisholm and Chance's departure came amid signs of a serious rift with Murdoch and the possibility that the media mogul, aware of his advancing years, was intent on putting his own daughter, Elisabeth, into the top job (she had already become head of programmes at BSkyB). US investors, particularly, were spooked by the apparent nepotism, and were in the vanguard of those who sold their shares in June 1997, when the departures of the two senior men were confirmed. 'Americans don't like nepotism,' Sam Chisholm himself told colleagues.

Despite these signs of weakness, some in the British broadcasting industry continued to see BSkyB as the devil. It helped that 40 per cent of the company was owned by Murdoch, the much-demonised media baron. But they blamed Sky for more than just its ownership: BSkyB had lowered the tone of British television, and had run roughshod over a slew of gentleman's agreements (thou shalt not poach another station's star programming by bidding more money, for instance). Worse, some members of the intellectual elite of television found the management at BSkyB uncouth: 'Not one of us'. And no one more so than the man who set the tone at Isleworth, BSkyB's utilitarian headquarters – Sam Chisholm.

Chisholm, on the verge of retirement, was relaxed about the sniping, although he clearly resented some of the more personal attacks. On BSkyB's monopoly position, his answer used to be: 'Anybody could have done what we have done: only Rupert Murdoch had the guts.' Later, as tensions between the two men rose, Murdoch won less of the credit from Chisholm, who worked incredible hours in the Murdoch cause, despite suffering from a serious respiratory disease, only to lose, in the end, his master's patronage.

In the pages that follow, the rise of BSkyB, and its recent falterings, is documented objectively for the first time. From a highly indebted fledgling company in the early 1990s, haemorrhaging freely, to the behemoth of today, BSkyB's story is as much about the changing face of television as it is about one corporation. It is about how Britain went from just four channels to 40, from Reithian certainty to market chaos. It is about soaps, cop shows, top football and bad US dramas. It is about Television Without Frontiers, deregulation, money and power.

About power above all. The power of the individual, of Murdoch himself, the master strategist, the ultimate risk-taker, the man who, despite his anglophile upbringing (and his Oxford degree), dismisses the English with the wave of a calculatedly outsider hand. The power of a government whose leader, Margaret Thatcher, saw citizens as individual consumers, unconnected to community, and whose world view was so beautifully matched by Murdoch's own relentless pursuit of money. 'There is no such thing as society,' Mrs Thatcher famously intoned. For the buccaneering Murdoch, intent on breaking the grip on British television maintained by the BBC and the commercial broadcasters, only to replace it with his own, the message was a welcome one. For Thatcher, Murdoch's willingness to attack those vested interests was equally to be applauded, particularly if it meant ending the vice-like hold on the nation's airwaves enjoyed by a liberal cabal at the BBC and spendthrift monopolists at ITV. Mrs Thatcher brought a group of broadcasters to a brainstorming session at 10 Downing Street in 1987, to discuss how British television could be reformed and become more competitive. It was more a lecture than a discussion: she had already decided that the strong broadcasting unions, and their generous benefits and work practices, must be broken, and she told the shaken executives as much. She was already inclined to change the comfortable, subjective basis on which ITV television licences were awarded to incumbent broadcasters, and replace it with market-driven 'highest-bidder-wins' rules. The ITV men did not know what they were in for. As they left her office, she peered out the window to the street below. 'Look at them all, climbing into their chauffeur-driven cars,' she said to an aide. How she must have longed for a Murdoch.

It was, in part, a marriage of political persuasion (Thatcher's) and commercial ambition (Murdoch's) that paved the way for BSkyB's success. The commercial television industry in the UK had been a carve-up: a series of cosy monopolies. Thatcher and Murdoch both knew that outsiders with money, sound management and strategic vision could take on the inefficient traditional broadcasting business, and could probably win, particularly if the government provided a regulatory framework, or indeed the lack of one, that gave outsiders an edge.

The story is also about the power of Murdoch's own near-monopoly: following long-established form, he fought hard to encroach on an existing, cosy market, only to defend his own territory once he had achieved the high ground. And about the power of sound if aggressive operational management, best exemplified by the dogged, determined, even bloody-minded commitment of Chisholm, like Murdoch an outsider in British media, to the company he helped turn around. And about the power of television itself, so pervasive a medium, so inclusive at its best moments (creating a commonality of experience that informs and sustains democracy); so fragmenting, too, in the form of niche broadcasting and the pay-per-view revolution that would one day allow us to watch more or less what we wanted, when we wanted, but at huge cost to social cohesiveness and collective experience.

This book is, above all, about the people – the outsized egos, the highly paid managers and their rows and strategems – and the way they conducted their business in the crucial seven years from Sky's inauspicious launch in 1989. Rupert Murdoch himself – feared, respected, loathed. Sam Chisholm, a man with a colourful vocabulary, rough charm, quick temper, astonishing focus, and a chip on his shoulder about the English (particularly the educated English). Chisholm's number two, David Chance, the smooth, earnest and deadly negotiator, the former satellite man (he cut his corporate teeth as UK marketing manager at Luxembourg-based satellite giant Astra) whom Chisholm turned to for details too mundane for the chief to remember. Elisabeth Murdoch, 29 – blond, striking, hard as nails (like father like daughter?), bright, with an ability to listen as well as to dispose. One insider says: 'She is incredibly cocky for someone who still has so much to learn about the television business.' Another warns: 'Don't underestimate her; she knows precisely what she is doing.' In many eyes, she was the heir apparent, not only at Sky but at News Corporation, her father's master company.

Outside Sky, the cast of characters is huge: senior executives in the cable industry, who may still manage to move their companies into direct competition to Sky, hustling for Hollywood film output deals and bidding up the price for cable and satellite programming. Or Roger Luard, the voluable showman at Flextech, the pay-TV packager, who snatched a joint venture deal with the BBC from under the nose of Murdoch and Chisholm, who themselves had desperately wooed the public service broadcaster. The regulators are crucial to the story: Don Cruickshank, of Oftel, whose job it was to regulate access to the brave new world of digital TV; or Sir George Russell, the now-retired head of the Independent Television Commission, and perhaps the man with the longest memory and the bluntest tongue in the industry.

In what follows, all conversations are based on the recollections of those present. As with any company run by men as ruthless, secretive, even Machiavellian as Rupert Murdoch and Sam Chisholm, there is usually more than one version of events. But through the scores of interviews upon which this book is based, a picture emerges of the way Sky was built, and the path it is now likely to take. Inside, we get the truth about the much rumoured falling out between Chisholm and Murdoch over the arrival of Murdoch's daughter, Elisabeth, to a senior job at Sky. We hear of Chisholm's health problems, the tensions surrounding his departure, his buccaneering management style, his growing rift with Murdoch, his abusive phone calls to rivals and journalists who displease him. We track the painstaking work done by Sky to herald the launch of digital television: the agonising negotiations about programming, satellite distribution and the setting of a digital standard for the set-top boxes viewers would need to gain access to the world of 200 channels. We learn just what went on that fateful Sunday in May 1995, when BSkyB suddenly all but bowed out of the running for the new Channel 5 licence, in one of the most unex-pected U-turns in recent memory. Or how Sky was exonerated over charges of anti-competitive behaviour during an Office of Fair Trading inquiry in 1996. In the end, we learn how a multi-billion pound company was built from the modest base of an industrial estate in down-at-the-mouth Isleworth, West London, and how its rise fundamentally changed the British broadcasting landscape. Just as tellingly, we see how a company that seemed at its height to be soaring inexorably skyward could have been brought so abruptly to back to earth.

The story of BSkyB is the story of an industry, a management team, new technologies, even new social forces. It was a company born in the Thatcher years, and it shows. Its success was due to breathtaking risks, light regulation and an uncanny knack for knowing just how much (and for what) viewers were willing to pay. British television has been radically transformed as a result. Here's how.

PROLOGUE:

The Guy From Sky

The astonishing news hit the newswires shortly after 7.30 am, 17 June 1997. Sam Chisholm, the 57-year-old chief executive of BSkyB, Britain's leading pay-TV broadcaster, would step down at the end of the year. It seemed to everyone even remotely connected to the media in Britain to be an announcement of huge significance. For many, BSkyB and Sam Chisholm were inextricably linked, and it was hard to fathom a future for the pay-TV broadcaster that did not include the short, blunt, bullying, indefatigable New Zealander. It was, in every way, the end of an era.

BSkyB's share price dropped, and the rout grew more impressive once it became clear that Chisholm's number two since 1994, David Chance, a younger, more temperate, but equally driven man, was also on his way out. Could BSkyB survive the departure of two of the executives (Rupert Murdoch must get credit, too, of course, alongside a number of senior managers, past and present) who made BSkyB into the corporate success story of the decade? And was the departure a sign that Murdoch was to take a more hands-on approach at BSkyB, either directly or through his daughter, Elisabeth, who, since early 1996, had held a senior position in the company?

Chisholm, in the top job since 1990, had seen BSkyB through its incredible turnaround, and positioned it for the high-risk move into digital television. He had implemented the merger of Murdoch's Sky and BSB, its pay-TV rival, and helped turn deep losses into operating break-even within just 18 months. He had been instrumental in signing up the Premier League of top football to a controversial and lucrative exclusive broadcasting deal. He had led the team that renegotiated the onerous deals that BSkyB's predecessor companies (Sky and BSB) had signed with the Hollywood studios for the rights to show movies on a subscription basis to UK audiences. And now, just as BSkyB was embarking on the fraught task of migrating its hugely profitable business from the analogue to the digital era, he was stepping down. Suddenly, the British media community would be without the man they had come to view as a quintessential part of the rapidly changing landscape of their business.

'Well,' he said to a media analyst on the morning of his resignation. 'That's it.'

Isleworth, barely on the edge of what most people would consider London, is vivisected by roads, badly served by public transport, but not far from the capital's Heathrow Airport. At an industrial estate called Centaur's Park, next to the Gillette Building on the A4 trunk road, sits the headquarters of Britain's most profitable broadcaster.

Just in front of the hangar-like buildings that house the studios and most of the offices of BSkyB is a newer building, called Athena Court. Inside the wide foyer of the main entrance, over the reception desk, hangs a large electronic bulletin board, revealing the BSkyB share price in real time, and the number of calls being handled by the company's cutting-edge subscription management service in Scotland. It was here that Sam Chisholm, the company's chief executive, had his headquarters.

His large office was designed by Anouska Hempel, the 1970s actress-turned-designer, whose calling card was the original, idiosyncratic Blake's Hotel in London. There was, amazingly, never any sign of paperwork, and certainly never a computer, in Chisholm's office. But on his desk lay one of the chief tools of his trade: the telephone. Like his one-time mentor Rupert Murdoch, Chisholm, routinely garbed in expensive Langevin suits, used the phone like a weapon, ringing contacts, gossiping with old friends, berating rivals, journalists and his own executives. Throughout the day, senior executives would come and go, assembled without warning for an impromptu meeting with the boss. Under Chisholm, BSkyB had one of the flattest corporate hierarchies of any major company. At the top, there was Chisholm himself, whose self-avowed policy was to 'delegate and then interfere'. At his side, even on long holidays, was usually David Chance, the former marketing director whom Chisholm promoted to the effective number two slot in 1994, whose knowledge of BSkyB was encylopedic, and whose energy was the match of Chisholm's. Chance had been with Sky very nearly since the beginning. In later years, he and Chisholm were practically inseparable. The two men decided virtually everything at BSkyB, and all the other senior executives answered directly to them. In negotiations, Chance was calmer but just as focused and relentless. It might have seemed a stifling life for Chance, whose public and private moments were completely dominated by Chisholm for virtually the whole of his career at BSkyB. But Chance appeared to do it willingly, at least until early 1997, when stomach pains telegraphed a biological warning that he could no longer ignore.

The circumstances surrounding the building of Athena Court tell a great deal about BSkyB and about Sam Chisholm. The property developers who owned the Isleworth complex had begun to build the addition without a word to BSkyB. They had assumed that the company, growing so quickly as it was, would be the obvious tenant in the new building. Chisholm watched with interest as the construction proceeded, and charted the progress each time his chauffeur-driven car deposited him at the office early in the morning. When the developers finally contacted BSkyB to offer the space, Chisholm told them no. And for months thereafter, the building remained unlet, until Chisholm finally relented, and offered to pay a risibly small rent. The desperate developers gulped, and accepted.

There are four other places Sam Chisholm liked to work. In his chauffeur-driven car (why waste time?), in the Enterprise pub in Walton Street, Chelsea (often in the company of his lawyer Bruce McWilliam, who worked for News Corporation and BSkyB), in his luxury flat in Hyde Park Square, London and at what everyone at BSkyB called 'the Farm', a palatial estate near Basingstoke, Hampshire, boasting an elegant facade and a car park big enough to receive the cars of the whole of the senior team at BSkyB. A good thing, too, as executives (ranging from marketing chief Jim Hytner to sales executives Peter Shea to David Chance and legal affairs chief Deanna Bates) were routinely asked to make the drive down to the Farm for brainstorming sessions.

Chisholm was always at the end of a telephone, wherever he happened to be. Supported by two full-time personal assistants, he was always at work, even while vacationing in the south of France or fishing off the coast of his native New Zealand. He was often in the company of his close friend Sue Ward, a publicity consultant at Sky, who had joined him from Channel Nine, the network he ran for mogul Kerry Packer in Australia, and his second-in-command, David Chance, usually accompanied by Deanna Bates, BSkyB's head of legal affairs.

The key to understanding Chisholm is to appreciate his incredible stamina. Despite a respiratory disease (he says asthma; others, including Rupert Murdoch, believed it to be emphysema), he worked long days, weekends, even bank holidays. He cut out the smoking when the disease became more threatening (although some claimed to have seen him light up even after he had formally quit), and in England he drank less – far less – than he had in Australia, where a day might have included a four-hour lunch and visit to the bar before returning to the office (and still he arrived back at Channel Nine early the next day).

A tale (unlikely to be apocryphal) has it that Chisholm used to fly to New York for English bank holidays because he could not stand the sight of empty roads, and no one working. His other chief characteristic was his reliance on instinct, rather than rote. He cared little for spreadsheets or research reports, or long strategy papers. 'It was in his gut,' says one of his sports executives. But above all, business for Chisholm was about winning. 'Sam's brashness or bullying or whatever you'd like to call it comes from that innate desire to win,' says Bruce Gyngell, the leading Australian broadcaster who worked with Packer and Chisholm at Channel Nine, and who later came to Britain to head the team that saved TV-Am, the morning ITV licencee, from financial ruin.

Chisholm's power emanated from his position as chief executive of Britain's fastest growing company. By the time he retired after seven eventful years, he had become, astonishingly, a member of the very broadcasting elite he so openly disparaged. He was not a typical British media executive (how could he be, given his Antipodean origins?), but he was every inch a television man. Unusually, he actually watched the medium, as often as he could. Not for him the rather precious view espoused by many in British media ('Television? I may make it, but I never watch it, darling'). He cared deeply about the look of Sky – from the on-screen promotions, to the boot room coverage of football and rugby, to the satellite feeds on Sky News, everything.

It was hard to imagine for those whose dealings with Chisholm were confrontational that he also had a sense of humour, even a rough charm. Bob Phillis, former deputy director general of the BBC and before that chief executive of ITN, the news provider for ITV and Channel 4, recalls a phone call from Chisholm, when Sky News was trying to decide which news supplier to use to supplement its own 24-hour service. Recalls Phillis:

'He said, "Bob, I'd like to come and see you for a brainstorming session".
I said, "What about Sam?" He said, "About ITN and Sky working together
on news." And, so, Sam arrived, with a few colleagues, and I had [senior
managers] Stewart Purvis and Richard Tait and a number of my colleagues
in the room there. And we sat there and [Chisholm] said; "Right, I rang
Bob up and I asked for a brainstorming session and these are the rules:
you've got the brains, I've got the storming".'

Many people did not see the charming side of Sam Chisholm. In negotiations, he could be threatening and abusive. In business, he was ruthless
on the attack and devious in retreat. Says a senior Sky executive: 'Sam uses
strength when he has strength and charm and humour when he doesn't.
Since he is in a stronger position than 85 per cent of the people he deals
with, he usually uses strength.' Still, he seldom stayed angry for long, and
was more likely to point out the 'mutual benefits' of a given deal rather
than browbeat his adversary into submission. Recalls David Elstein, head
of programmes at BSkyB from 1992 to 1996: 'He'd show a glimpse of steel,
and then go back to the velvet.' But was he really dangerous? Could he
cut short careers? He said so himself, and liked to think so. Realising
how powerful BSkyB had become, many believed him. Others, however,
believed the bark was worse than the bite. 'Strike back every time, that's
the way to deal with Chisholm,' said one broadcasting executive who
dealt extensively with BSkyB. Chisholm certainly appreciated bluntness,
and hated nothing more than English politeness. At a meeting with a
young independent producer in 1992, to discuss plans to make a promotional film for Sky Sports, he asked her: 'How much is it going to cost
me?' The producer said she would have to go back to the office and draw
up a budget. Chisholm started kicking her legs under the table, and said:
'When I ask for something, I expect to get it.' The producer kept her cool,
responding: 'Well, whatever it was, it has just doubled. And don't you ever
fucking kick me again.' She got the contract.

He made quick friends with those who spoke their mind, provided they
had something to say. He rated intelligence, because he had a fair quotient
himself. He tested people, constantly. It was a favourite trick to claim he
knew someone was crossing him, even if he had no real proof. He found,
more often than not, that his bluff was not called, or that he had been
instinctively right. He gave the impression of being omniscient and omni-
present. Middle-ranking Sky executives were always cautious on the telephone, because the rumour had gone round that Chisholm had tapped
all the phones (a suggestion vehemently denied by BSkyB management).

The press relations office of BSkyB was a joke throughout Fleet Street. No one but Chisholm could speak authoritatively about BSkyB, and the hapless press officer who might be quoted as a 'Sky spokesman' in the newspaper would get a dressing down when the story appeared the next day.

One favourite way of spooking his executives was to call at odd hours – just after a promo had run late at night on Sky 1, for instance, or very early in the morning, after the newspapers had arrived at Chisholm's London or Hampshire homes. He gave the impression of always being at work by ensuring that his two PAs could patch through calls to wherever he was. And he had Britain's most extensive list of home phone numbers. When he wanted to talk to someone, he could, he bragged, always get straight through. One was meant to be in awe of Chisholm: of his stamina, of his instincts, of his all-seeing, all-knowing management style. He wasted his honed act even on trade journalists and media correspondents – men and women who could not have had the slimmest effect on his business. Every slight meted out to Sky in the pages of even the least respected trade journal was likely to ignite a broadside from the chief executive's suite. Such calls would always start in a normal tone, quiet, even pleasant. The volume would increase with the incidence of bad language. By the end, there was often an explosion of sheer, unadulterated venom, punctuated by the shortness of breath that accompanied his respiratory disease. A minute later, Chisholm would calm down, and suggest to the journalist in question that, the next time a story about BSkyB might be contemplated, why not call him directly?

Chisholm clearly liked the cut and thrust of debate; even liked jokey, competitive banter – the kind you hear mostly in the pub after the third round. But when it came to business, he did not like being contradicted in public. The best place to win a debate with Chisholm was in private, when he was not performing to the crowd. Getting him alone, however, was not easy: he felt exposed without an entourage. *The Independent* asked for an interview in late 1995, at the height of the debate about sports on British television, when there was a chance the list of 'protected' sporting events reserved for terrestrial free television would be extended. Chisholm, unusually, agreed to the interview, realising he needed to defend Sky's huge market presence in broadcast sports. *The Independent* correspondent (me) arrived at Isleworth expecting a traditional interview with the chief executive, in the presence, perhaps, of a public relations officer, only to be confronted by a team of five senior Sky executives. Chisholm did nearly all the talking; the others were there merely for comfort.

Chisholm liked to be right, but was willing to admit when he was wrong. His first deal with Don King, the boxing impresario, was pitched far too high: Chisholm had been in awe of the man. He tended to be in awe of power and titles. He subsequently sent Trevor East, from Sky Sports, to renegotiate the contract. He sometimes appeared to pay too much for programmes, for instance for a multi-part series based on the Bible. But he was right most of time, especially when it really counted.

Chisholm's most powerful tool of all was his focus. He could keep several, often conflicting, agendas in his head at one time, never wavering from the ultimate goal. But he was willing to change tack suddenly, even retreat altogether, no matter how much work had already been done on a given project. To those used to more settled corporate cultures, he appeared mercurial. Sometimes, important matters were left unresolved until they grew into mini-crises. Then, suddenly, it was all action at Isleworth. But it all worked, somehow. There were mistakes, but generally not on the issues that really mattered for BSkyB.

Says Richard Dunn, formerly of Thames Television, and later based at BSkyB to develop Murdoch's non-US TV operations: 'The underside of it could sometimes be deeply unpleasant and genuinely counterproductive. I never minded being castigated or sworn at by Sam but I did mind when he would go for a junior minion, people who didn't know how to defend themselves and then dismiss them as fleas.'

Chisholm was a man much influenced by the two media moguls who figured so hugely in his 30-year television career. The first was Kerry Packer, son of Frank Packer, the scion of the family dynasty that dominates media in Australia. Packer and Chisholm worked together for the crucial early years of Chisholm's rise in Australia, in a kind of (sometimes uneasy) partnership. While Packer was always the boss, Chisholm himself created a virtual kingdom at Channel Nine, the national Australian TV network where he first made his mark.

The other great influence was, of course, Rupert Murdoch. The two men had a lot in common. They even sounded similar, and not only because they shared an Antipodean accent. Whether by chance or by long association, both men drawled out the word 'no', with a slight, rising intonation at the end. It was a tone one usually reserved for remonstrating young children. Both men, too, liked to lower the volume suddenly at the end of sentences, dropping into a conspiratorial near-whisper. They shared a rough vocabulary, with plenty of 'bloodys' and even stronger epithets.

And they both dotted their speech with the phrases, 'I promise you', when they wanted you to believe them, against the odds, and 'I suspect' to indicate strong convictions politely masquerading as doubts.

The two men shared, too, a buccaneering approach to corporate strategy. Richard Dunn says: 'I once asked Sam, "What is the strategy here?" and he said: "It's the options Rupert's got in his hand this morning". It's invigorating and risky and you make mistakes, inevitably; you've got so many options you're discarding all the time. So sometimes you lose a really good opportunity. But more often than not they got really good things in their hands and boy, did they play the cards well.'

In a day-to-day sense, Sam Chisholm was undoubtedly in charge at BSkyB. He was backed by a strong team of professionals, and was more reliant than he liked to admit on the accountants, consultants and advisers working at Isleworth. But only a very small circle (as small as Chisholm, Chance and McWilliam) knew everything. He was required, of course, to accept direction from Rupert Murdoch, the 40 per cent shareholder (50 per cent before BSkyB was floated on the stock exchange in 1994) and, crucially, the man with the official power, at least until BSkyB was taken public, to appoint the company's chief executive. But once BSkyB was a listed company, and had entered the FTSE-100, the index of leading British companies, in 1995, Chisholm had his own power base. That did not always sit well with Murdoch. Nor did the two men always agree on strategy and tactics. Chisholm was not averse to throwing his weight around: he must have been one of the few Murdoch executives able to stand up, at least recently, to the boss.

In the end, while the timing of his departure was his own, Chisholm may not have been able to cling on much longer even if he had wanted to. In the past, when relations between them were at their warmest, Murdoch publicly hailed Chisholm as one of the world's great TV executives. By the time Chisholm had agreed to leave, Murdoch's praise was more muted. 'I don't want to take away from Sam, he's a very effective executive but he is as territorial as hell,' Murdoch says. 'He calls the plays, and he gets it right more often than not. The problem is, he plays favourites, and he frightens people. He is a frightening man. He plays people off each other. But the combination of Sam and David together was fantastic. Sam likes to say that he is the thinker, and David is the doer, but David does a lot of Sam's thinking for him. Sam will give a rip-roaring speech, and then David will spend 20 minutes explaining it all. That's how they worked together so well.'

Chisholm's speeches were famous within Sky. He had a few common themes on which he routinely expounded. His problematic relationship with the English was one; his at-times disparaging view of the BBC, Britain's public service broadcaster another. After a few meetings with Chisholm, you began to recognise the set-pieces. 'Our deal with the Premier League [of football] is one of the great corporate romances of all time' was one riff, often repeated.

If Murdoch was cooler about his chief executive, concerned perhaps by Chisholm's increasing independence, and the tensions between him and Elisabeth Murdoch, other British TV executives paid warm tribute upon Chisholm's announced departure, even if most saw him as a bit of an unpleasant customer. 'Sam is amazingly able to hit the buttons, he knows just what matters,' says Gerry Robinson, chairman of BSkyB and of Granada, one of BSkyB's biggest shareholders after Murdoch. 'He is an excellent team motivator, and there is an awful lot of affection for Sam, despite everything. Underneath it all, he has taken them down the right path and they have all, individually and collectively, done well.' Roger Luard, chief executive of Flextech, the pay-TV company that has emerged as a potential rival to BSkyB in pay-TV programming supply, says: 'You choose a horse for the race. At certain points in the race you need a Sam Chisholm who's just going to bulldoze through all the bullshit, and take things head-on and he's an incredibly good man manager. Okay, it's a mixture of bullying and kindness, but ultimately, he gets the best out of his guys.'

Michael Green, the media-mogul head of Carlton Communications, rates Chisholm 'a very able manager, and you must not underestimate him. He proved that the public would pay for multi-channel television, and that they wanted more choice. He understands television, all aspects'. Even Greg Dyke, the head of Pearson Television, who as chairman of the sports committee of ITV was bested by BSkyB in the high-stakes bidding for the rights to the Premier League of top football in 1992, is grudgingly complimentary: 'What Sam will be given credit for is sorting it out on a daily basis.' Michael Grade, formerly chief executive of Channel 4, and later executive chairman of First Leisure, concludes: 'I like Sam, I get on very well with him, very very well. I wouldn't trust him an inch on a deal.'

But whatever the contributions of Sam Chisholm to the success of BSkyB (and they were, by any measure, huge), the real risk at the start was Rupert Murdoch's, who bet his extensive interests in global media on this one business: pay-TV in Britain. At least in the early years, Chisholm was a hired hand. It was Murdoch who exercised the real power, and laid one of the biggest bets in British corporate history.

PART ONE
Murdoch's Billion-Pound Bet

CHAPTER 1

A Gleam in His Sky

By 1997, Rupert Murdoch, arguably the world's best known media baron, owned an impressive array of US, UK and Australian newspapers, magazines, an Internet company, a US television network, a Hollywood studio, a book publisher – in short, a global media empire. But building it on the strength of an Australian publishing group, inherited in 1952, from his celebrated father, Sir Keith Murdoch, had not been easy. Two brushes with financial disaster accompanied his risky efforts to expand around the globe. Murdoch built his empire on a mixture of charm, ruthlessness, risk-taking, bravura and relentless energy. He was Machiavellian, an inveterate gossip, vain and even a little insecure. But his grasp of the sprawling business empire he constructed over 40 years was absolute: no other executive at News Corporation, his master company, knew precisely how it all worked together.

Many of the key investment decisions he took seemed not to follow any preconceived pattern. His global business was built as much on opportunism as on carefully plotted business plans. However, on at least one front – television – Murdoch was wholly consistent. He passionately believed that there was a natural road to follow from newspapers to broadcasting, in Australia, in the US and in Britain.

But Murdoch had long been frustrated in his attempts to win a position in British broadcasting. In 1969, shortly after he had bought the *News of the World* and *The Sun*, his flagship tabloid newspapers, he was already actively looking for a way of moving into TV. In his home country of Australia, the rules on cross-media ownership were restrictive (he would eventually manage to win control of a clutch of TV stations, only to be forced to divest some of his holdings when the rules were tightened). In the US, he was more successful, but it took the radical step of becoming an American citizen to cement his empire there. In the Britain of the

1960s, the relevant legislation was astonishingly vague, speaking only of the need for TV licences to be owned by individuals or corporations resident in the UK. The issue of cross-media ownership was subject only to 'public interest' tests, not specific, detailed regulation. Murdoch sensed an opening, and soon found one.

London Weekend Television, which controlled the ITV franchise at weekends in the capital, had run into huge financial difficulties by 1969, a year after it had won a six-year licence, hurt particularly by the competition for advertising revenues mounted by Thames, the weekday franchise holder. Tom Margerison, then LWT's managing director, met Murdoch by chance in London in May that year, and suggested the Australian might wish to invest in the struggling company. By the autumn, LWT's financial worries were serious enough to divide the company's board, and outside directors began to tire of the endless bickering about the failures. Arnold (later Lord) Weinstock, the chief executive of mighty GEC, decided to sell his 7.5 per cent stake in LWT, and offered it to Murdoch. With the approval of the Independent Television Authority, which regulated ITV and which had wide-ranging powers including the right to take broadcasting licences back, the deal was sealed, and Murdoch immediately began to canvas other shareholders to see whether they, too, might wish to sell. The need for cash at LWT had become acute, and Murdoch offered to invest £500,000 in the under-capitalised company. The board agreed to issue one new share for each three existing shares; if shareholders did not take up their allotments, Murdoch would be free to do so. He ended up with nearly 35 per cent of the non-voting shares, and the right to attend executive meetings.

It did not take him long to make his presence felt. Within three weeks, Murdoch had engineered the firing of Margerison, and announced that he would chair the executive committee. He began to interfere in programming decisions, and hinted at wholesale changes in the LWT schedule. The ITA issued an ultimatum in February 1970: LWT would have to submit programming proposals to the regulator; a managing director and programming controller must be named; and Rupert Murdoch could not become managing director of the company.

An angry Murdoch, who had decamped to Australia, told a local interviewer that the LWT troubles were 'all a bloody storm in a teacup'. Why should the ITA interfere on programming decisions?, he thundered. After all, wasn't that what managing directors were for? David Frost, the celebrated TV interviewer and a co-founder of LWT, interceded at this stage, suggesting that a compromise outsider candidate be named to head the company. His choice: John Freeman, former editor of *The New Statesman* and a diplomatic appointee of Harold Wilson to both India and the US. Murdoch agreed, but he continued to take a keen interest in the company.

A young John Birt, now director-general of the BBC and then a documentary film producer at LWT, remembers meeting Murdoch at the time. 'I was brought into the company [after Freeman took over] and subsequently asked to fulfil a franchise promise to start a current affairs programme, which became *Weekend World*. This was a very dry, serious, analytical current affairs programme. [I was told] one day that we had to go and have lunch with Rupert Murdoch and Larry Lamb [editor of *The Sun*]. I had all the arrogance of somebody in my late 20s. And I was making this dry intellectual programme, trying to wrestle with the great issues of the time, inflation, wars, price shocks and so on. Over lunch [I was told] what was right or wrong with *Weekend World*. And I thought this was a bit preposterous – not a critique coming from the right direction. Rupert Murdoch didn't say very much at the lunch, but Larry Lamb offered his critique. And I was fantastically aggressive back. I stood my corner, I didn't accept any of his critique and it was a rather tense and dramatic lunch. Rupert Murdoch had [never] even seen the programme, but he plainly approved of the fact that I was being so feisty. And I can remember at the time thinking: "It doesn't matter what these people think. I'm a programme maker".'

Murdoch never won the control of LWT he coveted. By 1980, following a decade during which he concentrated primarily on his print media interests, he agreed to sell out, at a (modest) profit. In the interim, he had moved, more or less full-time, to the US, taking an apartment in New York City. Looking back, he concludes: 'We just weren't allowed into [UK] terrestrial television. That door was closed to us. I saw then how the system worked. The management were more interested in pleasing the [regulator] than the shareholders. And the [ITA] was made up of a cross section, but they were the great and the good, and had a huge bureaucracy and they just extended the [BBC–ITV] monopoly.'

Looking back on that period, Peter Rogers, chief executive of the Independent Television Commission (the successor regulator), says Murdoch was badly treated: 'There was always that feeling on Murdoch, and about the Canadians in radio and television [Lord Thomson, the Canadian press baron, had bailed out Scottish TV]. There was a feeling of recognition that people who had done so much for broadcasting were suddenly no longer acceptable as owners of it.'

For Murdoch, the world of British broadcasting was hopelessly elitist, comfortable, fat and content. Commercial television, from the beginning, had been structured as a series of regional monopolies, licenced by the government. The regulator held incredible sway; but then, so did programmers, who felt they, and not the shareholders, were in charge. Licences to broadcast commercial television were awarded on a highly subjective, clubby and opaque basis. The BBC, meanwhile, was a law unto itself. Never mind that British television was generally viewed as being some of the best in the world – far better, anyway, than the great cultural wasteland of the American variant. Murdoch wanted to come in, and the great and the good would not let him.

Murdoch's LWT experience convinced him that the alternative he was seeking had to be outside the traditional contours of the establishment. And what was more outside, more unexpected, than satellite TV – unregulated, flexible, commercial? Not just in Britain, moreover. In 1983, Murdoch bought a struggling US satellite operator, Inter-American, which he then renamed Skyband, and began scouring Hollywood for ways of securing the key content he needed for a multi-channel service. (In America, too, he would have had trouble buying mainstream, terrestrial TV stations, owing to strict ownership rules barring foreigners from holding TV licences. He would get around this in 1985, by becoming a US citizen.) Skyband was dropped only six months later, at a loss of $20 million, when Murdoch determined the risks were too high. He would not revive seriously his plans for a US direct-to-home service until the mid-1990s, when digital TV was launching.

Having studied the US cable industry, which by the early 1980s had matured into a huge and profitable business (although one, he thought, that had already become over-priced as an investment), Murdoch understood early that programming would be the chief driver. It was movies, particularly on the Home Box Office (HBO) network, that really powered the cable industry to its dominant position. But winning a serious foothold in content would prove difficult and expensive. In 1983, he tried to buy Warner, the Hollywood studio that subsequently merged with publishing giant Time, but was seen off by management after several months of jockeying. A joint venture to make films with Robert Stigwood, the impresario who had produced *Jesus Christ Superstar*, among other theatrical and recording projects, also foundered. Finally, in 1984, Murdoch took advantage of weaknesses at Fox, the film studio, to buy a 50 per cent stake, thereafter taking full control and adding six television stations to his US media empire. With his Fox purchase, he also acquired the services of Barry Diller, the Fox studio head, and one of the industry's most accomplished and cleverest executives. Together, the two men would build a US TV empire – until, that is, they fell out, as Murdoch is eventually wont to do with even his most trusted senior executives.

Murdoch's TV strategy was starting to gel. He had Fox in Hollywood, the embryo of a major US network (eventually becoming, in effect, the fourth national channel), as well as his Australian TV interests. But Britain was still, frustratingly, untapped. Throughout much of the early 1980s, Murdoch often travelled with a technology guru, Peter Smith, who would routinely answer the boss's questions about the complicated world of satellite TV – encryption, conditional access, billing and the like. Based on these informal discussions, which often took place in airplanes traversing the Atlantic, Murdoch began to formulate a plan for European TV. The key, he believed, was the technology. In the 1970s and early 1980s, receiving satellite signals required a huge dish, and the transmission standards were still under-developed. Murdoch knew he wanted to get into British television, and was persuaded he would never be allowed to own a standard terrestrial licence. But there was no obvious alternative distribution platform available, since high-powered, or even medium-powered satellites, from which relatively small dishes suitable for the home would be able to receive the signals, had yet to be launched. Still, even when the technology was in place, he would need a broadcasting company, although he would have to wait some years before hitting upon a distribution strategy that made commercial sense. In 1983, he found the broadcasting vehicle he had been looking for: Sky Television. He would have to wait another four years before he found the right distribution platform.

With little fanfare, Sky Television, then a pan-European, advertiser-funded service, owned by Satellite Television (SATV) in which Lord Brabourne had a stake, had been launched in 1978, using a test signal on a low-powered, telecoms satellite, and primarily servicing cable networks on the continent. The schedule was dominated by repeats of British programming and cheap American imports, which practically no one in Britain was watching. The channel, first developed by Brian Haynes, a researcher on Thames' *This Week*, had its headquarters in Grafton Street, London, and had been owned in its earliest days by Guinness Mahon, the merchant bank, and Trident, the UK entertainment company headed by Ward Thomas, the veteran UK broadcaster, whose company held the Yorkshire and Tyne Tees ITV licences. (After an hiatus of several years, Thomas, by then in his late 60s, would return to the industry in 1993 to become chairman of Yorkshire–Tyne Tees, and later chairman of the Granada–Yorkshire–Tyne Tees ITV combine.) Also a shareholder was Lord Romsey, son of Lord Brabourne, an early believer in satellite television.

The original licence for Sky had been for a so-called 'point-to-point' transmission, from Finland to Malta. This had been the only way Sky could easily get around the various and old-fashioned rules enforced by Europe's Post and Telecommunications (PTT) agencies, which had the early regulatory oversight of satellite transmission. The Finland–Malta connection gave Sky a 'footprint' that extended over much of Northern Europe, including Britain. Anyone with a big enough dish – and they had to be big – could receive the Sky signal. (As a result, most of the customers received the signal via cable, relayed from the satellite.) The only potential revenues would be from advertisers, as there was no way to 'encrypt' (or scramble) the service in order to charge subscription fees.

'It was a very small involvement in cash,' Thomas remembers. 'We serviced it and provided some executive management and I was the chairman, which Rupert [Murdoch] always acknowledges, and we started a programme service.' The schedule was uninspiring, and the company far from profitable. 'The truth is we did not know what we were doing,' Thomas concedes. 'I thought it was very exciting and had potential, but I had no means of measuring it because there was no way of knowing who the hell had got the power to receive the thing.'

As exciting as it was for Ward Thomas to be in on the ground floor of satellite television, he soon realised that there was no way to make any money out of it – certainly not on the levels of investment the partners were then prepared to support. 'We were really just doing it to have a service and to see what on earth you did with it,' Thomas recalls. 'We were fumbling around, not really being very clear as to how to develop it, spending a lot of time going around talking to the European Space Agency, looking at rockets and things. But having got into it for a year or two you suddenly realised that you had to have a lot of money behind it if you were going to develop this into something that was meaningful.'

In 1982, Thomas attended a board meeting at tiny Sky. 'You know we won't capture Europe on the budget of Border Television,' Thomas told his fellow directors in reference to one of the UK's smallest ITV operators. 'We have either got to put up or shut up.'

Guinness Mahon had no interest in ploughing significant cash into the venture. Trident, for its part, had reached a crossroads. In 1982 the government, through the Independent Broadcasting Authority, which had taken over from the ITA in 1972, declared that no company could own more than one ITV licence outright, although a holding of up to 30 per cent in a second licence would be allowed. Trident then owned both Yorkshire and Tyne Tees, and was the only ITV company to hold two licences. 'I said, fuck it, if I can't keep [both], I don't want it,' Thomas says. 'So we sold off the two television companies and used the cash to go and buy the Playboy Casinos, and at that moment we said to Guinness Mahon, "You can have Sky," and we took ourselves out of the business and went off and played with [Playboy] bunnies instead.'

Murdoch ended up buying majority control of the struggling Sky service from the remaining shareholders for £1 plus debts in 1983. Even Murdoch, who by this time was committed in his own mind to launching a full-range satellite service in Europe, was unsure how to proceed. 'We had put in £3 or £4 million into it each year, but we were really waiting for a higher-powered satellite to be developed,' he recalls. By 1987, the accumulated losses stood at £20 million, and the company was earning less than £3 million a year in advertising revenues. Holland and Germany were its key markets, but ratings were abysmal.

Cable, which was just getting off the ground in the UK, was also a possible distribution platform for those wishing to avoid the terrestrial sector. There had been several early attempts to create channels for cable TV in the UK – one of them, Premiere, a movie channel backed by the Hollywood studios themselves, and another put together by Robert Maxwell, even then a controversial would-be media mogul. None of them worked.

As cable struggled, it would be quite a long wait for a satellite service to be up and running. But liberalisation was slowly creeping across much of Europe, in part as a reaction to ventures such as Sky Television. State-owned networks in France, Italy and Germany were being opened up to competition in the commercial marketplace. National governments were intent that home-grown companies, and not pan-European satellite providers, would reap the rewards of liberalisation.

All the same, there were several projected satellite services being discussed in the early 1980s in Europe, even if few of them seemed to be making any progress. One leading candidate, Société européenne de satellites (SES), looked attractive but risky. Could an effective medium-powered satellite be developed? Could it be successfully launched? A clutch of Luxembourg banks, in partnership with the Luxembourg government, was persuaded it could work. Then, in 1984, an unlikely source of investment money appeared on the scene, in the form of Thames Television, then run by Richard Dunn, the tall, patrician broadcasting veteran.

Recalls Dunn: 'Low-powered telecommunications satellites could provide one or two television channels if you had a dish the size of your greenhouse. High-powered, direct-broadcasting satellites (DBS) were soon to be introduced with dishes of 60 cm or less, but the technology was expensive. So at Thames we thought there was a role for a medium-powered satellite.' SES's Astra satellite, was in the early planning stages when Dunn went to Luxembourg in the course of 1984 and 1985 to see whether Thames might invest in the venture. 'I found out that they were planning a 14 or 15 channel satellite with medium power,' Dunn recalls, 'and a dish receiver in the UK of 80cm diameter or less. This looked pretty attractive.'

While Murdoch and Thames Television were hovering around the edges of medium-powered satellite television, the rest of the mainstream broadcasting sector was either planning applications for direct satellite or, at ITV, discussing the launch of a superchannel for Europe. The IBA, the statutory regulator of commercial TV, had long been intent on seeing satellite work in the UK. Five 'direct broadcast by satellite' (DBS) licences, using high-powered frequencies set aside primarily for Britain, had been awarded to the UK by the World Administrative Radio Conference in 1977 (known, thereafter, as WARC 77). These signals were powerful enough to be received on much smaller dishes than standard satellite transmission, making them ideal for home reception. The drawback was the limited capacity: five channels next to as many as 16 being planned by SES on Astra. The advantage, of course, was that the service would be targeted specifically at the UK, and would be, ostensibly, of higher picture quality. By targeting a particular national market, broadcasters would more easily secure rights to programming and develop convincing viewership figures with which to entice advertisers. Similar frequencies were awarded to other European countries, and the European Commission began to draw up proposals to ensure there was a single transmission standard across the Community.

It was not until 1980 that the Home Office began to look formally at the question of encouraging the development of a national satellite TV service, using the WARC 77 frequencies. By 1982, the government had hit upon a typically British solution, one that smacked of the 'industrial strategy' approach of the 1970s. The BBC was to be given two DBS channels for its exclusive use, and a new untested technology, the so-called D-MAC standard, was to be adopted for transmissions. Never mind market forces.

MAC stood for Multiplexed Analogue Component, and used the same number of lines making up a broadcast picture – 625 – as the European standard PAL. The idea was that the MAC system would improve picture quality and create a European lead in the next stage of evolution in broadcast technology, particularly to see off the Japanese, who had been developing a similar but incompatible system. (The IBA, which had developed the MAC, and held many of the key patents, remained wedded to the technology throughout the 1980s.) The BBC found the system far too expensive to develop on its own, and the idea foundered.

But the IBA was still intent on seeing the D-MAC technology used, and the standard was accepted for all direct-to-home satellite transmission within the European Community. Recalls Peter Rogers, chief executive of the ITC: 'Although it is true that the IBA engineers had invented it, having invented it they promoted it to a European standard. By the time it came to be used [in the UK], it wasn't just an IBA requirement, it was a legislative requirement because it was the *de jure* European standard for direct-to-home satellite. It wasn't just us, that was the standard that was agreed. At the time there was a lot of thought that we should be investing in the next generation of television, and investing in satellite broadcasting, to stay ahead of the Japanese.' Indeed, as late as 1993, the European Commission was still officially committed to D-MAC, despite the fact that just one of 30 satellite services in Europe actually used it. The requirement was quietly dropped that year.

In 1984, the government proposed the Club of 21, a joint venture made up of Thorn-EMI, Pearson, Virgin, the BBC and all the ITV companies. Again, the D-MAC technology was meant to be adopted; worse, the government insisted that the group use a British satellite, likely to cost far more than systems already developed in the US. A venture as unwieldy as this was bound to fail. By June of 1985, the Club had collapsed under its own weight, amid much acrimony. 'The absurd notion that you can get 21 organisations, including the BBC, 15 ITV companies, [Virgin chief] Richard Branson, Pearson and Uncle Tom Cobleigh and all, to make anything work was a complete and utter nonsense,' says Bob Phillis, then at Central Television. Finally, the IBA was asked by the Home Office to run a competitive tender for the DBS licences, inviting companies to bid for up to three channels. The winner would be given a 15-year licence and a three-year monopoly, after which time the two remaining DBS channels would be licenced, not necessarily to the incumbent broadcaster.

Thames' Dunn reluctantly took part in the Club of 21, as chief executive of one of the leading ITV companies, but remained convinced that medium-powered satellites were a cheaper and more efficient distribution platform for multi-channel television. He was not surprised when the venture collapsed, and he stepped up his efforts to secure a stake in SES. 'You don't want to be lumbered with some government-imposed transmission standard, like D-MAC,' Dunn says. His was a risky strategy, and not just on commercial terms. Thames appeared to be going against the wishes of its regulator, the IBA, which slavishly backed the five-channel D-MAC option. Thames also annoyed its ITV colleagues by refusing to support an investment in Superchannel, a pan-European service modelled on the successful 'super stations' being set up in the US, and directly aimed at countering Murdoch's small Sky TV venture.

Dunn and the regulator exchanged terse words when the prospect of a Thames investment in SES was first raised with the IBA. In a letter to Dunn, the regulator referred to SES as an 'organisation of doubtful legality', and counselled that the investment should not be made. Dunn sent a copy of the letter to the British Ambassador in Luxembourg, recommending that the issue be taken up with the Foreign Office. 'I suggested that the British regulator might be unwise to describe something being initiated and regulated by the Luxembourg Government as being of doubtful legality,' Dunn recalls. The IBA backed down quickly, but the relationship with Thames was clearly strained.

Ignoring the implicit disapproval of the IBA, Thames took a five per cent stake in SES in early 1986, with an option to buy an additional five per cent by the end of the year. Within a few months, Dunn had taken the maximum stake, for a total investment of £7 million, making it the largest shareholder after the Luxembourg government. Crucially, Thames also had a veto over other potential British shareholders; unless 75 per cent of SES's shareholders over-ruled him, Dunn could ensure that Thames remained the only British owner of SES shares. At the same time, Dunn formally ruled Thames out of the bidding for the DBS licences.

The IBA was not best pleased. All the ITV companies had been expected to back the DBS option, and Thames, one of the most important of the independent commercial broadcasters, was running a huge risk in upsetting the IBA's plans. Says Dunn: 'The IBA was very hostile to this move [into SES] because they wanted us to be in DBS.' The veto over shareholdings was a way of safeguarding Thames' SES investment, by ensuring that Thames would not be challenged by media rivals from Britain.

With Thames on the sidelines, other major British media and leisure companies began to look seriously at the DBS option. The IBA invited 'expressions of interest' in the autumn of 1985, and proceeded to call for applications in April the following year. Usefully, it appeared that the government was finally willing to relax the rules about using a British satellite, although D-MAC, inevitably, was to be the broadcasting standard. 'The logic of the thing was if you wanted high-quality pictures and so on, you would put your efforts into the high-powered satellite,' Peter Rogers, then finance director of the IBA, explains. 'This [would allow] relatively unsophisticated receiving equipment to be in the home. Certainly at that time, the engineering community used to say, "You'd never get a watchable picture out of a communications satellite. Everytime it snows, it'll go off, and every time it rains, you'll be able to see the rain". But of course, technology moves ahead, and it wasn't true.'

Several major players were interested in the DBS concept, including Rupert Murdoch himself, who finally joined one of the consortia established to bid for the available licences, after much hesitation. He had been looking at a range of other possibilities – including SES – having been convinced by his experience at LWT that he would not be allowed an official broadcasting licence in the UK. In the end, he overcame his doubts, having been swayed by John Jackson, the chief executive of Celltech, the biotechnology company and the guiding force behind Direct Broadcasting Limited (DBL). In addition to Murdoch's company, DBL brought together British and Commonwealth Shipping, Ferranti, Sears and Cambridge Electronic Industries. Even after he agreed to join the consortium, Murdoch harboured doubts. This was also the year of Wapping, when Murdoch had dismissed the print trade unions and set up a new production and print operation in the east end of London. The daily images of picketers and mounted policemen in conflict had done little to endear Murdoch to the 'chattering classes', despite (indeed, perhaps because of) Thatcher's firm support.

Murdoch said to Jackson: 'Look if we come in, it will be the kiss of death. The IBA will just knock it out.' When Jackson insisted, Murdoch merely shrugged his shoulders: 'Don't blame me,' he said. And, inevitably, the Murdoch-backed bid was indeed passed over.

By the eve of the DBS award, in December 1986, it was clear there were only two major contenders. British Satellite Broadcasting, backed at first by media company Pearson and ITV company Granada, as well as Richard Branson's Virgin Group, looked the stronger of the two. It had been created thanks to Chris Irwin, a BBC executive who had developed the public service broadcaster's satellite strategy. He convinced Pearson to come on board, in particular by enlisting Mark Burrell, who headed the company's new media fund. Granada soon followed, with Derek Lewis, the chief executive, taking a personal interest. Lewis was intrigued by, among other things, the possibility that Granada's extensive rentals division could benefit from what he hoped would be exploding consumer demand for satellite receiving equipment. ITV company Anglia Television, too, signed up, as did Amstrad, Alan Sugar's computer and home equipment manu-facturer.

BSB's only serious competition for the DBS licences had come from Carlton's Michael Green, the controversial would-be media tycoon who had failed to win a terrestrial broadcasting licence in 1980 and who had mounted an unsuccessful bid for Thames Television in 1985. He put together a satellite bid, called DBS UK, which included London Weekend Television, the ITV company holding the London weekend franchise, and Saatchi & Saatchi, the advertising agency run by Green's close friends, the Saatchi brothers Charles and Maurice.

The chief difference between the two bids had been glaring from the start. DBS, Green's group, believed that advertising revenues would be the sole source of revenues for the fledging direct-to-home market. BSB's proposals called for at least one subscription channel, with movies encryp-ted for viewing only by those who paid a monthly fee.

In December 1986, BSB was told by the IBA it had won the licence. Later, IBA officials would confirm that it was the promise of a mix of subscription and free services, as well as the commitment to original (and relatively expensive) programming, that clinched it for BSB. (As usual, the UK regulator would be swayed by promises of high quality and public service; no matter that the broadcaster, in the end, might not be able to deliver.) Immediately, Alan Bond, the Australian entrepreneur, called to offer his company as a partner to complete the extensive financing. Shortly thereafter, Chris Irwin signed up Chargeurs, the French media and textiles company, which had been impressed by the successful pay-TV (terrestrial) service owned by Canal Plus in France, with a three million customer base by 1986. Also brought on board after the licence was awarded was Reed International, the magazine giant, which had previously been owners of *The Daily Mirror.*

Before the financing was completed, Alan Sugar decided to pull out. The plain-spoken, barrow-boy entrepreneur already sensed that BSB was going to be a spendthrift company, too luxurious for a man who still ran his operations from downmarket Brentwood, in Essex. Sugar would tri-umphantly re-emerge on the satellite scene two years later – this time sitting next to Rupert Murdoch when plans to launch a competing UK service, Sky, were first unveiled. By the time all the partners were aboard, Bond had put in £50 million, Granada £35 million, Virgin £25 million, Chargeurs £24 million, Reed £20 million and Anglia Television £11.5 million. Smaller investors included London Merchant Securities, with a £10 million investment, Invest International Holdings at £5 million and Trinity, the Liverpool-based regional newspaper publishers, at just £2 million.

The partners raised more than £220 million in the first financing, of which £170 million would be needed to build and launch two new satellites. The investment was large, but the backers were relaxed. After all, this was to be a monopoly. In the view of the government, there was to be one official satellite network, tightly regulated.

But Murdoch had other ideas. Even while he had been negotiating his involvement in his doomed DBS bid, he had been reviewing other ways of getting into the British satellite market. At one point, the idea of beaming signals from the Isle of Man, complicatedly outside direct UK jurisdiction, had been seriously considered. But by 1987, his sights had become trained on SES. Dunn, meanwhile, was still anxious to protect his investment by ensuring that other British companies could not join him as shareholders of the Luxembourg company. Indeed, Robert Maxwell, the soon-to-be-discredited media mogul, had announced in Cannes in 1987 that he was going to launch a multi-channel service for Britain, and become a major shareholder in SES. As it turned out, Maxwell had been a bit premature, as Dunn managed to convince enough SES shareholders that Thames should remain the only significant British investor.

Murdoch, too, toyed with the idea of taking a stake in SES, if he could. But Dunn believed Murdoch was really more interested in securing transponders on Astra, and wouldn't necessarily want to take a non-

controlling position in the company. 'He knew that the articles of association of SES prevented any of the commercial shareholders from having
more than ten per cent,' Dunn recalls. 'The Luxembourg government had
a preferential position with a big shareholding and [Murdoch] understood
that [having a stake] wasn't essential. What would be the point? What he
needed was a shareholding friend.'

Thames, it transpired, would be that friend. The chairman of Thames,
Sir Ian Trethowan, was also a director of Times Newspapers, Murdoch's
broadsheet publisher. He put Dunn in touch with Murdoch late in 1987,
and the two men held a number of discussions over several months. The
first meeting, in November 1987, was held at Murdoch's offices at
Wapping. The same day, Patrick Cox, who had been helping to run Sky
TV, quit. He and Murdoch no longer agreed on the right strategy for Sky,
with Cox certain that pan-European, advertising-supported services were
still the best way forward. (Cox went on to run the European operations
of NBC, which subsequently bought the ill-starred Superchannel.)
Murdoch, for his part, was still wedded to the idea of advertising-supported
broadcasting, but believed he should concentrate on Britain rather than
on the whole of Europe. In the end, the windfall from pan-European
advertising predicted by some – with major brands like Coca Cola and
Nike lining up to buy space – simply failed to materialise. Advertising was
still largely national and regional.

In the UK, Murdoch was convinced that the 'comfortable duopoly' of
the BBC and ITV (supplemented in 1982 by the new Channel 4) could
be broken, and that the British television market was being woefully
under-served. His US experience had shown him the power of multi-
channel TV, and had proved that viewers were definitely attracted by
increased choice and flexibility. If Americans liked it, why shouldn't the
British? Throughout the course of 1987, Murdoch had begun to concentrate on a UK-focused service. In addition to his discussions with Astra
over carriage, which had dragged on for months before Dunn interceded
to provide help, Murdoch had also begun to negotiate with Eurosport, the
consortium of public-service broadcasters, about creating a sports channel
for the British DTH market. A news channel was also in Murdoch's mind,
as early as 1987. At the third meeting between Dunn and Murdoch at
Wapping, Murdoch took the Thames Television chief down a corridor to
what Dunn describes as a glorified broom cupboard. 'Look at all these
journalistic resources I have [at *The Times* and *The Sun*],' Murdoch said.
'I'm just going to put the journalists in there, and they'll read the news.'

Initially, Murdoch wanted two Astra transponders, with an option over a further two, allowing him to broadcast up to four channels, including his Sky TV general entertainment service. Even better from SES's point of view, Murdoch was willing to pay up front for ten-year leases. Dunn persuaded the other SES shareholders that a deal with Murdoch would be good for the company, as it would give the fledgling satellite operator its first real customer.

'I knew we would get momentum if a really important customer signed up two years in advance [of the launch],' Dunn says. 'My £7 million [investment] would look a little better that way.' Thames even considered taking a stake in the Sky channel itself, on the assumption that a carriage deal with Astra would give Sky every chance of succeeding in the British satellite market. But relations with the IBA were already strained enough, and Dunn did not want to antagonise further his regulator. As well, Murdoch had agreed a provisional deal with Thames, but suddenly suggested a much larger investment in all four channels – more than Thames could afford.

More importantly, in early 1988, the government announced it would alter the basis on which ITV licences were awarded in the UK, starting with the next franchise round in 1991. Until that year, the IBA and its predecessor, the ITA, had used a subjective and secretive process to select broadcasters for each franchise, giving rise to complacency and even profligacy. Henceforth, the licences would go to the highest bidder. The change was intimately connected to Thatcher's campaign against union power and what she viewed as entrenched interests in British broadcasting.

Even the regulators themselves realised that change was necessary. Recalls the IBA's Peter Rogers: 'I had some unease at the time about the subjectivity in the way we took our decisions. The government were right to say that that was a flaw and perhaps a fatal and decisive flaw in the way the IBA had issued contracts. To my mind, and this is to judge by the standards of today, it was too secretive and too subjective. The government were right in 1990 to seek to make a change. The specific form of tendering they went for was a pretty fair disaster, partly because, as we see over time with Channel 3, Channel 5 or local delivery licences [for cable], if you are tendering, you need to have some broad consensus about what the value is of the licence you are seeking. All the best brains have always been all over the place, and they still are. That was one of the things that was wrong with it. [But] at least it became more objective. The papers, internally here, were more analytic, and more within a coded proper framework.'

With the threat of competitive tendering for the first time, Dunn realised he would have to marshall his cash, and limit any non-essential investment, if he was going to be able to win a renewal for Thames in London. (It would not get any easier for Dunn, whose *This Week* series came into direct conflict with the Thatcher government in 1988, when it broadcast the controversial *Death on the Rock* documentary, which dealt with the way British special forces had shot unarmed suspected IRA terrorists in Gibraltar.)

A deal with Astra was struck by Murdoch in the spring of 1988. He would eventually have four transponders on the first satellite (and take another two later, when Astra 1B, the next in the series, was launched). Amazingly, he agreed to lease the transponders for ten years, giving Astra much-needed stability. 'That was a transformer of SES's business,' Dunn says. Also crucial to SES's success was the support of British Telecom, which as the national telecoms provider controlled the satellite uplink services, under the European rules on satellite broadcasting. BT broke ranks with other European PTTs, which had been campaigning against SES in Europe.

Meanwhile, BSB, the winner of the official DBS licences in 1986, was starting to set up its own operations, in expectation of a 1989 launch. Most of the shareholders did not seem unduly concerned about the planned Astra launch, assuming that the official status of the DBS operator in Britain would see off any competition. And after all, BSB had the leading-edge technology (small dish, high-quality transmissions) while the best that Astra could offer was a compromise service (big dish, inferior picture quality). But some British media executives expressed concern that Thames had gone its separate way in satellite television. 'It was rankling that Thames had gone off and backed a Luxembourg company that no-one had ever heard of for a satellite that wasn't yet built and with no customers,' Dunn recalls. (It was not yet publicly known that Murdoch had contracted to take his transponders on the Astra satellite.) Michael Green, who had headed the unsuccessful rival bid for the official DBS licences, was intrigued by Thames' move into Astra, and discussed it with Dunn. Virgin's Richard Branson, too, expressed surprise about Dunn's strategy, and asked to come in to discuss Astra. Branson's company had, of course, taken a stake in the winning DBS consortium, BSB.

'What did you do that for?,' Branson asked Dunn of the Thames' investment in SES. 'You know that BSB is going to be the bee's knees.' (Long before BSB's delayed launch, Branson himself would become so worried about the company's prospects that he would sell Virgin's stake outright, to the soon-to-be-struggling Australian, Alan Bond).

BSB still believed it could easily ignore a European service, Sky, that no one to speak of in Britain was watching. In early 1987, the official satellite broadcaster made its first appointment, recruiting Graham Grist, formerly at IBM, a man with no media experience at all. A few months later, Anthony Simonds-Gooding was appointed chief executive. Simonds-Gooding, a high-flyer, had previously been a marketing executive at Unilever and then at Whitbread's, the brewing and food giant, ultimately joining Saatchi & Saatchi to oversee the advertising agency's risky (and ultimately failed) attempt to build a global empire. BSB felt they needed a marketing man rather than a broadcaster in the top job. It was a measure of how quickly television was changing in the UK, as accountants and sales directors became more important than programmers and commissioners.

Still, BSB did recruit real programmers, enlisting Andy Birchall to run the subscription movie channel (he had launched an ill-fated cable movie channel in 1984, and had formerly worked as a development executive at Pearson) and Bob Hunter, who would eventually run the sports channel on BSB.

BSB's mood of optimism was dented in June 1988, when, his Astra carriage deal signed, Murdoch rose to address a packed house at a dinner sponsored by BAFTA, the British Academy of Film and Television Arts. Murdoch promised four channels of satellite TV for the UK, initially free. He would use leased transponder space on Astra, and would eschew the IBA-sanctioned D-MAC technology in favour of PAL. This was partly out of necessity, since the D-MAC technology had not yet been developed to commercial standards. His movie channel, too, had to be free because there was, as yet, no reliable way to scramble PAL transmissions. But Murdoch was not overly worried. He believed there was a significant market for advertising-supported multi-channel television. The trick was, he believed, to get as many dishes into as many homes as he could from the start. The rest of the business strategy could be worked out later.

Murdoch believed that he could beat BSB by being first in the market. The 'early mover' advantage would outweigh any suggestions that BSB's programming, and its firm support from the IBA, gave the official British broadcaster an edge. Murdoch assumed that advertising would ultimately represent the bulk of Sky's revenues, with the rest coming from subscriptions when a reliable encryption technology had been developed. Despite the lacklustre performance of Sky in its pan-European incarnation, he was still convinced he could wrest advertising business away from traditional broadcasters. (By 1997, only 12 per cent of BSkyB's revenues would come from selling advertising. This was to be, at root, a subscription business.)

Murdoch's decision to use the Astra system was inspired. Rather than bear the huge expense of launching his own satellites, as BSB had undertaken to do, he was able to secure four channels without committing as much cash upfront. Moreover, Astra had ambitious plans to launch yet more satellites, holding out the prospect of even more capacity for Sky if the market for multi-channel TV proved robust. Even better, Sky was a 'non-domestic satellite service' – in short, yet another example of Murdoch's uncanny ability to spot a regulatory loophole and muscle his way through it. Unlike the competition, Sky would not be wholly at the beck and call of regulators. Admits the ITC's Peter Rogers: 'Murdoch went down that road, and he [therefore] had no licencing locus with us in those days. It wasn't a British frequency, it wasn't a British satellite.'

Warming to his theme at the BAFTA launch, Murdoch revealed plans to add three new services to his Sky TV (later rechristened Sky 1) – news, movies and a sports channel (Eurosport, the joint venture backed by Europe's leading public-service broadcasters, including the BBC). There were promises of two more channels following the launch: Disney and an arts channel. Media correspondents attending the launch were breathlessly excited: not only did this mean good copy (Murdoch always meant good copy); it might mean the start of a satellite war that conceivably would run and run.

The task Murdoch had set himself – to launch three new channels and completely overhaul the original Sky TV service in just eight months – was daunting enough on its own. But Murdoch knew he would soon be under huge threat from BSB. Once it finally launched (late) in April 1990, the official broadcaster would spend even more freely to win satellite customers: its losses would amount to an incredible £10 million a week by the autumn of its launch year.

With Murdoch as a major client, Astra was soon able to sign up other broadcasters. Ultimately, it would carry a mix of services, including foreign-language channels, the Children's Channel, and Screensport (owned by retailer WH Smith and Robert Maxwell). But fully a quarter of Astra's capacity would be taken up by Sky – a huge risk for Murdoch, but a potentially lucrative one if the service won a significant number of customers in Britain.

The original team at tiny Sky Television, led by Jim Styles, was suddenly asked to go from running a single channel to launching a four-channel service nearly from scratch. It soon became clear to Murdoch that the team was out of its depth. Andrew Neil, the blunt-spoken Scot who edited *The Sunday Times*, Murdoch's flagship UK newspaper, was brought in as executive chairman. He joined a small team largely of Australians, including David Hill, the man responsible for revolutionising the coverage of cricket and rugby league in Australia (working for Sam Chisholm), and who would put an indelible mark on Sky's own sports programming in later years. Head of Sky News was the much-respected John O'Loan, a far less flamboyant man than some of the Aussies who worked for Murdoch. A few months later, Murdoch sent in some additional help, parachuting in Gary Davey, the Australian broadcaster then working at Fox in the US, and Pat Mastandrea, an advertising executive, also from Fox. The original offices of Sky Television in the West End were abandoned for the modern, soulless environs of Heathrow Airport, where hangar-like accommodation on a business park in Osterley would become the new headquarters. (Later, Sky would insist its headquarters were in Isleworth, the next-door, slightly less hideous, community. That was technically incorrect, but eventually 'Isleworth' became short-hand for Sky's head office.)

The premises were not yet ready when Neil and his team moved in, just two months before the February 1989 launch. The staff immediately embarked on a hectic schedule, working from what Neil later described as a 'construction site in the middle of a mud field'. Not only were the studios and broadcasting facilities not yet completed, but the four channels still needed to be scheduled. To save money and time, Murdoch had done a deal with Eurosport, which Sky would transmit as one of its four services. For the movie channel, he hired Stewart Till, who later went to Polygram, to negotiate with the Hollywood studios. Murdoch knew that BSB was also bidding for movie rights to transmit on its own film subscription channel, and was concerned about the spiralling costs. To cover the huge risk, he struck a deal with Disney, the giant US entertainment company, which also owned Touchstone Pictures. The partners would together cover the costs of movie rights, and Disney would contribute its own output (although not its extensive library) and later launch a Disney Channel on Sky, as a premium service. They would thereby share in the success of the Sky service.

The relationship with Disney was never smooth. Almost immediately, Michael Eisner, Disney's ruthless chief executive, balked at having to pay his Hollywood rivals the huge costs of securing movie rights, which had been driven up to unprecedented levels by the competition between BSB and Sky. BSB had taken out ads in the Hollywood trades, warning studios against dealing with the outlaw Sky. (Eventually, Disney would pull out of the joint venture, and Murdoch would slap a $1.5 billion lawsuit on the American company.)

All of this work proceeded even before the Astra satellite was operational. The launch was scheduled for 9 December 1988, but was delayed because of bad weather. Jonathan Miller, a *Times* executive brought to Sky by Neil, was sent to French Guyana to witness the launch. Also present was an extremely nervous Richard Dunn, of Thames. 'I watched £7 million of my shareholders funds tied round the nose cone of that damn rocket,' Dunn recalls. 'Fortunately it worked. It did what it was supposed to do. It opened its little solar panels, it flew into the right position and everyone breathed a very big sigh of relief.'

There were other problems to surmount, however. Alan Sugar's Amstrad, which, among other companies, had agreed to manufacture the all-important receiving equipment, had delayed the production line until Sugar was sure the satellite would be launched. He did not want to be left holding unsold kit. By the time the dishes were manufactured and shipped from the Far East, the birth of Sky was looming. There would be very few households with the necessary equipment to watch Sky Television. Neil maintains he was unbothered by this. 'When BBC-TV had begun its first broadcast in the 1930s,' he writes in his autobiography, 'only a few hundred homes had TV sets.' The lack of reliable encryption technology, then being developed by the Israeli-based News Datacom, a Murdoch subsidiary, meant that most of the movies Sky had contracted to broadcast could not be used. The studios, with the exception of Disney and, of course, Murdoch's Fox, would only allow the films to be shown on a subscription basis. It would be nearly a year before the movie channel could be encrypted, and smart cards produced for subscribers to unscramble the signal.

Against the odds, Sky launched on schedule at 6:00 pm on 5 February 1989. Precious few households could watch it; the response of the critics was vociferously negative ('trash, down-market'); and BSB, which had yet to launch its own five channels, mounted a huge and impressive campaign cajoling viewers to wait for the 'real' satellite service later that year. But unlike BSB, Murdoch actually had a TV business up and running.

CHAPTER 2

Toward Disaster

To Sky's relief and delight, BSB missed its launch target date by nine months and was only to appear in April 1990, giving Sky more than a year's headstart. The chief problem was the 'squarial', the home receiving equipment which BSB was pioneering: the prototype of the small dish, whose main advantage next to Sky was its unobtrusiveness, simply did not work, and required additional development to ensure that it could. However, BSB did get some welcome help from regulators, when the IBA awarded two more frequencies to BSB in June 1989, allowing it to expand its planned service to five channels – one more than Sky.

But during its first months on air, despite the lack of any satellite competition, Sky itself faced a host of problems. The worst was the dish shortage, due to the unwillingness of manufacturers to commit to large-scale production runs. The company was forced to delay its national advertising campaign on ITV and Channel 4 by two months, because there weren't enough Astra dishes in the shops. Partly as a result, Murdoch publicly announced he was cutting his forecasts for the first year, from 2.5 million homes to just 1.15 million (and even that proved optimistic).

The slow take-up was a blow to Sky's revenue forecasts, which were crucially dependent on satellite dish sales and subsequent advertising revenues. Because reliable encryption technology was not yet available from Israel, all four of Sky's channels were free, and relied solely on advertising. But until the company could deliver credible audiences, the advertisers were unwilling to commit large sums. Suddenly, Murdoch's vision of a robust future for satellite broadcasting looked highly doubtful.

Within a month of launch, Sky suffered its first management casualty, when Jim Styles, the managing director since the days of the old one-channel Sky Television, resigned. Pat Mastandrea and Gary Davey were appointed joint managing directors. The early losses were beginning to alarm Murdoch, who decided to attend more meetings at Isleworth and to take a far bigger role, much to Andrew Neil's annoyance. But even under Neil, who finally left in March 1990, to be replaced as executive chairman, briefly, by Rupert Murdoch himself, there was no mistaking the real power behind Sky.

'[Murdoch] had this system where he would go around the table, and every head of department used to have to give a report about had happened in his department that week,' Deanna Bates, Sky's young, Welsh-born legal director, recalls. Even when he wasn't present, his presence was deeply felt. 'All [Murdoch's] companies do weekly accounts, and in those days he would ring up Pat [Mastandrea] or Gary [Davey] and ask them very detailed questions about the last week's numbers,' Nick Carrington, Sky's chief financial officer, adds.

Murdoch was desperate, and knew he needed to put things right. He had spent two years and millions of pounds preparing and then launching the service. Key News Corporation lieutenants had already been parachuted in to help – notably Andrew Knight, who was running News International, Murdoch's newspaper company in the UK. But the early figures were bitterly disappointing. Despite all the investment, the hellishly expensive Hollywood movie contracts for Sky's film channel and the joint venture with the giant Disney Corporation, the company was teetering on the edge of disaster. Other parts of the Murdoch empire were beginning to feel the effects, with senior managers of News International increasingly frustrated at the huge cash demands of the sister company.

Sky's Carrington remembers the period well. 'Can you imagine it? Cash is haemorrhaging out of the business, and I'm having to phone up News International and say, "I need another three-quarters of a million, I need another million, I need another two million" every day. These guys are just not our friends. Rupert was coming along saying we need another £10 million for Sky, so we'll just take it from News International, so these guys were really bitterly opposed to us.' Adds another senior Sky source: 'All of the people at News International were seeing their costs were being cut; they were just there to generate cash to support us.'

The neophyte broadcaster was losing at least £2 million a week by mid-1989 – money that Murdoch needed to keep his global media empire afloat. Bankers were pressing, interest payments mounting and the money from Murdoch's dazzling array of media assets (television around the globe, publishing, and newspapers in the US, Australia and Britain) was not enough to cover him. He had rolled the dice on Sky, and the odds were mounting against him. 'This is my money you are losing,' Murdoch thundered at one of many crisis meetings at Sky in late 1989, banging his fist on the table.

'It all came at a bad time for us,' Murdoch explains. 'At the same time [as we were developing Sky], we had huge capital expenditure requirements in the newspaper businesses for new plant and equipment. In the 1980s, if I had taken better advice, I'd have borrowed money on the bond markets instead of from the banks. Now I seldom borrow from the banks. Maybe I have become too cautious.'

To make matters worse, the deal with Disney, which ought to have seen the launch of the Disney Channel within a few months of Sky's birth, imploded in May 1989 after months of wrangling over film contracts and programme deals. Murdoch launched a $1.5 billion lawsuit against Disney alleging that the US entertainment giant had used 'fraudulent tactics' to torpedo the agreement between the two companies. A month later, a truce was reached, and Disney agreed to continue to licence the broadcast rights to its films. (Disney would remain on the sidelines of the UK pay-TV market until 1995, when it agreed to put the Disney Channel into BSkyB's multichannel package.)

By mid-1989, Murdoch had reached desperation point. Despite having promised to fund Sky for at least five years, he was alarmed at the spiralling losses, and sought a more radical solution to the company's obvious problem: lack of dishes in UK homes. He was convinced that Sky had to take full advantage of its head-start on BSB. But consumers were simply not prepared to buy an Astra dish in case the 'squarial' emerged as the winning distribution method. 'Between them, Sky and BSB had managed to recreate the VHS/Betamax dilemma consumers faced when video recorders were first launched,' Neil conceded later in his autobiography.

Sky's first year's business plan forecast a million dishes in UK homes. But after five months on the air, only 10,000 had been sold. Sky had also managed to sign a cable deal with Robert Maxwell, to distribute the channels to cable homes, and later added a £3 million-a-year deal to add cable homes served by BT, the telecoms giant. The £5 million-a-year deal with Maxwell, arranged by Andrew Neil, was particularly one-sided. In effect, Sky was paying Maxwell to take the Sky channels. When Murdoch saw the terms of the deal, he muttered: 'If you lie down with dogs, you get up with fleas.'

Murdoch wanted dish customers, and he wanted them fast. 'The staff at the time were all broadcasters, and they put a huge amount into getting the four channels on the air,' recalls a senior Sky executive. 'At first, they thought the proposition was so hot that dishes would fly out the door, and the retailers would be thanking us for doing them a favour. When that didn't materialise, the management lost confidence in the retail distribution arm. They realised that actually the business was not just going to be about programming but was going to be about building a distribution system.'

After long debates, Sky elected to get into the satellite dish business itself, through a highly secret plan, dubbed Project X, to establish a direct sales force. Project X was the idea of David Johnson, a US consultant hired by Mastandrea, who convinced Murdoch it was the only way to encourage dish sales. (Johnson had formerly advised Murdoch on the launch of Fox Television in the US.) For £4.49 a week, viewers could get the Sky service without paying the upfront costs of a satellite system, originally nearly £300. Liam Kane, another Murdoch appointment (he subsequently left the fold to join first Caledonian Publishing then Mirror Group), was put in charge of implementing the project.

But the scheme required Sky to get into the business of direct selling to consumers, thereby bypassing the High Street retailers like Dixons or Curry's. 'That played right into BSB's [hands],' Bates recalls. 'BSB [which, by this time, had still not launched its own service] said to the retailers, "Oh my God why do you want to be selling Sky dishes? They're going to go into competition against you".'

It also created a marketplace ripe for picking by BSB. If viewers actually bought an Astra dish, they would be less likely to abandon it when BSB's squarial came on the market. But renting a dish meant customers weren't tied to Astra, and could be 'swapped out' more easily. David Chance, then director of marketing and distribution, was dead set against Project X, and said so, at the risk of losing his job. 'I almost got fired, because I vehemently fought the idea,' Chance recalls. 'I knew that if we went into direct selling, we were going to completely fuck off the retailers. I resisted it to the point that my job was in danger.'

Despite the anticipated pitfalls, Murdoch was adamant. Kevin Kinsella, now director of business development at BSkyB, remembers: 'When Murdoch came into one of these executive meetings and said we are going to go into direct selling, God a huge gasp went round the table. Here we were having just launched four television channels faster than it had ever been done before, and [there were] huge structural problems just trying to manage that operation and we were going to be in a completely new business selling and renting dishes with absolutely no experience of it at all.'

The lack of experience showed early. Recalls one senior executive: 'Pat [Mastandrea] said, "Well, what can be so hard about this. We have just got to get a warehouse on the M25 and we'll ship them out." There was no real understanding of what was required.' (Later, Sam Chisholm would remark: 'They had put broadcasters into the end-user business. They tried to be Stanley Kalms [legendary retailer, and the chief executive of Dixons], and they didn't understand.')

At first, Project X, launched in June 1989, was implemented through direct marketing, as Sky encouraged potential viewers to ring a toll-free number. But that approach only generated sales of about 10,000 dishes a month – not enough to suit Murdoch. Five months later, in October, a direct sales force was drafted in. In a matter of weeks, Sky had put a thousand sales people on the streets. The recruitment was done so quickly that the calibre of the sales force was an open question. 'Guess where they came from?' Carrington asks. 'These were the sharks of the industry, all former double-glazing salesmen who looked at us and thought, mmm, a chicken ready for plucking.'

Suddenly, Sky was getting as many as 50,000 dish orders a month, helped by promotional campaigns and the direct selling efforts. Merely processing all the contracts provided by the sales force was a huge task, made more complicated by the amount of fraud from sales people and supply problems from dish manufacturers. Customers needed a bank account in order to apply for the service. Insiders speak of one salesman who opened a thousand accounts with just a pound in each, who applied for upfront commission payment on an unknown number of falsified contracts. 'There was fraud on a huge scale,' says one senior executive.

Sky also had to create its own installation company and to provide incentives to some of the existing installers in order to keep up with the demand. The installation market was dominated by small, one or two-man shops: they simply couldn't cope with orders on this scale.

All the same, Project X certainly provided a boost to dish sales. 'It wasn't implemented very well, but what it did do was get dishes on homes very quickly, which BSB didn't have,' Kinsella says. But at a huge cost. By the time the dust had cleared, Sky had spent an incredible £140 million on the plan. Still, the dish campaign certainly frightened BSB, which was a few months from its own launch and desperate to convince consumers to wait for the squarial. Richard Brooke, then at BSB's finance department and now group finance director at BSkyB, remembers: 'Suddenly, you could see all these Sky dishes. It went just like that, from not selling anything at all, suddenly [they] were selling hundreds of thousands of dishes.'

Looking back, Murdoch believes the approach was flawed but the concept was right. 'I never doubted the demand was there for more choice but we weren't selling the dishes. And the team didn't really get it right. When they went out leasing equipment, they were going door to door, without credit checks. The concept was right, but the execution was flawed. It was done under enormous pressure, because every month, we were being told by BSB that they were going to launch soon, and we knew we had to get a head start. So we had a window of time, that we had to take advantage of.'

With hindsight, Sky would have been better off working through the retailers in the High Street, the company now concedes. David Chance concludes: 'When Project X finally went down, can you imagine going back into the Dixons and Curry's of this world and saying, "Look, I know we shafted you for the last 18 months, but actually now we would like you to support us rather than these [BSB] creeps".'

In the middle of it all, BSB finally launched its Marcopolo satellite, in August 1989, expensively sending a team of executives to Florida to witness the historic event. That same month, the company moved into its new headquarters – the fancy, quintessentially 1980s-style Marcopolo House in Battersea. From the start, BSB was a high-rent company, its car park filled with BMWs and Jaguars, its executives used to travelling first class.

BSB offered what nearly everyone conceded was the better technology, based on the D-MAC broadcasting standard and delivered by a purpose-built, wholly owned satellite. BSB was the Cadillac service; Sky the Volkswagen. Later, after Sky had turned the corner, Gary Davey, then the joint managing director, used a different analogy: 'Theirs was the Concorde, we were the jumbo jet. Ask yourself which one makes money.'

But BSB also had the backing of the British media establishment and the official stamp of approval from the IBA. Sky, by contrast, was the outlaw outsider. BSB exuded that confidence that came of being part of the establishment. A young freelance trade journalist was taken up to Leeds to see the company's subscription management service. Used to travelling second class, she was astonished when a first-class train ticket arrived from BSB. 'They told me that all travel for BSB over 40 miles had to be in first class,' she recalls. 'They were spending money like it was going out of style.' Anthony Simonds-Gooding, BSB's chief executive, told an investment banker at the time he was having fun 'spending other people's money'.

Indeed, until Simonds-Gooding brought in his financial director, Ian Clubb, there appeared to be no operating controls at all. Personal expenses ended up on corporate credit cards; producers managed to combine their own private business with BSB work; for every public campaign, no expense was ever spared. Recalls Michael Grade, then at LWT and later chief executive of Channel 4: 'Murdoch's people were on a mission, a mission to destroy the BBC, a mission to destroy ITV. A mission to destroy the old order. They were zealots. If you went to the BSB car park, everyone had a BMW and a chauffeur. They were all there on a gravy train, and they weren't focused at all.'

But why did the shareholders of BSB agree to the profligacy? BSB was a far more 'British' media company than Sky – not surprisingly, perhaps, given its shareholders. Pearson, the blue-blooded, family-dominated conglomerate that owned *The Economist*, *The Financial Times*, Penguin Books and other media assets, thought multi-channel television was the key media play of the decade. The great sponsors of the BSB investment at Pearson were James Joll, the finance director, and Michael (Viscount) Blakenham the scion of Pearson's controlling Cowdray family. Both believed that BSB would earn a fortune, and were willing to argue in favour of each and every cash call from the fledgling company.

At Granada, Alex Bernstein, the company's chairman, of the Bernstein family that had built a television empire out of a retail and rental chain, was equally sold on the concept, while Jerome Seydoux, the chairman of Chargeurs, the French media company, and Michel Crepon, the executive vice-president, had watched with envy the early success of Canal Plus in France, and were keen to be in on the ground floor of a similar pay-TV company. At Reed, both Peter Davis and Ian Irvine had been early converts to the prospects of satellite TV.

But from the start, oddly, the shareholders themselves kept their distance from the day-to-day operations. Indeed, even the application for the licence, awarded in 1986, was written almost entirely by paid consultants, in a small office in Rathbone Place, London. Virgin, which had been an original investor in BSB (but which subsequently sold out to Alan Bond), rented the office but executives from Richard Branson's group rarely put in an appearance, recalls Bruce Fireman, then at Charterhouse and a lead author of the licence application. He adds: 'For six weeks, we never saw anyone from Granada or Pearson.'

Janice Hughes, a media consultant at Spectrum, concludes: 'BSB was doomed to be a failure almost from the start, doomed to be a failed conglomerate of separate entities that could never really sing with one voice.' Worse, the service was being run by a mix of traditional broadcasters (particularly on the production side) and marketeers, many of them without television experience. It early became bogged down in intractable technical issues, not least the huge work of financing and co-ordinating the development of the squarial and the encryption technology needed to scramble BSB's movie service – an investment, ultimately, that topped £400 million. The combination would prove inadequate to the task. Says Sam Chisholm: 'It was ridiculous, really. They had no idea.'

Michael Grade, a longtime Sky critic, blames government strategy, just as much as BSB's management, for the debacle. 'It was incredible regulatory and government intervention that told which satellite to use, how to do it, what they wanted. You can't run a business, a new start-up business, on the basis of civil servants and politicians telling you what the structure is going to be. It was crackers. So it was doomed really before it started.'

Even before the company launched, it was time to seek additional financing. Already, £431 million of funds had been committed, but the original business plan called for a second round of financing bringing the total to more than £1 billion. There had been vague talk of a flotation, tapping the equity markets. But by February of 1990, it had become clear that the shareholders themselves would have to cough up more money. A complicated matching formula was agreed, whereby banks would supply £450m, and the shareholders would pledge their own companies' assets up to the same amount.

The hapless Alan Bond, who by 1990 was in desperate financial shape, did not take up his rights in the financing, and saw his stake diluted to just 7.5 per cent. Despite a search for other partners, that was widened to include Disney and Robert Maxwell, no one could be found to take up the slack created by Bond's problems. Carlton's Michael Green, along with *The Daily Telegraph* owner Conrad Black, the Canadian newspaper baron, was offered the chance to buy into the BSB consortium. Recalls Green: 'Conrad [Black] and I met Peter Davis and others at Millbank [Pearson's offices] and we suggested Michael Grade [then at LWT, and later chief executive of Channel 4] as a candidate to run the company.' But in the end, Pearson and Granada believed Green was asking for too much control, and no deal could be struck. The other partners – the big four of Granada, Pearson, Reed and Chargeurs – reluctantly stumped up enough to compensate for Bond's inability to pay – and the deal was finally done in May 1990.

BSB launched with five channels of entertainment, news and movies – Galaxy, Now, Power Station, Sports Channel and the Movie Channel – in April 1990, and, unlike Sky, had actually commissioned significant UK production. Another major difference: unlike Sky Movies, which were offered 'free to air' at launch, BSB's Movie Channel was a 'subscription-only' service from the start. Sky had finally managed to encrypt its movie channel from February 1990, just two months before BSB was on the air, and began to receive much-needed subscription revenues. BSB would get the benefit of monthly payments from subscribers from the start.

Sky had also built its subscription management service in Livingston, Scotland, in record time. Run by David Wheeler, to many the unsung hero of Sky's ultimate success, the service in Scotland would prove to be crucial to Sky's (and later BSkyB's) efforts not only to administer the pay-TV service but to reduce cancellations and to encourage viewers to upgrade their packages. ('Livingston is an absolutely wonderful set-up,' says a senior ITV executive, who looked into the idea of creating an ITV subscription management service for digital TV in 1996. 'If you haven't paid your bill, they will cut you off in the middle of a crucial Manchester United [football] game. Then, when you call to complain, they not only get you signed up for direct debit, but they even try to sell you another channel.') Chisholm himself was extremely proud of the Scottish operation. But he left nothing to chance. Whenever he had occasion to ring Wheeler, at Livingston, he used a public line in order to time how long the call took to be answered. If it was too long, Wheeler would know about it.

Livingston was a basic service when it started, however. Established in August 1989 to take calls from potential viewers following the introduction of Project X, there were just '12 people, lying on the floor, with telephones and bits of papers', a Sky insider remembers. 'There was only one desk, and that was for David [Wheeler].' Later, when all the basic channels were added and the premium sports channel was launched, the staffing levels would soar. From 1992, Livingston would be as much a proactive marketing tool (enticing subscribers to trade up the premium ladder) as a trouble-shooter or a bad credit agency.

Like Sky before it, BSB managed to launch into a marketplace where compatible receiving equipment was thin on the ground. Only a handful of squarial dishes were installed in time for the launch, and even two months later, the sales were risible. Nearly immediately, BSB hit a wall. Recalls Frank Barlow, the tough, former journalist who saw off the unions at Pearson's Westminster Press, and who represented Pearson on the BSB board: 'The biggest problem was getting the equipment, the dishes. Nobody was tooled up and everyone was very doubtful about producing them in bulk, and some of the early [dishes] didn't work.' The bank loans had been based on BSB hitting a series of subscription and revenue targets, and these proved hellishly difficult to reach.

But there were other problems. Many of BSB programmes, while still far cheaper than ITV or BBC fare, cost considerably more than Sky's mix of cheap US imports and second-string sport. The BBC repeats on Galaxy, for example, were only available for broadcast if BSB invested as much in British original programming as on acquisitions, under a complicated deal with Actors Equity, the trade union. At the same time, BSB had secured just half the Hollywood film contracts (the others, of course, were with Sky), at a phenomenal price. 'Hollywood didn't know what hit them,' a senior BSB executive says. 'It was like Christmas, with these Brits running all around town waving big chequebooks.' With such huge programming costs, BSB needed to convince viewers to buy squarials – and fast. Within two months of launch, losses were running at £8 million a week.

In the early months following the launch, the BSB shareholders held their nerve. The two rivals battled it out: in the High Street, in the newspapers, in Whitehall and even in the Houses of Parliament. BSB mounted a huge and sophisticated lobbying campaign, as the new Broadcasting Act (of 1990) was being debated in the House of Lords. So-called 'non-domestic' satellite services were excluded from the cross-media ownership restrictions that kept big newspaper publishers from owning TV assets. An amendment was tabled to bring such non-domestic services (meaning Sky) within the general ownership rules, which would have forced Rupert Murdoch to divest himself of his satellite venture. In the end, whether because of his close ties to the Thatcher government or because the Lords did not believe Sky was the domineering monster claimed by some, Murdoch escaped regulatory restraint – not the first or last time.

Sky also faced a host of technical problems, some of them linked to the high degree of regulation still in effect in the telecoms sector. For its Sky News, for instance, the company was obliged to use British Telecom as the supplier of uplink services. 'The result has been that our transmissions have to follow a bizarre path via fibre-optic cables to the Telecom Tower, and thence by microwave to the Docklands Teleport on the other side of London from our studios in London,' Ray Gallagher, head of corporate affairs, complained at the time. (Once the government abandoned its duopoly approach to telecoms, whereby just two companies – BT and Mercury – dominated, issues such as uplinking and electronic news-gathering were far easier to resolve.)

BSB believed that Murdoch was financially stretched (just how far they would only learn later) and that BSB had the richer parents. Each side knew that there would likely be only one winner. 'We knew this would take time, but we really thought we had the better programmes and the better technology,' says one BSB insider. 'We also had the money.'

But Murdoch had a huge advantage – his major UK newspaper titles. Michael Grade puts it bluntly. 'I'm not taking away from his skills at all but if [Murdoch] didn't own 36 per cent of the newspapers, supporting a Conservative Government at the time, he would never have got where he is today. The whole thing is based on that cosy relationship.' Whatever the truth about the connections between Mrs Thatcher and Rupert Murdoch, the support of *The Sun* and the *News of the World* in championing satellite television was probably crucial in Sky's ability to attract attention and, ultimately, subscribers.

By the summer of 1990, the huge costs of Project X were beginning to worry even Rupert Murdoch. A key meeting that month descended into chaos ('A real shouting match,' said one executive in attendance), as the results were dissected. By the end of the financial year, 30 June 1990, Murdoch's News International would report losses of £266 million, with Sky losing £95 million at the operating level, after £120 million in start up costs. Recalls Murdoch: 'When [BSB finally] did start, there were two kinds of technologies, offering the same programmes basically. We both had sport and movies. And the market just dried up. Everybody was waiting to see who would win. No one wanted to buy the losing system, or have to end up buying two systems.' That summer, the red ink flowing and the satellite wars still raging, Murdoch finally made up his mind. Fresh management blood was needed.

CHAPTER 3
Cue Sam Chisholm

One Saturday in late August 1990, early in the morning, Sam Chisholm, the veteran Antipodean broadcasting executive, secretly boarded a plane headed for Los Angeles. He told no one at Australia's Nine Network, where he was managing director, about his trip; and if he looked a little tired on the Monday morning, chairing the 8:30 am executive meeting in Sydney, no one could guess why. 'I had a busy weekend,' Chisholm told one colleague who asked him why his face was so drawn. 'I'll tell you about it someday.'

But it would prove to have been a crucial whirlwind trip. Chisholm's host on the West Coast was Rupert Murdoch, the global media mogul who would transform Chisholm into arguably Britain's most powerful broadcaster, and certainly one of its richest. Over lunch in LA, home to Murdoch's US master company, the newspaper, TV and publishing entrepreneur made his well-rehearsed pitch. Would Chisholm be willing to leave Nine after 23 years, most of them at or near the top, to help salvage struggling Sky Television in the UK? Could he bring himself to abandon his boss, Kerry Packer, the media tycoon who had just months before bought back Nine Network from the financially stretched Alan Bond, another of the seeming limitless number of swashbuckling Aussie entrepreneurs who at one point dominated Antipodean media? (Bond had been declared unfit to hold a broadcasting licence by the Australian government in late 1989, and subsequently had been forced to sell his TV interests.)

As usual, Murdoch had done his homework. He had sensed Chisholm might be ready for a change: certainly his extensive network of Australian friends had whispered that Chisholm was poachable. When Packer had returned to Nine after Bond's spectacular collapse, he had immediately ordered a cost-cutting exercise: the champagne culture (stars, cars and boozy nights) was to be replaced with austerity, a style to which the hard-working, hard-living Chisholm (he of the impressive stamina for long hours and the even more impressive expense account) did not necessarily want to become accustomed. Although he duly instituted the cost-cutting programme, and even agreed to impose a draconian one-hour limit on lunches, it was becoming clear Chisholm was increasingly uncomfortable. The turning point may have come when Packer appointed Bob Shanks, an American TV executive, as adviser on drama, an area where even Chisholm admitted there were weaknesses in the Channel Nine lineup.

Chisholm had already thought of retiring when Packer sold out to Bond three years before. 'We improved the rating of the network,' Chisholm says, 'but it had an horrific effect on the profitability. Television then went through a very competitive period, and all these guys then sold, having taken a terrible hiding.' When Packer, newly reinstalled as owner, started to crash the costs (banning alcohol on the premises too), Chisholm started having second thoughts. (Packer had got a fantastic deal when he bought the network back. He had sold to Bond for $1 billion, agreeing to leave $200 million in the company. When he returned, that $200 million was enough to secure 60 per cent of Channel Nine.)

But Chisholm's ultimate decision to leave was informed by more subtle motives. Then aged 50, Chisholm still thought he had some good years in him, despite the respiratory disease from which he was suffering. Maybe not at Nine, however, and if not at Nine, then not in Australia. And 23 years is a very long time to work anywhere, let alone in the mercurial world of Australian television. 'I had been there a long time,' Chisholm says. 'I really thought back then that I'd go to my grave there. I could drive to the place [blindfolded]: I knew it like the back of my hand.'

Murdoch had been keeping his eye on Chisholm for years. The New Zealander, public school-educated, the son of prosperous farmers, and a man too studiously like James Cagney to be taken seriously as a creature of the middle class (as, in fact, he was), was famous, even notorious, in Australian broadcasting circles, where he was credited with taking Nine to the top of the rating league, besting, among other networks, Murdoch's own Channel Ten.

Chisholm started his career as a salesman for Johnson's Wax, moving to a station in Melbourne, owned by Kerry Packer's brother, in the early 1960s. He joined Channel Nine, the national network, in 1967 to sell air time, rising by degrees to become managing director. By 1984, Nine was Australia's most popular TV channel, and the record remained unbroken every year thereafter. Chisholm's programming instincts were legendary. His mix of current affairs (he introduced the Australian version of *60 Minutes*), news and sport ultimately attracted 30 per cent of the TV audience and nearly 40 per cent of TV advertising revenues. Key to Chisholm's success was his mix of toughness and courtship. Stars were pampered at the 'Bollinger Channel', which routinely wrote out huge cheques to poach talent from rival networks. A tight group of senior executives drank regularly with Chisholm at fancy Sydney watering holes: it was here that much of the serious work got done. It was a pattern Chisholm would bring with him to Sky in London, where he quickly inaugurated the Friday Night Frolics at Chelsea bars such as the Enterprise.

But he was also ruthless, and applied punishment for every error he uncovered. 'Why aren't you getting things right?' he'd bellow at employees, even if they had done nothing obviously wrong. It was a way, he explained, of keeping them on their toes. A notorious workaholic, he routinely pored over the viewer complaint log at weekends, and watched programmes for even a hint of mistake. Paul Keating, later Prime Minister, met Chisholm while Federal Treasurer. 'I was very nervous,' he said. 'I mean people die in that office.'

Far from being an intellectual, Chisholm was nonetheless surprisingly well read, able to identify unlikely literary quotations. But he cared little for long, drawn-out discussions and micro-management. His approach was intuitive and brash – 'buccaneering,' says a former Sky executive. He was never very interested in detail. 'That is his style of management,' says Richard Dunn, for two years a senior television executive for Murdoch's News Corporation in London. 'He's always going to deputise somebody to do all of that [detailed] stuff and he'll kick arse if it doesn't get done and he'll praise – maybe – if it does get done.'

Murdoch had already won a reputation for choosing the right executive at the right time (and for dumping them when their usefulness was at an end). Chisholm himself was in the Murdoch mould: like Murdoch, the Australian-turned-American chairman of mighty News Corporation, the master company, Chisholm was blunt, sarcastic, oddly charming, ruthless and fickle. Like Murdoch, Chisholm had his favourites, but they went out of favour soon enough. When he wanted something, Murdoch knew how to court and woo: so did Chisholm. The New Zealander, too, preferred to run his company virtually alone, with only a handful of close associates (the uncharitable call them 'cronies'). He, too, delighted in keeping even shareholders and senior management in the dark over key strategic decisions. He, too, had something of the schoolyard bully about him, complete with a quick temper and a filthy vocabulary. He would later tell a senior programmer at BSkyB, who popped his head into Chisholm's office unannounced with some unsolicited marketing advice: 'What the fuck makes you think I want the opinion of a pommy cunt like you?' And he, too, was a natural strategist and masterful negotiator, seemingly born to it. Chisholm himself says his negotiating skills are 80 per cent intuition, 20 per cent perspiration. David Elstein, formerly head of programmes at BSkyB and now chief executive of Channel 5, explains: 'He's not thrown by the fact that circumstances might force him to tack away from a stated strategy, in another direction. He's obviously been heavily influenced, first by Packer, then by Murdoch, in how you deal in those situations. Basically, you climb aboard the beast and however much it bucks, you hang on and you don't step off. You have to ride it, you have to keep your nerve, you have to keep everyone else off-balance.'

Chisholm himself has this to say about his skills. 'You think about your own position, that's what you consider all or most of the time. You don't waste a lot of time, energy, thinking about the other guy's position. You concentrate on your own business, whatever that happens to be, at the time.' The single-mindedness, the clarity of vision, even the mercurial mood changes and fits of apoplexy, have time and time again flummoxed less driven rivals.

It may have come late, but given how much the two men shared, the Murdoch offer to Chisholm looked somehow inevitable. The invitation to lunch in LA marked the second time Murdoch had made a concerted effort to woo Chisholm away from Nine. In 1987, Murdoch had flown down to Sydney with Barry Diller, then the head of his Fox Hollywood studio, to sound Chisholm out about a different job. The three men went sailing in Sydney harbour to discuss the options.

Murdoch suggested Chisholm take over Channel Ten in Sydney, and advise Diller on Fox as well. Murdoch was about to sell the channel, and wanted a strong management team in place to secure the best price. Chisholm wasn't really tempted: having built Channel Nine, he didn't like the idea of working to tear it down as the head of a rival broadcaster. But nor did he want to shut the door on Murdoch. 'I said I'd think about it, because you never like to let a parachute go in this business,' Chisholm says. 'I thought, "How do I get out of this and still keep it as a backstop in case something happens?"' During the afternoon cruise, Chisholm said he would be happy to help Murdoch sort out Fox, but he didn't want to leave Nine. He did get a salary increase out of the offer, however, with Channel Nine agreeing to pay $500,000 a year. (Later, Diller, like so many Murdoch men before him, left the News family on fairly acrimonious – if highly lucrative – terms.)

Things were different by 1990. By the time Chisholm boarded his plane to Los Angeles that August weekend, he had already half made up his mind. He wanted a change, and preferred to leave Australia. He already knew the job that Murdoch wanted him to do. Everyone in broadcasting was aware of the crisis that was developing in the Murdoch empire, centering on the debilitating satellite wars in Britain. Ken Cowley, then Murdoch's key Australian lieutenant, had approached Chisholm in the summer of 1990 with a simple plea: 'We've got an enormous problem in Britain at Sky,' Cowley said. 'Are you interested in the job?' Chisholm said, 'I might be.'

Over Murdoch and Chisholm's lunch in Los Angeles, the conversation ranged across numerous subjects: mutual friends and associates in Australia, the state of the US media market. Eventually, Murdoch got around to Sky. 'I've already told Gary [Davey] I'm replacing him,' Murdoch told Chisholm. (Pat Mastandrea had already left, to return to America.) Chisholm agreed then and there to take the job. The salary would be £200,000 a year plus a potentially lucrative bonus – less in salary terms than Chisholm was making at Channel Nine but the bonuses and options won later, once BSkyB had been turned around, would vindicate the decision to move. (By 1997, Chisholm would have made nearly £20 million out of BSkyB, and probably more than £25 million counting consultancy payments from News Corporation.) There remained the question of telling Packer. The Monday following his trip to Los Angeles, Chisholm chaired the regular 8:30 am meeting, and then called his boss. Packer sensed immediately that there was no point trying to talk him out of it. (Indeed, a little fresh blood at Nine might be a good idea.) Packer asked Chisholm to stay on the board of Nine, however. 'Sure,' Chisholm responded. 'If its OK with Murdoch.' And it was, at least until Chisholm went onto the main News Corporation board in 1993.

A month later, Chisholm headed for Britain. He had been there several times before, as had most senior Australian broadcasters. He had even met Anthony Simonds-Gooding, the chief executive of Sky's rival BSB, some months before, on a courtesy visit when he was scouting out opportunities for his then boss and BSB shareholder Alan Bond. But he'd never worked in Britain; nor had he ever worked in pay-TV. So quickly had the decision to hire Chisholm been taken that no work visa could be requested and sent to Chisholm on time. When he arrived at Heathrow on the morning of 11 September 1990, a Sunday, Chisholm had to wait behind the customs barrier while David Hill, a Packer man wooed to Sky by Murdoch, argued with officials.

Hill took Chisholm straight to Isleworth, where Chisholm saw for the first time the operations he would be running. 'It looked like any other TV station,' he recalls. 'If you've seen one television station, you've seen them all. They look the same – like motor cars, unless you're an *aficionado*.' But this one *was* different: it was losing millions, and a bunker mentality had set in. The competition, BSB, had hired senior, seasoned marketers and a handful of broadcasters (at huge expense); Sky had turned to a younger, greener contingent. When BSB finally launched, the young Sky team felt the pressures.

'The biggest problem was simply lack of experience,' Chisholm now says. 'What these guys had achieved was amazing. It was real *Guinness Book of Records* stuff, [requiring] colossal energy, huge dedication and enthusiasm. They had massive self-belief which you could not help admire. But a tremendous amount of this energy was misdirected. You need degrees of management for degrees of company. These [people] were a brilliant start-up team: they [now] needed someone to carry the ball the next 100 yards, and to define and direct the energy of the company in a few more sensible areas.'

It was time for a new direction, a new broom. Chisholm, it would transpire, had the right bristles.

'Some of us were shaking,' recalls one Sky junior executive. 'Sam had no particular profile in the UK, but some of the Australians knew all about him. His reputation, at least among the Aussies, certainly preceded him.' One such Australian was Gordon French, then head of production (and soon gone), who had formerly worked for Chisholm at Channel Nine. 'Gordon was very nervous about Sam coming,' an insider recalls. 'His claim to fame was that he had had a stand-up fight with Sam, and that was one of the reasons he had left Australia. He took a swing and Sam stepped aside and [French] fell over. The next day he said good-bye, and flew as far away as possible, only to be followed...'

The press was filled with rebaked stories about Sam Chisholm: his temper, his sarcasm, the late-night drinking sessions. One of the few telling facts that actually turned out to be completely true was the plaque on Chisholm's desk at Nine: 'To err is human; to forgive is not my policy.'

Also true was Chisholm's standard line to his executives, which gave a clear clue to the way he operated. 'I am the wall against which you all have to push.'

But there were more fundamental differences of style between Chisholm and the rest of the British broadcasting industry. Adam Singer, who, as president of TCI International, John Malone's international cable and programming company, had worked extensively on both sides of the Atlantic, concluded: 'Chisholm came out of a truly competitive television environment. The whole of his strategy was that if any piece of programming looked like it might have a value at any time in the future, [you should] buy it and grow it or buy it and kill it. Nobody in the UK had been schooled in full-contact, fully competitive television, and the only place you can find these people in the English-language world is the US or Australia.'

Gary Davey told the staff about Chisholm's arrival a few weeks before he took over officially. 'The company has moved on to another level now,' Davey told them. 'We've got to get some serious responsibility in here. Sam Chisholm is going to do that, so I can start to have some fun again on the programming side.'

At the first executive meeting, Chisholm instituted his now famous 8:30 Monday sessions. He went round the room, asking everyone: 'Who are you, and what do you do?' It felt to one attendee like a 'defining moment', the start of a new era.

All senior managers had to go to the meetings, unless he or she was outside the country. And 8:30 actually meant whatever time Chisholm was ready to start. The quick learners saw the way forward: get there early. 'Like a game of musical chairs, I'm convinced Sam made sure that there was always one chair missing. Anybody who arrived late got the full treatment,' recalls a now-departed Sky employee. 'It became clear that Sam liked to engage in ritual humiliation. Every meeting, at least one person got it bad, and the rest of us just breathed a sigh of relief.' Recalls another: 'It was like Sam's victim of the week.'

Some women were reduced to tears. At least once, the treatment was so bad, even Chisholm himself felt chastened. He presented the woman in question with a watch of significant value, and a fulsome apology. But he still found a target at the next meeting.

David Elstein recalls: 'For some time I found it very unsettling and upsetting. It seemed completely unnecessary and miles over the top and there was an aspect of it that was just straightforward bullying.' But Elstein soon learned that the ritual humiliation was just one of Chisholm's tools. 'There were two things going on,' he recalls. 'One was his own dyspepsia, the build-up of bile and frustration. No doubt he was getting the same from Rupert most days, so passing it on to his troops seemed reasonable. But another part was conveying the sense of urgency, the sense of embattlement, the sense of permanent crisis and a sense of his ability to solve any problem. Individuals felt belittled and empowered at the same time.'

Chisholm immediately imported some other tried and tested techniques from his years at Nine. An executive rota was established, and from the start Chisholm invited a few key colleagues out for 'drink and discuss sessions'. There soon developed a gang of three: Chisholm, David Chance and Bruce McWilliam, Chisholm's lawyer (some call him the *consigliere*, akin to Rupert Murdoch's own legal adviser, Arthur Siskind). Gary Davey continued to take a hands-on role, as Chisholm's nominal number two, especially on developing programming.

Chance, particularly, became a crucial member of the inner sanctum. Young, public-school educated, and with US experience, 'David was almost like a son,' says one Sky insider who knows both men. 'Sam turns to David for the details, and expects him to remember everything.' Chisholm liked the fact that Chance had been the British-based marketing director for Astra, the satellite company that would prove crucial to Sky's dominance of the UK pay-TV market.

It was a measure of Chisholm's feelings for Chance that the marketing man was soon exempt from the grilling meted out to other senior executives at the dreaded Monday morning meeting. The last time Chance himself was on the receiving end of a public bollocking was 1991, during the summer, at a time when dish sales were sluggish. 'Dish sales are shit, and you are incompetent,' Chisholm thundered. 'What am I going to tell Murdoch?' Chance stood his ground, as the rest of the executives at the meeting looked down at their papers. 'It's hot, Sam,' he said, 'and people don't buy dishes in the summer.' Chisholm gave him a withering look. 'Is that the best you can do? Is that the best fucking excuse you can give me?' 'Yeah,' Chance answered. 'That's it.'

Chisholm kept up the pressure for another two meetings, having decided it was Chance's turn in the barrel. Exasperated, Chance told himself: 'This is not how I want to spend the rest of my life.' He asked for a meeting with Chisholm, walked into his office and shut the door. 'I'm the best guy to do this job,' Chance said. 'But if you think there is anyone else, you should let me go home and go and get him. If you want to motivate me,

I don't need to be harangued in front of my colleagues. I will work my ass off for you, and I do work my ass off for you.'

Chisholm sat Chance down, and said, 'I think you are brilliant, you are the best for the job. Obviously we are all under pressure to get these dish sales up. You're going to go a long way in this company: you are going to replace me.' That was the last time Chance got the ritual humiliation treatment.

Outside the inner group, even very senior people were kept out of the information loop. 'We were made to feel unreliable: we weren't to know what was really going on,' says one Sky executive. 'We had the impression there were always deals going on, shadowy things, and that somehow Sam would always come out on top. That was part of his power.'

Chisholm also began to take an interest in the smallest detail of the on-screen programmes. Anybody at Sky had to be prepared for a late-night berating phone call. At the 8:30 meetings, he routinely bawled out his team, accusing them of knowing nothing about television and of never heeding his commands.

'It's your relationship with people that makes it all work, and their relationship with you,' Chisholm says. 'You can't run companies by barking orders down the telephone. You've got to have an understanding of each other. It just makes life easier, and it makes it more effective too.'

Chisholm felt he was pushing against the nature of the British. 'You've got to pull people together by a variety of tactics, because good broadcasting should have good teams, and, in my experience, the English are not constituted by teams. The English are by nature individuals, and they don't fraternise in the same way as, say, Australians and Americans. You've got to get them to work all together and it's quite difficult, when they don't have this culture.'

Chisholm clearly had no great affection for the English. He was quick to adopt a 'posh' English accent when poking fun at rival broadcasters, bemoaning the elitism, the arrogance, of the British media scene. 'Oh, three cheers,' he often muttered, when anyone made what he regarded as a typically snooty 'English' observation. Remarks Adam Singer: 'Sam can be immensely charming, he can be very funny, very witty and he's managed to charm, bludgeon, impose himself on the British estab-lishment. But he has very little time for the English and England – he can't stand us basically.'

By the second meeting after his arrival at Isleworth, Chisholm was hitting his stride. He announced that costs were going to have to be cut –

and fast. Already a few executives were either left to leave or saw the writing on the wall. Murdoch slowly pulled back, waiting for Chisholm to start delivering on his promises. The phone calls from Los Angeles continued, and the pressures to cut, cut, cut were enormous. But day to day, Chisholm was basically left to get on with it.

For a man long associated with an open chequebook, Chisholm took to cost-cutting with unexpected glee. 'The first thing was no cheques got signed until [Chisholm] signed them,' recalls a senior executive. 'Anything over £10,000 Sam had to sign, and that was practically everything.' One independent producer had done some work for Sky, submitting an invoice. When he hadn't been paid for several weeks, he called the accounts department, where he could get no satisfaction. As the work had been directly commissioned by Chisholm, the producer placed a call directly to the chief executive's office. Chisholm came on the line. 'I am now going on holiday for two weeks, and the cheque book is locked in my desk drawer,' Chisholm told the producer. 'And that's where it stays until I get back.' For a time, only bills with writs actually attached were paid. Chisholm was intent on husbanding the little cash he had to play with. The draconian approach reached high and low in the company. Photocopy paper had to be used on both sides, and 'you couldn't get a paperclip in the company', one insider says.

Chisholm also set about appointing people he trusted, and figuring out whom of the existing staff he respected. He was immediately comfortable with David Evans, another Australian, who had run Packer's Melbourne TV station when Chisholm was in Sydney. Evans would stay on until 1993, when he went to Los Angeles on behalf of BSkyB, subsequently joining Fox Television. Evans decamped in 1997, wooed to John Malone's TCI. One of Chisholm's first appointments at BSkyB was Peter Shea, the ex-Thames ad salesman who was asked to sort out Sky's flagging sales efforts. The company had gone through six sales directors in a year.

Shea went to see Chisholm during the chief executive's first week at Sky. 'I had a very quick negotiation with Sam and we struck a verbal deal,' Shea recalls. 'And he said, "You can start now, you don't leave the room until you accept the deal".' Shea went straight to the Sky sales office near Victoria station, only to be turned away at the door. Chris Benson, then sales director, refused to see him. By the next day, Chisholm had fired Benson over the telephone, and Shea was put in charge.

'The first thing I had to do was to generate the maximum amount of cash possible,' Shea says. That meant ditching the 'Charter Advertiser' system that Sky had put in place, under which leading advertisers paid up front for promised air time. 'The problem was everybody knew what everybody else was paying,' says one member of the sales staff. Shea introduced short-term spot invoicing, which meant cash was coming in on a regular monthly basis. But advertising was simply not cash generative enough. Forecasts of the time proved woefully inaccurate about the strength of the advertising market for satellite television: indeed, even today, BSkyB earns a bit more than ten per cent of its revenues from advertisers. The business, at least for most the 1990s, was to be about subscription television, as both Murdoch and Chisholm had come to realise.

Cost-cutting, new staff appointments and tight controls on accounts payable were just the first steps. 'Sam took the company by the throat, and gave it a good shake to wake it up,' Ray Gallagher, head of public affairs, recalls. 'I worked long hours, because there were just so many problems,' Chisholm now says. 'It was so difficult to get to grips, having come out of a business where everything is so organised, and going into one that was so totally bloody disorganised. Everyone was pretty territorial. It took a lot of skill to finally get everybody pulling behind the things that I wanted.'

And behind the scenes, by phone and during regular visits to London, Murdoch continued to pressurise and cajole. He knew that the success of his global media strategy rested squarely on the prospects at Sky. Murdoch wasn't the only source of pressure on Chisholm and his executive team, however. At Battersea, at the swank headquarters of BSB, the rivals were gearing up for the battle of a lifetime. 'We are a fully loaded gun pointed at Sky's head,' Anthony Simonds-Gooding, BSB's chief executive, said at the time. When the smoke cleared, there could only be one victor.

CHAPTER 4

Satellite Peace

By the late summer of 1990, alarm bells were ringing at the corporate headquarters of Pearson, Granada and Reed. BSB had managed to sign up just 110,000 dish subscribers, using its much-ridiculed 'squarial' units as well as at least two other formats that eventually found their way into retail shops. Sky had 750,000 satellite subscribers to its four channels, which included Sky Movies, the film service. But Sky's headstart was not enough. Both companies were bleeding freely – so much so that the idea of abandoning their services was no longer even conceivable to their increasingly alarmed shareholders. So much was now at stake: not just the future of the far-flung Murdoch empire, but the financial viability of a clutch of Britain's most important media companies.

The chairmen of the four BSB investors -- Peter Davis, Michael Blakenham, Alex Bernstein and Jérôme Seydoux – decided that they had to get more involved. A committee of four was established, with Bernstein from Granada, Reed's Ian Irvine, Eric Guilly from Chargeurs and Frank Barlow, the former chief executive of *The Financial Times*.

Barlow's appointment in 1990 to second Lord Blakenham at Pearson marked a radical departure for the staid, family run company. Barlow was a definite outsider, what one Pearson confidante calls 'a counter-intuitive choice'. Next to chairman Lord Blakenham's Eton and Harvard and finance director James Joll's Eton and Oxford, Barlow was from another planet – born in Cumbria, educated at a grammar school and with a stint in Africa for *The Daily Mirror* under his belt. He had already paid his dues at Pearson, spending several years at Westminster Press, a regional newspaper group that Pearson subsequently sold, before taking on *The Financial Times*.

'We had lunch at Reed's office, and the first thing we did was to ask Simonds-Gooding to have regular weekly meetings [because] we had to be involved,' Barlow says. Simonds-Gooding, who had been used to running his own show, resisted throughout lunch, but finally gave way by tea time. After just three meetings, Barlow went to his chairman, Lord Blakenham, and told him that BSB wasn't going to work. The only solution, Barlow believed, was a merger.

Barlow had not been the first to suggest the companies come together. The idea of merger had been floated in the trade press, and many ITV rivals believed that BSB and Sky would eventually have to accept a marriage. Such a radical move looked impossible to achieve, however. A merger might have been possible before the two services launched. But with emotions running so high, and with the war of words (in newspapers, in the High Street and even in Parliament) it was inconceivable that either side would give in. More to the point, both had committed such large sums of money (at least £1.5 billion between them by the time of the merger) that neither could contemplate the concessions that a marriage would entail. Granada, among the BSB shareholders, had even graver worries about the idea of merging with an unregulated satellite service. The ITV licence holder did not want to upset the IBA, which oversaw not only the DBS licences but the ITV franchises as well. Granada, alone among the BSB shareholders, was already a regulated broadcaster, with its North of England ITV business. Pearson, for its part, had a stake in Yorkshire–Tyne Tees, another ITV franchise, and so was worried, too, about what the IBA might think. In a few months, Granada, along with the other ITV franchise holders, would be asked to submit competitive bids to win renewal of their licences, under the controversial Broadcasting Act (1990). Now was surely not the time to antagonise the regulator.

Barlow believed, however, that the crunch was not far away, and that there was every chance BSB could actually bring the founding companies crashing down. All four principal shareholders of BSB had been staggered by the continuing cash demands from Marcopolo House. 'They had been told they would spend X and they were being asked for X times N,' Barlow says. 'Everyone was getting huge pressure from their boards of directors,' recalls another BSB executive. Reed in particular was nervous, and even suggested to its partners that 'just getting its money back' would be enough.

Barlow prepared a memo for the Pearson board, suggesting that funding be arranged to allow BSB to carry on until Easter of 1991. By that time, he believed, a merger would be inevitable, and at least BSB would have a big enough business to have a real say in the terms of the marriage.

Versions of that same memo were presented to all four sponsoring boards, and the plan was agreed.

Meanwhile, at Sky, the prospects were just as dire. 'Nobody could bloody afford to spend money this way,' says one Sky executive. Even Chisholm himself wondered how long it could go on. 'They had simply spent themselves into oblivion, all of them,' he says. 'The truth was that both businesses were conceptual failures and they had failed the execution [too]. It hadn't just been a failure, it had been an appalling failure.'

BSB did not have to wait until Easter, however. US investment banker John Veronis, playing the honest broker, had engineered a meeting between Murdoch and Peter Davis from Reed that July. While the dinner meeting, at Claridges Hotel in London on 26 July, had led nowhere, it had opened up a line of communication between the two camps. By September, the two rivals were on the edge of disaster, with Murdoch under threat from his increasingly worried banks. A crisis meeting was called by Murdoch himself at the end of September, and BSB sent Ian Irvine to Murdoch's ranch in Australia. Looking back, Murdoch concedes he was worried about BSB's financial firepower. 'They [BSB] had some big share-holders, with deep pockets, and they could have continued to outspend us,' he says.

Murdoch and Irvine spent 48 hours thrashing out the bare outlines of a merger deal. 'A pretty vague understanding was reached that there would be a merger,' Barlow says. 'Rupert was rather vague, and that was tactical. What came out subsequently was that Rupert would have gone broke, but we didn't know that at the time. He was planning a merger, and he knew what he wanted out of it.'

The merger talks began in earnest in late October, at Lucknam Park, a luxury hotel in the Wiltshire countryside near Bath. Andrew Knight, chief executive of News International, and Peter Stehrenberger, NI's finance director, represented Murdoch, assisted by lawyers from Farrer and Co. Sam Chisholm and Gary Davey also attended the meetings, mainly to provide information about Sky, while the company's legal affairs director, Deanna Bates, sat in. The BSB side sent Frank Barlow, Ian Irvine and Derek Lewis, then chief executive of Granada, to negotiate, and brought in Ian Chubb, BSB's finance director, to provide additional information. Not once did Rupert Murdoch himself attend. But NI negotiators conceded later they had been in constant touch with the boss.

The talks were kept secret from nearly everyone on the staff of the two companies. Anthony Simonds-Gooding was told early, and sworn to secrecy, but was not invited to the merger negotiations. John Gau, BSB's director of programmes, was called in to provide details on BSB's movie deals, but was similarly told to tell no one. Ironically, a group of journalists was meeting in another room of the luxury hotel. Amazingly, word of the talks was kept out of the press until the very eve of the deal. But some middle-ranking executives of both BSB and Sky suspected something was happening. Sky insiders recall the numerous phone calls from Stehrenberger, the News International lawyer, demanding detailed financial information. They noticed, too, that both Chisholm and Davey were away from the office, and that even Bates, the Sky lawyer, was absent. Rumours began to fly around Sky's Isleworth headquarters. At BSB, too, some managers sensed that something was up, particularly when Ian Clubb disappeared.

Despite the huge egos involved (the biggest, indeed, in British media), there was a astonishing will to see the merger succeed. It was a measure perhaps of the scale of the financial pressures. But that did not make the negotiations any easier. Throughout the week at Lucknam Park, as the two sides argued over satellite contracts, movies, sport and the precise financial terms of the marriage, there were many times when it looked like the talks would founder after all. 'One of the big arguments everybody was having was which satellite we were going to use,' Deanna Bates recalls. 'The BSB side seemed to think that if you went Astra's way, Sky would have [been seen to have] won.' BSB shareholders were intent on ensuring that the merger was viewed as mutually beneficial: a true merger, in other words, and not a takeover by Sky. (After the fact, Peter Rogers, at the IBA, would comment: 'Merger is a public relations term. We knew it was a takeover.')

In the end, BSB agreed that the capacity limitations of the Marcopolo satellite would be a brake on future growth. Astra carried 16 channels, and the company was planning more satellite launches. BSB had a maximum of just five channels. From that concession, the logic of the merger unfolded inevitably in Sky's favour. Out would go the D-MAC technology, developed at such great expense; instead, Sky's PAL standard would emerge as the chief means of delivering satellite signals in the UK. That meant that the merged firms would have to use a PAL-compatible encryption technology when they came, later, to scramble virtually all BSkyB's signals. Usefully for Murdoch, his own company, News Datacom, had developed a PAL system known as Videocrypt, which would eventually emerge as the only functioning conditional access technology for satellite in the country.

The decision on which satellite to use was a disappointment to several managers on the BSB team. Many of them, including Simonds-Gooding, were convinced that the D-MAC/squarial technology was vastly superior to PAL/Astra. But not everyone saw it this way. Barlow recalls: 'One thing Simonds-Gooding was saying is that we should definitely stick to the squarial, because it was far superior. Now, as a matter of fact [I said to him], "Although you tell me that this has a better picture I really can't tell the difference". But there was a big thing about keeping the squarial.'

There were great debates, too, about how the eventual dividends (providing there were any) would be apportioned among the shareholders. While the final deal gave each side 50 per cent of the merged entity, Murdoch was promised a higher share of the initial pay-out once profitability was reached. 'That reflected [the fact] that News Corp had effectively a better business and they were entitled to an earlier pay out,' Richard Brooke, now BSkyB's finance director, and then on the finance team at BSB, explains. (As it turned out, subsequent refinancings meant that the unequal pay-out structure was never fully invoked.)

Crucially, Murdoch also won the right to appoint the chief executive of the merged companies, a request readily accepted even by the BSB shareholders, who believed that Murdoch was in the best position to make the new company a success. There was a difference of views, however, about the chairmanship. Says Barlow: 'I had a conversation with Ian Irvine [and said], "We must have the chairman", and they were saying, "no, we must have Rupert to run it." And I said, "Make no mistake, I want Rupert to run it, I want News to run it, and I realise the value of that, but politically, it's not acceptable." So it was agreed that we would have the chairman, that Ian Irvine would be [appointed].'

By the time the week's negotiation had been completed in late October, the shareholders had the bare bones of an agreement. The new company would be called BSkyB (but trade as Sky), and the chief executive would be Sam Chisholm. The company name was revealing: all that was left of BSB were the two bookend 'B's, surrounding the only truly pronounceable, and therefore memorable, bit of the title. (In the end, the merged company would have a lot to answer for in providing a progeny of equally tortuous corporate names around the globe: Murdoch would later choose ASkyB, ISkyB and JSkyB for his American, Indian and Japanese pay-TV ventures.) The Astra satellite would be used to transmit the combined Sky–BSB services, even if there might be a need to 'dual-illuminate' the two services for a time (meaning that the services would be available on either satellite system). But there remained a few stumbling blocks, not least how to handle the expensive movie contracts the two companies had reached with Hollywood studios.

'The shareholders of BSB didn't necessarily know what was going on [with the movie contracts],' Deanna Bates says. 'We had a look at [the contracts] signed with UIP and others, and it was billions of pounds over the time of the deal and it was twice as expensive as the Sky deals.' In the first five years alone, it was estimated BSB would have to pay Hollywood $700 million. Gary Davey had a private word with Ian Irvine to see whether BSB might come up with additional money to finance the movie contracts following the merger, given how much more expensive they were. 'Don't be so naive, so pathetic,' Irvine told Davey. In the end, however, the movie contracts would prove to be one of the most intractable issues on the table. BSB would end up agreeing to fund more than its share of the merged companies' operating costs, largely because of the drain represented by BSB's Hollywood deals.

The teams moved to London, and the offices of Freshfields, BSB's lawyers, on the last Monday in October, to finalise terms. That day, Murdoch went to see Margaret Thatcher, who for a few more days would be Prime Minister (a leadership review came just two weeks later, ushering in the government of John Major). At the end of their meeting, Murdoch told Thatcher about the merger plans. Recalls Murdoch: 'She was showing out a foreign visitor, and she said to him, "Here is Mr Murdoch, who gives us Sky News, the only unbiased news in the UK". I said, "Well you know it is costing us a lot, and we are going to have to do a merger [with BSB]", and she just nodded. This was a day before the announcement.'

By this time, there were growing fears that the news would leak out and set off a political storm. Granada was still very nervous about its relationship with the IBA, and Alex Bernstein, the chairman, tried to convince his partners that he should tell George Russell, the IBA chairman, about the merger plans. Barlow and Davis argued strenuously against the idea, and in the end Bernstein caved in. In the event, Russell was only told after the merger was agreed, much to his anger.

By now, the merger looked all but inevitable. The chief advantage lay in the fact that BSB had a separate financial structure, and could fund the combined operations for a time. Murdoch, it had now become clear, had virtually no money to pump in, and it was agreed that BSB would provide up to £100 million in financing – enough for a few months' more trading. By then, the partners hoped, the banks would be prepared to offer project financing to see BSkyB into profit. An existing £380 million non-recourse loan from Barclays Bank could be renegotiated, for example. Sky's Nick Carrington says: 'On a day-to-day basis the most important thing was that Granada and the other BSB shareholders effectively financed the whole venture for a few months. BSB had a whole financing structure, because it was a stand alone company.' In the end, however, the banks refused, sending BSkyB into yet another funding crisis.

That would come later. At first, the two sets of owners were ecstatic that they had managed to get the merger deal done. The official announcement was made at on 2 November, a Friday, but not until 9:00 pm, after the lawyers had finessed the last of the complicated clauses in the deal. Murdoch had flown in from Australia, where he had been attending the annual meeting of News Corporation, his master company. He invited his young son, Lachlan, who had recently joined his father's Australian operating company, to witness the formal signing of the merger deal. That night, the Sky camp celebrated their victory at a hastily convened party at Isleworth. The BSB executives, however, held something more akin to a wake at Marcopolo House.

Further details gradually emerged. BSkyB had inherited a total of nine channels: the four Sky services (Sky Movies, Eurosport, Sky 1 and Sky News) as well as BSB's five (Galaxy, Now, Power Station, the Movie Channel and the Sports Channel). Early in 1991, BSkyB applied, successfully, to the ITC to drop the number to seven, through the 'merger' of Galaxy with Sky 1 and of Now and Sky News. By April of 1991, following the launch of Astra 1B, the new satellite on which Sky had an option for two more transponders, Sky was ready to offer five channels for UK viewers: Sky News, Sky 1, Sky Sports (Eurosport was dropped, under duress from the European Commission, and the old BSB Sports Channel was moved onto Astra and renamed), and the two movie channels. Power Station, BSB's music video service, was also dropped. Despite vague promises that both satellite systems would remain in service 'while there was demand', it became clear only Sky would continue.

Within days of the merger, Sam Chisholm had written to retailers saying that only the Astra dishes should be sold or rented from then on. Manufacturers of the squarial, including Philips, immediately ceased all production runs, and began to consult their lawyers about the merger. Could BSkyB get away with dumping the squarial altogether, without compensating dish manufacturers? Sam Chisholm thought so, and wanted BSkyB to hold its ground. There was no reason why the two satellite services should continue to be operated. He was appalled the weekend after the merger announcement when Andrew Knight, chief executive of News International, promised on national television that squarial owners would be 'swapped out' at BSkyB's expense.

'I did not think it was courageous,' Chisholm says. 'It was the easy option, and I didn't think it was in the company's best interests. Andrew Knight came out and said we'll swap everyone out, and then we couldn't go back on this.' The cost of swapping 110,000 dishes rose to about £10 million in the end. Looking back, Chisholm is still highly critical. 'It was a questionable decision,' he says.

There was also pressure from the IBA, which looked for a time like it might flex its muscles. In the view of George Russell and the IBA members, the DBS licences had not been the property of BSB to dispose of. 'At the time of the takeover, our main concern, and considerable irritation, was not with Sky, which was not our licensee, but with BSB who were,' the ITC's Peter Rogers recalls. 'Effectively, they were in breach of their contract with us. The irritation was not with Murdoch, who was under no obligation to us whatever, but with those who were under obligation, who out of fear or whatever had abrogated that contract and not told us about it.' The new company, it reasoned, ought to at least offer to 'dual illuminate' the service on both Astra and Marcopolo for several months, perhaps as long as two years. And it should certainly offer to 'swap out' BSB's 110,000 dish owners.

The IBA even considered taking legal action against the merged company. Was it feasible to launch a claim for damages against BSB, for breach of contract? Was there anything in the relevant legislation that might help the IBA scupper the deal? Meanwhile, the new Independent Television Commission, the IBA's successor set up under the 1990 Broadcasting Act, which was already up and running in shadow form, also came out publicly against the merger, while the Office of Fair Trading, the competition watchdog, said it would investigate the terms of the deal. Looking back, (now Sir) George Russell says: 'We'd have given permission, had they asked. The IBA could not have taken upon themselves to reject it on those grounds. I think it was quite obvious that these two groups were in serious trouble, and we could see how they could get out of it. Would the IBA have wanted these two systems to go under? They must have been close to trading as insolvent as separate groups. The measures were of desperation. It was not a long-term strategy. It was the only strategy that gave them a chance.'

Because the BSB shareholders had acted without consulting the regulator, they were treated harshly. 'The BSB owners were in great danger of being defined as not fit and proper, because they deliberately for commercial reasons chose to reject the contracts and obligations they had undertaken,' Sir George recalls. 'I was prepared to take it through the boards of all the companies – the main board directors. It was a correct club that they knew I was prepared to use.'

He adds: 'We took a fairly hard line with them. Those who had an interest in the terrestrial side were willing to do a lot to make up for what they had done. Lots of things were agreed, including that two people called compliance officers were appointed. Murdoch has always had a view that you can do well enough without bucking the regulator. Go as near to the edge as you can, but stay within the rules.'

The fact that the IBA was in the process of passing the regulatory torch to the new ITC was, in fact, a crucial matter. Under the Broadcasting Act of 1990, which was only then coming into force, it might have been impossible for Murdoch's Sky to control 50 per cent of a new, merged company controlling the official DBS licences. But due to the way the Act was worded, there was an odd hiatus during which neither the IBA nor the ITC actually had the power to regulate. It was, suspiciously, during this tiny window that BSB and Sky merged. 'The control of satellite ownership did not come in for five days,' Sir George Russell recalls. 'I expect this move was known in the cabinet, but it was not known to us. She [Mrs Thatcher] knew before we did, and no information was passed to us. There was a strange gap, because the rules on satellite ownership had not yet come in. It was a clever move at the time.'

Politicians were vocal in opposition. Robin Corbett, then Labour's broadcasting spokesman, attacked the merger as a 'Skyjack,' telling *Marketing*: 'We are totally opposed to a satellite monopoly, particularly when controlled by a non-EC national [Rupert Murdoch].' Veiled threats from Isleworth – notably that BSkyB would simply transfer its operations to Luxembourg or another off-shore headquarters, using its 'non-domestic' Astra satellite licence to broadcast to UK audiences – particularly enraged critics. 'Bluff,' said Corbett. But the Tory government seemed relaxed about the merger. David Mellor, later National Heritage Secretary, whose department oversaw the television sector, said that market forces should be left to prevail. Two satellite companies could not make a profitable business: one on its own had a far better chance. When the storm settled,

Murdoch had, once again, correctly read the political mood. He would not be stopped by a Conservative government.

With the merger deal done, Murdoch and Chisholm lost little time. That Friday night, 2 November 1990, just hours before the merger was announced, Simonds-Gooding was told by Frank Barlow in a brief phone call that he was no longer needed. Over the weekend, BSB's personnel director, Jennifer Haigh, rang Simonds-Gooding to say that he should stay away from Marcopolo House. His personal belongings were removed and delivered to his home. (Haigh, herself, would also subsequently leave.) On the Monday morning, Chisholm went to the BSB headquarters, and a day-long board meeting began. Murdoch himself joined late that afternoon, as the discussions continued. He arrived a little late, having been stuck in the lift at Marcopolo House for ten minutes.

On the Tuesday, Chisholm and a handful of Sky executives were actually barred from entering Marcopolo House. 'Someone had told the security guards that no one from Sky should be let in,' an insider says. Chisholm was forced to return to Isleworth, where he made a few phone calls. Later that morning, the team returned, and the real blood-letting could begin.

Within days of taking over at BSkyB, Chisholm asked Arthur Andersen, the management consultants, to look through the books, to determine exactly how much the merged entity was losing. 'I remember giving [them] £20,000 because the company had no money, but I said I would make it up to them in years to come,' Chisholm says. Chisholm stood by his promise to Arthur Andersen, and was equally loyal to Herbert Smith, the lawyers, and particularly Charles Plant, who had done stellar work for the company. A previous law firm issued a statutory demand for £25,000, and never got another bit of business from BSkyB.

The results of the Arthur Andersen audit were sobering in the extreme: combined, the companies were losing £14 million a week. These losses 'were just absolutely unsustainable'. Chisholm says. 'That's when I rang Murdoch and said, "This is what the company is losing at the trading level", and so that's when the gloves came off.'

Having already cut costs sharply at Sky, it was decided that Chisholm would implement the same policy at the merged company. 'The first thing I did was stop all the cheques,' he recalls, 'you know, the usual stuff.' He also slashed jobs: virtually all the BSB's 580 staff were either fired or left of their own accord. Those who were on short-term contracts did not have them renewed. Even some of Sky's 700 employees were let go, leaving the combined payroll at least 50 per cent down. Notwithstanding the long-term lease on BSB's Marcopolo House, which BSkyB kept following the merger, the whole operation would be moved to Isleworth. Later, QVC, the home shopping channel part-owned by BSkyB, would take space. And in 1997, the winners of the digital terrestrial licence, British Digital Broadcasting, would agree to move in.

The first steps following the BSB-Sky merger were ruthless. 'I fired Ian Clubb [BSB's finance director] the first day,' Chisholm says, because he believed Clubb could not provide the financial information he required. A steady stream of employees visited Chisholm's office in the first week, to learn of their fate. Bob Hunter, who had been running BSB's sports channel, was another who lost his job. According to Sky lore (although disputed by Chisholm himself), Chisholm called him in, and announced gleefully that Hunter's contract had in fact run out, and that he was owed nothing. 'But you are a sporting man, and so am I,' Chisholm is said by some to have told Hunter. The two men would flip a coin: if Hunter won, Chisholm would pay him six month's salary. But if Chisholm won, Hunter would get nothing, and would agree not to sue for a pay-off. Hunter agreed and won the toss. Whatever the truth, Hunter certainly got his money.

Chisholm was always hard-nosed about sackings. When he later fired BSB veteran Ellis Griffiths, formerly chief engineer at Channel 4, who had stayed on board after the merger as BSkyB's head of operations, he offered no severance whatsoever. Chisholm was convinced that Griffiths was a 'fifth columnist', working on his own projects and revealing information about BSkyB to rivals and regulators. Chisholm even had Griffiths' phone calls recorded, in an attempt to unmask the conspiracy. Griffiths ultimately sued BSkyB and was awarded £90,000 in compensation because he was exonerated of all Chisholm's charges. But not without a long, legal battle. Chisholm just would not give in.

Chisholm attacked the cost-cutting in a style that many in British television outside Sky had never seen before. They were unused to the bullying, the shouting, the ritual humiliation. They hadn't experienced the odd mix of British, American and Australian customs that Sky had created at Isleworth – known, by some in the industry, as 'that Aussie drinking club at the end of the M4 [motorway]'.

Some shareholders were privately aghast at the swingeing cuts introduced by Chisholm, but were content to leave him alone. 'They'd all had a go at it and I think they found it the most depressing experience,' Chisholm now recalls. 'So they were prepared to let me do it. The tactics that I employed were probably not the tactics that they would have employed so it was easy for them to sit back and say, "Look, he's uncontrollable, this guy, he's tough". I was everybody's instrument of torture, but I made it very clear from the start, the quicker we can take this business back, the quicker we can take it forward.'

Even Murdoch, as ruthless an executive as they come, was taken aback at the cuts. 'Sam likes to talk about the turnaround, but remember, we put these two companies together, and the big losses only lasted for about a month because Sam was in there on the first day firing everybody. I think only two people survived from BSB. I'm sure some people got fired who shouldn't have been fired, but that is really the only way to do it in a business facing bankruptcy.'

The merger was effectively a takeover of BSB by Sky, but there were still casualties from among the Sky staff. Chisholm sent a note to staff at Isleworth, warning them not to be complacent. 'They had got a bit smart out at Isleworth and they thought that BSB were getting all the flack and they were scot free.' Virtually all of Peter Shea's sales team was asked to go, and Chisholm promised jobs to BSB employees to replace them. But the BSB team, *en masse*, eventually declined the offer. Shea, however, was not allowed to offer the old Sky employees their jobs back.

The initial months after the merger were a 'nightmare', a participant recalls. There was a huge outcry in Parliament, confusion in the High Street electronics shops, a raft of legal action from squarial dish manufacturers and a whispering campaign from the independent production sector, which had suddenly lost four channels of original programming when, ultimately, all but one (movies) of the BSB channels were dumped. Chisholm and his team ignored the fuss. Running now the only satellite service in the UK, they set about restructuring the channel lineup, cutting administrative overheads, and relaunching the marketing campaign. A single proposition, carrying six channels, was introduced in April 1991, backed by press adverts. The Movie Channel was added to Astra, giving BSkyB two, encrypted movie services on a single satellite platform. Recalls a senior Sky executive: 'Because you had one proposition in the market place, the consumers started to go out with confidence as opposed to just prior to the merger, [when] sales were very tough to generate.'

But despite all the advantages – a single satellite proposition, full support from the advertising community, a compliant regulator, and nearly two million cable and satellite customers – the business remained on shaky ground in 1991. It became clear that cost-cutting on its own would not save the company. Indeed, by March of that year, the company was in danger of being engaged in illegal trading, an offence punishable by a prison sentence imposed on company directors.

Frank Barlow, Pearson's representative on the board of BSkyB, was increasingly nervous. 'If you carry on trading when you have no money, you go to jail,' he says. 'I remember at this meeting, all the chairmen [of the parent companies] starting saying what I should do and what I shouldn't do, and I said, "Don't tell me what to do. [As directors of BSkyB], Ian Irvine and I go to jail, you don't".' Barlow explains the financial pressures that came to a head in March 1991. 'One of the theories behind the merger was that BSB was going to get a project loan from the banks, as well as the money coming from the shareholders. The great theory was that there would be no competition. I had a meeting with the chairmen of the four investing companies, when Ian [Irvine] arrived from a meeting at the bank, saying we wouldn't get a project loan. The banks realised now how stretched News really was. Even after the merger, it was too big a risk.'

Murdoch's own financial problems were widely known by then. In January of 1991, just two months after the merger, a massive restructuring deal was agreed by the News companies and their bankers. All told, $8.2 billion worth of debt was rescheduled. Under the terms of the debt deal, Murdoch could not use money from News Corp or News International, the UK operating company, to shore up the ailing BSkyB. Fully $800 million in the first year had to be paid to banks out of asset sales and increased profits. The strict covenants would prove to be a huge sticking point when, inevitably, BSkyB was forced once again to turn to its shareholders for more money. Barlow requested a BSkyB board meeting, and asked Herbert Smith, the lawyers, to explain the rules on illegal trading. The only way to rebalance the situation was to raise more cash, he told his fellow directors. The banks had refused a project loan even for £200 million, the minimum needed to keep the business afloat. One of the chief drains on cash was the money going to Hollywood for films. The two companies had competed with each other for studio rights, and between them stood to spend more than $1.2 billion over five years, and several times that amount over the whole of the multi-year contracts. Worse, some of the payments would have to be made whether or not the films were shown, and even if BSkyB could not attract enough paying viewers to cover the costs. These so-called minimum guarantees were the crippling aspect of several of the major deals done in the heady days of 1989 by the two rival services.

Barlow believed he could convince the four BSB shareholders – Pearson,

Reed, Chargeurs and Granada – to put up another £25 million each, provided Murdoch was prepared to offer £100 million to retain his 50 per cent stake in the merged company. That, in theory anyway, would give BSkyB the £200 million it needed to reach break even. 'If we don't succeed in this,' he told the BSkyB directors, 'then we will have to cease trading. We'll have to go to court and say we are in a parlous state.'

As the ground phase of the Gulf War carried on through early 1991, daily images from the battlefield were televised back to Britain. One eye on the TV screen, Barlow rang Murdoch's office in New York, demanding to speak to him. The secretary told him Murdoch was unavailable. 'Tell him its Frank Barlow, he'll be available for me,' Barlow said. A few minutes passed, and the secretary came back on the line. 'I'm sorry, he really isn't available.' Increasingly angry, Barlow told the secretary to find out where Murdoch was, and tell him to call London. Five minutes later, Andrew Knight, Murdoch's chief UK lieutenant, rang Barlow's office. 'I gather you are trying to get hold of Rupert,' he said. 'Yes, I am,' Barlow replied, 'and no offence, but you won't do.' Knight said, 'Yes, I understand that, but the problem is, it's Rupert's [60th] birthday, and he promised his wife he would take a holiday and not work. They are at a fitness resort in Arizona, and he promised he wouldn't interrupt it.' (Recalls Murdoch: 'I said to my wife, I don't want any bloody party, I would treat myself to one of these fitness places.') 'Look,' Barlow said, 'I must see him. Tell him I'll go to Arizona.' Knight patched Barlow's call through to Murdoch and the two men agreed to meet.

The trip was so hastily arranged that Barlow was questioned severely at the airport by officials. With the Gulf War raging, security was extremely tight. 'Why are you going to Arizona, and why did you purchase your ticket only yesterday?' the security officer probed. Barlow was eventually allowed to board the flight, and arrived in Tucson, where Murdoch's pilot awaited him to drive to the resort. He was surprised to see Sam Chisholm already there, going through budgets with Murdoch. Chisholm had just flown in from Los Angeles, where he had been attempting to renegotiate the onerous terms BSB and Sky had reached with the Hollywood studios for the rights to movies. Also present was Walter Valkey, the Swiss-born finance director of BSkyB. Clearly, Murdoch, too, knew that his problems were far from over, despite the merger. Murdoch's wife, Anna, was not to get her husband to ignore work after all.

Barlow, Chisholm and Murdoch had an informal chat about Sky, but Barlow kept quiet about the purpose of his trip. The three joined Murdoch's wife for a drink at the hotel, before Barlow and Murdoch adjourned for a private dinner. Barlow now wasted no time. 'Look, Rupert, Sky is broke,' he said. 'I'm going to get money out of the other shareholders, and if I get that, I want some out of you.' Barlow was prepared to accept some of Murdoch's payment 'in kind' – in the form of Murdoch's movie and programming rights at Fox, his US studio. 'And if you don't, and I get it from the others, then you will be diluted,' Barlow warned.

Murdoch asked for one other concession. Under the terms of the complicated merger deal, all money for the new company had to come from News Corporation or News International, and not from other News subsidiaries or directly from the Murdoch family. Could that rule be relaxed, Murdoch wondered? Barlow agreed. With a verbal deal in place, Murdoch asked Barlow to accompany Chisholm on his return to LA. 'Rupert thought that Sam was being too tough [in his dealings with the Hollywood studios] and that we needed a more sophisticated approach,' Barlow recalls. After a day of meetings with Paramount, the studio owned by Sumner Redstone's media conglomerate Viacom, Barlow and Chisholm took the flight home to London. During the trip, Barlow told Chisholm what he had discussed with Murdoch. Chisholm went quiet for a moment, and then turned to Barlow. 'So if you fail, then we're out of business and I'm out of work,' he said. 'Hmm, I haven't even got a [signed] contract yet.'

Upon his return to London, Barlow told the three other BSB shareholders what had been agreed. All but Reed were prepared to go ahead. 'I think probably Ian [Irvine] wanted to do it, and Peter Davis, too,' Barlow says. But the Reed board had long been alarmed at the mounting losses, and refused to go along with yet another financial restructuring. The dilution terms now had to be agreed, and the negotiations were fraught. Not only did Granada, Chargeurs and Pearson have to agree to raise their stakes to accommodate Reed's exit, but Sky had to deal with a handful of small minority shareholders that still remained on the books. (They were subsequently bought out by Murdoch.) The talks lasted several weeks, culminating in a marathon all-night session. The deal was finally agreed at the end of April 1991.

In the end, Granada stumped up the £25 million needed to keep its BSkyB stake at just under 14 per cent. Reed saw its position diluted to just 3.7 per cent from 10.4 per cent (and would ultimately sell the whole of its BSkyB stake). Pearson and Chargeurs went from 12 per cent to about 17 per cent each, coughing up £37.5 million each. Murdoch agreed to offer cash and 'in kind' payments worth £100m, keeping his 50 per cent stake.

Even then, Murdoch was hard pressed. 'He really got Sam by the throat, and credit was extended, and Rupert really put the pressure on,' Barlow recalls. 'It was a fantastic lesson in cash control.'

For Reed, the departure was difficult to justify to the City. Why bow out now, just as the future of the company looked somewhat more secure? In the words of one senior media analyst at the time: 'BSkyB looks to have a better chance of succeeding than at any point in the past.' Subscriber figures had breached the 2.3 million figure, while losses had been cut to £6 million a week from £14 million at the time of the merger six months before. There were 784,000 paying dish subscribers to BSkyB's two movie channels. But Reed's board was adamant. Peter Davis told *The Observer* in May that '£25 million is not a lot of money for Reed, but it was the third or fourth time we had been asked to inject money into the project, each time believing it would be the last time cash was needed. We still think it will be a long-term success but felt our resources would provide a better return if invested in the core publishing business'.

By allowing its stake to be diluted so dramatically, Reed's Ian Irvine was obliged to step down as chairman of BSkyB, to be replaced by Frank Barlow. At Granada, Derek Lewis was eventually forced to resign as chief executive, partly because of concerns over the cash needs of BSkyB.

The new financing in place, BSkyB began in earnest to tackle the remaining obstacles. The company faced three huge challenges in the course of 1991, with the ink on the merger deal and the refinancing barely dry: lawsuits galore from manufacturers and retailers, who had been stuck with BSB kit; still-sluggish dish sales, a victim of the recession; and the huge costs of the Hollywood movie deals. 'Coming out of the merger, you'd get up every day saying, "How are we going to get through this",' Chance remembers.

The lawsuits over BSB equipment were tackled in typically systematic fashion. All four of the major consumer equipment retailers and rentals chains – Granada, Thorn, Comet and Dixons – had launched legal action against BSkyB, arguing that they had been burdened with unsold equipment and considerable administrative costs. BSkyB reckoned that Granada, which was, of course, a shareholder in BSkyB, would be the easiest litigant to satisfy. The trick was to find a way of settling Granada's claims without paying cash, of which BSkyB had precious little. A legacy of Project X, the direct dish sales effort, was a base of 300,000 subscribers who rented their Astra equipment directly from Sky. BSkyB offered to assign the whole base, along with the associated cash flow, to Granada, which in addition to its broadcasting interests, was also in the business of renting consumer equipment. 'This was something we didn't know anything about, and Granada did,' Chance explains. 'It was a neat solution.'

With Comet and Dixons, BSkyB managed to convince them to settle their action in return for a rich package of incentives on the sale of Astra dishes in the future. 'We basically told them, "Let's think about the future, not the past",' Chance says. For every 200,000 dishes sold, Comet and Dixon's were rewarded with marketing incentives – much of it in the form of cash and deep discounts. Consumers were encouraged to buy dishes at full price, but were offered a year's free subscription to Sky Movies. Meanwhile, manufacturers such as Amstrad and Pace Microtechnology were given subsidies to ensure that the retail price point fell to a more affordable £199, rather than £299, for receiving equipment. BSkyB also had 300,000 dishes in warehouses, left over from the days of Project X. These, too, were placed on the market at a cut-rate price.

The problem of dishes exercised Amstrad's Alan Sugar, who had made a huge commitment to the Astra system, and was worried throughout 1991 and 1992 about the market for satellite TV. John O'Loan and Lis Howell, at Sky News, were asked to come to Chisholm's office at that time, to argue for an increased budget to send a news crew abroad. When they arrived, Chisholm was on the telephone, but motioned them in. He proceeded to scream down the line, swearing liberally. 'I don't care how many dishes you've got in your fucking warehouse,' he said at one point. The conversation continued in a similar vein for some minutes, ending with 'Fuck you'. Chisholm turned to O'Loan and Howell, with a smile. 'That's the problem with Alan Sugar,' he said. 'He's got no small talk.'

At the same time, BSkyB was obliged to meet the costs of 'swapping out' BSB equipment. Under its agreement with the TV regulators, all BSB's 110,000 dish subscribers had to be given the opportunity to exchange their dishes for Astra. To cut costs, BSkyB offered free subscriptions to Sky rather than free Astra dishes or cash compensation, provided viewers purchased their own Sky equipment. BSkyB also largely settled legal suits totalling £200 million from manufacturers of squarials, including Philips, Ferguson and Nokia, although the cases dragged on for years.

On the expenditure front, BSkyB was also tackling the huge costs of the movie deals – the legacy of the hugely competitive battle between BSB and Sky in the late 1980s. Sam Chisholm himself took the lead, spending an incredible 84 days in 1991 at the Four Seasons Hotel negotiating with Disney, Warner, and other major studios. But a better deal from Hollywood was not enough, and Murdoch and Chisholm both knew it. BSkyB needed a 'killer application' – programming that would launch Sky into orbit. The answer, it transpires, was football.

CHAPTER 5

Films and Football

The Hollywood films deals reached by BSB and Sky in the heady pre-launch days had been easy enough to negotiate, but proved hellishly difficult to undo. Chisholm knew, however, that he could not afford to continue to pay minimum guarantees per film to the studios out of what was still less than £100 million in revenues a year from movie subscribers in the UK.

Between them, Sky and BSB had signed up every major studio to supply their respective film channels. Sky had won the Fox contract, of course: Murdoch was the studio's owner. They had also managed to sign up Warners and Disney, which also owned the Touchstone brand. BSB had signed up most of the other major studios, including Columbia, MGM, Paramount and Universal. Between them, the two companies were contracted to pay about $1.2 billion to Hollywood over five years, of which perhaps half had to be paid whether or not the films were shown, under the punitive minimum guarantees (MGs) insisted upon by the studios. These meant that a payment – typically $750,000 – had to be paid per film, irrespective of the number of movie subscribers. And many more hundreds of millions would be due over the full term of the contracts, stretching well into the next century.

Chisholm set himself the challenge of knocking at least 40 per cent off the MGs, bringing them down to about $250 million over five years, or $50 million a year. All told, including the per-subscriber payments, Chisholm hoped to lower his total commitment over the life of the contracts (most of them running 10 to 15 years) by at least $1.2 billion. Chisholm took the same hotel room at the Four Seasons hotel in Los Angeles on each of his 84 days and nights in Hollywood in the spring and summer of 1991. 'I'll give you a typical month,' he says. 'We were going every week back and forth and running the company [at the same time]. With all the problems back here [in London] it's amazing looking back how we ever did it all. It's a wonder we're all still here.' Also on most of the negotiating trips were Bruce McWilliam, Chisholm's trusted lawyer, and Stewart Till, the head of movie acquisition at Sky (and now a senior executive at Polygram, the European-owned studio). Graham Woodhouse and Walter Valkey, in the finance division, kept track of the financing modelling in London.

Chisholm and McWilliam had already met most of the Hollywood executives. Before Chisholm left Australia, he had made several visits to Los Angeles to try to renegotiate contracts the Nine Network had made with the studios, at a time when all the Australian broadcasters had been bidding madly for film rights. McWilliam had been lawyer to Packer in Australia, heading to London shortly after Chisholm to take care of BSkyB's legal affairs. He was famous at Isleworth for the contents of his briefcase – all the documents Chisholm might ask for – and his ability to draw up a legal document of mere paragraphs, but one which would stick in a court of law. He had also negotiated Chisholm's salary increase at Channel Nine.

As the BSkyB–Hollywood talks dragged on, Chisholm became increasingly exasperated. 'They were all guilty of a herd mentality,' he remembers. 'No one wanted to go first.' But some of the studios had every reason to resist. The more financially stretched of the main Hollywood companies had listed the value of the BSB–Sky deals on their balance sheets, and were unwilling to write them down. They were also concerned that the formerly competitive UK market in pay-TV had been transformed, at a stroke, into a monopoly, and fervently hoped a rival – perhaps the cable companies – might appear on the scene. Nor did they like the fact that by helping BSkyB they were helping Murdoch, the man who through his Fox studio was one of their main movie competitors.

At the start, BSkyB didn't have many negotiating cards. In some cases, the minimum guarantees were backed either directly by the shareholders of BSB (Granada, Pearson, Reed and Chargeurs) or a letter of credit. The studios knew they could probably get at least some of the money out of the company's backers, even if BSkyB itself continued to be loss-making. But Chisholm wore them down by repeating a simple point. 'The basic theory was that they couldn't replace our money,' he recalls. 'We said, "Look if we go under the next guy who comes along is going to offer you five per cent of what we're offering you. This is a high-risk business, so you'd better go long with us and keep the business alive".'

Chisholm knew that if one studio capitulated, the others were likely to fall into line. He trained his attentions on Columbia, where he negotiated with Arnie Messer, head of Columbia's pay TV interests. The studio had served BSkyB with a statutory demand for $15 million because the payments had stopped, and BSkyB was in arrears. Chisholm had no money to play with, and told Columbia so. In the end, BSkyB hit on a novel solution to the problem, and agreed to mortgage the Marcopolo satellite in part-payment. 'Honestly,' Chisholm says, 'things were so desperate, the [satellite] was the only collateral we had, we had nothing else.' The mortgage raised £20 million, enough to cover the £8 million owed in arrears to the studio and to secure the current year's broadcasts. (The two BSB satellites were subsequently sold to Scandanavian companies.)

For Disney, which had already split with Murdoch over the original Sky Movies deal, the negotiations proved just as difficult. In the end, BSkyB played on Disney's desire to launch its Disney Channel in the UK, and offered to do Disney's subscription management for just £1 a subscriber – a price at which BSkyB would be making a loss.

In the case of UIP, which had reached an incredible five-year, $800 million deal with BSB on behalf of Paramount, Universal and MGM, the studios had been granted a letter of credit, and UIP was demanding that the terms be honoured. UIP steadfastly refused to budge, even after other studios had agreed new arrangements. BSkyB then decided to take a different tack. The company's lawyers, Herbert Smith, were asked to prepare a court case arguing that the UIP structure was anti-competitive and in breach of European Union law. 'They just didn't believe us, so we sent them our case, hundreds of pages, and they called back very quickly,' Chisholm recalls. The case actually went to court, but the parties subsequently agreed to settle their differences. The renegotiated UIP deal was reached at the very highest levels, with Murdoch, Paramount's Martin Davis and Universal's Lew Wasserman all involved in reaching the final agreement.

Warner was the last to sign, in late 1992. The studio appeared arrogant in the extreme, Sky insiders say. Recalls McWilliam: 'This finance director came to London to see Sam from Warner Brothers, and he said his division was so well run that no one in the world owed him more than $1 million. And Sam waited until he got out of the room and then rang the [BSkyB] finance director and said "Can you confirm to me how much we owe Warner brothers", and it was $12 million. So he went into the hall, where the Warner brothers guy was waiting for the lift, and he said, "You are to be congratulated on such financial controls".'

The deal was delayed because Warner had a clause in its contract that gave it far better terms if BSkyB hit two million subscribers by 1992, which it might have done, had Alan Sugar, the Amstrad chief executive, not had supply problems in the Far East. There were not enough dishes in the shops to keep up with the demand. Warner believed that BSkyB had deliberately tried to slow down the growth in subscribers, in order to put pressure on the studio to renegotiate, a charge BSkyB denies.

The Hollywood reshuffle was the first sign since Chisholm had arrived in Britain that he could negotiate with the big boys. His early tests at Sky and then BSkyB had been about cost-cutting, brinkmanship with regulators and ruthlessness with staff. With the Hollywood negotiations, he had taken more money out of the film industry than anyone had ever managed to do outside a courtroom. 'Deal making is not as complicated as some people think it is,' Chisholm says. 'You can make it complicated or you can make it simple. The secret to getting things done is attention to detail. You'll probably do all these things at twice the speed, if you're prepared to rely on your innate skills. The workaholic knows the formula that works for him and he sticks to it if he's clever. He knows what wins.'

By 1992, the renewed Hollywood contracts largely in place, the costs cut to about £400 million a year, and the staff down to just 700 people, BSkyB was beginning to look far more stable. Operating losses were running at about £1.5 million a week, on revenues of £330 million, although the accumulated debt was still stuck at nearly £2 billion and the interest payments were mounting. More than 1.8 million people received BSkyB programming on satellite, with another 430,000 on cable. Of these the majority were taking the subscription movie services.

'Nobody is going to have to put up money because it should soon become largely self-financing,' Gary Davey, then Chisholm's number two, said at the time. Indeed, by April of that year, 1992, BSkyB had actually reached operating break-even for the first time. With the cash flow now improved to the point that debts could be adequately serviced (albeit painfully), Murdoch and Chisholm began to think about the next stage.

There had long been arguments within Sky about the need for original British programming. Could the broadcaster afford to buy significant domestic content? And would such fare shift dishes? During late 1991, Chisholm had held a number of talks with Thames Television, which had famously lost its London franchise in the competitive ITV bidding round of that year, and which would end its broadcasting life on 31 December 1992. Thames made such successful programmes as *This is Your Life* and *The Bill*, the popular cop soap, and was prepared to offer its best programmes to the highest bidder, now that it was no longer to be part of the ITV system as a broadcaster. Chisholm thought it made sense to take some of the Thames programmes; indeed, for a time, he and David Chance, then marketing and distribution director, thought Rupert Murdoch might be convinced to buy Thames outright. Its 58 per cent owners, Thorn–EMI, the music and rentals group, were eager to sell, and had been so disposed even before the licence was lost. It is possible BSkyB could have had the whole company for about £70 million, at a time when the pension fund had a surplus of at least £50 million. Murdoch balked, however, believing that BSkyB should concentrate its attentions elsewhere. (In the end, Thames was sold for £99 million to Pearson in 1993, and might have been worth £300 million by 1997.) The acquisition having been turned down, Dunn and Chisholm continued to talk about what Dunn dubbed the Big Deal ('Make it big for Rupert,' Chisholm advised) which would have seen nearly all Thames programming go to BSkyB.

'Our pitch was you could licence *The Bill* and a whole range of [our] other programmes,' says David Elstein, then head of programmes at Thames. 'You could start running [repeats of] *The Bill*, waiting for the [series] to become free at the end of 1992. And Sky could have bought a whole pile of [advertising] air-time from Thames in London at that point, which was important because Sky couldn't get on to ITV, which was far too expensive.' Elstein recalls a key meeting with Murdoch, Chisholm, David Hill, Gary Davey and Andrew Knight. 'Richard [Dunn] and I did our pitch, but in the end Rupert decided it was just too expensive: the price of *The Bill* was just too high.' The Big Deal simply looked too rich for a company that had only just moved into operating profit and still had huge debts, and eventually Thames sold its major programmes to the BBC and ITV. Chisholm began to look elsewhere for fresh programmes to bolster Sky's business.

In its earliest days, BSkyB, and Sky before it, had found it difficult to shake its down-market reputation. Those of the chattering classes who thought about satellite TV at all assumed it was largely a working-class phenomenon, of interest only to those living in council flats. In fact, as early as 1992, more than 12 per cent of BSkyB's subscribers were ABC1s (the much-cherished socio-economic demographic), and there was good penetration among housewives with children, an attractive market for advertisers of fast-moving consumer goods. Whatever the truth of the market perception, Chisholm was intent on widening Sky's appeal.

Partly with this in mind, he brought Tony Vickers in from TV-Am, the morning ITV company that had lost its licence in the 1991 franchise round, to run the advertising department. In the end, Sky would get several TV-Am executives, under a deal Chisholm reached with Bruce Gyngell, the TV-Am chief executive, following the failure of the broad-caster to win renewal of its morning franchise. BSkyB would also get a boost in credibility when Gyngell agreed to buy news services from Sky News for the last year of its licence in 1992. Many TV-Am news executives, including Stephen Barden, who would become general manager at BSkyB and later chief executive of News Datacom, took jobs at Sky as a result of the supply deal, which was worth about £7 million a year.

But Chisholm knew he needed a trump card to put Sky firmly on a growth path. In the US, sport had always been a powerful magnet for audiences. Indeed, the emergence of pay-TV in the US market, particularly from the mid-1970s, had already proved the point. There were really only three kinds of programming that people were willing to pay extra for: movies, sport and pornography (and, as Frank Barlow says, 'not necessarily in that order'). In the UK, diehard football fans were drawn traditionally from the working class, but the sport nonetheless had broad national appeal, at least among men. The grounds attracted a largely male, young, 'C1 and down' crowd, although significant numbers of well-heeled fans would attend, even on the terraces. This was less true, however, in the 1980s, when hooliganism at England matches reached its heights and families – a target audience for football clubs, if they could be enticed – wouldn't have dreamt of going to the stadiums. But long before pay-TV was introduced in the UK, the TV audience for football tended to be impressively broad in demographic, gender and class terms. Even at its low point, as the images of violence became routine at football matches, the game attracted vastly more TV viewers than any other sport. For broadcasters, this was a market worth tapping, and ITV had done well out of football since it won the League contract in 1988. Chisholm learnt, too, that in the 1960s, *Match of the Day* would routinely draw huge audiences for the BBC – as high as 15 million. BSkyB saw a market here, if it could wrest the rights away from terrestrial television.

Even better from BSkyB's perspective, as it considered making a bid for the exclusive live rights to football, was the incontrovertible fact that ITV's coverage of Sunday live soccer was uninspiring, lazy and flat. By injecting new excitement into the game, BSkyB might be able to broaden the game's appeal and build its subscriber base throughout the country and into more middle-class homes.

Sport had always been part of Murdoch's vision for multi-channel television. Originally, the Eurosport deal was seen as a temporary measure, and it had always been assumed that a British-based service could one day be developed. (Andrew Neil had argued for a dedicated British sports channel as early as 1989.) Sky had also worried about the huge losses it was making on Eurosport. Under the original deal, Sky could bail out once its share of losses topped £40 million, which finally occurred in 1991. For the first two years, Eurosport actually broadcast out of Sky's studios in Isleworth. But Screensport, the now-defunct Astra competitor backed by WH Smith, formally complained to the European Commission about the arrangement, claiming it was anti competitive. 'We were actually quite happy the Commission said we had to get out of Eurosport,' a senior Sky executive recalls. 'It was losing money and now we had our own sports channel [BSB's] to broadcast.'

After the merger, BSkyB inherited some of the executives originally hired to provide BSB's Sports Channel. Chief among them was Vic Wakeling – the easy-going, slightly shambolic, sports-mad producer, who had, through Mark McCormack's TWI, been supplying a sports news strand for BSB. Wakeling met David Hill, head of sports at Sky, shortly after the merger, who asked him to join BSkyB as head of football. Also brought in from BSB was Andy Melvin, who would eventually be executive producer of BSkyB's Premier League football broadcasts.

BSB had a contract to broadcast certain minor football matches, as well as rugby. Sky, for its part, had secured the rights to Sunday cricket and to England's overseas test cricket matches, although these had been broadcast on Sky 1, rather than on the old Eurosport. But there was no doubt that top football would be the prize format for pay television, and huge management effort was directed, from early 1992, into securing as many football rights as possible, despite the likelihood that ITV would be a powerful rival for the television contracts.

Football had always attracted large audiences for the terrestrial broadcasters, but the game itself never managed to secure much of the money on tap. The two main broadcasters, the BBC and the ITV, had been running a cartel, alternating the rights in order to keep the price down. Frank Barlow says: 'I knew there was a great arrogance in television. It is unbelievable to remember it now, but the BBC used to have *Match of the Day*, and the Football League asked for more money, and the broadcasters said, "Don't be ridiculous. If you carry on this way, we are going to walk out of football". They actually threatened that they would stop carrying football! I realised how they were being exploited, and so I took the view that ITV wouldn't bid enough.'

Ironically, it was partly through the efforts of ITV, and Greg Dyke, then head of light entertainment at LWT, and Trevor East, head of Sports at ITV, that the Premier League concept, whereby the top teams would set up their own, breakaway fixtures, was born. Dyke, the man behind Roland Rat, was also the chairman of the sports committee at ITV, and had convinced most of the Channel 3 companies that they should try to win the rights to top football for the post-1992 period. A group of football executives, including David Dein, of Arsenal, met Dyke and Trevor East for dinner at LWT's London headquarters in early 1992, to discuss the idea of picking off the top 22 clubs, using a lucrative broadcasting contract as the bait. Dyke relied to an extent on East's contacts in football, built up over a career in journalism and ITV. Several of the top chairmen had been canvassed by East, about their interest in creating a new, top tier of football. Over dinner, the plan was discussed. The top five clubs would be offered £1 million a year each for four years, in exchange for live rights to home games. The deal would then be offered to the next five clubs, and so on. In the end, Dyke believed he had the rights to the top clubs for about £12 million a year, plus money for overseas matches. ITV would broadcast a live match every Sunday, with the kick-off at 4:00 pm.

But BSkyB was already laying plans to disrupt the agreement. When the Premier League was officially formed, Sir John Quinton, the former head of Barclays Bank, was appointed chairman. An accountant from Manchester, Rick Parry, who had spearheaded the unsuccessful effort to win the Olympic Games bid for Manchester, was named chief executive of the new league, and given the mandate to secure as lucrative a broadcasting contract as possible. He talked to many potential partners, and had even discussed the idea of launching a football channel, backed by the Premier League and sponsored by Chris Akers, then at Swiss Bank (later SBC-Warburg, the merchant bank), who later went on to run Caspian, owners of Leeds United, the football club.

The Akers proposal was looked at by Thames, too, which had options on satellite transponders through its SES shareholding, and which was looking for ways of offsetting the loss of its London ITV franchise. Even BSkyB was brought in, as a possible partner. In the end, Thames was left out of the Akers bid, which withered on the vine. But it did bring together Sam Chisholm and David Elstein, then a senior executive at Thames, and a bright, ambitious and accomplished programme maker. 'At that point, I found myself having occasional chats with Sam about what he was going to do [about football],' Elstein remembers. Those early chats would eventually lead to Elstein leaving Thames, and joining BSkyB.

Vic Wakeling at BSkyB was told by David Dein, of Arsenal, that the Premier League was about to be formed. Wakeling told his colleagues at Sky Sports, and Chisholm was informed. Rupert Murdoch had lunch with Quinton early in 1992. 'He said we should bid, because they wanted to make sure there was competition for the rights,' Murdoch recalls. 'But the real work was being done by Sam [Chisholm], who was talking the money, and David Hill who was telling them all the great things we would do with the broadcasts.' Others remember it a bit differently. According to Barlow: 'Of course Rupert got deeply involved. He was having dinner with Alan Sugar [Tottenham chairman and dish manufacturer] and all that.' Murdoch also invited several football club chairmen to Livingston, BSkyB's state-of-the-art subscription management service in Scotland, to prove how effortlessly the company could manage paying subscribers to football matches. Even back then, there had been talk of pay-per-view services for football, and the promise of untold wealth for the top clubs.

Chisholm went to see Quinton, too, and asked him what the rules would be for the bidding. Quinton answered: 'There are no rules. There is a knock 'em down, drag 'em out negotiation, and the last man standing is the one who wins.' It was just the kind of challenge Chisholm loved.

Chisholm, Gary Davey and David Hill decided early on that Parry would be the key to BSkyB's negotiating tactics. 'We dealt with Parry, Parry was the guy we put our money on,' Chisholm says. 'ITV put their money on the old guys that they knew from before – guys like David Dein of Arsenal – and they worked through them.' Says Dyke: 'Parry had fallen in love with Murdoch. He was a little man from Manchester who got wooed by Murdoch. It was not the first time that had happened.'

From the start, the main shareholders were supportive of the Premier League bid. Pearson's Barlow, for one, was convinced that football was absolutely critical to BSkyB's prospects. 'When we were bidding for the Premier League, all of Sky was basically Australians, and I'm not sure they realised the importance of soccer in the UK, [although] now they [do] of course. I remember Sam saying, "We may not be able to afford the Premier League". I said, "If you are going to have a sports channel in the UK, you have got to have the Premier League". I think if we hadn't got [it], the chances are [BSkyB] would have failed again.'

There were debates about how much BSkyB ought to pay for the rights, however. Chisholm, by this time, had decided that the company's future was inextricably linked to football. He recalls: 'It was something we decided to bet the company on. We decided to get the Premier League no matter what.' But he was cautious – against type – because the financial position was still precarious, even if BSkyB had actually moved into operating profit. There were still huge debts to service, and he was concerned about the state of the economy and of the market for direct-to-home satellite dish sales.

By the Spring of 1992, Murdoch had agreed to put in a bid. But he wanted Chisholm to explore the possibility of a joint offer from ITV and BSkyB. Chisholm was happy to do so, having realised that BSkyB could still make money even if it shared the rights with another broadcaster. He rang Greg Dyke, at LWT, and asked him to lunch at Langan's Brasserie, in the West End. According to Dyke, Chisholm asked: 'How are we going to keep these bastards in football from robbing us?' Dyke was dismissive of the Antipodean TV executive, and openly caustic about BSkyB. 'You may have been a big deal in Australia but you're a bit of a non-event here,' Dyke told Chisholm. 'Well, think about it, because we're pretty determined and we'll do it,' Chisholm answered.

Dyke said he would consider the option, and agreed to get back to Chisholm in a few days. When he hadn't, Chisholm called him again, and Dyke put him off, telling him: 'I'm still thinking'.

'In retrospect, we should have done a deal [with BSkyB],' Dyke says. 'There was certainly a deal on the table. We could have got the Sunday live and [BSkyB would have had] the Monday live.' Still, Dyke believes a deal with BSkyB would have ended in tears. 'Anyone who does a deal [with Murdoch] ends up being shafted in the end,' he says.

Chisholm decided at that point to leave Dyke out of his plans, and approached the BBC, with which he had already held tentative talks. BSkyB offered the BBC an attractive deal: Sky would broadcast the live games of the Premier League, while the BBC would get highlight rights, enabling it to revive *Match of the Day*. 'It was a question of using their respectability and our money,' Chisholm says.

From the BBC's perspective, there was no point in trying to compete with satellite television for the live rights to the Premier League. 'These forces are inevitable,' John Birt, the BBC director-general, says. 'The technology allows, for the first time, rights holders – soccer, movies, whatever – to extract more of the value of their product from the consumer. And the simple strategic analysis showed that it was impossible for the BBC to follow that. Our alternative strategy was to recognise that some of these sports would inevitably go to sports subscription services, and that's the process which will continue in the future. We needed a strategy to protect the licence fee payer's interests. What was it? It was to see high-quality recorded sport, in the case of soccer. So we thought we served the licence fee payer's interests by negotiating to maintain *Match of the Day.*'

In the weeks before the bids were due in May 1992, BSkyB spent a huge amount of management time trying to second-guess the strategy of ITV. Chisholm was absolutely determined to bid above – but only just above – the ITV offer. Vic Wakeling was asked, for example, to talk to his contacts in football and broadcasting, to attempt to work out what ITV might be willing to pay for the Premier League rights. But BSkyB also had a secret weapon, in the form of *Footballer's Football*, a long-running BSB pro-gramme that had continued on Sky Sports following the merger. Wakeling explains: 'It was a programme where we would invite certain players and managers or coaches in [for interviews]. As we were getting our [Premier League] bid together, we made sure we had a few chairmen in like Ken Bates, Ron Noades, David Dein or Martin Edwards. And, of course, they were led away and had a couple of drinks and they would tell us what they thought was going on.' (Trevor East, at ITV, saw the Sky programme, and told colleagues: 'We have a problem'.) As well, Sam Chisholm himself developed some close contacts among footballers, at least at the senior level. But despite the excellent intelligence, the close contact with Rick Parry, and a firm commitment from Murdoch that the Premier League was worth going after, it was not at all clear whether BSkyB could afford the sums needed to ensure that it, and not ITV, would win the contract from 1992. 'People say now that, perhaps, we got it cheap,' Wakeling says. 'But at the time, it didn't seem like that.'

In late April, ITV was convinced they had done enough to ensure victory. East had visited all the club chairmen to deliver a simple message: only ITV could give football the national coverage it needed. He was sure that he had the support of at least 11 football chairmen – not quite enough to win (14 was the magic number under the Premier League's own system) but close enough to be comforting. He had also invited Parry to join him in Manchester, for a major boxing match involving British boxer Chris Eubank. In the bar beforehand, East made his final pitch, insisting that the offer from ITV was almost sure to be the richer of the two options. And why would the Premier League want to risk its future with an untried, money-losing, limited-audience service like BSkyB's? East had privately been worried that the final ITV bid was too 'light' in the early years, with most of the serious money only coming on stream three or four years out. He raised this with Parry in the bar in Manchester. Parry said he was unbothered, and added that this was a bid he believed he could support. East reports that the two men shook hands on the deal at that point.

But there were still some machinations to come. The two camps were asked to put together their final bids, and to make presentations to the football chairmen at White's Hotel, in London, on 14 May 1992, a Thursday. Sam Chisholm made the opening remarks for BSkyB/BBC and left David Hill and Gary Davey to describe the brave new world of football broadcasting on offer. Hill had worked for Sam Chisholm at Channel Nine, where the two had revolutionised the coverage of rugby league. When Frank Barlow, worried about the effect of pay-TV sports on stadium attendance, had asked Chisholm how the Rugby League deal affected gate receipts in Australia, Chisholm played him a promotional video. 'He told me that the gates had actually increased, and the teams got so rich in the end they could afford to get [singer] Tina Turner,' Barlow recalls. 'And there she is in a short dress with these fucking great Australian forwards, and that's how they promoted it. They were in a different league to ITV and BBC in [terms of] promotion.' Great riches were on offer, too, for the Premier League. All they had to do was sign on with BSkyB.

Just before Chisholm rose to leave after giving his pitch, he turned to the 22 Premier League chairmen. 'Do you think this is our last bid?' he asked. 'Well, it isn't.' He left the door open to a sweetener, just in case ITV was planning a final, deal-making offer.

That Friday, Chisholm was convinced that everything had gone 'too quiet', and that ITV was up to something. Meanwhile, at ITV, the same mood prevailed. Dyke called Trevor East in the Peak District on Friday, interrupting a family holiday. East returned to London on Saturday, and prepared for a final round of discussions with Dyke about the bid. Dyke spent the weekend on the telephone with senior ITV executives, trying to convince them to cough up a sweetener. Dyke remembers: 'Suddenly the story was going around that clubs were switching sides. We [also] discovered that there was a degree of collusion between Murdoch and Parry. [So] we decided to make a late bid.'

Dyke had faced a huge problem at ITV. Because of the notorious London split, whereby two different companies broadcast in the capital, one during the week and the other at the weekend, there was far from universal appetite for a higher bid to purchase programming that would benefit the weekend more. Moreover, the amount that Dyke wanted to add would have paid for a Sunday night drama throughout the year. Getting an extra £27 million had been extremely tough, and it was unlikely that the ITV companies would agree to go any higher. On Sunday, East was asked to go to Dyke's house in Twickenham, in the presence only of Dyke's personal assistant. The two men worked until 1:00 am, Monday, 18 May, adding £27 million to the bid, bringing it to £262 million, including the overseas and highlights rights, over five years – enough, they thought, to top anything BSkyB and the BBC could produce.

Chisholm was itchy on Monday morning. At 7:00 am, he rang Rick Parry, who was staying at White's Hotel in London. 'Have you heard anything?' Chisholm asked. Parry said no, but agreed he would stay in touch.

Parry rang back an hour later, with some amazing news. East (later poached by Sam Chisholm to work on sport at News Corporation and BSkyB), had arrived at Parry's hotel at just after 8:00 am, with an envelope, enclosing the fresh offer from ITV. East told Parry he would be handing out similar envelopes to each of the chairmen at the door of the Royal Lancaster Hotel, as they arrived for their summit meeting to make a final decision. Parry looked inside the envelope, and realised the sweetened bid would be enough, by several million pounds, to top BSkyB and the BBC. He then, controversially, told BSkyB about the upped offer from ITV.

The revised bid was pretty rich for BSkyB. 'We got together and thought, Hell,' Chisholm recalls. An emergency meeting was held with BSkyB's advisers, Arthur Andersen, who cautioned against going too high. How could you make money on these ludicrous terms? At 9:00 am, ignoring his staid advisers, Chisholm called Murdoch in New York, where it was 4:00 am, and woke up the boss. 'We're going to put another £30 million on the table,' Chisholm said. Murdoch grunted his approval, and went back to sleep. BSkyB then rewrote its bid, and sent it by fax to Parry, at the Royal Lancaster Hotel. The new offer, topped up with more money from overseas rights and the BBC's contribution for highlights, was worth £304 million over five years, easily a record for sports rights in the UK. BSkyB was also offering an unmatchable advantage over ITV. With more hours of broadcasting time available, the pay-TV company could ensure that more games were transmitted live and in their entirety. ITV could not dedicate hours and hours of time to football, because it risked alien-ating the millions of viewers who were not football fans.

Parry had delayed the start of the 10:00 am meeting of the chairmen, waiting in a side room for BSkyB's new bid. East, meanwhile, was passing out his envelopes in the foyer, as the chairmen arrived. Paul White, the commercial director of Nottingham Forest, arrived at three minutes to ten, wearing casual trousers and carrying a sports bag. 'You're a little late, aren't you?' East asked him, as he proffered an envelope. 'And where is Fred Reach [chairman of Nottingham Forest]?' 'He's not coming,' White replied, as he took the envelope. 'Did he brief you?' East asked, his heart sinking. Nottingham Forest had been down on Dyke and East's list as being 'definites' in favour of the ITV bid. 'No,' White said. 'Christ,' said East. 'Look, I've got 30 seconds to convince you that you are about to make the most important fucking decision in the history of British sport, I guarantee you, your chairman said he would vote for us.'

White then joined the other chairmen at the meeting, and East waited in the lobby, increasingly nervous. Terry Venables, then at Tottenham Hotspur, handed the envelope he had received to Alan Sugar, his chairman, and, as a manufacturer of Astra dishes, a direct beneficiary of BSkyB's success. Sugar took one look at the ITV bid, and quickly left the meeting. He rushed to a payphone in the hotel lobby, where he was overheard by Trevor East. 'Blow them out of the water,' Sugar was heard to shout down the phone. (Sugar said later he had been talking to his girlfriend.) He returned to the meeting room.

Parry then read out the two bids he had received, one by envelope and the other by fax. 'The fax beat the man with the envelope,' Chisholm says. 'If you do your business by quill and parchment, you can't expect to keep up with modern technology.' Of course, it helped that Chisholm had a man on the inside, Rick Parry, who had told him about ITV's late offer. And even if Parry hadn't already been in touch with BSkyB, it is likely Chisholm would have known about the last minute ITV manoeuvre, thanks to Alan Sugar.

The assembled chairmen then took a vote on whether Sugar, given his potential conflict of interest, should be allowed to vote on the television contract, a point raised by Liverpool. The clubs voted 20 to 1 (with Tottenham, obviously, not voting) to allow him to take part. They then proceeded to vote on the two offers: ITV's £262 million, and the £304 million from BSkyB and the BBC. On the final tally, 14 of the 20 clubs that voted (two abstained) went for the BSkyB/BBC offer, the minimum required for outright approval. Of the then Big Five (Tottenham, Arsenal, Everton, Liverpool and Manchester), only Tottenham voted for the BSkyB side. Sugar's vote, therefore, turned out to be crucial. The smaller clubs liked the 'cascading down' effect of the rights money, under which even less successful clubs would benefit. Even low-rated teams would get significant airtime under the BSkyB/BBC deal. The others were nervous that BSkyB might not be able to deliver on its promises, and that there might be a backlash against putting matches exclusively on satellite and cable. Sir George Russell, chairman of the ITC, says: 'Had the BBC not taken the decision of going in with Sky, I don't believe the Premier League would have gone in with BSkyB. On *Match of the Day*, all the hoardings give major exposure to sponsorship. It would never have worked without the BBC.'

ITV was not given an opportunity to beat the new BSkyB bid. Dyke concedes he might not have been able to wring any more out of the ITV companies. But he maintains to this day Parry ought to have given him an opportunity to counter-bid. 'Either the bids should have been sealed or they should have come back to us,' Dyke says.

Back at Isleworth, Sam Chisholm had taken a call from Murdoch, now awake in New York. 'What did you do, then?' Murdoch asked. Chisholm told him about the revised deal. Later, Murdoch would say: 'The Premier League was the really big move, it gave us a huge boost. That was a big deal, and it took off straight away.' But at the time, it seemed an astonishing amount of money.

Just before noon on 18 May, the phone call came from Parry to say that BSkyB had won. 'This was the turning point of the company,' Chisholm says. 'It was a staggering achievement for Sky, because nobody expected it for a second.'

'Greg [Dyke] clearly underestimated what Parry could do or what Parry might do,' ITV's Barry Cox says. 'I think he was genuinely surprised that all his careful planning and all the [support] he had secured turned out not to be enough.' Dyke himself was gutted, but called Chisholm personally to congratulate him. He told his staff, however, not to worry. There was no way BSkyB could make a profit on that kind of investment, Dyke believed. Later, he would change his mind. 'The single most important thing [BSkyB] did was football,' he says. 'It turned them. It was inevitable that pay-TV was going to make more [out of football] than non-pay.'

Almost immediately, the backlash began. Editorials filled the newspapers about the 'theft' of Britain's national sport by the upstart pay-TV broadcaster. Millions of soccer fans would be deprived of the chance to watch their team's matches, said Craig Brewin, of the Football Supporters Association. 'Fans will be frustrated because they won't be able to afford a satellite dish,' he claimed. Opposition Labour politicians called on the government to act. But there was no mood at Downing Street to intervene in what was seen as a commercial matter. Efforts by the ITV to seek a High Court injunction to reopen the bidding, on the grounds that BSkyB had been unfairly told of the revised ITV bid, failed, because it was decided that Rick Parry had done nothing wrong.

The furore about sport would continue, in muted fashion, for several years. Michael Grade, then chief executive of Channel 4, called the Sky deal 'a rip-off' of the consumer in 1993. The government would have to fight off a concerted effort in 1995 to extend the list of so-called 'listed' events (those sporting events like Wimbledon or the FA Cup Final which must be broadcast on free, terrestrial television). Even more recently, in 1996, a campaign was launched Europe-wide to prevent the rights to key sporting events from being bought up by pay-TV broadcasters. The Labour government elected in 1997, meanwhile, suggested it would review the list of protected events, to see whether it might be widened beyond Wimbledon, the FA Cup final, England cricket and other so-called 'Crown jewels'. And the Premier League deal with BSkyB and the BBC would be reviewed by the Restrictive Practices Court, on the basis that it was anti-competitive for the Premier League to sell its broadcasting rights collectively.

With the Premier League on board, BSkyB began preparations to encrypt its sports service, creating a second subscription revenue stream after movies. By August, on the eve of the football season, BSkyB had signed up nearly one million subscribers willing to pay up to £5.99 a month for the sports channel. 'It was absolutely unbelievable. Up in Livingston [BSkyB's subscription management service], there were sackfuls of mail arriving everyday,' Chisholm recalls. 'It was like Christmas.'

Sport would prove to be BSkyB's strongest suit, and not just in commercial terms. After a slightly embarrassing start, when BSkyB experimented with cheerleaders and other US innovations, the company settled down to providing a superior broadcasting service. Within just two seasons, BSkyB revolutionised coverage of football, eventually bringing in celebrated players as commentators, introducing US-style slow motion replays and multiple camera angles. Along with football, Sky Sports also had cricket and rugby league, and would later bid for major golf events and boxing too. Sport would soon be the prime driver of BSkyB's business in the UK, and would be part of the company's core marketing activities.

Billboards around the country would hammer home the message: Sport was Sky, Sky was sport.

Sir George Russell, chairman of the ITC, says: 'Had they not got the Premier League, I don't think they would have made it. After they ran out of the major films, which they bought at a very high price, they couldn't have afforded to renew the rights. Films meet only modest demand. It was sport that drove them.'

Football would receive a windfall, allowing teams to afford new stadiums and to bid for world-class players. Attendance at the grounds shot up over the course of the first BSkyB rights deal, and the popularity of football soared even among middle-class families (although women were less susceptible than men to the trend). The BSkyB coverage helped create new stars, and added fresh excitement about the game. Still, some traditional supporters bemoaned the fact that the times and dates of matches were moved to coincide with Sky's scheduling needs. There was a risk of the game being taken away from the real, committed fans.

Financially, too, the deal was transforming. BSkyB had found a second leg for its pay-TV stool, to supplement the appeal of subscription movies. The vast majority of new subscribers to Sky would henceforth sign up for at least one premium service, with many of them taking both sport and movies. The press coverage continued to be negative in some quarters, particularly in the non-Murdoch broadsheets. But even the furore over the 'theft' of the national game eventually died down, at least until 1997, following a huge price increase for the Sky Sports channels which ignited another backlash. Murdoch concludes: 'Our problem was, and still is to some degree, that 70 per cent of the press [were] sneering at us for a very long time. And it is only now that some of the sports lovers acknowledge what we have done for sports.'

Most significant of all the effects of BSkyB's Premier League win was the dawning realisation among many traditional broadcasters that pay-TV might prove a real threat. In the earliest days of BSB and Sky, many traditionalists assumed that no significant market existed for pay television in Britain. 'We have the best television in the world,' went the argument. 'Why would anyone pay extra to watch repeats and cheap programming?' When the ITV companies were preparing their bids for the first competitive licences, awarded in 1991, most put in a line or two in their business plans about the growth of BSkyB. But many senior executives did not believe it. The Premier League triumph changed all of that.

'When they bought the Premier League contract, [that was] the psychological moment when, suddenly, they showed their purchasing power, their imagination, their ability to take away something from terrestrial television,' says John Birt, director-general of the BBC. 'All of a sudden, something very attractive indeed was created on subscription services, which materially changed the balance between ourselves and the satellite broadcasters.'

Says ITV's Barry Cox: 'It was a big shock to the system. These guys thought they could spend all this money and make it work. It was the arrival of pay-TV. Suddenly the strategic focus for some of us switched [and we began to say] that BSkyB is the enemy, no one else is.'

The most dramatic judgement, however, was Sir George Russell's, reflecting on the impact the deal had on the BBC. 'Once you lose your major sports, and have to go to Parliament to beg for the little bit left [by arguing for legislation on terrestrial rights to major sport], you can see already the long trail of those who argue, "Why are we paying the licence fee when we don't get the things we want to see?" Everything stems from that moment [when the BBC did the Premier League with BSkyB].'

Getting the Premier League contract had cost dearly, and it was not yet clear whether enough subscribers could be encouraged to pay for football. But perhaps there was another solution to the need for increased revenues. BSkyB management had long understood that subscription television, and not advertising, would drive the business. It was time to see whether the company could convert all of its channels to a pay basis, and to encourage even third parties like Viacom or TCI, the US entertainment giants who had invested in UK cable and satellite, to put their channels into a subscription-only package. If BSkyB could charge a basic subscription fee to everyone, insisting they buy the basic channels before getting premium sport and movies, the economics of the business would take a huge step forward. Then, it wouldn't matter as much if sport costs had risen sharply, since there would be a new revenue stream derived from basic subscribers.

In the second half of 1992, with Sky Sports firmly launched on an encrypted basis, BSkyB began in earnest to create the multi-channels package. It helped that Thames Television, bereft of its licence, had decided to launch its own satellite service, UK Gold, in league with the BBC. The channel, which featured repeats from the Thames and BBC libraries, was one of the ways Richard Dunn at Thames hoped to offset the effects of having lost his broadcasting franchise. Dunn had options over two transponders on Astra 1B, the second of the SES satellites, which he had secured thanks to his shareholding in SES. With the programmes lined up, and with distribution via Astra, Dunn negotiated with BSkyB in early 1992 to add UK Gold to Sky 1 and Sky News as a basic offering of non-premium programming, jointly marketed. Thames would be paid 15p per subscriber per month by BSkyB on the deal, which saw the satellite launch of UK Gold in November 1992.

It had not been an easy negotiation. Thames had toyed with the idea of launching UK Gold as a 'free', unencrypted channel, and then as a separately serviced pay channel outside BSkyB's subscription management service. To Chisholm's annoyance, Thames had also done a deal with the BBC to offer movies from Warner on UK Gold in the 'satellite window,' which looked like it was treading on BSkyB's own exclusive movie distribution deals. But Chisholm realised that, if Thames was intent on launching its Gold service, BSkyB would be better off as a partner than as a competitor.

Throughout the negotiations on UK Gold, in which he took little direct part, David Elstein had also been talking to Sam Chisholm about a job at BSkyB. Thames was about to lose its broadcasting licence, and Elstein, a respected programme maker (on, among other programmes, the *World At War* series for Thames) was weighing up several options – not least the key position of programme director at ITV Network Centre, for which he was interviewed. In the end, he began to think seriously about BSkyB, much to the surprise, even incredulity, of friends and colleagues. 'Why go somewhere which is failing or marginal, peripheral to the whole of British broadcasting?' Elstein remembers his friends asking. '[But] that was just not understanding what Sky was about and not beginning to get a sense of how far Sky had moved from 1990 to 1992. I had tracked [it] pretty carefully and I was pretty confident that Sky was going to emerge very, very quickly.'

But what would Elstein, the ultimate programmer/commissioner, do at BSkyB, where most of the programmes were bought in? 'What is there for you to do at Sky? They're not going to suddenly release lots of money to make drama shows,' his friends quite sensibly argued. However, Elstein had spent seven years commissioning and scheduling programmes, and 22 years before that making them. 'It looked to me very interesting to move to a company which had a much more strategic approach to broadcasting and which absolutely believed what I had long believed in: multi-channel subscription TV, a direct relationship with the consumer, and breaking the cartel on sport,' Elstein says. At the same time, he says he felt less and less comfortable 'being part of the cartel, part of this lumbering, cumbersome thing called ITV'. He was tired of the complacent view that 'terrestrial TV was so good that nothing else could possibly attract the consumer'.

All the same, deciding to turn his back on ITV to face an uncertain future at BSkyB would be difficult to contemplate. Elstein was one of a clutch of similarly aged TV executives, men like Michael Grade and the BBC's Alan Yentob, who had considerable power within commercial and public service television. Did he want to break ranks and join Murdoch? Moreover, Elstein was still hopeful that the Independent Television Commission would agree to award a new licence in 1992 for a fifth terrestrial channel, Channel 5, for which Thames was the sole bidder. Elstein, who would later become chief executive of Channel 5 when it was finally launched in April 1997, had long harboured the dream of running his own TV channel.

But lack of adequate financing doomed the first efforts to get Channel 5 off the ground, and the ITC decided not to award the licence to the single bidder. In October 1992, Elstein met Sam Chisholm for a brief meeting. The two men had discussed a number of issues in the past, including football (Thames had been initially involved in the Chris Akers proposal for the Premier League), Channel 5 (in which BSkyB had considered taking a stake) and, of course, UK Gold, the golden oldies channel which BSkyB agreed to carry along with Sky News and Sky 1 in its 'basic' package. Chisholm wooed Elstein with the promise of taking part in the great BSkyB adventure. '[Chisholm] does a proper courtship; he phones, he cajoles he flatters and occasionally goes cold a bit,' Elstein says. '[But] he put more pressure on once the Thames licence was running out and I was beginning to have to choose between a number of different options.'

That first meeting proved inconclusive, and the trail went temporarily cold. Elstein remembers that the concern was really BSkyB's desire to block UK Gold's movie deal with Warner. But by December, Elstein was ready. At Chisholm's request, Elstein flew to Los Angeles that month to meet Rupert Murdoch, flying out on Virgin Atlantic. The two men spent an hour discussing how BSkyB could move forward on the planning front, and Elstein was convinced there was a shared view about the need for a mix of programmes – sports, yes, and all the American imports (*The Simpsons*, *Beverly Hills 90210* and *Melrose Place*). But he was also promised an Arts Channel, a concept close to his heart (although BSkyB consistently put off its launch in later years).

Elstein's deal with BSkyB was completed with Chisholm in the plane on the return trip from LA, where the two men sat in British Airways' first class. Also on board was Bruce McWilliam, Chisholm's lawyer. 'By the time we landed, we had a contract that I was happy with,' Elstein says.

BSkyB had scored a major coup getting Elstein, a *bona fide* member of the broadcasting establishment. Quickly, he became an indispensable part of the BSkyB publicity machine, representing the 'acceptable face of Sky'. At conferences, on radio and on television, it was Elstein, more often than any other Sky executive, who defended the company against what was becoming a chorus of disapproval and criticism.

Elstein took on responsibility for acquisitions, including the movie contracts. Most of these had been renegotiated, but there remained some work to do on the Warner and Disney deals. Elstein was also encouraged to sign up other, small film companies, including Polygram, Rank and British Screen. Sport and news were run quite separately, however, with their own divisional heads. As soon as he arrived, Elstein was also pushing the idea of buying Thames, which was still up for sale. He saw an obvious fit between the two companies: at a stroke, Sky would secure the kind of original programming that was always popular in Britain, while Thames would be assured a future after the licence ran out on 31 December 1992. Murdoch still believed, however, that Thames was too expensive.

Elstein merged the operation of the movie channels, and moved all the movies to the same time: 6 o'clock, 8 o'clock, 10 o'clock. BSkyB started a campaign to convince people to take the whole movie service, in a successful attempt to narrow the gap in subscriber numbers between Sky Movies and the Movie Channel. But one of Elstein's main tasks was to commission and schedule Sky 1, the general entertainment channel. Recalls Elstein: the task was to 'rationalise the schedule, to make a better sense of the material that was already there, schedule it properly, to get rid of some of the gungier material, to find some new product, although there wasn't a lot around and to commission a little but not big scale'.

With additional management, and a new channel in the form of UK Gold, BSkyB's prospects had been strengthened. But there were a dozen other channels in the satellite and cable market, some of which might have been potential competitors in a rival package of subscription television. Could BSkyB convince them to join the Sky multi-channel package? That was the challenge the company now set itself.

CHAPTER 6

Making a Bundle:
The Birth of the Multi-Channel Package

Having a sports channel would provide a fresh revenue stream, Sam Chisholm knew. But the other channels generally available on satellite in the UK were also a definite draw for consumers: even better, you didn't have to pay for them. Astra satellite homes were enjoying 'free' access to such popular programming as MTV (the music video channel), Bravo, Nickelodeon, CNN (24-hour news), the Children's Channel (TCC) and several others, once householders purchased (or rented) the receiving equipment. Even Sky 1 and Sky News were available free. Could BSkyB convince all these other operators that a pay-TV package of basic channels was in everyone's interests? Could they then convince non-subscribing satellite homes that they should pay for Sky 1 and most of the other formerly free services?

Recalls David Chance: 'We thought we needed a multi-channel package. We thought we would generate an income flow from people who weren't taking the premium channels, and that would provide an income boost.' BSkyB also hoped it would be able to convert more subscribers to the premium channels, once they had signed up for the basic package. Most importantly of all, the company would be able to raise prices in the future with great ease, by adding new channels to the basic package each time to convince subscribers they were getting value for money. The key concept they hoped to get across to premium customers was that the basic package came 'free' once you took sport and movies.

But the desire for a multi-channel package was driven as much by fear as by strategy. BSkyB was worried that other big players in multi-channel TV, like TCI and Viacom, would create their own packages, complete with a rival subscription management service and proprietary smart cards. If a competing platform was developed, then future channels coming into the marketplace would have a choice: there would be two ways of getting into satellite homes (and by extension cable homes) on a subscription basis. Recalls David Chance: 'Sky was potentially pretty exposed at that time. It had movies and was just getting sport. If somebody else had gotten together a basic tier – Viacom or TCI – we would have taken a bath.'

BSkyB's biggest fear was that it would no longer be able to charge a large premium for sports and its two movies channels. For example, by the end of the first full year of the multi-channel package, BSkyB was charging £9.99 a month for the basic, £14.99 for one premium, £19.99 for two premiums and £21.99 for all three. Therefore, the notional price for one premium channel (having accounted for the £9.99 basic package) was £5. If a rival had emerged to offer most of the basic channels available in the marketplace, Sky could never have charged such aggressive prices for the premium services, and its finances would have been severely weakened.

The trick would be to sign up enough channels to ensure that only BSkyB's multi-channel package could survive, and newcomers would have to deal with BSkyB to enter the market for DTH subscription television. The two main non-BSkyB players in the multi-channel market in 1992 were both American. TCI, the giant pay-TV company, had moved into the UK cable market in the 1980s, via its United Artists subsidiary (later Telewest). By 1992, it controlled the biggest cable network in the country. It also had a group of channels, including Bravo and Discovery. Later, it would add Family and the Children's Channel. The stable had been some time in the making, and had relied on the work of another, much smaller company, to bear fruit.

Flextech, an oil services company run by Roger Luard, had been looking to expand into the media business in the 1980s. 'Flextech was looking for another leg to compensate for its then primary business,' Luard recalls, 'which was subject to all the sort of volatility that goes with being in the oil industry.' Luard, unusually brash and peripatetic for a UK businessman, received a visit from a close friend, Peter Orton, the tall and garrulous TV man who had built up a business in the UK based on the rights to programmes made by Jim Henson, creator of the Sesame Street puppet characters (the business was known as Hit, or Henson International Television). Disney had been interested in buying the Henson companies, and Orton told Luard: 'Look, I don't want to work for Disney. I think there's a great opportunity in this industry. Would you back me?' Luard answered: 'That's terrific, Peter, but we're not in the venture capital game.' Still Luard was intrigued enough to sit down with Orton and look at investment opportunities in the media, particularly in the growing multi-channel market.

Having studied the US, German, French and Scandanavian markets, Luard says, 'I could not understand why pay television in the UK was going to be any different in terms of choice and variety and desire on the part of the consumer than anywhere else in the world.' Luard's Flextech took a 25 per cent stake in Hit, Peter Orton's company (since sold at a large profit). Flextech also began to apply for cable franchises, which until 1992 had been amazingly easy to get, and at a low price, because so few players were willing to take the financial risk. Recalls Luard: 'I knew how to sign my name at the bottom of the application form.'

Flextech paid around £300,000 for its handful of franchises, which Luard eventually sold on for £65 million, when largely US telecoms operators began to take an interest in the UK cable market. He had by then decided he would concentrate on the programming side of the business. 'In programming, you don't have the enormous upfront capital cost,' Luard explains. But it meant that he needed to ensure his programming would be distributed somehow. 'Pay-TV is rather like when you buy a house, [when] you talk about location, location, location,' Luard says. 'When you're in the pay-TV game it's distribution, distribution, distribution.'

It proved to be oddly easy for Flextech to build a programming business. A number of mainstream broadcasters, including Thames, Central and telecoms giant BT, had invested – albeit gingerly – in pay TV programming interests. Flextech was able to buy stakes in enough channels to create the embryo of a significant pay-TV company, including home shopping, the Children's Channel and the Family Channel. Recalls Luard: 'We bought these off traditional people who, today, are clamouring to get back into the bloody [pay-TV] market.' Luard got assets on the cheap. 'They [BT] gave [TCC] up at no cost,' he says. 'I bought my initial stake in the Children's Channel for £1.5 million. I took control of 75-odd percent, for about £6.7 million.' Luard then sold 25 per cent of TCC to TCI, for £5 million, proving (not for the first time) that programming in the emerging pay-TV market was the key element.

For its part, TCI, run by John Malone and his key UK programming executive, Fred Vierra (head of United Artists European Programming), had been looking generally at channel opportunities in the UK, having helped to develop several formats in the US. By the early 1990s, TCI owned the Discovery and Bravo channels in the UK, offering documentaries and cult TV series respectively. Later, it would take a stake, via its Telewest cable affiliate, in CPP1, the first effort by the cable operators to create cable-exclusive programming that might, eventually, vie with Murdoch, for the pay-TV pound. (CPP1 would eventually create its own channel, and then sell out to the Mirror Group, which created L!veTV.) The TCC investment alongside Flextech would mark the start of a more serious investment in UK programming, ultimately leading TCI, in 1994, to reverse UAEP into Flextech, thereby taking a majority stake. That gave TCI a range of UK channels, and meant the company, could, conceivably, create its own pay-TV platform.

TCI had been educated in the US market, where the cable industry was indisputably in control of pay-TV distribution. TCI, for instance, bid up the prices of channels to win the best line-up possible. But at the same time, the company had taken stakes in the channels themselves, and so benefited from the higher carriage fees offered by other cable operators around the country. Recalls Luard: 'Controlling the cable industry [in the US] means that [Malone] controlled the motorway, and however good your car was, in terms of programming, you needed to pay his toll. He paid you [for programming], but he leveraged equity out of you, he controlled the prices. The money went round in a big circle where he was concerned.'

Murdoch, who by then had made his commitment to satellite TV, did not want to see the same situation develop in the UK. Or, to put it another way, if someone was to control the 'big circle', he preferred it to be BSkyB. Says Luard: 'Sky was developing the means of allowing the consumer to access multi-channel television without having to wait for them to build the cable past their house. Murdoch had seen the dominance of cable in the US. In the end, Murdoch certainly didn't want to allow the cable industry to build and develop and dominate in the same way that it did in the US.'

Perhaps he needn't have worried. The conditions that obtained in the US during cable's big expansion in the 1960s and 1970s were never present in the UK. For a start, many US viewers took cable because they could not get a reliable terrestrial signal. In addition, the great cable boom occurred in the US before the growth of the video hire market, and so the early movie subscription channels did not compete with the Blockbuster's down the street. In the UK, the VCR was nearly ubiquitous by the time the cable operators began in earnest to build their UK networks.

Viacom, meanwhile, was having similar thoughts to Flextech's about the UK market. Sumner Redstone's media giant, and the owner of the Paramount studio, had three branded channels – MTV, VH1 and Nickelodeon – and was in two minds about whether to seek a subscription business or to continue to rely on pan-European advertising. MTV (housed in Camden Town, at the old offices of TV-Am, losers of the morning ITV franchise in 1991) had been an unexpected runaway success in Europe, having reached its break-even point far earlier than originally anticipated by its backers, Viacom (Maxwell, who had been the majority partner in MTV Europe at its launch, had eventually sold out). MTV Europe had been set up and run by Mark Booth, a young American broadcaster, who would return to Britain in 1997 in an unexpected role.

But there was a big question for the head of MTV Networks in Europe, Bill Roedy, an ex-marine: whether to go 'clear' (available to anyone with a dish) or encrypted (available only to those who paid a subscription fee). MTV was broadcast first on Eutelsat, a competing satellite system, and was available throughout the continent. Encrypting for the UK meant doing the same in other countries. Channels such as TCC and Bravo were primarily targeted to UK audiences, and did not much worry about losing a small continental audience. Back in the US, the parent company of MTV, Viacom, had two other channels – Nickelodeon (for young people) and VH1 (aimed at the slightly older generation of would-be rock 'n' rollers). How would these channels be introduced to the UK market? Not altogether surprisingly, the various channels under the Viacom umbrella did not always agree about strategy. That proved to be an opening that BSkyB could exploit.

The other channel operators were making their best efforts to upset the developing BSkyB monopoly in pay TV. Recalls Joyce Taylor, one of cable's early pioneers and later head of Discovery Europe, the TCI channel: 'There were all kinds of people in rooms [negotiating].' Among them: Travel, run by Richard Wolfe, CNN, MTV, and all the TCI-backed channels. 'But it got bogged down in the technology and the encryption system, the [smart] card and who would get paid what,' Taylor says. 'It was a real precursor of what has gone on ever since with everybody within the cable industry. Here you had a group of people in a room who didn't have one person driving the vehicle, so it always ended up in a squabble. "My channels are worth more than your channels". Or "My channels are 24 hours and yours are only eight". So you always got bogged down with these small issues and therefore it allowed Sky to [dominate].'

There was another problem with creating a competing system. The industry was beginning to realise that only movies and sport could really drive subscriptions. Without premium programming, it would be difficult to convince subscribers to take a second smart card. Says Taylor: 'Nobody was in a position to do the movie and sports deals that Sky could do, so there was [nothing] that could drive an alternative package. You didn't have anybody who could drive the vision of going out and buying sports rights and film rights.'

Admits Adam Singer, later executive chairman of Flextech, and then with TCI's international operations: 'The great mistake we all made was [that] the UK cable industry had a chance to lock up sports and movies, long before News Corporation turned up, but it failed to grasp that [opening], because it never actually had a content mentality. The brilliant thing that Sky had done was to persuade everybody to forget that it's a [wireless] cable operation, and [to believe] it's a content operation. Sky is a dead straight wireless cable operation with an unbelievably well built-up brand and everybody thinks of it as a content play not as a distribution play.'

Finally, it was unlikely that Viacom, TCI, Time Warner and other giant US companies would co-operate in the UK when they were so ruthlessly competitive in their home market.

Still, Isleworth was worried. A rival package of multi-channel television, even if it did not contain movies and sport, would have made it impossible for BSkyB to charge higher rates for its premium programming. David Chance explains the strategy. 'We had to get a system where there was enough channels [in our package] that the secondary channels would get concerned about being left out,' he says. 'With that in mind, we targeted two entities – TCI and Viacom.' On offer was entry to Sky's own platform, and the chance to secure additional revenues from the Sky subscription base. An added bonus would be Sky's undoubted marketing expertise.

BSkyB, not surprisingly, chose TCI first. The US company had both cable operations and channels in the UK, and was therefore concerned not only about its content but about its distribution. On the cable side, TCI, through its Telewest cable associate, knew that BSkyB held all the rights to Hollywood movies and (thanks to the recent Premier League deal) to top football. Both programming strands were seen as absolutely key to the prospects of the cable operations.

Explains Adam Singer: 'Sky came along and said: "We are going to have to encrypt [our basic channels], and clearly we have got some powerful channels in the guise of Sky 1 and the Movie Channel and Sports channel, but we need capacity fodder and [more] basic channels".' He adds: '[Even though] we were fairly heavily involved in trying to create more basic programming, the issue that was facing us was that we had a fairly significant cable investment.' That meant that TCI could only rely on subscription revenue for its channels from cable and not from DTH, since its satellite signal was received 'free' in UK-equipped homes. At the same time, Telewest was buying Sky's movie and sports channels, for distribution via cable. BSkyB kept most of its supply arrangements on very tight terms: a 12-month contract was considered the maximum. That made it difficult to plan ahead, and to convince the banks (and indeed equity markets) that it had the long-term stability needed to underwrite its expensive network construction.

Recalls David Chance, who, with David Evans and BSkyB's lawyer Deanna Bates, led the negotiations on the multi-channel package: 'They [Telewest] needed certainty of where their pricing was going to be in order to get the funding to build the network. They needed to know what the pricing levers would be.'

Parallel negotiations began with TCI-Flextech and with Telewest to reach a deal, with the final negotiations taking place in Los Angeles. Throughout the multi-channel negotiations, Chisholm himself took a back seat. But his reputation was constantly used by Chance. 'If we needed to reinforce the point that the answer was no, we could turn to Sam. Or if someone called Sam up, and said "Look, Chance is being impossible", then Sam would say, "If I join these negotiations, its going to be another 5p off the table". He was very helpful in that sort of approach. His reputation is such that it is quite easy to carry a lot of force. We could say: "This is all we are going to do, that's all the money I can get", and they'd believe it, because of Sam's reputation.'

With Telewest, a four-year deal was agreed for the supply of Sky's premium programming, at prices that were set at a pre-determined discount to the price paid by retail satellite subscribers. At the time, TCI had pressed for this kind of pricing structure, although later, the cable industry would unite to fight the 'discount-to-DTH' price in the wholesale market because it gave BSkyB the ability to dictate prices throughout the pay-TV system.

'The interesting thing about the deal was, of course, it was two parts to the equation,' Singer says. 'Telewest was a customer for Sky's channels [and TCI-Flextech were suppliers] so it was a supply and a purchase arrangement, it wasn't just a straight supplier arrangement. [From the

Sam Chisholm (on right), Chief Executive of BSkyB, and David Chance, Deputy Managing Director of BSkyB, both until December 1997.

Rupert Murdoch at the Multi-Channel Launch, 1993

Mark Booth Chief
Executive, BSkyB
as of December 1997

Vic Wakeling, Head of
Sports at BSkyB

David Elstein
Former Head
of Programmes
at BSkyB, Now
Chief Executive
at Channel 5

Elisabeth Murdoch,
General Manager of
Broadcasting and
Head of
Programmes
at BSkyB

Dinner hosted by Sam Chisholm for Mark Booth to celebrate his wedding:

1 Nick Pollard, 2 Jonathan Sykes, 3 Tony Vickers, 4 Peter Shea, 5 Ian West,
6 Jon Florsheim, 7 Bruce McWilliam, 8 David Chance, 9 Trevor East,
10 Jim Hytner, 11 Vic Wakeling, 12 Raymond Jaffe, 13 Sam Chisholm,
14 Mark Booth, 15 Bruce Dunlop, 16 Bruce Steinberg.

First Premier League match on Sky TV 1992 – Nottingham Forest v Liverpool

BSkyB 'Free System' campaign

free SKY system
when you buy a PC this Xmas

X-Files - December on Sky 1

http://www.sky.co.uk

Spend over £299 on electrical items at participating stores and you will get a free Sky satellite system.
Subject to subscription to any of Sky's Channels for 12 months. Subject to conditions. Offer closes 16th November.

From left to right: footballer Ian Wright; David Chance; Sam Chisholm;
Sky personality Anna Walker and Richard Brooke at the flotation of BSkyB, 1994.

BSkyB's Livingston operation, Livingston, Scotland

Gerry Robinson,
Chairman of BSkyB
and Granada

At signing of agreement between British
Sky Broadcasting, Bertelsmann, Canal+,
and Havas. Pierre Lescure, Chairman,
Canal+; Rupert Murdoch, Chairman and
Chief Executive, News Corporation;
Michael Dornemann, Chairman and
CEO, Bertelsmann AG; Pierre Dauzier,
Chairman and CEO, Havas; Sam
Chisholm, Chief Executive, BSkyB;
Rolf Schmidt-Holt, President
TV Film Europe, UFA

programming side], Sky was essentially a wireless cable operator and it was just a quick way of reaching the market fairly effectively.'

The negotiations took several months, with some within the Telewest–TCI camp favouring remaining cable-exclusive for subscription television. Recalls Singer: 'I think there was some concern that we were creating a competitor [by going into the Sky platform].' But in the end, logic and realism prevailed. 'We understood that the only quick way you could achieve a market which could support programming would be through rapid growth of a distribution base. The easiest base would be DTH [which reached far more homes]. Clearly [supporting DTH] was not a comfortable decision. I suppose if direct-to-home satellite had never come into being and we could have just provided programming to cable, it might have been better for us [in the long run]. On the other hand, we'd have lost an awful lot more money.'

Even with the advantage of hindsight, and in light of BSkyB's over-whelming dominance in the pay-TV marketplace, Singer believes the deal with Sky was the only option. 'How do you reach the home? You had to be on Astra. Advertising revenue wasn't sufficient, so how do you get sufficient revenue? You had to encrypt. How did you actually make sure that you would get that subscription revenue? You had to be hovering close to a movie and sports package. What drives cable – either wireless or otherwise? Movies and sport. Therefore we had to be part of a movie and sports package. The only movie and sports package in town was them.'

The original BSkyB–TCI deal was pitched at 15p per subscriber per month, with pre-determined increases year by year. 'The prices were less than what cable was paying,' Singer concedes. 'But if you look at it on a volume-discounted basis, it wasn't that different.' DTH was a much bigger market than cable. 'As soon as subscription was introduced you had a great joy of being a Flextech or TCI shareholder and you could just drive past houses [with satellite dishes] and say there's 50p there's 50p there's 50p,' Singer says. 'Of course Murdoch could say it's a much bigger figure [for him].'

Getting the TCI–Flextech channels was the breakthrough Chance and Chisholm had been seeking. Says Luard: 'We probably should have done a better deal. Once they'd locked us in, then everybody else who was at that time entering the pay-TV universe had to come in. I could have played hardball with them, and maybe I should have done. I was naive and I didn't know as much as I do now. But at the end of the day, hey, I'm happy. And there ain't no one else who is getting [as much as we are] from Sky.'

BSkyB then turned to Viacom, and targeted MTV first. But the music channel proved a much harder nut to crack. Bill Roedy, who led the negotiations for MTV, initially asked for 75p per subscriber per month, a huge amount by UK pay-TV standards. He was concerned to get as much as possible in return for losing significant audiences when the channel became 'encrypted' throughout Europe. It was a sign of desperation on Sky's part, perhaps, that the counterbid from Isleworth was a still-princely 25p, much higher than the deals done with TCI.

When Roedy refused to budge, Chance went to Nickelodeon, MTV's sister channel, which had not yet launched in the UK. His offer was simple: why not launch the channel in a 50–50 partnership with BSkyB? In exchange, Chance promised that BSkyB would not launch a competing kid's channel. That deal proved much easier to conclude, and MTV was now isolated. 'We knew that if we could land Nickelodeon, there was no way that Viacom would allow MTV to go on a competing platform,' Chance says. 'Then the stampede started.' Four more channels, Family (part owned by Flextech), Country Music TV, UK Living (the sister channel to UK Gold) and the shopping channel QVC (in which BSkyB took a stake) all did carriage deals with BSkyB to come into the basic package.

There were hold-outs, however, The Travel Channel, owned by Landmark, the US broadcaster, ultimately refused BSkyB's terms, preferring to remain cable-exclusive. Insiders at Travel insisted that BSkyB was only willing to do a deal if it could have equity in the channel, a charge made (but never publicly) by other channel operators as well, and consistently denied by Sky. Landmark had originally approached BSkyB in December 1992, with plans to start a UK version of their successful US format. 'We thought travel was one of the few niche opportunities that was quite interesting for us to take an equity position in,' Chance says. 'So in our discussion with Landmark [we raised the concept] of a joint venture approach.' But Landmark was unwilling to sell any part of the company. As the negotiations dragged on, the US channel reached carriage deals with several cable operators, which they believed would give them leverage in their dealings with BSkyB.

Chisholm denies there was any untoward pressure put on Landmark to agree an equity deal. 'It needs to be born in mind that these guys [channel operators] had gone, they had left the market when things were tough. [Then, after] we'd been through this agony [of creating] a market, then they re-emerged. We then kick-started the business, got the software and that's what [everyone else] really ran off the back of.'

BSkyB would later seek other equity deals, in those niche areas it believed had real potential. By 1997, it had stakes in several channels, including History, Paramount and Granada Sky Broadcasting, a joint venture with Granada. Many channel operators complained about Sky's demands for a stake in exchange for carriage, although none would say so publicly, for fear of offending the 'gatekeeper' in pay-TV. 'They would bully us, and they would do it openly, knowing how powerful they were,' recalls a senior cable channel executive. Channel operators also complained about BSkyB's unwillingness to provide cross-promotional opportunities on other Sky channels, and about the reluctance of Murdoch's newspapers, particularly *The Sun*, to take advertisements from channels that would not play ball. 'They were running the show, and they knew it, and they made sure we knew it too,' the senior channel executive says.

In the end, the negotiations with Landmark were broken off. According to BSkyB, a chief reason for the failure to agree terms was a demand from Landmark that Sky not show any competing travel-related programming, even on Sky 1 or Sky News. A year later, BSkyB launched its own travel channel, on satellite only. According to Chance, the appeal of travel was as much about the future as the present. 'We felt that travel was going to be a very important part of a transactional service that we would offer to our subscribers down the road.'

With the basic package now in place, and a deal signed with Viacom's Nickelodeon, BSkyB returned to MTV. The price on offer from Isleworth had now dropped to the standard 15p, rather than BSkyB's opening shot of 25p. But the music channel was still unwilling to commit, chiefly because it had yet to secure carriage of MTV on a pay basis in Germany, one of its biggest markets.

BSkyB put the deal on the table, and set a deadline for encryption. When the date came and went, Chisholm decided it was time to turn up the heat. 'Sam suggested that instead of maintaining the rate at 15p, since they missed their deadline we should drop the fee structure down to 3p,' Chance recalls. 'That was one of the most interesting meetings I've ever had, [going] into MTV and [saying], "Look guys, instead of paying you 15p the fee is now 3p". I mean, the guy just about lost it.' MTV would only encrypt in July 1995, getting a rate of 'somewhere between 3p and 15p', Chance says.

The Sky multi-channel package was launched in the autumn of 1993, at an introductory price of £6.99. To encourage new subscribers to sign up, a special price of just £2.99 was set for the first six months. Dish subscribers would still get a few channels 'in the clear', including Sky News, CNN, Eurosport, the Cartoon Network, TNT and foreign-language services. But a significant number of dish homes that had not subscribed before agreed to sign up as paying customers for the first time.

Sky managed an astonishing feat at the same time. The original launch of Sky, back in 1989, had been as much about Astra, and the other channels, as it had been Murdoch's celebration. By the time the multi-channel package had been put together, and the extravagant party to mark the event had been planned, Astra was nowhere to be seen. 'Sky did [it] magnificently, the taking over to the Sky brand,' Discovery's Joyce Taylor says. 'You look at the pictures of Rupert Murdoch when Sky launched on satellite, [and] the room was full of Astra logos. Then you look at him on the multi-channel launch and there wasn't an Astra logo to be seen.' A company that was really just a distributor, with a handful of owned channels, had become a brand. It was the Sky satellite, not Astra. It was Sky Television, and not Nickelodeon, or Bravo or MTV.

The launch of the multi-channel package had an unintended consequence. New subscribers to the basic tier tended to take premium channels too – in far greater numbers than BSkyB had anticipated. Recalls Chance: 'Not only were we getting non-subscribers into basic, but it was also the catalyst for getting them up to the premium channels as well. That really delivered a substantial financial boost.'

The package also gave the whole of the pay-TV market a boost. There was now a significant number of pay-TV channels available on both DTH and cable, earning subscription revenues for the channel operators. 'It was without question Sky's programming and Sky's creation of multi-channels which actually saved the UK cable industry,' Singer concludes. 'I don't think there should be too much doubt about that.'

But the introduction of the multi-channel package had a negative effect on Sky 1, the general entertainment channel. Recalls David Elstein, the head of programmes: 'From the day that multi-channels launched, as had been predicted for some time, the Sky 1 share of the viewing [in multi-channel homes] dropped sharply; it dropped back to seven per cent and even six per cent [from as high as nine per cent]. Then, the struggle was to hold on to five or six per cent.' This was no great surprise. 'We'd brought in a lot of competition,' Elstein points out. 'Sky 1 at one point had a 15 per cent share in kids viewing of satellite programmes on a really cheap schedule but with no opposition. Suddenly there were a load of opposing specialist kid's channels.'

But, overall, the new pricing structure would prove a boon to BSkyB. The company had secured its position as the leading pay-TV broadcaster, co-opted the potential competition, and created an effortless way of increasing subscription fees year in and year out. There were blue skies ahead.

PART TWO

Into Orbit

CHAPTER 7

Floating Sky

With the multi-channel package launched, BSkyB now had in place a pricing structure that would power the company to ever higher profits. As Barlow says: 'It is marvellous. What you do is give people more of what they don't want, but it allows you to put the price up. It's so clever.' From 1993 on, Sky put the price of its channels up every year, each time adding services to the basic package as a way of convincing subscribers they were getting value for money. The initial basic package of ten channels (not counting the free Sky News) rose to 15 in 1994, 20 in 1995 (plus Disney, offered as a bonus channel to movie subscribers) and 31 in 1996. (Counting all the premium and bonus channels, the total package was nearer 40 channels). Meanwhile, the subscription prices for BSkyB's top programming rose by far more than the rate of inflation. In order to get the full array of services in 1991, for example, you would have paid £14.99 (nominally for the movies, as the rest of the Sky lineup was 'free'), rising to £16.99 in the autumn of that year. When sport was added in 1992, the top price was £19.99, for the two movie channels and Sky Sports. By 1997, when Sky was offering 40 channels, this had risen to £29.99.

With the ever higher revenues, a tight control on costs and a growing subscriber base (helped, in later years, by the steady if unspectacular growth of cable), BSkyB soon saw its operating profits begin to shoot up. By late 1993, Sky was making £2 million a week, and the full-year pre-tax figures for the year to June were in positive territory for the first time. This meant BSkyB was actually making a profit even after meeting the huge costs on its sizeable debt. The incredible success of Sky Sports was one reason. But from 1993, it would be the successful marriage of basic and premium channels that would really fuel the growth.

At the same time, the pricing system had an added benefit for BSkyB: it kept the cable industry hopelessly pinned down. Cable needed sports and movies, which were sold in the wholesale market at a set discount to the retail satellite price. That price was dictated by BSkyB, and meant that cable operators earned far narrower margins. At the same time, BSkyB offered the full discount only if cable operators took even unpopular channels such as Sky Soap and Sky Travel (both introduced in late 1994). Flextech's Adam Singer, whose parent company owned a large stake in Telewest, the cable operator, says, 'What's being created is a wealth trans-ference mechanism, which transfers the wealth from the subscribers' pockets to Murdoch's and doesn't touch our pocket in the middle. Good for them: it serves us right for not getting movies and sports sorted out.'

Regulators, until much later, would not act. And why should they? BSkyB was still a tiny player in the television business, at least in terms of audience share. Sir George Russell, then chairman of the ITC, is blunt. 'We took the view on multi-channel packaging at the time: what was the penetration, and what was the size of Sky? We couldn't overturn all this if their market share was only three per cent or something. How could we act on a competition basis? How could this be massively anti-competitive at this market share? They still aren't at a market share that causes trouble.'

Murdoch was eager to see BSkyB's success replicated elsewhere in his empire. His Star-TV, based in Hong Kong, critically needed attention, and he had already sent Gary Davey, one of the original co-managing directors of Sky, out to the Far East to deal with the problem of launching a successful pay-TV network for Asia. Increasingly, Sam Chisholm was also spending time in Hong Kong, much to the annoyance of BSkyB's chair-man, Frank Barlow. From 1993, Chisholm had a *de facto* role, supported by a management services contract, at News Corporation, responsible for Murdoch's non-US international TV operations.

In London, BSkyB had beefed up its management, having brought in David Elstein at the end of 1992. By early 1994, with Chisholm heavily involved in the Asian operations of News Corporation, Murdoch looked to bring in extra management resources at Isleworth. His choice struck many in British broadcasting as odd in the extreme: Kelvin MacKenzie, then 45, the brash, controversial editor of the downmarket *Sun*, who cheerfully told everyone who asked that he knew absolutely nothing about television.

It was MacKenzie who had claimed, on the front page, that it was *The Sun* 'wot won' the 1992 election for the Tories. It was he who penned the heartless 'Gotcha' headline upon the sinking of the Argentinian ship, the Belgrano, during the Falklands War. He seemed destined to remain forever in the rather grubby world of tabloid journalism, which appeared to suit his character and his tastes. But Murdoch obviously had other ideas.

It was a common tactic of Murdoch to move his executives around the empire. He had done it (successfully) with Gary Davey, for example, who went from Fox in the US to Sky and then to Star-TV. In other cases, the changes weren't as productive. Andrew Neil, for instance, was offered a job in US television, making a current affairs programme, after his long stint at *The Sunday Times* and his two years at BSkyB. It ended badly, and he and Murdoch had a terrific falling out.

Murdoch approached MacKenzie in November 1993, and asked him: 'How long do you wish to continue editing *The Sun*?' Murdoch knew that MacKenzie, easily the most successful tabloid editor of his generation, was tiring of the game. Says MacKenzie himself: 'After 13 years editing newspapers I was seeing many of the same issues coming at me that I dealt with before.'

The two men had a 20-second conversation, during which it was agreed he would be managing director of BSkyB, number two to Sam Chisholm, in effect replacing Gary Davey. The chief executive had no strong views on the matter, and professed to have been quite relaxed about MacKenzie's appointment. Indeed, the two men had often spoken in the past: Chisholm would ring MacKenzie to discuss news developments and News Corporation politics. But those who knew the two men could barely believe they would actually work together under the same roof. How could MacKenzie and Chisholm get along in business? Both had quick tempers and used strong language, and shared a reputation for bullying. Both insisted on running the show, and hated long, drawn out strategic arguments. Both managed by intuition rather than rote, and preferred quick decisions to collegiality. Both bawled out inferiors, and used trenchant sarcasm to belittle and so control. And both were intelligent and capable: more so than their rough styles might have suggested.

MacKenzie knew within seconds of arriving at BSkyB in January 1994 that, faced with having to work with a man as driven and as idio-syncratically difficult as Chisholm, this had been a horrible mistake. The chief problem, was, of course personality. Chisholm clearly didn't like MacKenzie, nor did he like the former editor's attempts to put his mark on Sky from the very start. MacKenzie, for his part, had a similarly dismissive view of his new boss. 'Having seen a class act like Mr Murdoch, I simply thought that Chisholm was a little prick,' he says. Of that first day, MacKenzie recalls: 'I had worked for News Corporation in London and New York for the best part of 20 years, and I had nothing but a creatively attractive atmosphere. This I found missing at Sky.' MacKenzie believes now it would have been better for both men if he had been appointed number three in the sports department. 'In the newspaper business, there would be very few people who could tell me how to run a newspaper,' he says. 'However, when I went to Sky, I knew nothing. Even the tea lady knew more than I did because at least she knew her way around the building.'

MacKenzie soon realised what he was up against in Sam Chisholm. While the chief executive never crossed MacKenzie openly, he would undermine him in subtler ways. Sometimes, MacKenzie would appear for a meeting outside the office and find that Chisholm had already spoken to those in question on the telephone the day before. MacKenzie wonders why Chisholm bothered. 'I was no threat to [him]. He'd been in TV for 30 years. I'd been in it for 30 seconds.'

MacKenzie appealed to Murdoch, himself as willing as his two executives to be gruff, dismissive, tough and unpleasant. Murdoch then rang Chisholm and asked him to support the new executive. While the undermining became less sustained, the two continued to dislike each other intensely. Several issues flared up between them, including MacKenzie's attempts to inject more populism into Sky News (which ultimately led to the departure of Ian Frykberg, a close friend of Sam Chisholm, who had been running the service at the time). There was also huge disagreement over the £6 million deal MacKenzie signed with Chris Eubank, the British boxer, which Chisholm believed to be excessive.

Other Sky executives watched the bitter fight with interest. David Elstein, for instance, believed MacKenzie had been out of his depth throughout his brief time at BSkyB. 'It's not that surprising because it's a very difficult business to understand and every different facet of it is perplexing,' Elstein says. 'You know, piracy – what do we do? The studios – what do we do? Rights – what do we do? The government – what do we do? The regulator – what do we do? There's a zillion things that can go wrong with Sky and when you bump into one for the first time [you think], "What's this coming down?" I remember being called in to some urgent meeting by Kelvin, and he was just going through piracy and [rate] card charges and the cost of it, [and asking] how are we going to solve this fucking thing?'

For Elstein, Chance and the other senior executives, this was nothing new. BSkyB had always been run in chaotic fashion. Issues were left unresolved for months, and then were attacked with vigour when Chisholm focused on them. It was done 'almost to preserve his [Chisholm's] power', Elstein says. MacKenzie was unused to it, however. 'He was used to getting the paper out day after day after day,' Elstein says. 'He would make decisions that were two-thirds right, one-third wrong but it's history within a day. Here you're making strategic plays, parallel strategic plays, overlapping strategic plays, conflicting strategic plays and you've got to keep them in balance and you've got to understand how they bounce off each other and you keep a situation open as long as possible; don't close off until you're ready. All those things were quite hard to get used to. I took some time to get used to that fluidity in the whole way in which Sky was managed.'

In August, just eight months after he had joined, MacKenzie sent a fax to Murdoch in LA, saying he was no longer willing to work at BSkyB. In it, he described Chisholm as someone who would 'smile up but shit down' within the corporate hierarchy. Ten days later, MacKenzie and Murdoch had breakfast, during one of Murdoch's frequent visits to London. 'Look,' Murdoch said, 'people go half-way round the world not to work for Chisholm.' Murdoch then offered him a TV job in the US, which MacKenzie declined. 'If I took such a job, and was within News Corporation, I would be tempted whenever I could to give a whack to Chisholm,' he said. Murdoch adjusted his glasses, and looked at MacKenzie thoughtfully. He said nothing. MacKenzie left with no pay-off ('Why should I?', he says. 'I fired Sky, not the other way around'), and in early 1995 joined Mirror Television, as its managing director, responsible for L!ve TV, the cheap and cheerful City TV network. MacKenzie would re-emerge as a thorn (*albeit* small) in the side of BSkyB when Mirror Group supported efforts by the cable operators to create their own pay-TV programming, notably bidding for rights to sport events and attempting to set up a pay-per-view movie service in 1995.

Meanwhile, at BSkyB, the 1993 financial figures had been good enough to allow the company to pay a special dividend to the long-suffering shareholders. Most of the debt on the books was either owed directly to the sponsoring shareholders or guaranteed by them, and it was agreed that pay-outs would be made as and when possible to repay the funds. The excellent results also emboldened Sky management to start thinking about a flotation of the company – something that had long been planned but that had been postponed in the wake of the disastrous early years.

Murdoch had been sceptical about the idea of a flotation, assuming that the other shareholders might not back the plan. He was eager, however, and pleased to see whether Chisholm could convince the others. 'He needed the money, because he always has a requirement for capital,' Chisholm remembers. 'I just don't think he thought the other shareholders were going to go along with it.'

But Chisholm was convinced the timing was right, and that shareholders would be able to realise some of their investment. 'The flotation cost me a holiday,' Chisholm remembers. He came back to have lunch with Barlow at Cecconi's, the venerable Italian restaurant in London's West End, in a bid to get the chairman's support for the flotation idea. Barlow approved, on behalf of Pearson; Granada, too was eager. The rentals and TV company had recently brought in new management, in the form of Gerry Robinson, the Donegal-born Irishman, who had made his reputation at Compass, the catering company he'd helped spin off from Grand Metropolitan, and Charles Allen, a young Scottish accountant and long-time Robinson colleague. The two men had inherited Granada's investment in BSkyB, but initially took very little direct interest. 'I just took the view at the point of arrival at Granada that to me [BSkyB] looked like something that was going to sort itself out,' Robinson explains. 'It felt like [it was] going somewhere, and had stopped calling for cash. It certainly looked to me that we should leave it alone. We had seen the worst of it and [there was] now probably some upside.' Robinson, indeed, did not even go onto the BSkyB board when he was appointed chief executive of Granada, leaving it to Henry Staunton and Graham Wallace, the finance director, who subsequently decamped for Cable & Wireless Communications, the cable and telephony company.

Robinson was an odd choice, in some ways, to head a company with such extensive media interests (Granada, LWT and, of course, its stake in Sky). But he was of a new breed in ITV, more concerned about the bottom line than about programming; charming, quick to laugh and conspiratorial in his way, but far from being a traditional media luvvie. He had ruffled the feathers of the media establishment, moreover, during the aftermath of his company's controversial takeover of LWT, completed in early 1994. The cost-cutting exercise that followed, which saw the departure of eminent broadcaster David Plowright, led John Cleese, the *Monty Python* actor, to call him an 'ignorant upstart caterer', a reference to Robinson's earlier career at Compass.

Robinson and Granada chairman Alex Bernstein, early converts to the concept of a flotation, threw their full weight behind the idea. Chargeurs, the French media company that had patiently backed BSkyB (and BSB before that) was the one hold-out on the flotation. Why, Jérôme Seydoux, the Chargeurs chairman, asked, would we want to dilute our interest now, just when BSkyB appeared to be on a winning course? But faced with Granada's desire to realise some of its investment, and Pearson's firm commitment to bring in public shareholders, Chargeurs acquiesced.

Chargeurs had been perhaps the most committed of all the shareholders to BSkyB, having never once wavered despite all the cash calls, the early losses, and the shakeup that followed the BSB–Sky merger. When BSkyB held a celebration in Paris to mark the flotation, the assembled crowd gave Chargeurs executives a resounding round of applause following fulsome remarks by Chisholm on the steadfast support the company had received from the French. 'There's a lot of sentiment in television about what makes it all work,' Chisholm says. 'These are the guys that have made this company work and I suppose it is part of our ethos [that] we don't forget them.'

BSkyB's advisers, Goldman Sachs and BZW, began the work on the flotation in mid-1994. It was soon agreed that the company would offer the public and institutions 334 million shares, or 20 per cent of the company, to raise as much as £867 million. On that basis, BSkyB would be worth an astonishing £4 billion in all. Not bad for a company that just three years before had been losing millions of pounds a week, had still carried £2 billion in debt, and had been in danger of trading illegally. The turnaround was all the more impressive for having taken place during a recession, when one might have questioned the likelihood that significant numbers of consumers would spend up to £275 a year on imports and movies (mostly American), news, sport and general entertainment.

Not everyone believed BSkyB was worth that kind of money. Some analysts put the value at closer to £2.5 billion, and questioned the more fanciful valuations produced by investment houses which were to join the share syndicate. Because the flotation was so large, several big City firms were asked to work on the deal, either as brokers or as members of the share distribution syndicate. Of the top ten media analysts in the 1994 rankings by Extel, only three worked for firms outside the ranks of BSkyB's corporate advisers and sponsors.

To get anywhere near a £4 billion market capitalisation, the City reasoned, BSkyB would have to double its profits and its subscriber base. Even if BSkyB traded on the same multiple as the market accorded other star media companies, such as giant Reuters, the financial information provider, the broadcaster would be lucky to hit £3 billion.

As the float neared, leading national newspapers, too, were skeptical. Many City commentators questioned the valuation, while others pointed out that the City was being asked to accept 'pie-in-the-sky' forecasts for the growth of multi-channel television. Some of the knocking copy could be put down to an anti-Murdoch campaign, however. Murdoch's own newspapers had launched a brutal price war, which was beginning to cause acute pain at rival companies. It was galling to some Fleet Street publishers that cash flow from BSkyB might be shoring up News International, Murdoch's newspaper arm, where profits were being hit by the deep discounting on the cover prices of News International titles. (Of course, those with longer memories will have remembered a time when it was News International that had been bailing out Sky, as the then-struggling broadcaster was bleeding freely.)

Management at BSkyB, backed by their big advisers, were unrepentant. They believed that BSkyB was *sui generis* – the only company of its kind. Its contracts with the Premier League and Hollywood studios were the bricks, while the superb marketing department, and the state-of-the-art subscription management service, were the mortar. BSkyB would go from strength to strength, having created what Chisholm called the 'virtuous circle'. As subscriptions grew, BSkyB had more money to spend on programming. Additional programming attracted more subscribers, whose payments then helped boost the programming budget yet further. Even better, management argued, BSkyB now had two distribution platforms: satellite and cable. The cable industry was still growing slowly in 1994, but had ambitious plans to spend up to £10 billion by the end of the decade to connect as many as six million homes to cable TV and telephony. While they concentrated on their network expansion, cable operators, in the main, did not expend much management effort lining up cable-exclusive programming with which to entice potential subscribers. Instead, the companies turned to the obvious suppliers of pay-TV programming – including BSkyB. As a consequence, an industry which might have been an effective rival for pay-TV viewers had become a distribution arm for Isleworth, paying BSkyB for the right to carry Sky programming. Satellite subscribers might have generated better margins for BSkyB, but the additional revenues from the cable operators were welcome indeed.

On the eve of the float, in typically robust fashion, Disney, the erstwhile partner of Sky, pounced. The studio had long been concerned about the cost of launching a subscription channel in the UK, which had been in the works since 1989, prior to the original launch of Sky. Disney now held out for a better deal on subscription management, and told BSkyB it would not proceed unless more money was put on the table. BSkyB, worried about the float, acquiesced, and Disney ended up with one of the best per-subscriber fee structures of any third-party channel in the UK.

The flotation would see three of the four principal BSkyB shareholders dilute their stakes. Murdoch would go to 40 per cent from 50 per cent, although he would retain 'management control' of the company – not officially of course, but through the willingness of other shareholders to allow him to take the lead. Pearson would drop from 17 per cent to 14 per cent, and Granada to 11 per cent from 13.5 per cent. Only Chargeurs, which had held out against the flotation in the first place, would buy shares in the new issue in order to keep its stake at 17 per cent.

During preparations for the flotation, a serious rift began to develop between Frank Barlow, the chairman, and the rest of the board, particularly the News Corporation appointees. Some of the other directors were tiring of what they saw as Barlow's incessant nagging about relatively unimportant matters. Barlow had been particularly vocal about the amount of time Sam Chisholm spent outside Britain, doing business for Murdoch. Recalls Gerry Robinson: 'I think that Frank had been through the really tough times, all that bitter twisting, turning and arguing over all kinds of bits and pieces. He probably lost what was important to argue and what wasn't important to argue and I think he irritated a lot of people in the place. There is a point at which if you protest at everything people will stop listening to you, it's as simple as that. [Having] small arguments as to how much time Sam Chisholm should spend in the country is complete nonsense.'

Barlow concedes he had arguments about Chisholm's position, balanced between News Corporation and BSkyB. '[News Corporation] used Sky staff to investigate [the prospects] at Star TV [in Asia], and I said, "Look, I don't mind you using these people, but you have to provide the names, the dates, and you have to pay a commission".' It may have particularly rankled Barlow that Chisholm was working on Star TV, a company that Pearson, too, had been interested in buying. During the long, drawn out negotiations in 1993, Barlow found himself beaten to the prize by a typical lightning pre-emptive strike from Murdoch. The final deal was signed in Hong Kong, on a boat moored in the harbour, while Pearson's Barlow was in town. Richard Li, the 26-year-old scion of Li Kai Shing's media and property dynasty, kept leaving the table during the final negotiations, suffering from sea sickness. The Star TV deal brought together Chisholm and John Thornton, managing director of Goldman Sachs, for the first time. Thornton would also act on behalf of Bertelsmann when News Corporation bought into Vox, the German music channel, in 1994, and would eventually become a director of BSkyB.

Barlow knew that fighting Murdoch on the BSkyB board was probably a hopeless cause. 'It's Rupert's technique to use the power of the management,' Barlow says. 'Let's say we are partners, and I have 40 per cent and you have 60 per cent, but I have the management. You can't physically stop me from doing things. The only way you can stop me is to go to court. And so, News wanted to run [BSkyB] as a News subsidiary.' But Barlow persevered nonetheless, and refused to be brow-beaten by the collective strength of the Murdoch appointees on the board. 'I spent my life fighting the trade unions,' Barlow says. 'There had been nothing more intransigent than a print union leader. I would insist that certain things would come before the [BSkyB] board. So I gave the News directors a very hard time.'

Barlow had particularly blazing rows with Arthur Siskind, Murdoch's highly-rated lawyer, who sat on the BSkyB board. 'Arthur really couldn't stand Frank,' recalls one director. 'They went at each other all the time.' Siskind, who had been a corpulent man, suffered a heart attack, and lost considerable weight. Shortly thereafter, he and Barlow had another of their famous arguments, shouting across the boardroom table. 'Look,' Barlow said to Siskind, 'my heart can stand it, can yours?'

Barlow also had a series of run-ins with Sam Chisholm, although Barlow insists their relationship was sound. On the matter of the float, however, the two men violently disagreed. The issue: flotation bonuses for the senior executives of BSkyB. The original proposal from the bankers, which had Chisholm's full support, was to establish a bonus scheme worth £24 million for senior staff, in the form of shares and cash. 'That was ridiculously high,' Barlow complained. 'I didn't disagree with bonuses, especially for Sam. But it was quantum.' Not only was the scheme too rich in Barlow's view but it extended too far down the management chain of command. 'There were movers and shakers like Chisholm and Chance and Gary Davey, who deserved it,' Barlow says. 'But people who were drawers of water and hewers of wood were in line for huge bonuses. I was against it.'

Chisholm believes some of the shareholders (notably Pearson) were trying to do a deal to cut out some of the management. 'The deal was: "Let's just see if we can buy Chisholm out and give him a big slug",' Chisholm recalls. 'And I said, "No deal, you've got to look after the whole outfit or no float". We didn't forget the management and everyone [who] had gone through it all.' He fingers Barlow as one of the culprits. '[Barlow] thought it was a great idea to float the company and then he said, "Yes we would certainly look after the management because they'd all worked like hell". [But] when we set out to see that everyone was properly rewarded, then he became extremely difficult.'

Murdoch himself says he thought the bonuses and option scheme were a bit rich. 'I was amazed at this idea of a flotation bonus,' he recalls. 'But I was talked into it, the merchant bankers said it was standard, and they supported it. I didn't like it.'

Barlow recalls being largely isolated at the time on the issue of the management bonuses, however. He believed that the two Granada executives, Henry Staunton and Graham Wallace, were not all that happy, and Chargeurs, at least initially, backed Barlow's position. But Murdoch did not intervene, and in the end the increasing prickliness between the detail-obsessed Barlow and the other directors left the Pearson man with few friends. Although the package was watered down to a degree, the management got its flotation bonus. In addition, one per cent of pre-tax profits were to be set aside for senior executives, and of this, Chisholm was in line for half. (Later, this would be changed to 1.5 per cent, with Chisholm in line for a third.) In the first set of public results after the flotation, it was revealed that Chisholm received £4.7 million in the year, making him one of Britain's best-paid executives. In a cheeky article in *The Sunday Times*, Murdoch's flagship weekend quality newspaper, Chisholm topped the list of the most over-paid executives in the UK. Catching wind of the story before publication, Chisholm called Murdoch to complain. Murdoch declined to intervene, suggesting to Chisholm that if he was that concerned about his image, he should consider giving the money back.

In retrospect, Chisholm is magnanimous in victory, even if he damns Barlow with faint praise. 'My main criticism of him would be that he was erratic,' Chisholm says. 'But I liked him and I thought he was actually a very good chairman and a very, entertaining character. He's good company, but he lacked consistency.' On the flotation, Chisholm says: 'These guys [the shareholders] have done spectacularly well, because everybody's got his money back and then some. Plus they've still got a position in the company.'

The flotation debates would prove to be the breaking point for the main shareholders of BSkyB, who had decided by early 1995 that Barlow would have to go. In Murdoch's words: 'There was just so much bad blood, and on the flotation, there was terrific bad blood. It would all get fixed, and then he started nit-picking. It was very, very annoying. I had a word with Chargeurs, and said shall we change chairman, and they said, yes, and let's act while we are still angry. Frank didn't know how to control Sam either.'

The request to Barlow to step down, done publicly and with little ceremony, was embarrassing to all concerned, although Murdoch did not seem to mind. In early February, Murdoch greeted Frank Barlow at BSkyB, and asked him into a small office next to the board room. Recalls Barlow: 'He was never rude to me. He took me aside, and there was Gerry Robinson and Jérôme Seydoux, and they asked me to stand down.'

Others recall that Murdoch was blunter. 'I have the votes and we want you to step down, Frank,' he said. Barlow responded: 'I want time to think about it.' But he soon realised there was no point in taking it to the full board, as the main shareholders held such great sway. Gerry Robinson was asked to become chairman, and was duly appointed 4 February 1995. Barlow says that Robinson has done nothing as chairman to ensure that Murdoch did not unduly interfere in the company. 'Rupert is the great seducer. He seduced Gerry and he seduced Chargeurs. He persuaded the two to take his line. Robinson didn't want to fall out with Rupert. Rupert can be charm itself. He has charmed so many people. Rupert will hire executives, and convince them, you are the best friend. They all go at some point.'

Robinson, for his part, saw no conflict in becoming chairman of BSkyB, even at a time when ITV, in which he was a significant player, was mounting an increasingly vocal campaign against the pay-TV broadcaster. The only time, indeed, that Granada's position within Sky might have been construed as a problem in Robinson's eyes was during the bid for the Premier League, when ITV was up against BSkyB. Even when Robinson took on the chairmanship of ITN, the news provider, in addition to his roles at Granada and BSkyB, he insisted that there were no outstanding issues.

'There might have been the odd grumbling from the sidelines about where Granada was really, but I don't think it was much of an issue,' Robinson says. 'It only became an issue when BSkyB started to become a serious player in the field and then there were concerns as to whether [we] could be into both camps. That turned out to be ridiculous, because everyone was trying to be as many camps as they possibly could.' And, he maintained, the BSkyB–Granada connection was incredibly useful to his company. 'It would have been madness for us to have lost that connection – crazy, because it was an enormous advantage to be in there.'

The flotation of BSkyB marked a huge step forward in the company's history. Now, its financial progress would be charted quarter by quarter by 'teenage scribblers' in the City, and its share price would be a daily testimony to the success or failure of the management at Isleworth. The shares were listed in December 1994, and BSkyB became a quoted company for the first time. Despite an initial dip, the share began to power ahead, on the strength of a string of positive news. In January, the company agreed a £400 million revolving credit, giving it far greater financial manoeuvring room. A month later, BSkyB unveiled a joint venture with Reuters, whereby the news giant would supply the bulk of Sky News, the one channel that had continued to be a serious drain on company resources. At the end of February, the company won an important legal case, which gave it far more power to stop the pirates who had been supplying fraudulent 'smart cards' with which illegally to receive Sky's scrambled signals.

All this news was voraciously consumed by an interested stock market. Suddenly, Chisholm and his staff were the focus of intense analysis in the City, and were set to generate thousands of column inches in the financial pages of national newspapers. BSkyB was by now making about £5 million a week, enough to impress even the most jaundiced of critics. It was also drawing much more fire from its broadcasting rivals, who now understood that pay-TV was not going to go away, and that BSkyB was a force to be reckoned with. Too late, perhaps, its rivals began to respond.

CHAPTER 8

Rivals Respond

With a few exceptions, including Barry Cox at ITV, there had been little effort by either the ITV companies themselves or the BBC to react to BSkyB's incredible growth. In one sense, ITV, the main commercial broadcaster in the UK, could afford to be complacent. After all, BSkyB had made very little headway in the advertising market, and was earning nearly all its revenues through subscriptions. When the various applicants submitted their bids for the first competitive ITV bids, in 1991, most had expected BSkyB to take at least some advertising business away from the Channel 3 broadcasters. No one had expected that BSkyB would, in fact, create a brand new market – subscription TV – on such an impressive scale. For its part the BBC had been preoccupied by the preparations for the renewal of its Charter, which necessitated considerable, time-consuming contact with the government. But by the beginning of 1995, there was increasing awareness in commercial television and at the BBC that the main broadcasters had seriously missed a trick. Sky was on its way to breaching the £1 billion mark in revenue terms, and might indeed close in on ITV and Channel 4 by the end of the decade. How could the traditional broadcasters, themselves eager to tap the pay-TV market that BSkyB had pioneered, win their share?

Some at ITV had been worried about BSkyB for several years. The Premier League contract was a turning point, and in July 1992, a campaign was launched to petition the government to revisit the Broadcasting Act of 1990, enacting changes to rein in the Murdoch empire. In a letter written to media executives by Nicholas Boole, an executive at ITV's PR advisers, Hill & Knowlton, it was announced that the lobbying campaign would intensify that autumn. Meanwhile, Barry Cox, then at LWT, was pushing ahead on a second front – attempting to convince the government that digital terrestrial television could prove to be a viable alternative to BSkyB, allowing the ITV companies access to pay-TV revenues without having to do business with BSkyB. As early as 1992, some in ITV believed BSkyB had emerged as a gate-keeper in pay-TV, and any other company wanting to tap this new market would have to do a deal with Murdoch. That view seemed to gain credence following the creation of the multi-channel package in 1993, when BSkyB took equity stakes in channels. BSkyB's public affairs team, led by Ray Gallagher, vehemently denied this was so, pointing out that any company could create a pay-TV system, set up a subscription management service, and market set-top boxes to consumers. By 1993, the European Commission was openly exploring ways of regulating pay-TV, particularly with reference to establishing standards for digital television, then being discussed as a viable market in Germany, Italy, France and the UK. In the UK, a digital working group was established, involving the ITV companies, the BBC, retailers, manufacturers and, eventually, even BSkyB. But even if they were ostensibly co-operating with Sky, the ITV companies particularly (not counting BSkyB shareholder Granada, of course), were still worried about how to pre-empt BSkyB in the digital age.

The mainstream broadcasters were not the only companies worried about the competitive threat from Isleworth. The country's cable operators were feeling increasingly squeezed by BSkyB's brilliant pre-emptive strike in 1992–93, when it secured carriage deals with all the main channels in the market, thus allowing it to dominate the subscription TV business in the UK. In order to get the premium sport and movie product BSkyB was supplying, cable operators had to pay through the nose.

The cable industry in the UK had already gone through difficult periods. An initial hopeful phase in the 1980s had delivered little in the way of a vibrant market. It was only in 1992, when the government changed the rules to allow cable companies to offer telephony services as well as cable TV, that an effective market had been created. For the initial few years after 1992, the emphasis had been on building the network and competing with BT, the dominant telecoms supplier.

Channel owners, too, were increasingly frustrated by BSkyB's dominance of the marketplace. Tales were told of secret pressure brought to bear by BSkyB on channel operators seeking carriage. In order to get into the Sky multi-channel package, critics complained, Chisholm and Chance were demanding equity in the channels for BSkyB. Such demands were never put in writing, the channel operators maintained. But it was clear what BSkyB wanted as the price of providing satellite carriage in the multi-channel environment. Sky management denies this was ever the case.

BSkyB had three huge advantages over any potential rival in the pay-TV market. It had secure control of the two main drivers of subscription television – sport and film. It had long-term carriage deals with Astra for transponders on the main satellites, a supply that had become impossibly tight by 1995. And it had the country's only functioning encryption technology for satellite viewers, provided by News Datacom, the Murdoch subsidiary. If a channel wanted to scramble its signal in order to generate subscription revenue from the direct-to-home market, it either had to invest in the huge infrastructure required for subscription management services (SMS), or do a deal with Sky. Cable-exclusive channels did not have this problem of course, as the cable operators ran their own SMS. But satellite had more than three million subscribers by 1995, compared to barely a million for cable. The economics of pay-TV meant going, ideally, for both platforms, but at the very least for the bigger satellite universe.

Cable operators, those who were investing billions in digging up roads in Britain to lay broadband connections to UK homes, had been concentrating on network construction, rather than on programming. As a result, they had meekly accepted the terms offered by BSkyB for access to its premium films and sport. And by most reckonings, the terms were harsh indeed. The sting was in the structure of the wholesale market for Sky's programming, where costs were set as a percentage of the retail (or direct-to-home, DTH) price. For instance, a satellite (DTH) customer wanting Sky Movies in 1995 would have paid £19.99, which included a notional payment for the 'free' multi-channel package. After all, satellite customers could only get the premium product if they 'bought through' the basic package. In the wholesale market, the cable operators paid between 50 and 60 per cent of the DTH price for Sky programming, depending on the percentage of their customer base that took premium channels (the so-called 'pay-to-basic' ratio). In the case, for instance, of Sky Movies, BSkyB set the discount wholesale fee on the basis of the £19.99 retail price paid by satellite customers, who would get the movie channel and the basic package for that amount. The cable operators, however, would only get the movie channel, and would then have to pay separately for all the channels in the multipackage, which included a number of third-party providers like MTV, Nickelodeon and Discovery. From the cable industry's point of view, this meant they were paying for the basic channels twice – once as a notional payment folded into the price for the premium channels they got from BSkyB, and again in payments made directly to the suppliers of the channels. As a result, they were penalised from the start, and had difficulty creating a retail proposition that could compete, on a price basis, with satellite. (Consider, for example, that the top price for BSkyB's channels was £29.99 in late 1997, compared to £37.99 in some cable franchises.) It was only through combining cheap telephony and cable TV that an effective retail package could be created.

It did not help, either, that the UK cable industry was dominated by North American engineers, sent over by parent companies such as the Canadian Videotron or the American Nynex to build networks, who knew nothing about marketing, and even less about the UK consumer. Or that cable was divided by region, and, unlike BSkyB, did not offer a single, national proposition.

Even worse, from cable's point of view, BSkyB offered additional deep discounts on the wholesale price only if the operators took all of Sky's channels. Thus to get the full discount, cable companies were obliged to carry, for instance, Sky Soap and Sky Travel, neither of which were particularly popular with viewers. And to cap it all, if a cable operator took a channel, it had to ensure that it was available to 100 per cent of its serviced homes. The terms were onerous, and benefited BSkyB inordinately.

BSkyB claimed it was just too difficult to set the prices of the wholesale supply of premium programming any other way. How could Sky know what the trend might be in the price of premium programming in the future? It could only commit to a long-term pricing regime if the wholesale offering to cable was linked directly to the prices BSkyB, itself, set in the marketplace, in recognition of its changing cost base. Indeed, BSkyB argued, it was at the request of certain operators themselves, in the early 1990s, that the wholesale payment structure was first devised. Chief among them was Telewest, the TCI-backed operator, which wanted a long-term supply agreement for movies and sport as a condition of putting the TCI channels (TCC, Bravo and Discovery) into the Sky multi-channel package. If you want long-term supply, BSkyB argued, then the price must be linked to something over which Sky had control: namely, the retail price for the satellite offering.

The cable industry was working on two fronts in late 1994 and early 1995, eager to present a united response to BSkyB's undoubted power in the pay-TV market. The first was programming. The main cable operators, led by Telewest, Nynex CableComms, Videotron, General Cable, and International CableTel, agreed to work together to bid for sports rights and to set up a pay-per-view (PPV) movie service. PPV, which had not yet been launched in the UK, was not covered by the output agreements BSkyB had reached with the Hollywood studios. US entertainment companies had pioneered the fragmentation of the market for broadcasting rights into a series of windows. A film would go to the cinema first, then to the 'video-for-purchase' market, then to the video hire shops. Thereafter, a pay-per-view window was available, in which the Hollywood studio would share the revenues from single viewings with the broadcaster. (This market had already been developed in the US, Canada and elsewhere.) A few months later, the films would be available to subscription movie channels (like BSkyB's Sky Movies and the Movie Channel) before being offered for 'free' broadcast on mainstream television. A new venture, called Home Box Office was set up by the cable companies, and headed by Steve Wagner, then the commercial director of International CableTel. The company began to negotiate with Hollywood studios to win the rights to the pay-per-view market for movies in the UK.

At the same time, the cable operators were looking to develop a sports channel, emboldened by their success in winning the UK rights to the World Cricket Cup held in 1996. Originally, the Sportswire service was part of Wire TV, a cable-exclusive channel owned by a group of London cable franchises. Mirror Group, publishers of *The Daily Mirror*, *The Sunday Mirror* and *The People*, essentially bought Wire TV (without its sports programming) in early 1995, in order to distribute its own L!ve TV, launched in the autumn of 1995. Only pay-TV was open to Mirror Group, because of strict cross-media ownership rules prohibiting major newspaper publishers from buying more than 20 per cent of a mainstream TV company. Sportswire was retained by the cable operators, and continued to look for buying opportunities in sport broadcasting.

The second front for cable was regulation. In early 1995, based on complaints from the cable operators, the Office of Fair Trading sought 'informal undertakings' from BSkyB on the terms of its supply of programming in the wholesale market. A 'rate card' would be agreed, subject to OFT approval, under which the Sky channels would be sold to cable on an open and transparent basis. These undertakings would be in lieu of a full-scale inquiry into BSkyB's near-monopoly control in the pay-TV market.

Murdoch was impatient about the BSkyB–cable relationship. 'The government forces us to sell our programming to the cable industry, and doesn't force cable to sell their programming to us. We are meat in the sandwich. What they are about is building an alternative to BT. The better ones are getting better, but they are selling telephony, not cable TV, they're making their money out of telephones. Cable ought to work harder, and sell more channels.'

BSkyB was clearly worried by the competitive rumblings from the cable industry. For the first time, the cable operators, which were nearing the one-million mark for subscriptions, looked like being a serious potential rival to Sky's own position in pay-TV. As well, the industry appeared to be getting the ear of regulators, for the first time. Cable was already becoming an important new source of revenues for BSkyB, since it was connecting new customers at an accelerating rate. Sky, for its part, was beginning to sense some resistance in the direct-to-home market for satellite dishes. (By 1997, nearly two-thirds of new connections to Sky's pay-TV channels would come via cable.) And the last thing BSkyB wanted was regulatory interference: having finally moved into serious profit, now was not the time to see the company's potential to earn an adequate return for its early risk-taking jeopardised.

The informal undertakings agreed in March 1995 would not suit the cable operators, who believed that they could win yet more concessions from BSkyB. Pressures continued to build throughout the spring of that year.

Behind the scenes, Chisholm and Chance were feverishly seeking a way around the threat from the cable industry. They knew that two of the backers of cable's bid for sport and film rights, Telewest and Nynex, were eager to sign new long-term carriage agreements with BSkyB, in order to reassure investors that they could sustain a business over the medium term. Nynex, particularly, was vulnerable, as its backers, the US telecoms company of the same name, were taking the UK operating company public, and were seeking the support of City institutions. BSkyB's approach was clever (typically so). They had already realised how effective it could be to 'divide and conquer' – the approach that had proved so successful during the negotiations that led to the creation of the encrypted multi-channel package in 1993. Chisholm and Chance offered long-term agreements – ten years for Telewest, which had already gone public – and eight years for Nynex, under which both companies would be supplied with the key movie and sports programming that had proved so crucial to the success of subscription television. In return, the cable companies had to agree to drop their support for Home Box Office and Sportswire. Indeed, the long-term carriage agreements, announced in May 1995, just days before Nynex's public share offering, included explicit 'non-compete' clauses. (One cable operator complained that Telewest attended a meeting of the cable programming group on 3 May 1995, and delayed signing a crucial contract for the pay-per-view channel. Two days later, the long-term BSkyB agreements were announced. 'We were betrayed,' the executive says.) The signatories to the BSkyB deal agreed not to support any pay-per-view movie services in direct competition with BSkyB.

Upon signing the deals, Nynex and Telewest pulled out of all the nascent efforts by the cable industry to create competitive programming. The other operators in the consortium, particularly International CableTel, Videotron and General Cable, were livid, and immediately complained to the Office of Fair Trading. At least three operators also made a formal complaint in May 1995 to the European Commission's DG4, the competition directorate, assuming that Brussels could then put pressure on London to act. It was hoped that the government of John Major, in power since Thatcher resigned in 1992, was less in thrall to Murdoch, and might be willing to disturb BSkyB's cosy near-monopoly.

A month later, the OFT ruled that the Nynex/Telewest contracts contained clauses that were 'significantly anti-competitive,' and called on the signatories to refashion their agreements. By then, however, the damage had been done. Even if the OFT insisted on changes to contracts, Nynex and Telewest had no intention of antagonising BSkyB, and dropped their support, unequivocally, for the cable-exclusive programming efforts.

In August 1995, the OFT formally approved the new rate card for BSkyB's supply of programming to cable (the second rate card to be so approved by the regulator). The industry was unimpressed, and privately opined that there must have been some kind of secret deal with BSkyB and Rupert Murdoch. How could the competition watchdog approve a scheme that allowed BSkyB to set prices for the whole of the pay-TV market? Industry insiders muttered about Downing Street plots and Whitehall deals, pointing out that a new Broadcasting Bill was likely to be debated within the year in Parliament. What had Murdoch promised Major? And more importantly, what had Major promised Murdoch?

BSkyB, for its part, was scathing. 'The rate card has been approved, published, renegotiated, approved and published for a second time in 1995.' What does it take to see reason?

The pre-emptive side deals with Nynex and Telewest had done their work, however. By October, the cable operators backing Sportswire had accepted the inevitable, and closed the service. Its portfolio of mostly minor sports rights was sold.

BSkyB had been busy on other fronts, too, in 1995, a year in which its pre-tax profits had soared to £155 million. In May, Rupert Murdoch announced that he had made an offer for three television stations owned by Silvio Berlusconi, the former Italian Prime Minister, who had been forced to seek partners in Italy in order to resume his political career, following the threat of a series of referendums on media ownership that might have gone against him. Murdoch was offering $2.8 billion for 51 per cent of Berlusconi's three TV stations and his TV advertising company Publitalia (grouped as Mediaset), with an option to buy the rest if local media ownership rules were reformed.

The move in Italy came as a surprise, as it marked the first time Murdoch had seriously tried to expand on the continent (although he had invested in a small way in Germany, via his Fox subsidiary, taking a stake on Vox, the lifestyle channel, in co-operation with Bertelsmann and Canal Plus – a deal negotiated by Sam Chisholm). More controversially, he was putting pressure on BSkyB to support the Italian purchase. In the eyes of some on the board of BSkyB, Murdoch was acting as if the company were his, and not 60 per cent owned by others. 'We were not convinced this was a good move for BSkyB,' one director says. More intriguingly, Chisholm himself was against the investment. He spent several weeks looking at the operations and reviewing the accounts, and believed there were severe problems – too severe to overcome.

Murdoch himself had some doubts about Berlusconi, but admired the way the Italian mogul had side-stepped regulations in the 1980s by beaming his television service into Italy from Monte Carlo. That was reminiscent of Murdoch's own approach with Sky, when he used the Luxembourg-based Astra to conquer the British pay-TV market. Despite his own Page Three titilation at *The Sun*, the downmarket tabloid newspaper, Murdoch did not think much of Berlusconi's programming, however, which was dominated by cheesy innuendo and scantily clad women. The Italian venture was just one of several TV prospects Murdoch had been reviewing, including Latin America, India and Japan. In May 1995, Murdoch had done an impressive deal with MCI, whereby the US telecoms giant would take a 13.5 per cent stake in News Corporation, for $2 billion. The two companies would jointly develop ASkyB, a US version of BSkyB. The extra money, along with $1 billion in the bank, emboldened Murdoch to hit the acquisition trail. 'We would like to repeat the success of Sky

Television elsewhere, but with local partners,' he told *The Sunday Times* in mid-May.

The Italian deal was complicated by Berlusconi's own hesitancy. Mediaset was also talking to Leo Kirch, the Bavarian mogul, Time Warner and even Prince al-Waleed Bin Talal, the Saudi investor, about selling them minority stakes. Murdoch thought it was worth pressing ahead, and wanted to use BSkyB to make the Italian investment, if terms could be agreed. He told the BBC's *Money Programme* on 22 May 1995 that he did not know yet whether any such deal would be made through News Corporation or BSkyB. Behind the scenes, however, there was consternation. The non-executive directors on the board of BSkyB, led by Gerry Robinson, strenuously opposed the proposal. Says one director: 'We did not like what we saw of the figures, and BSkyB had plenty of opportunities still to explore in the UK.' Chisholm supported that view. He told his lawyer, Bruce McWilliam: 'Italy is a great place to eat pasta and take holidays.'

Recalls Murdoch: 'Sam was always frightened of the Italians, and in retrospect, he may have been right. For a time Berlusconi wanted to get out of this business to become Prime Minister. We did look at that, and looked at the books, and it looked like a God awful mess, and probably was. Still, it was an opportunity we missed.'

In the end, Berlusconi and Murdoch disagreed over the issue of control, with Murdoch publicly insisting that Berlusconi would have to exit completely, to be replaced by other Italian partners. The Italian mogul elected instead to bring in minority partners, including Prince al-Waleed. But while the deal may never have happened, Murdoch was cross that BSkyB's board had withheld their support. The Italian venture was the first signal that Chisholm's BSkyB was quite prepared to go its own way on key strategy.

The share price of BSkyB, meanwhile, had performed strongly, rising from 150p in late 1994 to nearly 400p by late summer of 1995, on the back, particularly, of the OFT approval of the new rate card and on BSkyB's stellar operating results. Pearson, run by the man Murdoch dumped as chairman of BSkyB, Frank Barlow, had by now decided to cash out of the business, convinced that the wild valuations implied by the share price could not last. By selling a near ten per cent stake, Pearson would receive £492 million, on top of the special dividends it had already booked from its investment. Some commentators believed at the time that Pearson was set on dumping its BSkyB stake ever since Barlow had been unceremoniously dumped from the chairmanship. But Barlow disputes this reading. 'I thought the analysts' valuations were ridiculous, and the profits never lived up to that,' he says. 'In fact, I thought it was a good price, and no one ever went broke taking profits.'

The sale by Pearson of its stake was enough to put BSkyB into the FTSE-100 list of top British stocks. The criteria were simple: size and extent of so-called 'free float', the number of shares that could be freely traded on the exchange. The Pearson sale to institutions freed up enough shares to ensure that BSkyB now qualified as a bona fide FTSE-100 stock. This had important implications for the future, as it meant that many institutional funds which invested on the basis of pre-determined 'weightings' in different market sectors, would now seek to take larger positions in BSkyB. This demand for shares – the so-called 'technical position' – would underpin BSkyB's share price for many months to come. Buoyed by the increased institutional interest, BSkyB shares reacted far more quickly to good news, and were less likely to plummet on bad news, as there were always investors around who were 'underweight' in BSkyB, and were looking for an opportunity to top up their positions.

Animosity between Barlow and Chisholm, and the view at Pearson that BSkyB was already overvalued, were perhaps not the only reasons for Pearson's decision to sell. The company had, in May of 1995, put in a bid for Channel 5, the fifth terrestrial channel, which the government again put out to tender after the embarrassing reversal of 1992, when the single bid was rejected on financial grounds by the Independent Television Commission (ITC). BSkyB, too, had put forward an application in the new round, as a member of a separate consortium. Pearson believed that a terrestrial channel would make considerable money in the UK, despite the recent growth of pay-TV. Pearson consultants explained that BSkyB, available in 20 per cent of UK homes, would never be as extensively watched as a terrestrial channel, even one, like Channel 5, that would reach only 60 to 70 per cent of UK households. Did Pearson want to jeopardise its chances of winning the bid by being involved in two, competing consortia?

The Channel 5 adventure was one of the high points of the 1990s in the media sector. The ITC had hesitated for months to readvertise the licence, worried about another embarrassing climbdown. But big media players advised the ITC that there was indeed an appetite for the franchise. Advertisers, too, were keen, as the addition of another national channel would increase the number of minutes available for commercials, and might put some downward pressure on the spiralling costs of ads on ITV and Channel 4. Meanwhile, the ITC's engineers had re-done much of the planning work left over from the aborted 1992 attempt to award a fifth licence, and could ensure applicants that, despite the crowded frequencies, the transmission patterns would ensure coverage of at least 70 per cent of the UK.

As with most licences for government-mandated TV franchises, there was a scramble as consortia formed, fell apart and reformed. From the start, David Elstein, the head of programmes at BSkyB, was intent on being part of a Channel 5 bid. He had been involved in the 1992 effort as director of programmes at Thames, when Thames and partner Time Warner had been the sole bidder. He was convinced that a BSkyB bid, in league, of course, with politically acceptable partners, stood a good chance of winning. BSkyB could provide films, sports, canny scheduling, marketing prowess – in short, it could help bring multi-channel sensibilities to the mainstream TV market. In the early months of 1995, a series of negotiations took place, mostly at Isleworth, to see whether a consortium could be put together. Granada, already a BSkyB shareholder, signed up. Even TCI, run by American cable tycoon John Malone, was a potential partner, even though Malone, one of the giants of US media, was not always on good terms with Rupert Murdoch, with whom he competed in America. Yorkshire–Tyne Tees Television, which a little more than two years later would be bought by Granada, also looked seriously, but Ward Thomas, YTT's chairman, was put off by the technical challenges of making a fifth channel work. Polygram, the film studio owned 75 per cent by Philips, the Dutch electronics giant, agreed to join the group, while Goldman Sachs, the international merchant bank, signed on as a financial investor.

Ward Thomas' doubts about the project were perhaps well founded. Channel 5 would be transmitted around much of the country on frequency 37, which was commonly used for the playback signal of video recorders in the UK. Little else was available on the crowded radio and television spectrum. (Later, after the award was made, a second frequency, 35, would be released for Channel 5's use.) Whoever won the licence would have to undertake to retune as many as ten million VCRs, up and down the country, to ensure that viewers did not experience interference on their home recording equipment. The winner would also have to provide customer services support for those viewers likely to ring in to complain about the interference when (and if) it happened.

Still, despite the technical challenges, four consortia eventually formed to bid for the licence. The prospect of broadcasting even to just three-quarters of UK homes, whatever the retuning costs, was too attractive to pass over. Of the main ITV companies, only Michael Green's Carlton decided against bidding for the licence.

When bids went in on 2 May 1995, BSkyB, Granada, TCI, Polygram, Scandinavian broadcaster Kinnevik and Goldman Sachs, in a consortium called New Century, faced competition from Virgin Television (Richard Branson's Virgin, newspaper giant Associated, publishers of the Daily Mail, Philips and HTV); UKTV (the Canadian broadcasters Canwest, with support from SBS, the US-owned Scandanavian TV company, independent production company SelecTV, and Ten Network, Canwest's Australian subsidiary); and Channel 5 Broadcasting, backed by Pearson, MAI (Lord Hollick's company, soon to merge with the owners of the Express newspapers to become United News & Media), Luxembourg-based broadcaster CLT and financial investor Warburg-Pincus.

Under the rules of the Channel 5 tender process, bidders had to offer a cash payment per year, for the ten years of the licence, and the highest bid, subject to a quality threshold, would win. Unlike the 1991 ITV licencing round, which had also been awarded on a 'highest bid' basis, the amounts on offer would be disclosed on the day the bids were received. This was to avoid the situation of 1991, when the bids were meant to be kept secret, and the enterprising doyen of media business correspondents, *The Financial Times'* Raymond Snoddy (later to move to *The Times*), managed to ferret out and publish virtually all the bids for the licences on offer.

There was general shock on the day the ITC published the bids. The highest bidder by far was UKTV, the Canadian-backed consortium, which offered more than £36 million. (No surprise, here, perhaps; the Canadian bid had been put together at the last minute, after another consortium, of Mirror Group, SelecTV and an American partner, fell through. The high bid was probably a sign of high desperation.) In second position, there was a tie, with both Channel 5 Broadcasting (Pearson and MAI) and Virgin TV bidding £22,002,000 precisely (pure chance, said the principals; and we were forced to believe them, despite all the conspiracy theories tossed out at the time). But the biggest shock came from the BSkyB-backed consortium, which came in at just £2 million a year. In the view of many media commentators (and not a few industry executives), New Century had by far the best bid, offering as it did movies, sport, general entertainment and a realistic retuning plan, to deal with all those VCRs.

Channel 5 Broadcasting, the Pearson/MAI group, suggested the country's home equipment could be retuned for a paltry £55 million, while New Century put in a more realistic £120 million. (In the end, the final retuning bill for the Channel 5 winner would be more than £150 million.)

Sir George Russell, then chairman of the ITC, remembers: 'When [a colleague] opened the bids, he said: "You're not going to believe this. The outsider is first, the favourite is last and we've got a dead heat for second". I couldn't believe it. No one could. It was so incredible. Nothing in the investigations that followed showed that [the tie] was anything other than a fluke. Anyone who would rig it wouldn't have rigged a tie. If I knew what your bid was, the last thing I would do was match it.'

Greg Dyke, of Pearson Television, said his joint bid with Clive Hollick's United News & Media had been set at £22 million. But the two men decided to add £1,000 each to the bid because they didn't like the round number. If their boards had been balked, they agreed, they would pay it themselves. A similar 'no round number' explanation was provided by Richard Branson's Virgin TV.

A more intriguing question, in the end, was: why did the BSkyB consortium bid so low? According to David Elstein, a driving force behind the bid, 'Sam [Chisholm] was an enthusiast for Channel 5 from very early on.' Indeed, Chisholm played a key role in convincing Gerry Robinson and Charles Allen of Granada, both of them sceptical at the start, that the retuning problems could be overcome, and that a terrestrial outlet for BSkyB, not to mention an additional platform for Granada itself, would be worth a fortune. 'Sam wanted a terrestrial outlet,' says one of the principals in the Channel 5 bidding group.

But Murdoch was not so sure. He harboured great doubts about terrestrial television in the UK, born of his disappointing stint as a major shareholder of LWT in the 1970s. He sincerely believed that the best bid in the world would not be accepted by the ITC if BSkyB (for which read 'Murdoch') was a member. 'Every one of those things is a set-up, and they still are,' Murdoch says dismissively. Murdoch also believed that he should not have to pay a licence fee for a terrestrial channel. Says Elstein: 'I think Sam was nervous of Rupert's approach to it, and always felt that Rupert would take quite a lot of persuading. [Chisholm] was quite content on the one or two occasions that the subject would come up – when Rupert was on the phone or was visiting – for me to take over and explain why it was of strategic interest to Sky.' Chisholm was also a bit nervous about his discussions with TCI, with whom Murdoch did not always see eye to eye (although the two companies would work together in South America and on a sports channel in the US). In the end, Murdoch had no objection to TCI's involvement.

The New Century bid was largely written by David Elstein, with advice from Bruce Fireman, a consultant at Guinness Mahon, the City merchant bank. Chisholm took an interest, however, and soon determined that a bid of at least £25 million a year would be necessary if the licence was to be won. Chisholm also went to bat for Elstein during the negotiations among shareholders about the staff for the new channel. Most of the shareholders agreed that Elstein should be chief executive, were New Century to win. But Yorkshire–Tyne Tees, which was then still in the frame, demurred, because Ward Thomas believed that programme people did not make good chief executives. Thomas attended a meeting with Gerry Robinson, Sam Chisholm, Kevin Kinsella and Bruce Gyngell, managing director of Yorkshire, and suggested that Gyngell would be the best candidate. Granada's Robinson agreed. According to one participant: 'Sam was sort of looking around, saying yes, yes and he'd look you in the eye and you knew he was lying, you knew he had promised it to David [Elstein], but he was willing to go through this charade of saying, "I agree with you". He just carried on looking at you, and everyone could see that we knew that he knew that we knew he was lying.'

Even Elstein, who had won Chisholm's support on this occasion, harboured no illusions about his chief executive: 'I don't trust him and his word is not his bond and there are times he offers you his hope rather than anything else, in terms of ability to deliver and basically he'd double cross anyone if it suited his purpose.'

Once Yorkshire dropped out, Chisholm worked on Gerry Robinson, insisting that Elstein was the best man for the job. Granada only agreed once BSkyB accepted Granada's Charles Allen as chairman of New Century. Elstein was reasonably relaxed, as he had been approached by Richard Dunn of Pearson Television to be chief executive of the Pearson/MAI Channel 5 consortium, and had also been offered the top job at Canwest's UKTV consortium. The Canwest approach to Elstein – through a firm of headhunters – had come late, just ten days or so before the bids were due to be submitted. The BSkyB consortium had been wondering what Canwest's boss, Izzy Asper, had been up to, and were worried that a serious bid could be in the offing. Bruce Fireman told Chisholm and Elstein that he knew 'there was a submarine out there, but all I can see is the periscope. I don't know if it's armed'. When Elstein received the call from the headhunters, he told Chisholm and Chance: 'I've got a sonar reading.' Elstein met Izzy Asper's son, David, to discuss the bid, and came away reassured that it was not likely to be a threat. He was particularly unimpressed with Canwest's plans for retuning VCRs.

Elstein kept his head down in the last few days before the bid deadline, running over the business plan. New Century was promising to spend £130 million a year on programming (more than the winners), and had approached David Liddiment, then at Granada (and later head of programmes at ITV Network Centre) to be controller. Two weeks before the bids were due, Elstein invited Liddiment to Isleworth to look at the business plan. Chisholm happened to call Bruce Fireman, who was also at Isleworth that day, for a chat, and Fireman told him Elstein and Liddiment were in a nearby office, reviewing the business plan. 'What, he's showing the figures to the help?' Chisholm said.

There was one more hiccup on the way to tabling the New Century bid. Polygram was holding out for 20 per cent of the company, in line with the Granada and BSkyB stakes. Chisholm again stepped in to smooth the waters, convincing the European film company to settle for 17.5 per cent.

At a board meeting on 27 April 1995, the directors of BSkyB met to consider the company's participation in the Channel 5 bid. Funding of £270 million, implying a bid of up to £25 million a year, won approval from all those present, including Gerry Robinson and Sam Chisholm. Greg Dyke, representing Pearson, where he had become chief executive of Pearson Television, did not vote, pleading a conflict of interest, since Pearson was backing a rival consortium. (It would prove to be one of Dyke's few appearances at a BSkyB board meeting; a few months later, Pearson would sell its BSkyB stake and Dyke would leave the board.) That weekend, Chisholm spoke to Izzy Asper, the chairman of Canwest, who had been asking to join the New Century consortium. Chisholm told Asper that a bit more than £35 million would be necessary to win Channel 5. It was a classic bit of manoeuvring from Chisholm, who knew that an irresponsibly high bid, particularly from a company that had so hastily put together its programming plans, was likely to antagonise the ITC.

On the following Sunday, Peter Shea, the sales director, David Chance and Richard Brooke, the finance director all joined Sam Chisholm at the Farm in Hampshire for a brainstorming session. A call came from Rupert Murdoch. He had been looking at the Channel 5 situation, and was unwilling to put in a high bid. Explains Murdoch: 'Our people said we had the best application, and that we should bid £25 million, and maybe if we had, we would have won but I doubt it. I would not agree to anything more than £2 million. I said we should not bid more.'

Chisholm, according to some insiders, knew when to argue and when to withdraw when it came to dealing with Murdoch. In this instance, he didn't see the advantage in arguing the point. He did worry, however, about the relationship he was trying to forge with TCI, particularly, which might have soured if the bid was all but abandoned. On the issue, Chisholm will only say: 'I didn't have any real religion about Channel 5.' Robinson, BSkyB's chairman, provides additional insight. 'I think Sam took the Channel 5 decision independently of Rupert at one level. I don't think Rupert himself was ever warned about [the level of the bid] and that didn't help. I think Sam followed his own instinct, but [it was] the combination of Sam's own doubts and the [concern] of getting it wrong and Rupert not being an enthusiast.'

Robinson adds that it was, in part, Chisholm's management style that led to the last-minute about-face. 'The thing about dealing with Sam, which makes it very difficult, is his [initial] enthusiasm about everything. I honestly believe that, at the 11th hour, Sam believed it was not worth more than a token bid. At that stage, having done all the work, we knew we were not going to win it. And, in a funny kind of way, [bidding low] might have been the right decision. The retuning of videos and the marketing [have proved] more costly. In the end, I think [it was] Sam's judgment and Rupert's luke-warmness that got us there. But it's the style of Sam's decision-making that makes it feel as if he had suddenly switched at the last minute.'

When the rest of the New Century shareholders heard that BSkyB had decided, at the last minute, on a low-ball bid, they were livid. The announcement was made to the other shareholders and to David Elstein on Monday, 1 May, the eve of the bid deadline. All the documents were altered to accord with a £2 million rather than a £25 million bid. Murdoch concedes: 'Some of the others were pretty unhappy about it. [But] they could have thrown us out, and put together their own bid, but I just wasn't convinced it was worth it. I think the transmission problems, the technical problems, were just too great. I've always assumed that anyone with a system out there that doesn't reach every home just cannot compete.' Months later, Murdoch told Elstein: 'Well, it wouldn't have mattered what we'd have bid. They would have ruled us out anyway.' He was convinced that the British broadcasting establishment ('they') would never let him in.

It was, by everyone's calculation, too late to reform the consortium and submit a higher bid without BSkyB. Granada considered doing so, but did not want to jeopardise its relationship with Sky. In the end, the bid was pitched at Murdoch's preferred £2 million. When the award was finally made, in October of 1995, not altogether surprisingly, the Canwest bid for Channel 5 failed the quality threshold. So did the Virgin Television application. (The two would seek a judicial review of the decision, but the action, as was usual in actions against the regulator, failed.) Of the remaining two, New Century (BSkyB and partners) and Channel 5 Broadcasting (Pearson and MAI), the highest bidder, Pearson/MAI, was awarded the licence. Had Murdoch supported the £25 million bid, nearly £3 million higher than the eventual winners, would he have won after all? Conspiracy theorists had a field day, suggesting that the Major government had intervened, telling Murdoch he would escape ancillary regulatory retribution if he stayed out of terrestrial television. That was certainly Michael Grade's view.

Even before the bids went in, it had been rumoured that BSkyB would be among the bidders. Grade, then at Channel 4, had been horrified about the prospect. He delivered a speech at the Journalism Review, warning about the dangers of Murdoch being given a stake in a terrestrial licence. He arranged with three newspapers – *The Guardian*, *The Daily Telegraph* and *The Independent* – to run excerpts of his speech. The articles helped set off a political storm.

Grade is convinced that the government leant on Murdoch at that point, warning him that he would be likely to face a competition review if he won Channel 5.

Peter Rogers, the chief executive of the ITC, says: 'I would have awarded it the licence [had it been the highest bidder]. Around the place, there would have been a whole lot of teeth sucking. But if that application had have been the highest bidder, it would have to win, save for exceptional circumstances, and I find it hard to see what the exceptional circumstances would have been.'

'They'd have got it,' Sir George Russell says. 'There was no question as to whether Sky should or shouldn't get it.'

Elstein was bitterly disappointed. 'I could have cheerfully strangled Sam, but after a while you recognise that, however close a project is to your own heart, in the broader scheme of things, Sky is involved in dozens and dozens of deals, projects, possibilities, and you win some, you lose some. Sky, on the whole, won in the deals that mattered. It had screwed up in this particular case, alienated its fellow shareholders, and done something quite hard to understand. After a while you just get on with it. There's no point crying over spilt milk.'

Elstein was now out of contract, having put off renewing his agreement on the expectation of leaving Sky to run New Century. He waited a few months before making any radical decisions, pending the outcome of the judicial review mounted by Virgin and Canwest. He had also hoped that Chisholm could deliver on a much-discussed plan: to put himself in the chairman's seat, allowing him to spend half his time in Australia with his family, including his wife, Rhonda, a former Miss New Zealand who had not moved with him to England and to promote Chance to chief executive and Elstein to deputy chief executive. But by this time, early 1996, Murdoch had already decided to appoint his daughter, Elisabeth, to a position at BSkyB, and did not want to see a major management restructuring. Says Elstein: 'In the absence of [Chisholm's] ability to deliver [on the new structure], we never got round to signing a contract.' Within six months of the Channel 5 award, Elstein would step down from BSkyB, to become chief executive of the winning consortium, Channel 5 Broadcasting.

But not before BSkyB embarked on yet another campaign. In May of 1995, the Department of National Heritage, under Stephen Dorrell, and later Virginia Bottomley, had published its proposals on cross-media ownership, which would be enshrined in a reformed Broadcasting Bill, to be debated over the first six months of 1995. The new bill was meant to repair some of the damage done by the 1990 legislation, which introduced competitive bidding for ITV franchises and laid out complicated and quite restrictive rules about cross-media ownership. The Bill was specifically aimed at relaxing the rules prohibiting newspaper publishers from owning television networks, and vice versa. The rationale was simple, if not wholly uncontroversial: in order to compete in the 'global marketplace', British media companies needed to be allowed to grow bigger, and to become more integrated. The biggest British companies – Pearson, Granada, and the like – were minnows compared to the Bertelsmanns, Time Warners and News Corporations of the world.

For BSkyB, the danger was that the new Bill might include amendments aimed squarely at reining in the dominant pay-TV broadcaster. BSkyB was exposed on several fronts: the proposed market for digital TV (where Sky's control of the 'gateway' of conditional access would come under attack); on ownership (in light of Murdoch's 40 per cent stake in BSkyB; and on sport, where its exclusive rights deals had sparked widespread negative comment.

Most crucially for Murdoch, if not for BSkyB, not all companies would benefit from the liberalisation of ownership promised by the government. In general, a ceiling of 15 per cent of total television audience was to be set as the upper limit; below that, companies could own as many commercial TV licences as they wished. But the government added a second limit, specifically designed to contain the biggest newspaper publishers. Owners of more than 20 per cent of the national newspaper market could not take more than 20 per cent in a regulated terrestrial TV business, even if they were well below the 15 per cent ceiling. The move hit just two companies – Mirror Group and, of course, News International. Murdoch was livid, and approved an amazingly intemperate press release, responding to the government's proposed changes. He argued that the new rules would protect 'the old vested and often unsuccessful interests', and sniped: 'We hope for a constructive dialogue with this supposedly free-enterprise, pro-competition government.'

As the government consulted on the new ownership rules through the autumn of 1995 and into the new year, preparing for the debate on the Broadcasting Bill, BSkyB geared up for a major lobbying campaign. It would have to see off a concerted effort not only from backbenchers and the Opposition, but from other broadcasters, who saw the new Bill as the perfect opportunity to push for the key changes they had been seeking since at least 1992: tougher rules on sport rights and an open-access framework for digital TV.

But as 1995 drew to a close, BSkyB was tossed what might have ended up being the ultimate grenade. After months of delay, discussion, negotiation and posturing, it was announced in December 1995 that there was to be, after all, an official Office of Fair Trading inquiry into BSkyB's supply arrangements with the cable industry. At the same time, BSkyB and the BBC's agreement with the Premier League was at risk of being reviewed by the Restrictive Practices Court, on the assumption that it could be deemed to be inherently anti-competitive. It looked, suddenly, as if BSkyB's charmed existence, its Teflon-like relationship with regulators, was coming to an end.

CHAPTER 9

The German Polka and the Premier League Rematch

Five men dressed in blue suits sat in the Craven Arms pub just outside of Coventry in June 1996. They looked out of place, next to the workmen in their overalls and the junior office staff enjoying a drink after work. The five were the men who had just pitched for one of the biggest deals of their lives – the renegotiated rights to the Premier League until 2001. Among them was Sam Chisholm – nervous as none of his colleagues had ever seen him. Next to him were Vic Wakeling, head of sports, Trevor East, responsible for the Premier League coverage on Sky, Bruce McWilliam, the lawyer, and David Chance. This was the big challenge: could Sky keep the rights to the sport that had powered BSkyB into the stratosphere? Could the company see off the challenge of well-financed rivals, who for the first time looked like challenging Sky's dominant position in pay-TV? BSkyB had put a knock-out bid on the table at a luxury hotel on the outskirts of Coventry just minutes before, but would it be enough? McWilliam kept an eye on his mobile phone, willing it to ring.

The preparations for the rebidding had started in early 1996. At Isle-worth, BSkyB's clashes with regulators were never allowed to be seen as an excuse to avoid the serious work of sustaining and extending the core businesses. As it embarked on the months of work an Office of Fair Trading inquiry would entail, not to mention a major court case on the Premier League deal and the ongoing debates about the Broadcasting Bill, BSkyB executives were already thinking about the next round of football contracts. The 1992 deal was scheduled to run until the 1997 season, but in early 1996, it was becoming clear that the Premier League was ready to start negotiating a renewal. This time, however, there was to be even greater competition. As well, Chisholm was spear-heading efforts to expand in Germany, where digital TV was soon to launch. Having disagreed with Murdoch about Italy and the Berlusconi deal (at some cost to their working relationship), Chisholm was far more comfortable with the German market, at least initially.

BSkyB had already ruled out France, where Canal Plus reigned supreme, and where cultural xenophobia would have made it difficult to enter. Richard Dunn, who had joined News Corporation in 1995 to manage Murdoch's non-US and non-Asian TV interests, recalls: 'Germany was different. Germany was a real opportunity and the more Sam looked at it the more he saw that it could be an opportunity like the UK. And I'm sure the guys in the City were saying to him if you can come up with something good for BSkyB and digital in Germany, the share price will go up, which it did. That's exactly what happened. So this was absolutely central to Sam Chisholm's bloodstream.'

Dunn had very little to do with the German negotiations, however. By this time, Chisholm was spending virtually all of his time on BSkyB affairs, and very little on News Corporation. And fair enough, thought most of the directors of BSkyB, including the Chairman, Gerry Robinson. BSkyB was a FSTE-100 company, worth more than £10 billion on the stock exchange. It required the full-time commitment of its management, whatever Rupert Murdoch might have preferred. As a result, there was now far less contact with Gary Davey at Star, or with the executives at Murdoch's struggling Foxtel operations in Australia. Given Dunn's role as a News Corporation executive, Chisholm wanted him to stay out of BSkyB's German deal. Bruce McWilliam recalls: 'Sam didn't want to answer the telephone at 2:00 am to respond to a call from Australia or Hong Kong.'

For the better part of a year, throughout all of 1995, Chisholm and Chance had been spending most bank holidays and many weekends in Germany, scouting opportunities in the digital TV sector. There were two main players in Germany – Bertelsmann, the global magazine, television and newspaper giant, and Kirch Group, run by Munich-based Leo Kirch. Murdoch, too, was interested, having decided that continental Europe was a possible new market. The early experience with Sky TV, the pan-European service, had convinced him that News Corporation could make a business in Europe; now he had a model, in the form of BSkyB, to drive his ambitions forward.

Murdoch was congenitally drawn to Kirch over Bertelsmann. The Bavarian media tycoon had spent a career buying rights to television and movies for the German market, and had also lined up some of the top sporting rights. He was an entrepreneur very much cut of Murdoch's cloth. But Kirch, a devoutly religious man not above broadcasting soft porn, had not made much progress in developing his digital plans, and Murdoch (with Chisholm) soon determined that the faster path to a position in the German digital market lay elsewhere. Bertelsmann owned a stake in Premiere, the pay-film channel also backed by Canal Plus, of France, and Kirch. That was the first option BSkyB seriously looked at. 'David [Chance] and I and a couple of others went every bank holiday rather than sitting round here,' Chisholm says. 'We went to Germany and finally we looked at Bertelsmann.'

In March 1996, BSkyB, prematurely as it turned out, announced that it was a partner in a new $270-million venture in Germany to promote digital TV. The partners were Bertelsmann, Canal Plus, the French pay-TV giant, Havas, the French media holding company, with BSkyB agreeing to take a stake in Premiere. Murdoch flew in for a signing ceremony, which brought together some of the leading figures of European broadcasting: Canal Plus chairman Pierre Lescure, Michael Dornemann, chief executive of Bertelsmann, Pierre Dauzier, chief executive of Havas, and Rolf Schmidt-Holtz, president of TV, at UFA, Bertelsmann's TV subsidiary. BSkyB would contribute its marketing and programming expertise to the new venture, and benefit from the launch of a digital movie, sports and general entertainment service.

But there was an immediate problem. Leo Kirch held the rights to most of the major movies and sports for the German market. For instance, he had secured exclusive claim to deals worth £117 million in 1996 for sports and for films from Warner and MCA/Universal, forecast to rise to nearly £200 million in 1998. 'Kirch had the rights, and Bertelsmann had the platform,' said one continental analyst. Kirch immediately threatened to scupper the BSkyB-Canal Plus-Bertelsmann alliance, vowing to veto any sale of a stake in Premiere, the film channel, to Murdoch.

The stand-off was immediate, and devastating. Murdoch himself travelled to Germany to discuss the options with both Bertelsmann and Kirch. In July, BSkyB announced an astonishing about-face. It was to drop the Bertelsmann alliance in favour of Kirch. 'He had the rights, and Bertelsmann and Canal Plus were moving far too slowly,' a BSkyB director said at the time. Behind the scenes, there was also increasing frustration on the BSkyB side with what they viewed as Bertelsmann's slow, careful approach to business. 'It was like the civil service,' said one senior Sky executive.

Under the new deal, BSkyB would take a 49 per cent stake in DF1, the digital platform being launched by Kirch. It was assumed by Chisholm and Murdoch that, ultimately, Premiere, the film channel, would be merged with DF1, to create a single, compelling proposition in the digital market. But for a second time, BSkyB's aspirations would be undercut by the jockeying within the German market. This time, Bertelsmann launched an attack on Kirch, tabling a law suit aimed at scuppering DF1.

As 1996 dragged on, BSkyB found it harder and harder to justify a German investment. The European Commission announced it was looking into the market in Germany, wary of what looked like a carve-up of the market among the main players. Meanwhile, DF1, which had launched in July with 25 channels, plus pay-per-view services including Formula One racing, managed to sign up just 30,000 customers by Christmas, compared to forecasts of 200,000. Worse, from BSkyB's perspective, the Premiere movie channel was still outside the DF1 bouquet, while the two German rivals, Bertelsmann and Kirch, continued to disagree about the conditional access technology that ought to be used for digital transmissions. Nor could Kirch secure a cable distribution deal with Deutsche Telekom, which would have given it access to 16 million homes.

Murdoch summoned Kirch to New York, in an attempt to break the deadlock. 'We wrestled and wrestled with them, and could not get a business plan out of them that made any sense at all,' Murdoch says. 'I met Kirch in New York, and he came to London once or twice. We couldn't get figures, and we couldn't get assurances about who was buying the Hollywood product. Were we buying it [in the joint venture] or was Kirch buying it and selling it on to us at a profit? It was all so complex, and he was under the thrall of some Hungarian technician [Gabor Tott], and he didn't want to use our technology.' Technology would often be the rock on which Murdoch's TV deals foundered. A deal with Echostar, the US direct-to-home satellite service, that ought to have ushered ASkyB into the increasingly crowded DTH market in 1997, fell apart when the two sides could not agree on which encryption standard to use. Murdoch, of course, wanted Videocrypt, the technology developed by his News Datacom subsidiary, which was used by BSkyB.

Kirch wanted to use a module rather than a smart card. But the module would cost £100 to replace if damaged; the smart card just £8. The set-top box was also too expensive, the BSkyB side believed, and they were amazed that Kirch had done a deal with just one supplier of boxes – Nokia – which meant no other manufacturers would enter the market and compete with lower prices. Kirch was also loading far too much of the costs of its own programming library onto the joint venture, at prices BSkyB believed were exorbitant.

The breaking point in Germany, however, was the lack of progress on Premiere. Chisholm was convinced that the movie channel had to be folded into the general digital package, to avoid confusing consumers. At the BSkyB results press conference in February 1997, Chisholm warned that he would not go ahead with the deal unless 'important issues' were resolved. A month later, Kirch and BSkyB issued a terse press release, saying they had 'mutually agreed to terminate their heads of agreement for the establishment of the DFI pay television platform in Germany because of failure to agree on a number of fundamental issues'.

After the fact, Chisholm was more forthcoming. 'In Germany, you've got 28 broadcasters [while] here, you've got the BBC and a couple of old monopolists, so Germany is [comparatively] a very difficult market to get into. You've got 28 guys putting movies on every night.' Chance adds that German television showed 462 movies over the Easter weekend 1996, all of them free. 'The banks could not make sense of his business plan and neither could we,' Chisholm says.

So would BSkyB ever consider returning to the German market? Maybe, Chisholm says, as long as 'you get everybody together'. He assumes, however, that, in a reference to the BSB-Sky merger six years before, 'everyone will have to do a bit more bleeding, and then Ian Irvine will have to go down to Australia, and they can all get together at Lucknam Park, and then maybe we will go back in'. (By 1997, the German digital market was still in disarray, although there were signs that the former rivals were finally working out their differences, having agreed a common platform.)

The retreat from Germany had an initially negative effect on BSkyB's share price, because some analysts and investors had believed that expansion outside Britain had been crucial to the company's growth prospects. Indeed some City houses put a valuation on DF1 of as much as £1 billion. Later, however, reason prevailed. The risks of going into a highly competitive market, already well-served by free television, clearly would outweigh the short-term benefits. Yet again, it looked like the peculiar structure of the UK market when Sky launched in 1989, and most particularly the relatively under-developed nature of multi-channel TV, was not going to obtain elsewhere. Only Britain, so far, could provide the incredible profit opportunities that took BSkyB into the stratosphere.

Through the first half of 1996, the debate on the Broadcasting Bill continued to rage. BSkyB had largely weathered a concerted campaign in the Lords in late 1995 to tighten restrictions on sports rights, particularly the list of protected events such as the Grand National, Wimbledon and the FA Cup. (Unusually, the government had decided to table the new broadcasting legislation in the Lords first). In the previous Broadcasting Act (1990), the listed events could not be shown exclusively on a pay-per-view basis. Now, many politicians wanted to prohibit exclusive broadcasts on pay television generally. The Lords forced a showdown on the issue, and the government caved in. As the bill made its way through both houses and the various stages, amendment after amendment was tabled by the Opposition Labour party in an effort to rein in BSkyB. The BBC was particularly active in briefing MPs during the passage of the Bill, much to the annoyance of BSkyB. Indeed, Chisholm wondered why the public service broadcaster, which benefited from its deal to show highlights of the Premier League on *Match of the Day*, was so keen to target BSkyB on so many different fronts – sports rights, ownership and the rules on establishing digital TV. Fumes Chisholm: 'It is an appalling state of affairs if the public service broadcaster is allowed to use tax payers' money to fight for causes that are not in the public interest, but are only in the sectional interest of the BBC. The public interest is best served by opening up the spectrum and letting in more choice. The BBC is using everybody's money to deny them a service and to maintain the status quo.'

The uneasy relationship between the BBC and BSkyB was exacerbated by small nuisances as well. When BSkyB showed the first ever pay-per-view event in Britain, the boxing match between Frank Bruno and Mike Tyson in March 1996, nearly 660,000 people paid either £9.95 (early-bird discount) or £14.95 for the privilege. The event was seen at Isleworth as a test run for the whole concept of PPV programming. Would viewers pay extra for special events? The answer would be crucial to BSkyB's digital plans, since it had hoped to create a new service, Sky Box Office, showing films sporting events and concerts on a pay-when-you-watch basis.

The BBC immediately complained that BSkyB was withholding the highlight rights to the Bruno–Tyson bout unnecessarily, not even allowing scenes from the match to be broadcast on newscasts in a timely fashion. A public brawl erupted, with both sides briefing the press and taking increasingly wild pot shots at the other.

But there were more fundamental differences of opinion. Since the early 1990s, the BBC had embarked on a revolutionary new strategy – restructuring its interests and pursuing commercial opportunities with far more vigour. It had decided that it would need to justify its call on the universal, mandatory licence fee by being as efficient, popular and responsive as possible. At the same time, it realised it could not effectively compete with private-sector broadcasters in crucial areas, not least the battle for sports rights. The architect of the new *realpolitik* was BBC director-general John Birt, sponsor of the controversial 'producer's choice' reforms and a former commercial TV executive himself (at LWT). In its dealings with BSkyB, the BBC was to follow its own, carefully balanced interests, sometimes in co-operation, sometimes in competition. Birt explains: 'We needed a strategy to protect the licence fee payer's interests. What was it? It was to see high quality recorded sport, in the case of soccer [rather than bid for exclusive rights]. So we thought we served the licence fee payer's interests by negotiating to maintain *Match of the Day*. Over and beyond that, we have not shirked from going to the regulators in Brussels and the UK and to the European Commission and to the government here. Where we thought there was a regulatory interest, we've argued fiercely and passionately for effective competition regimes in respect of the digital gateway. We have been more rigorous than anybody else in identifying the issues.'

These issues came up again and again in the debate on the Broadcasting Bill (and would, again, be debated in the autumn of 1997, by the Labour government). Among the amendments tabled during the Spring of 1996 were several on sport and broadcasting (calling, among other things, for new powers for the Secretary of State to void any sports rights contract found to be against the national interest); many on conditional access and subscription management services (one, for example, on guaranteeing access for public-service broadcasters to conditional access systems free of charge); and one on the extension of the television tax regime to include non-domestic satellite broadcasters (meaning BSkyB).

In the end, nearly all the amendments were defeated. Anti-Sky campaigners claimed one important victory, however. Following an incredible vote in the Lords in December 1995, which went against the government, the final Bill included an amendment aimed at strengthening the list of protected sporting events. The furore had reached fever pitch, however. Recalls Sir George Russell, then chairman of the ITC: 'Ever since Premier League, the BBC has been on the run. All the attempts to go to Parliament have been looking for a way to protect the BBC from Sam [Chisholm]. That's what it amounted to. The word Murdoch was used. But in reality, it was Sam's extraordinary capability. He was putting the pressure on.

You saw the House of Lords trying to overturn Parliament [through the amendment on the listed events], you had a whole constitutional issue, because it looked as if someone was going to lose Wimbledon. He has played a much bigger role [than many thought]. What has happened to the BBC was Sam.'

BSkyB shrugged off even this setback. Sky sources pointed out at the time that the company had never bid for any of the protected sports, and had been unlikely to do so. 'A seven-minute horse race isn't much good to us. We need to fill 12,000 hours,' a senior sky Sports executive says.

More damningly for Murdoch and BSkyB, the government's strict cross-media ownership rules were duly passed, prohibiting News International, which controlled 36 per cent of the national newspaper market, from owning more than 20 per cent of an ITV company or of Channel 5. Only one other company was caught by the conditions – Mirror Group, the publishers of *The Daily Mirror*, *The Sunday Mirror*, and *The People*, and 46 per cent owners of Newspaper Publishing, publishers of *The Independent* and *The Independent on Sunday*. (Mirror executives were bitterly disappointed, believing that the Conservative government was punishing the group for its pro-Labour editorials in the *Mirror*). The Act was passed just before the summer break, and came into effect in late 1996.

Significant management time at Isleworth had been taken up dealing with the debates on the Bill and on putting together submissions to the OFT, on the issue of programming supply to the cable industry. But there was plenty of time left for BSkyB to train its sights on the most important prize of all: the renewal of the Premier League contract of top football.

The 1992 contract with the Premier League had radically transformed BSkyB's financial fortunes, and created a huge, new market for top football in the UK. In addition, it provided the basis on which BSkyB could develop a full range of sports coverage, including golf, cricket, rugby league, boxing, tennis, even basketball. In 1994, it added a spill-over channel, Sky Sports 2, to accommodate the additional coverage (at the end of 1996, it would add a third sports channel). Also key was BSkyB's use of its sports channels to cross-promote other programming on the Sky platform – for instance, advertising a movie or a new series on Sky 1.

By early 1996, the Premier League let it be known that the renewal would not be automatic, despite a controversial clause in the original contract with BSkyB (since referred to the Restrictive Practices Court), giving the incumbent broadcaster the right to match the best offer on the table. BSkyB still believed it had the obvious inside track, because it had done so much for the game. Indeed, senior sports managers at BSkyB make even greater claims. Says Vic Wakeling, head of sports: 'There's been a huge explosion in sports interest in this country and I would argue that Sky has had a lot to do with that. Everybody in Fleet Street has said, "Hang on, look at their subscriptions – 4.2 million subscribers to Sky Sports alone!" Everybody is now doing pullouts, whether it be *The Telegraph* or *The Sun*. And there is a demand there: you've got Eurosport and you've got the BBC and ITV still churning out sport.'

Early in 1996, several media and sport companies began to look at the prospect of stealing the Premier League away from Sky. A small group of sports rights specialists, located in an office off Pall Mall, were among them. They had hoped to convince a large merchant bank to put together a £1-billion slush fund, out of which a knock-out bid for football could be stitched together. The plan had been to secure transponder space on Astra or Eutelsat, two satellite operators, then sign up the major cable companies. There was also the prospect of using Premier League as the basis of a new digital terrestrial television service, in partnership with the football clubs themselves.

Also exploring the prospects for Premier League were Greg Dyke, at Pearson, and Lord Hollick at what was then MAI. Dyke had been on the losing side of the ITV bid for top football in 1992, having been beaten by the last-minute higher offer from BSkyB. This time around, Dyke wasn't convinced that traditional broadcasters could win the rights. 'BSkyB has to have it, because [otherwise] all these guys with the basic package will just walk away,' he argued. Chisholm and Murdoch would bid whatever it took.

In the end, Dyke stepped aside, although he was prepared to supply programming to the eventual winner, should any of the other BSkyB rivals emerge victorious. By this time, Dyke was chief executive of Pearson Television, the independent producer created following the purchase of Thames Television by Pearson in 1993. He was happy, therefore, to supply programmes to any and all who were willing to pay.

Lord Hollick, the Labour peer, stayed in, convinced that football could be the embryo of a new series of pay-TV channels for MAI. The company already owned two ITV licences – Anglia and Meridian – as well as financial services. In February 1996, MAI became the first company to take advantage of planned changes to cross-media ownership rules outlined in the Broadcasting Bill (which was not yet law). Lord Hollick merged his company with United News & Media, Lord Stevens' media giant, which owned the Express Newspaper group, as well as regional newspapers, magazines and a conference and exhibitions subsidiary. The merged group, which retained the United News & Media name, started in earnest to plot its Premier League bid in February 1996, shortly after the merger.

One other serious bidding group was also forming, led by Michael Green's Carlton, owners of the London weekday and Central franchises. Green was equally convinced that football was a driver in pay-TV, and wanted, desperately, to position his company for the launch of digital services, as planned under the Broadcasting Bill. He agreed to work with David Montgomery's Mirror Group, which had the year before launched L!ve TV, and which had for months been looking at acquiring sports rights in the UK. The odd pair of Kelvin MacKenzie and Michael Green thus took up the battle against BSkyB: MacKenzie, the former BSkyB executive, still with a large axe to grind and a real hatred of Sam Chisholm; Green, the focused, articulate, arrogant entrepreneur, who demanded to be taken seriously in British media.

Throughout the spring of 1996, the consortia developed their plans. The premium was on secrecy: above all, the serious rivals (Carlton/Mirror and United) did not want anyone at Isleworth to know what they were planning. Football and broadcasting are both small worlds, however, and news trickled out. A series of articles in *The Independent*, revealing some of the Mirror/Carlton plans, incensed Michael Green, who immediately rang Kelvin MacKenzie and said the consortium would be dissolved if there were any more leaks. Meanwhile, the football clubs themselves, along with their many advisers, were talking openly about their expectations, with some saying the rights would go for £1 billion over five years this time, compared to £304 million in 1992.

Alan Sugar, of Amstrad and Tottenham, who was named by the Premier League owners as the chairman of the television rights committee, ran into Michael Grade, then chief executive of Channel 4, during the lead-up to the renewal of the contract. Grade recalls Sugar saying: 'I've put a figure on it. And I shocked Sam Chisholm when I told him how much we wanted.' Grade answered: 'I'm sure you know what you're doing Alan, but if I was negotiating it, I would go to Sky and say not how much I want for the rights; I would tell them how much I would let them keep.'

The Premier League knew they were on to a good thing. Their own studies had shown that the market for pay-per-view matches might be worth more than £2 billion a year. They knew, moreover, that BSkyB had absolutely no choice. It had to win the rights if it wanted to safeguard its most important driver of subscriptions. Lord Hollick, David Montgomery and Michael Green, too, were aware of BSkyB's need to win. Even if a rival could not pinch the contract away, the competition would drive the price Sky had to pay to unbelievable heights. That would suit broadcasting rivals, who were intent on countering BSkyB's incredible strength in pay-TV.

The negotiations on behalf of the Premier League were again being handled by Rick Parry, the man who had been so helpful to BSkyB the last time around. Parry believed that a short-term contract would suit them best. Digital TV had not yet been launched, and there were still a few years before pay-per-view services could be offered. When channel capacity allowed, the Premier League teams wanted to create their own channels, rather than go through an intermediary, so a long-term contract would be out of the question. The 1992 agreement had included a clause on pay-per-view, giving BSkyB the right to negotiate a PPV deal. The 1996 agreement would include a similar clause, whoever ended up winning. But there would be no promises from the Premier League about the final form of any PPV deal.

BSkyB management put on a brave front that spring, but it was clear they were worried about losing the crucial football contract. All Sky Sports staff were asked to keep their ears open, and to report back any intelligence they heard about plans in the rival camps. Vic Wakeling recalls: 'We had heard all the rumours, and I've got to tell you I think that Sam was on top of it right from the beginning. But I was getting very edgy about it. There were lots of stories about various syndicates who were getting together.'

That suited Parry's purposes, as he was worried that rivals would back out in the end, allowing BSkyB to win the rights with a low-ball bid. Parry rang both United and Carlton/Mirror, to assure them the rights were indeed available to the highest bidder, despite BSkyB's matching clause. He also stayed in touch with the shadowy group at Pall Mall, which had convinced Merrill Lynch to back its football rights plan (in the end, they would disband). 'Parry played us like a violin,' MacKenzie would tell a colleague when it was all over.

United put a large team on the bid, taking up a wide, open area at Ludgate House, its Blackfriars Bridge headquarters. The Mirror/Carlton bid was mostly put together at Carlton's Knightsbridge head office. Both sides spent considerable time securing transponders on satellite systems, as they realised the Premier League was unlikely to go for a bid that did not include satellite customers – the core audience of the existing televised matches.

For its part, BSkyB played on the weaknesses of any 'greenfield' bid. Having worked with Sky to build a business for pay-TV football, did the Premier League chairman really want to do it all again from scratch?

The final bids were scheduled to be presented on 13 June 1996, at a luxury hotel outside Coventry. A few days before, Chisholm called in his senior staff to his office at Athena Court, and gave them fresh instructions. He created two groups, one headed by Trevor East, who was responsible for the Premier League coverage, and the other by John Bromley, a consultant who, on behalf of Sky, had held the hands of the club chairmen throughout the previous four years. 'Right, you go and talk to all the clubs, and find out what you can about the opposition bids,' he told them. 'Remind them how Sky has kept its promises over the past four years.' He asked Wakeling to ring a few select contacts in football, while Chisholm himself would also hit the phone.

Says Wakeling: 'None of us picked up a single thing on money, how much money was going against us. [But] we had a fair idea of what was being talked about.' The day before the final offers were due, Chisholm held a meeting in his office, and went through the running order. Chisholm himself would make the opening remarks, telling the chairmen how much football had benefited from the existing BSkyB contract. Wakeling would then take them through the broadcasting plans, while David Chance was on hand to sum up, and to discuss the future of digital television. Wakeling had asked his football team to put together a film a few days before, which he then produced. '[It was to] remind everyone exactly what we'd done,' Wakeling says. 'Not only the coverage and everything we'd introduced, but all the support programming, and the way we promoted the fixtures.' Chisholm agreed that the film would be shown to the chairmen the next day. He then ushered most of the others out of his office, leaving him alone with Nick Carrington, the financial officer, and David Chance. Chisholm had already rung Murdoch to discuss the final bid, and had cleared it with the BSkyB board. It was agreed that Chisholm himself would make the final offer, using his best judgement. (Some at BSkyB believed that Chisholm finally did get wind of what the competition was up to, the night before the bids went in. One story had it that Kelvin MacKenzie had mentioned it to a football executive, and it had got back to Sky that way. Another version had it that Rick Parry told Chisholm that night, a suggestion that has never been substantiated.) The final bid was faxed to Parry on 12 June 1996.

The next day, all three groups made their way to Coventry. Of the three,

United News & Media was up first, unveiling a £1 billion, ten-year deal, with aggressive profit-sharing for the clubs themselves. The bid had been the result of months of work, and was fully costed, and impressively presented. But United had been pushing against a firmly shut door. Even with all the promised revenues on tap, the clubs were absolutely adamant. They were not going to accept a long-term offer. They saw the way the market for broadcasting rights was developing, and were convinced that, within a few years, the rights holder, and not the broadcaster, would be in the pole position. Why lock themselves in over such a long period of time?

Next to present was Mirror Group and Carlton, with Michael Green himself making the main presentation. The bid was professional and convincing, offering £650 million over five years. But it soon dissolved into farce, when two members of the Carlton/Mirror entourage began to argue openly in front of the chairmen, and when Alan Sugar and Michael Green exchanged sharp words about the consortium's choice of satellite (Eutelsat, rather than Astra). Mirror Group would complain later that BSkyB had made it impossible for any rival to gain access to the Astra platform; 'they may as well have owned it outright,' one senior Mirror executive complained bitterly.

Meanwhile, the BSkyB team had arrived in two cars, and pulled up early in front of the hotel. Wakeling, Trevor East, Bruce McWilliam, David Chance and Sam Chisholm stopped briefly, and decided to go around the corner and wait until the appointed hour for their presentation – 5:00 pm. They pulled up in a small country lane, and Wakeling got out to smoke. 'Imagine the scene,' Wakeling recalls. 'A farmer drives up, and sees the two limousines, and several well-dressed gentlemen. There's these guys in dark blue suits standing around the cars looking into the distance. He must have thought, "These are gangsters. Where are the violin cases?"'

'Can I help you,' the farmer asked, clearly worried. 'No, no,' Wakeling answered puffing on his cigarette. 'Just getting some fresh air.'

The group returned to the hotel at 5:00 pm precisely, and headed into the meeting room. As planned, Chisholm gave the opening remarks, which he ad-libbed as usual. He then said: 'You see in front of you what our bid is.' But none of the chairmen had been told, and there was no paper in front of them. Chisholm said, 'Fair enough', and leaned back to Bruce McWilliam, who produced some papers and handed them to Chisholm. The final bid, £670 million over five years, was then read out. Chisholm then gave Wakeling a tremendous build up, calling him the man 'who has made English football into what it is. He's the best producer in the world'.

Wakeling gave a short speech, and then moved toward the VCR. The senior of Chisholm's two PAs, Alexandria Wight, had arranged for a Sky technician to install the machine in the room that afternoon, and to ensure it was working. She had also asked him to remain in case anything went wrong. As Wakeling began his presentation, he realised there was no technician in the room. Suddenly, he became seized with an irrational fear. 'I'm not going to be able to do this,' he thought. 'So I'm getting up from the table and continuing the speech with the tape in my hand, pushing it into the machine, pressing the button,' he remembers. 'And I'm already making apologies and saying [despite] what great technicians we are and what great television we make, I wish I'd brought my 12-year-old along because she could probably operate this machine better than me. I know all you guys have the same problem at home. So I put it in and I can't get the bloody thing to work.'

Chisholm looked over at the struggling Wakeling, and said, 'No problem. David [Chance] is going to tell you about the digital future and the possibility of new things that might come along.' As Chance began to talk, Wakeling caught the eye of Trevor East, who had been watching from the back of the room. Wakeling mouthed, 'Find the fucking technician,' and East hurried out.

As Chance continued, Wakeling noticed the door opening, and saw a man with overalls enter the room. 'Run it when I say,' Wakeling whispered to him. Chance started to wind up, and turned to ask Wakeling, 'Are you ready?' Wakeling nodded yes, and motioned to the technician to start the tape. This time, the film ran. Afterward, Wakeling summed up, his enthusiasm mounting. It was all going to be fine, he thought. Just before he finished, he looked up at the chairmen and said: 'And just think, not a hint of topless darts on Sky Sports,' a reference to the Mirror Group's infamous L!ve TV programme.

'Cheap shot,' Chisholm said, *sotto voce*. 'Oh fuck,' Wakeling thought.

The Sky team left the meeting room and headed for the lobby. On the way, Chisholm turned to Wakeling. 'Where's that technician?', he asked. 'I don't know,' Wakeling answered. 'Well, when you see him, tell him he's sacked,' Chisholm growled.

In the lobby, they came across Kelvin MacKenzie pacing up and down, clutching a drink. 'Get the cars, and let's get out of here,' Chisholm said. (Recalls Chisholm: 'That's the way we liked it – arriving at the last minute, and leaving straight afterward. That's Sky – you don't know what they are up to, you don't know what they're thinking.') The five men were driven to the nearest pub, which turned out to be the Craven Arms, on the outskirts of Coventry. They ordered pints, and sat drinking quietly. Wakeling leaned over to Chisholm after the second pint and apologised for his topless darts line. 'Don't worry about it,' Chisholm said, distracted. Then, suddenly, Bruce McWilliam's mobile phone rang (Chisholm never carried one of his own). It was about 6:30 pm. 'Yes, yes, yes,' McWilliam said in a quiet voice. 'You'd better speak to Sam.' It was Parry, to say that the chairmen had voted, again, for BSkyB.

As soon as Chisholm told the group the news, there was an explosion. 'All of a sudden, [we knew] we'd got it,' Wakeling recalls. 'And suddenly, in the middle of this pub, in the middle of all these guys off the building site, the blue suits suddenly [begin] jumping up and down, hugging each other, punching the ceiling. Everyone is looking at us and thinking, "What the hell is that all about?"' Chisholm turned to one of the locals and said, 'We are Sky, and we just won the Premier League!'

Everyone in the BSkyB team reached for his mobile phone and started calling friends and colleagues back in London. Chisholm told the group to drink up, and hustled them back to town, where a party was laid on at the Bell and Crown in Chiswick. Chisholm called Murdoch with the good news, and joined his colleagues at the pub. At one point in the evening, he found Wakeling, and took him aside. 'You know that technician?' he asked. 'Yeah,' said Wakeling. Chisholm paused, smiled, and lifted his glass. 'Don't sack him,' he said.

The Premier League extension gave BSkyB the rights to top football until 2001, but at a great cost. Rupert Murdoch told Lord Hollick, when he saw him at a function some months later, 'You cost me a lot of money.' Michael Green, after the fact, told colleagues, 'I was a wimp.' On the record, his only comment: 'We were too cautious. We could have had it if we had paid another £50 million.' The higher costs for football would cause BSkyB serious problems once the new payments kicked in. But the Sky camp knew they had no choice. Says Elisabeth Murdoch: 'this market is so competitive now. Look what happened to the Premier League contract. It didn't multiply in price because we wanted it to. It multiplied because there [were] healthy competitors out there who challenged us.'

A few days after the Premier League deal was sealed, Sky Sports again pounced, reaching a highly controversial, £87.5 million deal with the Rugby Football Union, based at Twickenham, which also covered

England's home matches in the prestigious Five Nations Tournament. After a long, drawn out battle, played out mostly in the newspapers, BSkyB offered to extend the deal to include the other British rugby nations and their matches in the Five Nations. And a month after the football triumph, BSkyB managed the triple: it was exonerated in the OFT inquiry into programming supply to the cable industry.

The OFT inquiry was the most exhaustive ever carried out in the UK pay-TV market. It lasted six months, and took up extraordinary amounts of management time, not only at BSkyB but at all the cable operators whose prospects were so closely entwined with the results. The main complaint from the cable industry was about the terms under which BSkyB's channels were supplied to competing platforms. But the OFT went further, looking at BSkyB's general position in the pay-TV market, the barriers to entry, the possibility that BSkyB was cross-subsidising its distribution and programme supply businesses, and the structure of the wholesale pricing in pay-TV. On virtually every measure, BSkyB emerged unscathed. There were only four main complaints of the cable companies that were (partially) addressed. The first concerned Sky's dominance in the market for sport rights. This, the OFT believed, must be addressed by the Restrictive Practices Court, which was due to rule on the issue of Sky's Premier League contracts in 1998. The second was the designation of channels as 'bonus channels' – only available if subscribers took other services first. This 'bundling' skewed the economics of the market, especially when it came to the purchases by cable of bundled programming from Sky. Here, the OFT passed the buck to the Independent Television Commission, which launched an extended inquiry into the issue in the summer of 1997. On the third issue, the so called '100 per cent carriage rule', the OFT was able to deliver some limited relief. Under BSkyB's rate card for the sale of programming, cable operators taking a given Sky channel had to ensure that the channel went to 100 per cent of their network. The OFT agreed that this was excessive, and lowered the percentage to 80 per cent. Finally, it ordered that a new rate card, meeting the fresh conditions, be issued (and agreed, here, to insist that BSkyB alter the terms of the card to ensure that success by cable companies in increasing basic penetration, as opposed to premium penetration, would still be rewarded in the terms offered by BSkyB).

And that was that. A six-month inquiry into the company that earned 90 per cent of all revenues from pay-TV in 1995, ended with just two substantive changes (a change to the 100 per cent carriage rule, a new –

but only marginally changed – rate card), and two passings of the buck (the referral of Premier League contracts to the Restrictive Practices Court and the inquiry by the ITC into the bundling of channels). BSkyB was living a charmed existence. For how long?

PART THREE
Storm Clouds Gathering

CHAPTER 10

The Digital Dance

The renewed challenge from cable and the traditional terrestrial broadcasters seemed hardly to dent the confidence at Isleworth. The team there was convinced that the power of BSkyB could only grow, provided governments did not unduly interfere.

The great challenge would be to prepare for the digital revolution. Digital was already a reality on the continent and in the US. Germany, Italy and France had all seen digital services launched by 1997, although with mixed results. In the UK, the government itself was keen to see digital take off, and at least part of the Broadcasting Act of 1996 had been aimed at providing a regulatory framework for the new transmission systems.

The attraction for governments was the likelihood that the old analogue spectrum could be auctioned off to other users (mobile phone operators, for example) once the transition to digital had been engineered. Digital was also a far more efficient way of transmitting image and sound, allowing far more data to be broadcast within a far narrower spectrum.

Digital entailed breaking down the signals into a series of noughts and ones, which could be compressed, transmitted and then reconstituted. The picture standard would be high, the sound quality excellent and the sheer capacity huge. For the consumer, digital TV promised a true revolution. For a start, viewers might get as many as 200 channels of programming (as well as interactive services like the Internet). The huge capacity of digital also offered the prospect of significant pay-per-view programming (for instance, with films and sport available nearly on demand around the clock).

One of digital's great attractions was the prospect of providing viewers with interactive services. Consumers could order goods over the television, instantaneously, with the payment automatically deducted from a bank account. They could download games, check their bank statements, watch a favourite film, order a major concert or sporting event, even draw up a schedule of programmes they would like to watch one evening, in the order they preferred. In addition, an incredible array of data and video could accompany the main programming services: a resume of recent plot developments on their favourite soap, for example, or a pre-game interview with the managers of two Premier League teams about to play a crucial match. All of this would be available from a keypad or a remote control.

A debate had already begun in 1996 and 1997 in Britain about how all these services would be provided. The cable operators insisted that only cable could be truly interactive and instantaneous, since only fibre-optic, broadband cable could carry signals in both directions. BT and other major telecoms providers insisted that much could be provided over the normal phone line, provided regulators and governments approved. BT was to be kept out of providing broadcast services on its existing phone network until 2001, however. Satellite operators, meanwhile, dismissed suggestions that interactivity was impossible via direct-to-home distribution systems. A satellite service would be supplemented by a modem and a separate phone line, providing a 'return path' that would instruct the satellite service provider.

But it was not just telephone companies that threatened to move into broadcasting. Bill Gates made broadcasters around the world nervous in 1997, when he bought Web-TV, a start-up company offering the Internet over the television. Broadcasters such as BSkyB could probably see off the threat of cable; but a serious push by the information technology giants, offering video services backed by the financial might of a Bill Gates, was a far more serious challenge.

Britain had three digital platforms in the planning stages in 1997: digital terrestrial, digital cable and digital satellite. In the end, after much debate, all three would be available via a single set-top box, even if a few adjustments (and perhaps the purchase of a 'side car' plug-in component) might be necessary. But which of the platforms would win? Even by the autumn of 1997, nobody was taking bets.

One thing was certain, however. Whatever happened in British pay-TV, BSkyB would be there. Rupert Murdoch may have been facing severe problems in other markets – in Japan, where JSkyB was facing a rocky launch, in India, in Hong Kong and even in the US. But in Britain, his company was still the pay-TV broadcaster against which all the others would be judged.

Murdoch's experience in other markets had been depressing. His efforts to get ISkyB, in India, off the ground, were indicative. Star-TV, Murdoch's analogue Asian direct-to-home service, had been broadcasting, successfully (if unprofitably) into the fast-changing sub-continent market. Now, Murdoch wanted to upgrade the service to digital, and created ISkyB (another offspring of the BSkyB model). His approach was vintage Murdoch, reminiscent of his efforts in China in the late 1980s, when he was eager to see Hong Kong-based Star pay-TV take off on the mainland: he hired senior Indian civil servants who had been working on broadcasting issues, and lobbied the national government ceaselessly. His chief executive in India was Ratikant Basu, formerly with the Information Ministry, and the director-general of Doordashan, the Indian equivalent of the BBC. Murdoch secured transponders able to carry as many as 70 channels, for £15 million a year, and agreed an operating budget of more than £500,000 a month for administration.

The government, belatedly, decided that there had to be some legislation to cover the advent of digital television, and banned any services until a new Broadcasting Bill could be debated and passed. The decision infuriated Murdoch, who had already offered ten channels to Doordashan as a sweetener to get the digital service off the ground. He threatened to sue the government. But by the autumn of 1997, ISkyB was still in limbo.

In Australia, Murdoch had done a deal with Telstra, the telecoms giant, which gave him access to Telstra's broadband cable network. In late 1997, it appeared that the government would finally allow the struggling Australia's DTH service to be merged with Foxtel, to provide a single pay-TV proposition in Australia.

In Japan, Murdoch had moved cautiously, signing up local partners, including Fuji, the electronics and broadcasting company, to help create JSkyB, for which Mark Booth, formerly at Foxtel in Australia, was named chief operating officer. Booth, who would later be named chief executive of BSkyB, to replace Sam Chisholm, worked on the launch of JSkyB from the beginning of 1997. Using local partners, and broadcasting to discrete national markets, were two of the lessons Murdoch had learned from his early experiences with Sky. A pan-European service, supported by advertising, had looked to be a gold mine in the early planning stages. But Murdoch soon realised that subscription television, beamed to particular markets, would be the more lucrative option.

In America, Murdoch found his ambitions thwarted. His ASkyB managed to win a DTH digital licence, at great cost, but he had found it difficult to find the right US partner to help develop a digital service. MCI, which had taken a large stake in News Corporation in 1996, declined to back plans for a multi-channel bouquet. Murdoch believed he had found the right partner in the US in late 1996, when he signed a deal with Echostar, the struggling Denver-based DTH broadcaster. The partners intended to offer the normal array of pay-TV services, including pay-per-view movies and sport. But they also wanted to carry local television stations, broadcast to the nation. The huge capacity of digital satellite would allow scores of local services to be distributed around the country. However, dis-agreements over technical issues – not least which conditional access technology ought to be used by the new venture – scuppered the deal, which collapsed among acrimony and lawsuits.

Murdoch was nervous. He had been eyeing two deals to develop more content for pay-TV: the purchase of the Los Angeles Dodgers, which would have given him a leading American baseball team, and the Family Channel, the back-to-basic-values service owned by TV evangelical host Pat Robertson, once a candidate for the US presidency. Murdoch already had his Fox studio output, as well as the Fox TV network, which was creating successful TV programmes. He was also attempting to roll out Fox News in the US. He wanted to ensure that he had both content and distribution in the US.

When the Echostar deal fell through, Murdoch says: 'We were forced in the end into asking ourselves, were we going to be programme and channel providers or distributors? We really faced a decision. I wouldn't have dared buy the Family Channel if I couldn't be sure that we could have cable carriage.'

His answer, uncharacteristically, was to swallow his pride and do a deal with the 'enemy'. In the US, pay-TV distribution had been dominated by the cable industry, which had impressive penetration in the marketplace. In the UK, cable operators managed penetration rates (i.e., the percentage of those homes passed by a cable network that actually take the service) of about 23 per cent. In the US, the figure was closer to 70 per cent. The cable industry, led by such giants as John Malone's TCI and Time Warner, were the effective gatekeepers in the US market for pay television. They had seen their biggest growth in the 1970s, with the introduction of subscription movie channels such as HBO. The launch of pay-movies had, crucially, predated the explosion in take-up by US households of VCRs, and the growth of the local video hire shop. Cable was the only way of getting movie services such as HBO.

But the early lead of cable over other distribution platforms was in danger. Most cable systems were old and of limited capacity, able to carry perhaps 60 channels and no more. Upgrading the networks to be fully digital would cost billions of dollars. Worried that DTH services via satellite, with their offer of up to 500 channels, might erode their power base, the major cable operators had, themselves, created a consortium to supply digital satellite services. Primestar, owned in part by Time Warner and TCI, was the result. When he could not deliver a deal with Echostar, Murdoch began to take seriously the prospect of signing up to Primestar.

'With Primestar, at least we know that we will get our money back,' Murdoch says. But the cable operators were in no mood to concede any advantage to News Corporation. 'It was a pretty humiliating deal, but once we decided we had to do it, we just went ahead.' Unusually, Murdoch was denied a voting stake in the venture, despite taking a 31 per cent interest and folding his DTH licence. His only benefit would come from the anticipated profits from Primestar; he would have no managerial control.

In Britain, meanwhile, his position was far stronger. BSkyB had control of the main drivers of pay-TV, the biggest single distribution platform, and the best subscription management service in the country. The question would be: could BSkyB's dominance of the analogue market be extended into digital? Or would the combination of regulators and rivals finally begin to erode the incredible power BSkyB had amassed?

CHAPTER 11

Cloudy Skies

Looking back, BSkyB may have reached its absolute apogee in October 1996, just before Rupert Murdoch shocked investors, not least his partners Granada and Chargeurs (now called Pathé), by raising $1 billion through a convertible share issue, putting up ten per cent of BSkyB as collateral.

Just six weeks before, BSkyB had put its retail prices up yet again, pushing the cost of the top package (the basic channels, movies and sport) to £26.99. As in the previous year, the blow was softened by the introduction of new channels for the basic package, including several new strands from Granada Sky Broadcasting, the joint venture between Granada (60 per cent) and BSkyB (40 per cent). The cable operators started wailing again about the increases, and about the introduction of new channels. Capacity was already tight, and the cable industry had its own programming ideas it wanted to find room for. BSkyB introduced Sky 2, a second general entertainment channel, which many operators refused to carry. They saw it as a blatant attempt to get more out of the cable industry, without significant fresh investment on BSkyB's part. Most of the material on Sky 2 had already been bought, but could not be scheduled on Sky 1 owing to lack of hours. Admits a senior Sky executive: 'Sky 2 was a marketing ploy to get more money out of the cable operators. It was also a financial ploy where we had more programming than we had slots. So we said, why don't we run them rather than write them off.' In the fraught negotiations about carriage, cable operators complained that BSkyB was in full, arrogant threatening mode. If the cable networks did not agree to carry the new channel, it was intimated, then Sky would shift all the popular Sky 1 programmes (like *The Simpsons* and *The X-Files*) onto Sky 2. That would have caused outrage among some cable retail customers, as Sky 1 programmes were among the most popular in the entire non-premium pay-TV lineup.

BSkyB seemed invincible. It had the programming, the distribution, the money and the talent. But Murdoch's financial manoeuvre sent a shudder through the market, from which BSkyB would take a long time to recover.

The news trickled out late on 23 October 1996, as City journalists heard increasingly convincing details of the $1 billion convertible issue, fashioned by giant US investment bank Merrill Lynch. At first it seemed inconceivable that Murdoch would, in effect, risk seeing his 40 per cent stake in BSkyB diluted to such a degree. After all, the UK broadcaster was the source of Murdoch's only serious profit in the pay-television sector. Did he believe that the shares, then trading at nearly £7 (for a market capitalisation of more than £12 billion) would go no higher? And if Murdoch thought it was time to realise some of BSkyB's towering value, should not other shareholders follow suit?

Indeed, some did. When the convertible share issue was confirmed on 24 October, blazoned across the City pages of *The Independent*, nervous investors wiped £1.4 billion off the company's stock market value. The other shareholders, notably Granada, were upset by the move, and Gerry Robinson even consulted his lawyers about the share issue, wondering whether he might have some legal recourse against Murdoch.

At Isleworth, company executives were worried. Part of BSkyB's success had been its incredible stock market following, which fed a confidence – even arrogance – that the company could do no wrong. Hadn't BSkyB seen off the OFT? Hadn't it avoided red ink in Germany, even at the price of withdrawing altogether from the German digital market? Hadn't it managed to emerge relatively unscathed from the Broadcasting Act (1996)? Hadn't it already begun to lay the best plans for the launch of its own 200-channel digital service? Hadn't it seen off competition from United News & Media, Carlton and the Mirror Group, cannily (*albeit* expensively) re-signing the Premier League to a five-year, £670-million deal?

So why was Murdoch bailing out? Quite simply, he needed the money. 'Rupert always needs money,' says a senior executive at a leading ITV company. In the US, his dream of creating an American version of BSkyB was going to cost millions; meanwhile, his Star TV was hungry for cash. It was a typically Murdochian solution to his problems: realising value in one part of the empire to feed his ambitions elsewhere. The old Sky Television was treated the same way in the late 1980s, when the newspaper interests grouped under News International were used to subsidise the early pay-TV losses.

And it was not the first time Murdoch had used the convertible share device to realise value and to raise cash. He did the same with his near 20 per cent stake in Pearson, the media conglomerate, which he had threatened with full-scale takeover in the late 1980s. Then, as with his BSkyB deal, he reserved the right to retain the shares if he bought the convertible shareholders out when the issue came due. But in the end, the Pearson stake was allowed to go. There were suggestions that at BSkyB, too, the 10 per cent stake used to back the debt-raising exercise would end up in other hands, diluting Murdoch's stake to just 30 per cent.

But there were signs that Murdoch believed the shares had risen far beyond their true worth. (Indeed, some six months later, he would tell *The Sunday Times*, his own newspaper, that the shares had been 'grossly' overvalued, and that the correction which came in June 1997 should have surprised no one.) Says Murdoch: 'I remember looking it up last year, and thinking, "Holy shit, this is selling at 40 times prospective pre-tax earnings. This is Microsoft territory, and they don't have regulators!" And so I decided I would raise some money and we banked $1 billion. The other shareholders could have done the same thing. They didn't, and that's not my fault.'

From the outside, it looked as if BSkyB was willing to shake off the doubts surrounding Murdoch's intentions. The team at Isleworth kept its head down, working to launch a digital service as the next stage of BSkyB's growth. But for perhaps the first time since the flotation in 1994, BSkyB looked less than impregnable in the pay-TV market.

It hadn't helped, either, that the BBC had chosen Flextech, and not BSkyB, as its partner for the digital future, despite a long and drawn out series of negotiations throughout the whole of 1996. The BBC, wise to the commercial value of its brand and programming library, had been intent on finding a private-sector partner with whom to develop a group of pay-TV channels for the digital age. The BBC had lost the argument with the government about the need for a higher licence fee to help offset the costs of the digital transition, and was forced to look again at extra cost savings internally and higher revenues from the commercial sector.

The commercial sector had never been particularly profitable for the BBC, despite its stellar reputation. BBC programming had helped make a millionaire out of John Hendricks, the founder of Discovery, the US cable channel that features hundreds of hours of BBC fare. But very little of the value accrued to the BBC. Recalls John Birt, the director-general: 'We were selling our programmes to new outfits like Discovery and A&E [the Arts and Entertainment Network]. We've allowed them to build up into huge businesses, highly capitalised. But we don't have a stake in those businesses; others built up big businesses on the back of our catalogue archive.' That had to change, the strategists at Broadcasting House, London, insisted.

The BBC and Flextech, majority owned by TCI, had already been partners, through UK Gold, the repeats channel created by Pearson, the BBC, and other partners in 1992. But a single channel, with only limited access to the BBC and Thames Television libraries, was not enough to give the BBC real presence in the pay-TV market. The BBC had the world's best TV library and an excellent brand name. How could it expand?

Early attempts to get BBC channels onto pay-TV systems abroad had met with mixed results. BBC World and BBC Prime, the two satellite and cable channels, were available in Europe, but getting carriage in the US market had proved impossible. Against that background, Adam Singer, then head of Tinta, TCI's international arm (and the vehicle through which TCI held its 51 per cent stake in Flextech), arranged to have dinner with Bob Phillis, chief executive of BBC Worldwide, in September 1995. The two men discussed the BBC's global aspirations, and the prospect of creating new channels for the UK subscription market. Singer told Phillis: 'You are sitting [on] the best library of English-language production in the world [but] it's under-utilised. We could actually create with you a much bigger, more important asset base.' At the same time, the complicated shareholder structure of UK Gold could be worked out, allowing the BBC to take some money out of what had been a modest success. Even better, Singer said, by doing a deal with Flextech in the UK, the door would be open to a similar arrangement with TCI in the US, giving the BBC the carriage on US cable networks it had long coveted and a new partnership with the partner of Discovery and other stellar brands.

Phillis, who had been under pressure at the BBC to make the commercial operations more profitable, was intrigued. Singer set up a meeting with Roger Luard, the chief executive of Flextech, and the man who would ultimately drive the deal with the BBC. Luard told Phillis a deal with Flextech would give the BBC a way of finally realising some of the value of its UK Gold stake. But the real benefits would come in the future, from the creation of a raft of new channels, distributed on digital platforms.

In February 1996, Phillis travelled to Denver, headquarters of TCI, for a series of meetings with John Malone, Fred Vierra and other senior TCI management. An agreement in principle began to take shape, whereby the BBC would do two deals – one with TCI (and Discovery) in the US and globally; the other with Flextech in the UK.

Luard felt confident from the beginning that a deal with the BBC could be struck. 'I actually had a relationship with the BBC and UK Gold, and more importantly I had locked their programmes [up] for another seven years. They had very limited ability to access programming if they went with another partner. Two, [by this time] they were in deep and dark discussions with Discovery and they had an enormous desire to work with Discovery to develop more programming on a co-production basis and looked to them to help them develop and build equity value in businesses that they could drive in other territories. Three, they also have had a desire to get into the US. You cannot get into the US in pay-TV unless you do a deal with TCI. There are no other means in there. Time Warner is not a means in there, it's too confused, too bureaucratic. So if they wanted to get into the US, there had to be a TCI involvement.'

By the spring of 1996, Chisholm and Chance had caught wind of the developments at the BBC. Indeed, BSkyB had already been looking at doing a similar programming deal with the public service broadcaster, and had asked Richard Dunn, to put together a proposal. Chisholm realised that BBC pay-TV channels would be a key element in the digital platforms then in the planning stages at BSkyB. He vowed to disrupt the BBC–Flextech arrangements, and to insert BSkyB as the commercial partner for the BBC.

It would be a uphill climb. As Luard says: 'If Sky had ended up with the sports, the movies, the control of DTH, 36 per cent of the print media industry through Rupert Murdoch, and the next headline was: "Sky buys the BBC", it might just have been a political decision too far.'

Still, Bob Phillis at the BBC was not averse to negotiating with BSkyB: the more rivals for the BBC's attention the better the final deal would be. Consistent with its public service character, the BBC dealt openly with both sides. At the BBC, the key negotiators were Mark Young, Matthew Symonds, formerly of *The Independent*, Dick Emery, and Phillis. Patricia Hodgson, head of Policy and Planning, also played a crucial (some believed determinant) role in setting the BBC's pay-TV strategy. For BSkyB, David Chance took a managerial lead, but much of the detailed work on the Sky–BBC proposal was done by Richard Dunn, a close friend of Bob Phillis, and the main creator of UK Gold back in 1992, when he had still been at Thames Television. Chisholm was convinced that Dunn could deliver the BBC.

But BSkyB was working with two distinct disadvantages (setting aside the political sensitivities of the BBC doing a deal with Murdoch). The first was the programming licence agreement between the BBC and UK Gold, which had another seven years to run. It would be extremely difficult to unwind, and yet any new Sky–BBC pay-TV service would need easy access to the BBC's programming library in the early years, as the costs of creating new, quality programming to supply cable and satellite would be far too high at a time when there were very few subscribers. Archive material was absolutely crucial. Second, Flextech could deliver cable carriage throughout the US, thanks to parent company TCI's huge cable network. Murdoch had trouble enough getting his own news network, Fox News, onto American cable networks.

By early summer, with both sides wooing the BBC, the public service broadcaster looked to be in a strong position. Either way, it would get private-sector funding to develop its digital strategy, without putting the licence fee revenues at financial risk. But the BBC had not reckoned on the negotiating tactics of BSkyB.

By 1996, BSkyB had developed incredible power in the UK pay-TV marketplace. But with that power came a certain degree of arrogance. Said one insider involved in the BBC-Flextech talks: 'They felt they were totally unconquerable, [that] no one could fart without asking their consent.' David Chance approached Roger Luard, a personal friend, in early summer, and suggested the two of them work together on the BBC deal. Sky would contribute its distribution platform and its marketing prowess. Flextech would bring its programming packaging skills, and the BBC would fuel the deal with its library and production capabilities. The BBC was not told about the approach, and Luard and Chance had several meetings and telephone calls. (Luard's driver used to say: 'Ah, we're gonna have another of those clan-get-eye meetings.') BSkyB's initial pitch to Flextech had been simple: 'Let's not bid this up, let's work together and split the spoils,' Chance said. 'Good idea, maybe we should,' Luard answered.

Flextech managers say they had never taken the idea seriously, but believed it made sense to keep talking to BSkyB, in part to learn what Isleworth was up to. The BBC was surprised when BSkyB's ardour for the pay-TV deal seemed to lose steam; Sky even started to talk down the price, increasingly confident that a three-way deal would finally be achieved.

Dunn, for his part, continued to develop the pay-TV proposals on behalf of BSkyB. Initially, the BBC had thought BSkyB's approach had been all talk and no action. Eventually, Phillis concedes, 'They were talking about a sensible and serious set of proposals for partnership with them.' But the BBC side noticed a difference of approach between the top management and Richard Dunn. 'Sam [was the] wonderfully amusing sort of stop/go man and I think Richard was ploughing on and pushing on and wanting to play it in a slightly different way. But that happens in any organisation,' Phillis says.

It was often Chisholm's style in negotiations he was not handling personally, to have more than one executive making more than one approach, and to involve himself fully only at the last moment. Dunn recalls, 'After Rupert's fiasco with Berlusconi, Bruce McWilliam and I were trying to find another position in Italy for Sam. Any pay-TV partnership there was going to depend heavily on soccer and the rights were up for grabs. We had arranged two visits to Rome for Sam and I to meet potential partners for our bid, but each time he had cancelled at the last minute. Finally with cloak-and-dagger secrecy lest Rupert found out about the extravagance, Sam hired a Gulfstream jet and we flew to Rome to meet Letizia Moratti, then chairman of RAI. It was only the day before the soccer authority was making its decision so we had less than 24 hours to construct a bid from scratch, with a partner we'd only just met and having only briefly talked about the strategy for the first time when in mid-air. Extraordinary. But Sam is a law unto himself. Needless to say, RAI wouldn't play ball and we missed the deadline.'

In early August, newspapers caught wind of the negotiations between the BBC and Flextech, and Luard's company was forced to make a stock exchange announcement that it was in discussions. At that point, BSkyB realised that a three-way deal was probably not Flextech's preference, and Chance and Dunn began again in earnest to woo the BBC separately. The price of a BBC deal, insiders say, began to soar, as BSkyB desperately tried to halt the momentum that was gathering behind Flextech. 'It was hell,' Singer recalls. 'The worst part in the whole deal [as we were] getting the wretched thing closed was actually [in August] when we knew we were fighting Sky.'

Adds Luard: 'They used Richard Dunn's relationship with the BBC, and just drove that price up and up. There was a very sweaty time.'

But the BBC was still leaning toward Flextech. Explains Birt: 'the main reason was financial. Flextech offered us a better deal. And they offered us something further which was really important to the BBC – through TCI, not only a way of funding our commercial services in the UK, but developing a strategy across the world of introducing channels in which we had an ownership stake. What we want to do over the next ten years is not just have income, by selling our programmes to many more channels, but to create value through that process.'

In September 1996, heads of agreement were reached between the BBC and Flextech. Up to eight channels would be developed and launched, including a revamped UK Gold, a documentary strand, arts and education. The minority shareholders in UK Gold, including Pearson, US greeting card and TV company Hallmark and Cox, the US cable operator, would be bought out, in return for shares in Flextech. The partners would then be free to sell their Flextech shares into a liquid market. The BBC, too, would realise its investment in UK Gold, receiving Flextech shares that it could subsequently sell.

But a final announcement could not be made until after a board meeting at Discovery, in the US, the next day. On the eve of the deal's approval, Luard, Singer, Fred Vierra and Kelvin MacKenzie, a friend of both Luard and Singer, met for a few drinks. They then went on to the autumn launch of EBN, the business news channel operated by Flextech. A little worse for wear, MacKenzie, Singer and Luard went into the studios and began to broadcast – internally – about Fred Vierra's sex life. It was only later that Luard realised there were several journalists in the building, assembled for the autumn launch. The next day, MacKenzie called Luard at Flextech's offices. 'Have you seen *The Standard*?' MacKenzie asked. Horrified, Luard rushed down the hall, shouting at Singer, 'We're all over the newspapers!' Singer looked up: 'I don't want to know,' he said. Luard rushed downstairs to get a copy of the early edition of *The Evening Standard*. 'I'm history,' he thought. Right on the edge of the biggest deal of his career, with the staid and serious public service broadcaster, he was going to be made out to be an irresponsible high-liver. He raced back to the office, flicking through the pages of *The Standard*. 'I can't find it,' he yelled. He then looked up, and saw a huge sign on the wall. 'Gotcha!' it read. (Kelvin MacKenzie and Brent Harman, Luard's deputy, had been behind the stunt.)

Word came in from the US in the early evening that the deal had been agreed. Flextech's final offer was worth £140 million. Another £450 million would eventually be invested by TCI in the US and elsewhere. It was a huge boost for the BBC, a watershed deal for Flextech, and a bitter disappointment for Sam Chisholm.

From his own sources, David Chance had heard early that morning that the deal was likely to go to Flextech. He called Luard, and offered to come in as a third partner even at that late stage. Meanwhile, Chisholm called Fred Vierra, of TCI, who was staying at the Laneborough Hotel. 'Fred, we want in,' Chisholm said. 'We can work it together, and we'll make great money.'

When Chisholm realised that BSkyB had lost, he called Chance and Richard Dunn into his office. Dunn remembers getting a mild bollocking, and was made to wait while Chisholm made the call to Murdoch. Chisholm told his boss that the deal had gone to Flextech, but at a high price, and that BSkyB would nonetheless be able to carry the new BBC pay channels on digital satellite. Chisholm then called Bob Phillis, who recalls: 'It was a very overstated incredulity: "How could you? What happened to you? How could you have done such a thing? I can't believe it". He was disappointed, of course, and he made it clear that he thought we had made the wrong decision. He made it quite clear that he felt that in his view it wouldn't happen unless there was a three-way cut to it and that they should be cut in. That would be the sensible way to go forward.' (Even by the autumn of 1997, it was not clear whether the BBC channels would get carriage on BSkyB's planned digital service, as the negotiations dragged on.)

Insiders at BSkyB believed that Sky could have done a deal with the BBC had it moved more quickly and decisively. Chisholm had not concentrated enough on the details, they thought. But in the end, Chisholm was not altogether convinced about the BBC channels. They were important, yes, but would they drive the take-up of digital receiving equipment? And anyway, could BSkyB have matched the global offer from TCI–Discovery–Flextech?

Remembers Richard Dunn: 'At the time there was disappointment that we didn't get it. And, yes, I was crudely criticised in the way that Sam does. He felt that Bob Phillis had let me down badly because Bob Phillis is a friend. It was just stupid because Bob was doing what he thought was best for the BBC and I was doing what I thought was best for Sky and it didn't come off.' Indeed, Dunn isn't even sure he was sorry the deal got away from him, given the great costs involved in developing pay-TV channels. 'These channels at the BBC are mostly of questionable commercial value in a very, very crowded spectrum,' he says.

Phillis himself felt triumphant. But the deal did not improve relations between him and his bosses at the BBC, particularly Sir Christopher Bland, Chairman of the BBC's board of governors, who did not get along with Phillis. Within a year, Phillis would leave the BBC, to join the Guardian

Media Group as chief executive. But he left the legacy of the BBC's first serious foray into the world of pay-TV.

Chisholm soon got over the loss of the BBC deal. He had a harder time with Murdoch's controversial share issue in late 1996, which marked a further deterioration in relations between him and the boss. Disagreements over Murdoch's foray into Italy aside, the first real tensions had come in early 1996, when Elisabeth Murdoch, then 27, was appointed general manager, broadcasting at BSkyB. Chisholm had agreed to the appointment – as chief executive, he probably could have blocked it, although at some cost to his already frosty relationship with the boss. But he didn't like it. Was Elisabeth a spy? Was she there to check up on Chisholm, who was running Sky like he ran Channel Nine in Australia – as a fiefdom?

It didn't please Chisholm, either, that Murdoch had tried to poach his number two, David Chance, to take up the job of chief executive of ASkyB, the copy-cat company Murdoch hoped would be the 'battering ram' to realise his designs on the pay-TV market in the US. Chance said no, sensing that ASkyB would be a disaster – as indeed it proved. (Chance was paid a loyalty bonus of £1 million to stay on board at BSkyB, not so much in return for having turned Murdoch down but for having declined a far more lucrative position in the US, as head of At Home Entertainment, a pay-TV company that ultimately went public. Chance might have made $40 million out of the job upon flotation.)

But it was the arrival of Elisabeth that really got Chisholm's goat. She, with her husband Elkin Pianim, the Ghanian-born investor and publisher, had spent 16 months managing two television stations in California, bought for $35 million in 1994 with a loan from Rupert Murdoch. (Before that, the pair, who had met at college, worked for the 'family firm', Fox). In California, they set about cutting costs ruthlessly, and managed to turn the stations around and sell them just a year and a half later for a $12-million profit – proof, thought her father, that she had real talent for running TV operations.

Pianim, who studied Marxism at Vassar, the college where he met Elisabeth, was every inch the entrepreneur when the couple arrived in England in 1996. He and his brother Nicholas, in league with Elisabeth, had established their own investment firm – Idaho Partners – and began to look at opportunities in the UK. Capitalised at $10 million, the company financed the launch of *The New Nation*, a newspaper for Britain's black community, and was on the lookout for 'media-related companies with positive operating cash flows and established technologies'.

Elisabeth was assured and articulate, very much a creation of her upbringing and her education. Vassar, the formerly all-women college that was her alma mater, educated many young women of the elite in America – gave them poise, articulacy, opinions. Elisabeth had all three. She also had the privilege (or the curse) of being born into the Murdoch family, with a demanding if affectionate father, who engendered in his children the will to succeed, to astonish him. 'It wasn't an easy place to grow up,' says a close friend of the Murdoch family. 'The children were judged – not necessarily harshly – but judged all the same. Could any of them live up to the expectations of a canny, unyielding father? Thank God for Anna', Murdoch's second wife, the mother of the three youngest Murdoch children (there was a daughter, Prudence, from his previous marriage).

Elisabeth speaks with the accent of the educated American: a preppie accent (akin, perhaps, to Britain's Sloanie, but with a far richer vocabulary). Unlike many Americans of her age, she also speaks in complete sentences, eschewing the ubiquitous 'like' or 'she goes, and then he goes, and then she goes', which many of her generation cannot seem to avoid. Extraordinarily, while she shares her father's assumption that people want to hear what she has to say, she also listens intently. From her arrival in Britain in 1996, she realised there were many cultural allusions that she was likely to miss. Better to say less and listen more.

Approaching his 70th birthday, Murdoch was clearly grooming his children to succeed him – Elisabeth at BSkyB, her brother Lachlan, 25, in Australia, and James, 23, the youngest, in New York. So much was made abundantly obvious when all three children were interviewed for a piece in *Vanity Fair*, published in the spring of 1997. It looked as if Murdoch was running a competition, asking his children to prove their worth by making a success of a part of the family empire: Lachlan in Australia, where he worked under Ken Cowley, a long-time News Corporation executive; James in New York (later Los Angeles), where he worked on News Corporation's new media interests; Elisabeth in London, at BSkyB.

Already by 1997, it was the children, rather than Murdoch, who were beneficial owners of the Murdoch family shares in News Corporation. Explains Murdoch: '[the succession at News Corporation] depends on how long I stay *compos mentis*. Basically we have or will have more than 35 per cent of the votes. That's enough to control it, unless you screw it up. So these kids have those shares now. It will be up to them, to those three that are really in the business.' He adds, however: 'I would say currently it is their consensus that Lachlan will take over. He will be the first among equals, but they will all have to prove themselves first.' On Elisabeth, he is less forthcoming. 'She has some things to work out. She has to decide how many kids she is going to have, where she wants to live. Elkin [her husband] wants to make money, and he finds that easier in the US. But they find as a mixed [race] couple, it is easier to live in London, and to make friends there.'

At BSkyB, Elstein was curious about Elisabeth's appointment. Chisholm assured him she would not be involved in programming. 'I really had very little to do with her,' Elstein recalls. 'It was like she had been given a title, Minister Without Portfolio – trouble shooting, sorting out some logistics, working on the budgets, really getting to know the business. Her ambition was to run the whole of Sky and she was doing a tour of the company finding out everything there was to know about it. It looked like glorified work experience at that stage.'

Chisholm himself referred to her as the 'management trainee' in private. But he realised there was not much mileage in fighting Murdoch on the issue: the media tycoon was, after all, owner of 40 per cent of BSkyB. Typically the board, including Gerry Robinson, the non-executive chairman, had no strong views.

Says Elstein: '[Elisabeth] is bright. She understands a lot of things very quickly. But being so new to UK TV, there's an element of risk the more responsibility you give her. But you know the shareholders have a mouth. If they don't like it they've got board meetings, and they can say it. The non-execs can say it. If Sam objected, which he could have done, she couldn't have got it. So once Rupert had pressurised Sam to take her, who is Gerry Robinson to say she cannot [come]?'

Those close to Chisholm say he was 'hurt' by the appointment, and realised that tensions were building, that Murdoch was no longer a champion, and that he was no longer Murdoch's 'favourite broadcaster'. There were fewer phone calls; there was less interaction, less consultation. In the words of one executive who knows both men well, 'At News Corp, there are many courtiers but there is room for only one [Prince].'

Says Adam Singer, at pay-TV rival Flextech: 'News Corporation in the last five years has changed from a one-man entity with a very interesting team of people he's had around him for a very long time into an Asian dynastic company. Sam has created this very formidable operation. The trouble is, he is a major, major prince but he isn't the emperor.'

A senior News Corporation executive explains it in simple terms: 'As much as anyone builds profits and develops the business, he can still be fired the next day. It is the shareholders who own the company. Sam did not own the company, although sometimes he acted as if he did.'

Says a senior British broadcaster, who has met both Murdoch and Chisholm many times, 'Murdoch chooses his favourite sons and then treats them obsessively, calling all the time, asking their advice about everything. I think Sam was very much in that category. Then when it became apparent that BSkyB was going to be extremely successful, Rupert found that difficult to deal with. Sam stopped being the favourite son. He's a sensitive enough guy, despite the bluff, and he was feeling pretty rejected.'

Elisabeth herself was feeling dejected, too, by the obvious bad blood between her and the chief executive. She had hoped to find in Chisholm a mentor, akin to the role Ken Cowley had played for her brother Lachlan in Australia. Instead, she believed that Chisholm was threatened by her presence. According to a close friend, she 'underestimated how threatened Sam would be, and [how he] would systematically attempt to undermine her. It's only coming out now, that some people trust her and she has her own friends [at BSkyB]'. According to her friends, colleagues have told her: 'I have been raked over the coals for speaking to you.' Elisabeth has told friends she gets along with Sam on a base level. She finds him witty and funny. But being her father's daughter, she would remind everyone that he wasn't the ultimate boss, and he can't operate if it isn't clear that he is the ultimate boss. Says Rupert Murdoch: 'Elisabeth thought that Sam would teach her everything, but he didn't. He tried to cut her out. He thought she was talking to me, and she was. But she doesn't tell tales. She loves the business – the programming and the scheduling, every bit of it.'

Elisabeth once asked Chisholm why, if he was such a strong person, he always worked for someone else? Chisholm waved the question away, but Elisabeth Murdoch believed it was proof that Chisholm was a bully. Bullies, she believed, always work best when they work for strong people, as a necessary stop-gap to their own inability to stay within boundaries.

Says David Elstein: 'As he found with Kelvin [MacKenzie], once the virus is in the body, what do you do with it? You tolerate it a bit and then you work out your defence mechanisms and then you wait to close in for the kill. But with Elisabeth, you can't kill it so you have to manage the situation, you have to look on in wonder, [you have to give her] a lot of slack in the hope that she'll screw up.'

Another reason for the apparent rift between Murdoch and Chisholm was the latter's increasing public profile in the UK. It was Chisholm (and to a lesser degree Chance) who was identified as the architect of BSkyB's phenomenal growth. Certainly after BSkyB's entry into the FTSE-100 group of top companies in 1995, the broadcasting giant had become a huge success in its own right. Chisholm liked running a major company, basking in glory. He saw, too, that pay-TV operations elsewhere in the Murdoch empire had yet to match BSkyB's success. 'BSkyB is the success story of the decade,' Chisholm liked to tell analysts and selected journalists. Murdoch couldn't match that. Star-TV was still losing huge sums of money, while ASkyB, Murdoch's US digital satellite company, could not get off the ground. So much for a 'Murdoch TV strategy'. In fact, only BSkyB was an undoubted pay-TV success, and that was down to three factors: loose regulation, lack of competition and sound management (notably Chisholm and Chance). BSkyB's strengths were confirmed by a simple, arresting fact: the UK company was worth more, in market capitalisation, than News Corporation, at least until the share-price rout of mid-1997.

There is no doubt that there was competition between Chisholm and Murdoch – a race that Chisholm, the hired hand, could never convincingly win. Murdoch saw BSkyB as just one of his many global companies – even if he only owned 40 per cent of it. He wanted Chisholm to be a team player, but the New Zealander would answer: 'I'm not a team player, I am a leader.' From Chisholm's perspective, Murdoch appeared jealous. From Murdoch's perspective, Chisholm appeared vain and obsessive. 'Sam came up with half the ideas, and Rupert came up with the other half,' says a colleague of both men. 'But Sam took the credit, and wanted more of the credit than he deserved. You'd think Rupert, in his position, wouldn't care. But he does.' The two men were surely heading for conflict.

Moreover, Chisholm used the press well, despite his public stance of being press-shy, and his oft-stated low opinion of journalists. 'They're an irritant, at times very time-consuming,' he says 'It's a horror story: there are too many newspapers, too many journalists, too little information.' Only one newspaper in the UK – *The Financial Times* – had regular access to News Corporation and to Murdoch. But Chisholm talked regularly to at least four national newspapers: *The Financial Times*, *The Independent*, *The Observer* and, to a lesser degree, *The Times* (owned by Murdoch) – always off the record, of course. His view of developments thereby usually found their way into print.

Chisholm even talked to trade journalists when the mood struck him.

The best way to get Sam Chisholm on the line was to write something he didn't like. There can't have been many journalists writing about BSkyB who hadn't received irate calls from the chief executive. 'Do you think anyone gives a fuck what you write in your shitty little rag?' he bellowed at one national journalist.

Chisholm's growing profile in the UK was unlikely to have pleased Murdoch, who guarded jealously his own authority within News Corporation's family of companies. And with good reason. His ability to take quick decisions and to run huge risks was intimately tied to the authority he wields, even though his family now owns just 35 per cent of the master company. Chisholm was an employee: a good one, no doubt, whose ruthlessness had been critical to the turnaround at BSkyB. But no employee was irreplaceable.

And Murdoch was increasingly annoyed by signs that Chisholm was more committed to BSkyB than to Murdoch and News Corporation. The Italian disagreement aside, there were other, subtler indications that Chisholm was becoming highly proprietorial about his UK-based company. He did not like to be told at the drop of a hat to fly off to some far-flung part of the world to advise on News Corporation's various operations. Nor did he want to threaten the undoubted success of BSkyB by seeing the company used as a vehicle to advance Murdoch's other interests. Some of his unwillingness to travel could be put down to the state of his health: his asthma (or emphysema) was a limiting factor for a chief executive of a global media company, obliged to board a plane at next to no notice. But Murdoch expected such energy and availability in his executives: Chisholm's signs of independence, even recalcitrance, did not go down well in Los Angeles. 'Sam kept threatening to resign for a year, showing me these doctor's certificates saying he was dying.' Murdoch says. 'I said, "it's up to you, don't tell me that you are going to work at half pace. I don't think you know how".'

Such corporate tensions aside, there was no doubt that personality was playing a huge part in the growing estrangement between Murdoch and his UK chief executive. Chisholm had been a diplomat early on, never missing an opportunity to credit Murdoch for his vision and his guts. But after 1995, when BSkyB matured into a serious, quoted company, Chisholm increasingly sought to take the credit himself (with due reference to his own management team). Each attempt by Murdoch to rein in his chief executive made Chisholm angrier and more frustrated. He believed he was owed more from Murdoch after years of hard work than intermittently abusive phone calls from Los Angeles, and relentless pressures from competitors, regulators and the press. He believed he understood more about broadcasting than Murdoch, and that News Corporation should let him get on with the job.

But in the end, it was the question of dynasty and succession that brought matters to a head. When Elstein finally left BSkyB in August 1996 to become chief executive of the new Channel 5, it was only a matter of time before Elisabeth would get a chance to get her hands on Sky's programming. By October of that year, she took on responsibility for scheduling, and a few months later ordered a revamp of the lineup on both Sky 1 and Sky 2. With her number two, former Nickelodeon executive James Baker, she imported the US concept of 'appointment television', a stripped and stranded schedule whereby similar programmes were shown in a block on specific days. The results were mixed: indeed, ratings actually went down, at least initially.

Elisabeth Murdoch is unrepentant. 'The rescheduling was important yet only one part of a longer term strategy,' she explains. 'Which is that we have to have original programming. That obviously takes longer than rescheduling.'

Her first move was to look at viewers' habits. 'Why have an audience that is 50 per cent men and then lose them by scheduling a woman's show right afterwards?' She then set out to create consistency in the schedule and to create excitement among viewers about the programming they could expect on a particular evening. The new Sky 1 lineup is 'a much easier schedule to handle for the viewer, than one that changes all the time,' she says.

A crucial part of her strategy was to give Sky 1 as much a 'premium' feel as the sport and movie channels. 'People don't part with their money easily, and we must remember that we are a pay-TV service. So even with a general entertainment channel, they have to pay [as part of the basic package]. You have to create "must watch" television. You can get your promotional hands around that. For instance, [consider] Super Sunday. We used the leverage of the other channels, by moving viewers over from Sky Sports to *The Simpsons* and *X-Files* on Sky 1, [in an] attempt to own Sunday.'

Elisabeth's US experience appeared to be crucial to her approach at BSkyB. The demise of network television had been predicted for more than a decade in the US, in the face of the competitive challenge from pay-TV. 'Everyone said the same thing, but look at the [US] networks,' she says. 'They have a coherent sense about them, and you gain loyalty to channels even more than to particular programming. That is a lesson we should all learn. A general entertainment channel has to have a sensibility, and it has to create expectation. The terrestrials here tend to schedule like the old fashioned networks, and I think they are going to have to change.'

Elisabeth was also responsible for Sky 2, the second general entertainment channel. Says a senior Sky executive: 'We didn't want to cannibalise Sky 1 just to get *The X-Files* onto Sky 2 now and then. So we said, look we have an opportunity here. What do we want to make Sky 2 into? We decided to make it the young channel, the alternative, the campy stuff – *Hercules, Beverly Hills.*'

When Elisabeth left on maternity leave in early 1997, to give birth to her second child, Chisholm ordered a review of the schedule, much to her irritation. When she discovered what was happening, she asked her father to intercede, and the review was stopped.

From then on, Chisholm appeared resigned about the future. His health was no better, and he was still working insane hours. Moreover, he knew that digital would be a long, hard slog, akin to the incredible challenge of turning BSkyB around in the first place. Leaving before digital was launched was attractive: it could mean going out on a high tide. Chisholm was wary of digital altogether. Turning around BSkyB fueled the corporate success story of the decade in Britain; launching a digital service, at a time of increased competition and closer regulatory attention, would put those achievements in doubt.

The question was: could Chisholm leave on his own terms? And could he ensure that his chosen successor, David Chance, stayed on? In the early months of 1997, Chisholm laid his plans.

CHAPTER 12

The Beginning of the End?

The first public sign of Chisholm's intentions regarding succession came in the form of a nearly unprecedented interview granted to *The Guardian* in May 1997. In it, Chisholm managed to create two impressions: first, that David Chance was the natural successor; second, that Elisabeth Murdoch was not yet ready to take on a senior management job. By this time, it would later emerge, Chisholm had already told Murdoch he was ready to step down as chief executive. And as it transpired, Murdoch himself did not think that Elisabeth was ready for the top job – at least not yet.

Meanwhile, the digital preparations continued apace. Since late December 1996, the market (and the media industry generally) had been waiting for signs that BSkyB would launch its 200-channel satellite service on time in late 1997. But Chisholm and his digital team were moving carefully: they had seen the problems arising in Germany, Spain and elsewhere, where digital satellite had been launched to a disappointing reception. 'Digital is a theoretician's delight and a practitioner's nightmare,' Chisholm told his staff. 'We've learnt one or two things along the way,' he says. 'Experiences [like launching Sky] are something you only do once in your life. I mean a bit of self flagellation is good for the soul, but doing it all again would be ridiculous.'

Explains David Chance: 'Let's not rush this. What are the things we must do to get this to work? Most people who have done it have underestimated the challenge; maybe we are underestimating the challenge. What must we do to give it the best chance of success? And so we are taking our time.'

BSkyB's approach to the digital launch was typical of the company's operational strategy. A small team of executives, including Ian West, head of digital development, spent much of 1996 working on the blueprint, supplemented occasionally by consultants. Chisholm himself paid little attention to the details, but periodically called together the team – either at Isleworth or at the Farm, Chisholm's Hampshire estate – to review the progress. Three broad fronts were determined: programming (more channels and pay-per-view services), technology (the electronic programme guide, conditional access and subscriber management) and interactive services (home shopping, home banking, arcade games, information).

Digital would bring as many as 200 channels of television, pay-per-view movies and events, and interactive services. If BSkyB played its cards right, it could emerge into the digital age with its near-monopoly intact. All it needed was secure sources of programming, adequate carriage on the new digital satellites being planned by Astra, and a careful marketing strategy that would not lead to the collapse of the analogue market during the crucial transition phase. The question of digital carriage was answered by long-term arrangements with Astra, under which BSkyB put up some of the costs of the satellite launch, in return for lower per-year transmission bills. On programming, BSkyB began to talk to a raft of channel operators, ranging from Bloomberg TV, owned by the financial information company of the same name, as well as Granada, its large shareholder, about a range of digital channel concepts. On marketing the new service, it was agreed early that BSkyB would attempt to convince existing subscribers to keep their analogue systems for use as a second TV service (in the children's bedroom, for instance), and upgrade to the digital service for the main lounge. The company also started to talk to BT, the telecoms giant, about forming a joint venture to subsidise the costs of the new receiving equipment, particularly the set-top box. It was believed that a stand-alone company, with partners, could soften the blow of the migration to digital, by offering a range of interactive services (home banking, games and home shopping), leaving BSkyB itself to provide the television side.

Meanwhile, the legal and regulatory affairs divisions, led by Deanna Bates and Ray Gallagher, were consumed by the ongoing battle over new guidelines for the digital age. A huge lobbying campaign had been mounted by traditional broadcasters on the vexed issue of conditional access, just as the government was finalising its guidelines on digital TV. Critics of BSkyB's huge power warned that digital broadcasters would be forced to turn to Murdoch for access to the new broadcasting environment: BSkyB would be the 'gatekeeper', thus maintaining its monopoly position.

The ITV companies, as well as the BBC, had been worried about the growth of BSkyB, and had long before highlighted the crucial issue of the gatekeeper's role. Earlier attempts to create an ITV2, for instance, had led to preliminary discussions with News Datacom, Murdoch's conditional access company, when the issues of market dominance and access were first made obvious to ITV.

As a consequence, ITV and BBC both launched a high-profile, and expensive, campaign to ensure a level playing field in the digital age. The key player would be the Department of Trade and Industry, and its regulatory offspring, Oftel, the telecoms watchdog. But the British broadcasters went via the backdoor, heavily lobbying the European Commission, which was then working on a directive on television.

'Where we thought there was a regulatory interest we've argued fiercely and passionately for effective competition regimes in respect of the digital gateway,' the BBC's John Birt says. 'We have been more rigorous than anybody else in identifying the issues, and actually achieving change. No one group is instrumental, but we were certainly very influential in getting the directive from Brussels that obliged the British government to regulate [in the autumn of 1996]. We argued fiercely for a proper regulatory regime.'

The Directive from Brussels insisted that all broadcasters should be given fair, open and non-discriminatory access to digital platforms. The UK government of the day responded by reforming its initial guidelines on digital access, notably giving Oftel, the telecoms regulator, a crucial role in ensuring that access to digital networks was open and guaranteed to be fair. While BSkyB argued strenuously against some of the more interventionist positions put forward by its rivals, it was forced in the end to accept a new regulator (Oftel) and to abide by the 'free and open' provisions agreed in November 1996.

'What we have managed to do, what was crucial, was not stop pay television but to make sure it was an open market and in the UK people other than Sky could benefit from it and that you didn't have to go cap in hand to get in,' Barry Cox, the head of the ITV Association, says.

BSkyB insiders openly derided the BBC, complaining that 'hundreds' of lobbyists and consultants had been brought in by the Policy Unit to organise the campaign on digital access in the autumn of 1996. The BBC dismissed such criticisms. 'We had no external lobbyists, just the small team in corporate affairs. As for all the numbers that are given for the Policy Unit, they are just made up,' Birt says. 'There are all sorts of different people, and of course the Unit has different obligations. But ask Patricia [Hodgson, head of Policy and Planning] to tell you how many people are involved in each of these and how many people actually turn up at negotiations and how many turned up from Sky for negotiations. And a somewhat different picture emerges. It's presumably because they find us effective [that] they're trying to undermine our effectiveness by suggesting that things aren't as they are.'

The digital guidelines were only formally approved in early 1997, but the framework was in place by early December 1996. Don Cruickshank, the director general of Oftel, would be the prime regulator of 'access to networks', as he himself put it. Cruickshank could not see how Oftel could regulate the provision of TV services in digital – that would be down to the competition authorities. He would focus his attention on the networks themselves – the set-top box, the electronic programme guide – to ensure no player was acting as an anti-competitive gate-keeper.

As the year was drawing to a close, however, there was still no news from Isleworth about Sky's digital launch. There was even a theory, believed by some very senior media executives at rival companies, that BSkyB had no intention of launching its digital satellite service. True, BSkyB had agreed to pay £100 million upfront and £8 million a year for ten years to lease transponders on Astra's new digital satellite. As well, it had conducted negotiations with channel operators ranging from Bloomberg TV to Daily Mail & General Trust to Virgin on the terms of digital carriage of new niche TV channels. It had also pushed ahead on creating British Interactive Broadcasting, the key joint venture with BT, the telecoms giant, to commission and market the set-top boxes needed to receive digital signals. But the analogue business was so good for Sky, and the question marks surrounding digital so obvious, Chisholm for one was not wholly convinced of the wisdom of BSkyB's digital strategy. Murdoch, who had a global vision for digital TV, was all for it; Chisholm and Chance, who believed the digital revolution could risk the incredible record of BSkyB, may not have been so firmly committed.

But if digital was to come, Chisholm wanted to get two elements of his strategy working together: digital satellite and digital terrestrial. 'Sky is in everything,' Chisholm explains. 'I mean it's a horizontally integrated business, that's why it's in digital terrestrial, cable, satellite you know smoke signals, what ever the platforms are, we're a programme deliverer.'

On that basis, BSkyB continued to plan for a digital satellite launch, but decided to delay it until 1998. Meanwhile, in late 1996, Chisholm opened a second digital front, deciding to approach the one company which seemed wholly committed to what many considered to be a dead-end technology: digital terrestrial television (DTT).

The government had been working on the launch of DTT in earnest since 1992, and the Broadcasting Act of 1996 had laid out the process for the award of licences. The main attraction lay in freeing up the analogue capacity, for use by other commercial operators. Broadcasting is an inefficient use of spectrum, requiring huge capacity to transmit quality images and sound. Digital technology, coupled with compression techniques, allows far more programming to be transmitted in a much narrower band frequency. But DTT's capacity was limited next to that of digital satellite or cable. With BSkyB such a strong competitor, and with its digital satellite plans, if delayed, already well advanced, there were doubts that DTT could even get off the ground.

The terrestrial technology had some undoubted advantages. Viewers did not need new equipment other than a set-top decoder, and the signal could be broadcast over existing (*albeit* upgraded) hill top transmitters. That meant DTT could be marketed to the 15 million homes in the UK that had so far eschewed cable and satellite, provided attractive programming was on offer. But what programming? BSkyB had the rights to top football and to Hollywood films, the only proven drivers of pay-TV. It had by the far the most experience in the marketing of paid-for TV services. And it had the technical expertise needed to get a new service off the ground (not least the conditional access technology so crucial to subscription TV).

Until late in 1996, most media commentators had all but written off DTT. BSkyB's near-monopoly control of premium programming, and its undoubted pole position in pay-TV, looked unassailable. Two hundred channels of digital TV from BSkyB's satellite proposals would easily trump the 30 or so channels possible on DTT. But not everyone was so pessimistic. Indeed, some ITV companies had been looking at DTT for five years or more, as a way of getting into pay television without having to go through Murdoch. Barry Cox recalls: 'Some of us believed that terrestrial digital was the only way you could actually be guaranteed [a way] into pay. If we can get that, then whatever Murdoch does he cannot stop you, he cannot use his gate keeper position.'

The ITC invited bids for DTT in November 1996, and set a deadline of 27 January 1997. There were to be six 'multiplexes' (or groups of channels) in all on the DTT platform. The first, dubbed Mux 1, was gifted to the BBC, for its sole use. Mux 2 was given to ITV and Channel 4, with capacity reserved for Teletext, the holiday and information text service. Licence A, the third multiplex, was half-reserved for Channel 5 and S4C in Wales, with the remaining capacity available to commercial broadcasters. The last three multiplexes, dubbed licences B, C and D, were also available for commercial bidders.

The ITC engineers predicted that the DTT platform could support about 30 channels (more if advanced compression techniques were employed). Of these, half would be supplied by existing broadcasters, who were obliged to 'simulcast' their normal (analogue) service on the new frequencies. The BBC, ITV and Channels 4 and 5 would then be free to use their gifted additional capacity as they wished, subject to normal rules on content (particularly taste and decency).

In late 1996, there was increasing anxiety at the ITC. Would anyone come forward to apply for the licences? Would the prospect of 200 digital channels from BSkyB on satellite scare off any potential DTT bidders? There had to be some doubt. DTT would support only a fraction of digital satellite's offering, and would have to be financed for several years before making a profit. BSkyB, with its installed base of analogue subscribers, had an edge in convincing customers to 'upgrade' to digital. The winners of the DTT bidding process would need to create a greenfield business, and would likely have to subsidise the costs of the all-important 'set-top' boxes (or decoders) needed to receive the digital terrestrial signal.

Throughout late 1996, speculation was growing that at least two bidding groups were forming to apply for licences for B, C, and D. (There was less interest in Licence A, which had sitting tenants in the form of Channel 5 and S4C. And the ITC had limited a single owner to just three licences overall.) Of the likely commercial bidders, the more certain was International CableTel, the US-owned cable operator that had bought NTL, the national transmission company, in 1996.

The other potential bidder was a far more serious player. Carlton, owners of the London weekday, Central and Westcountry ITV franchises had been working on the prospects for DTT for several months. Michael Green, Carlton's chairman, was convinced he needed a new growth path for his company, which had often been overlooked in the unforgiving City. It galled him that his company traded at a discount to other media companies, despite its strong profit growth. Some analysts warned about the reliance of the company on television services, and on video and film duplication, a market that might, one day, be supplanted by new technology like digital video discs and on-line delivery of films.

Carlton had put a team on to DTT early in 1996, even before it made its failed bid for rights to the Premier League. Green's optimism was matched by that of Nigel Walmsley, his director of broadcasting, who helped to put together the early business plans prior to the bid. 'We invested time, effort and resources looking at the business,' Green says. 'I asked people to go full throttle and look at every angle. Once I knew the good and bad points of DTT, then I would make a decision.'

In addition to his major presence in ITV, Green had already invested in a small way in pay-TV, buying a cable channel, SelecTV, in 1996, relaunching it as Carlton Select. He later added the Carlton Food Network. In addition, Carlton would buy the film rights to the Rank library, giving it another source of programming for a new TV service.

Two weeks before Christmas 1996, Green received an unexpected phone call. Sam Chisholm wanted to know whether BSkyB might come in as a partner in Carlton's bid for DTT. Green was immediately suspicious. What was Chisholm up to? For months, BSkyB had been rubbishing the idea of DTT, scoffing at suggestions that anyone would want 30 channels when they could have 200. But Chisholm had realised that Carlton was serious about its DTT bid. For the first time, there was a chance that a well-funded, well-managed competitor to BSkyB might enter the pay-TV market, and the prospect worried Chisholm.

Chisholm and Chance went to Carlton's headquarters in Knightsbridge for a meeting with Walmsley and Green. 'We know you're going for this, and we know you've got some American partners you're thinking of bringing in,' Chisholm told Green. 'Why don't you dump them and we'll come in with you?'

BSkyB thought Green had been negotiating with Warner about a joint venture bid, although Green denies this was so. BSkyB's relations with Warner were not all that good, after the launch of the US company's pay-TV channel in the UK was cancelled. To Chance's annoyance, BSkyB had pulled the channel following a huge battle between Murdoch and Time Warner in the US over whether Time Warner would carry Fox News on its cable network in New York City. It was another example of how Murdoch's international interests could sometimes interfere with BSkyB's operations. Oddly enough, Murdoch subsequently offered to revive plans to carry the Warner channel in the UK. This time, Ted Turner, the vice-chairman of Time Warner, said no.

Green was still wary, and wondered whether there might have been a hidden agenda. Chisholm was shown the business plan Carlton had been working on, and realised the bid was serious indeed. 'He realised we were not shadow boxing, that this is real,' Green recalls. All the same, Green was prepared to consider a deal with BSkyB, for obvious reasons. Everyone knew that sport and film were the only drivers of subscription television. It would be a huge risk to create a brand new broadcasting platform without the two chief drivers. Who would pay a subscription fee for a group of lifestyle and repeat channels? Green was also hoping to do a deal with BBC-Flextech, to get at least a few of the new pay-TV channels being planned. But even with the BBC name, the DTT platform would look weak next to the powerhouse satellite service BSkyB was aiming to launch.

Chisholm suggested a 50/50 split for the new company, to be called British Digital Broadcasting. An agreement in principle was reached, and Chisholm left for a holiday in New Zealand. Gerry Robinson, chairman of both Granada and BSkyB, was astonished to learn from his own market sources that BSkyB and Carlton were going into DTT together. (Outsiders had every reason to be amazed as well. How could the chairman of the company not know about a possible bid that might cost as much as $100 million?) Robinson rang Chisholm in New Zealand and asked if it was true. Chisholm admitted it, and Robinson immediately asked for a stake for Granada. He told a colleague later: 'I would have kicked myself if these two had made a go of it.' Robinson had been unimpressed with DTT since the concept was first kicked around the ITV companies in 1992. But since then, he had taken Granada into the satellite business, via the seven-channel Granada Sky Broadcasting joint venture, and was looking at prospects for rolling the new channels out on digital platforms. He realised that if BSkyB was a partner, and BDB won the licence, there was a distinct possibility DTT could work after all. If it did, Granada would get an inside track on the new distribution opportunities.

Chisholm agreed to put the idea to Green. Carlton took some convincing. Recalls David Chance: 'Carlton had gone from a position where they were driving the whole process, to them being a 50/50 partner with Sky, which helped them because of our [programming] contacts, to then being asked to go to a position where they are going down to a third. And the third partner was going to be one of their [rivals] from ITV.'

BSkyB said that Granada would have to be accommodated, or BSkyB would pull out. Says Chance: 'I think they increasingly came to realise that having Granada in as well really gave the bid enormous strength overall. [It was] better to have a third [of a company] that was hopefully likely to succeed, than not.'

The revised shareholding structure of BDB was formally agreed just after Christmas 1996, and a large team was put to work on the DTT bid at

Carlton's Knightsbridge offices. Carlton concedes that BSkyB's presence was of enormous benefit. BSkyB had already done a phenomenal amount of work on digital TV – developing an electronic programme guide, lining up channels and modelling the financial implications. The team worked so furiously that there was no doubt an application for multiplexes B, C and D would be ready on time. It was quickly agreed that BSkyB would provide three premium channels (Sky Movies, Sky Sports and the Movie Channel), as well as Sky 1 and a truncated version of Sky News. Carlton would bring its Carlton Select channel onto the system, and create two new channels – Carlton Films and Carlton Entertainment. It would also produce a true-crime strand, Public Eye. Granada would offer Granada Plus, its 'gold' channel, and Granada Home Shopping.

Carlton then approached the BBC, and asked whether BDB could have four of the planned Flextech-BBC channels. Negotiations were launched in late December, with the hope of getting Horizon (documentary), Arena (art) BBC One TV (music) and Showcase (later merged UK Gold) onto the DTT platform. With some of the programming strands sharing channels, the total package would provide 12 basic channels and three premium.

But the BBC and Flextech were also talking to the rival DTT bidders. Digital Television Network (DTN), owned by International CableTel, was promising an innovative mix of new channels and interactive services, making creative use of digital's greater flexibility. Its chief executive, Jeremy Thorpe, offered a rich fee to the BBC if it would agree to offer its channels to DTN and to no other bidder. It was bonanza time again at the BBC, as the two rival bidders wooed the public service broadcaster.

In the negotiations between BDB and BBC/Flextech, BSkyB was clearly the dominant force on the BDB side. Recalls one participant: 'At these meetings, there was Ian West [head of digital], David Chance, Nigel Walmsley [Carlton's director for broadcasting], the lawyers and a Granada representative, who I am convinced to this day is actually a tailor's dummy and they pinched it out of the Selfridges' window, because he didn't open his mouth for all the meetings that I was there. And when Nigel Walmsley spoke and answered one of the questions put to him, invariably Ian West or David Chance would turn round to him and say, "Now Nigel, I'm sure you didn't quite mean that did you?" So, they [BSkyB] were pulling the chains.'

Initially, Carlton did not tell anyone at BBC Worldwide about BSkyB's presence in the BDB consortium. But when it looked like BBC-Flextech would succumb to an attractive offer from DTN, Green acted on his own.

He rang Sir Christopher Bland, Chairman of the BBC's Board of Governors, at Broadcasting House, and said he had to meet him. That night, in early January, John Birt was holding a drinks party for media journalists in his office. Green was whisked into a room just next to the party, where at least 50 journalists were chatting with senior BBC executives.

Green told Bland, Birt and Phillis about BSkyB's involvement, and asked for a commitment that the BBC-Flextech channels would swing to his consortium. Phillis was surprised but pleased about Sky's involvement. The BBC itself had already determined that DTT would be an extremely tough proposition if it did not include major sport and Hollywood films. After further negotiation, the BBC and Flextech agreed to put their channels into the BDB bid, in exchange for a high fee (35p per subscriber per month for each channel) and minimum guarantees on subscriber numbers.

On 27 January, the ITC announced that two consortia had bid for the three main commercial licences – BDB and DTN. The City immediately marked up the shares of BSkyB, Carlton and Granada, and declared the bidding war over. Clearly, BDB had the upper hand. The ITC would not make a decision for several months, however, and when it did, the outcome shocked the industry.

Chisholm believed in early 1997 that he had played most of his cards right. The digital satellite preparations were far advanced, and even if there was risk attached to moving subscribers from analogue to digital, BSkyB, with its sport and films, had the edge over potential competitors. He had managed to battle his way into the DTT bid from Carlton. If BDB won, BSkyB would pre-empt the emergence of a well-heeled pay-TV rival. If DTN won, Chisholm was sure he could easily vanquish the under-financed, poorly organised consortium. He also believed that the cable industry was still firmly under foot (he used to joke that the best place for cable is 'six feet under'). Even the creation in October 1996 of a new cable giant, following the merger of Mercury, the telecoms company, with three cable operators to form Cable & Wireless Communications (CWC), did not unduly bother him. Cable was still fixated on the telecoms side of the business, and needed to deal with BSkyB when it came to pay-TV programming. Indeed, there was every chance that CWC would do digital deals with BSkyB, buying programming, including pay-per-view movies, from Isleworth, leaving the cable operator to concentrate on its telephony business.

Chisholm had even found a way of limiting the potentially crippling costs of launching his digital satellite service, through the joint venture he had long been negotiating with BT. When British Interactive Broadcasting was finally unveiled (in May 1997), it would prove to be an innovative answer to the question of financing the digital revolution. The company would be owned 32.5 per cent each by BSkyB and BT, with Midland Bank taking 20 per cent and Japanese electronics manufacturer Matsushita 15 per cent. Together, the partners would invest as much as £400 million subsidising set-top boxes (a million were ordered in May 1997) for the consumer. These decoders would be useable regardless of which distribution platform the consumer preferred (cable, satellite or DTT). BIB would offer home shopping, home banking, computer games and even Internet connections over the television set, linked to a modem and a telephone 'return path'. BSkyB would provide the main TV service, including simulcasts of the existing analogue service, time-shifted programming, new niche channels and pay-per-view movies, concerts and, eventually, even sport.

But Chisholm knew, as did David Chance, that there were some clouds on BSkyB's horizon. It would be incredible if Sky managed to secure the same degree of dominance in the digital age as the two men had helped to achieve in the analogue world. There would be more players, and more money, arrayed against them. Regulators would take a close look at questions of access and technology.

BSkyB could have launched digital as early as 1997. Indeed, Murdoch might have preferred that schedule. 'I didn't think [BIB] was the right approach, although I went along with it,' Murdoch says. 'Everyone said the box would cost £500 each. And so they went off and invented this idea of an interactive company, that would subsidise the boxes. And in that time, the cost of the boxes was coming down. So we really lost a year or more working out the software, and negotiating with BT. We could have been in digital with 200 channels a year ago. I'm not sure there is a big market for interactive services in the UK, at least not initially. I mean, even in the US, there is only a small percentage of homes with PCs that actually use the Internet regularly.'

But Chisholm was cautious about an early digital launch, not least because he saw how damaging the digital migration could be to his existing business. There was, perhaps, another reason why he did not want to see a premature move to digital. By early 1997, Chisholm had more or less made up his mind to leave. He had overseen the incredible expansion of BSkyB, and realised that the growth rates he had achieved were unlikely to be sustainable. Some of his critics within Sky said that he did not do enough to extend the company's market – for instance, by investing in original British programming. Instead, Chisholm concentrated on making as much as he could out of the narrow base (about 24 per cent of homes) that took pay-TV. He wanted to leave on a high note. Why jeopardise one of the country's unquestioned corporate success stories?

Even Murdoch believes more could have been done. 'The idea at BSkyB is to push the profits, and to push the subscription rates. We haven't pushed the penetration, and so our profits have maxed out now. We are about to have the costs of digital, the new Premier League deal. I expect we have plateaued, and that we will see a couple of years of flat earnings.'

But no one could criticise the turnaround Chisholm had achieved. His record, were he to step down, would be spectacular, and those who followed in his footsteps would be handed a serious, perhaps impossible, challenge. Perhaps, in the end, that is what Chisholm wanted. A legacy impossible to match.

CHAPTER 13

End of Blue Sky

The precise moment at which Sam Chisholm decided to bail out may never be adequately pinpointed. He himself talks generally of his desire to leave, and the declining state of his health. It appears, however, that Chisholm finally told Murdoch that he wanted 'to change his role' in December 1996, when he wrote to both Gerry Robinson and to Murdoch.

From Murdoch's perspective, the departure came as no surprise. For the better part of a year, Chisholm had been complaining about his health and about the punishing effects of his hectic schedule, particularly all the air travel. His respiratory disease had been getting worse, and he was in hospital at least once in 1996. 'He had certainly had a few real scares,' says a close colleague. At the unveiling of BSkyB's results in August 1997, Chisholm said that he did not want to embark on the digital launch, only to have to give up half-way because of his health. 'You don't start climbing Mt Everest and then stop on the way,' he said.

'To be fair,' Murdoch says, 'his health really isn't that good. If Sam had flown in here [LA] a few days ago, he couldn't walk from here to the commissary. He cannot work at the current pace.' Murdoch was not all that unhappy to hear that Chisholm was finally ready to go. The relationship had become increasingly prickly, and on several occasions in 1996, Murdoch had actually been enraged by Chisholm's behaviour. For instance, the efforts that year to create a Super League of rugby, led by Chisholm, ended up costing £15 million a year, far more than News Corporation had expected to pay. Chisholm rubbed salt in the wound, declaring that BSkyB, which would broadcast the matches in the UK, would pay nowhere near that. Murdoch himself says: 'What annoyed me, a real irritation, between every News Corporation executive and Sam was when he bought the Rugby League in Australia and then he wanted to lock up England. And having agreed £17 million for Australia, he said that

BSkyB could only afford £6 million in the UK, leaving News Corporation to pick up the rest.' When Murdoch realised that even other executives in the wider group were upset with Chisholm, he began to wonder how long the chief executive was going to last.

Chisholm had already gone to Murdoch some 12 months previously to suggest his favoured succession plan: Chisholm as chairman, David Chance as chief executive and David Elstein as managing director. Murdoch swiftly turned it down. 'At dinner once [Chisholm] said over the third bottle of wine, and I decided to be deaf, that he wanted to be chairman,' Murdoch recalls, 'I wasn't prepared for that.' But it had been made clear, at last, that Chisholm did not expect to continue in his chief executive's role for much longer. Indeed, the previous year, he had relinquished his role as senior executive for Murdoch's non-American global TV interests. Increasingly, he saw BSkyB and not News Corporation as his primary responsibility. Frank Barlow's earlier concerns about the grey areas between Murdoch's own interests and those of BSkyB were ultimately shared by BSkyB's own chief executive.

Murdoch was not inclined to stint Chisholm, who had, after all, helped turn around BSkyB, to Murdoch's own huge benefit. A fair pay-off, at the very least his salary until the end of the two years still to run on Chisholm's contract, would be on offer. Even better, two years' worth of bonus was also available (at Chisholm's controversial 0.5 per cent of pre-tax profits). There can be no doubt that Murdoch had tired of Chisholm; equally, it was clear that he was not about to dump his successful chief executive without due ceremony.

Murdoch was also getting tired of Chisholm's independence, and his increasingly public profile. Says one of Murdoch's closest advisers: 'When Sam said once too many times that he disagreed with the boss, and that he didn't want to do what Rupert wanted, and that he wasn't well, then Rupert was blunt. "If you are really that sick, then maybe we ought to call a halt," Murdoch said. "Maybe we should," Chisholm replied' – surprised, perhaps, that all his hints that he was going to step down next week, next month, next year were suddenly being taken seriously. (Close colleagues say Chisholm first started to talk about stepping down in 1994, when the company was taken public. 'It was something Sam was always saying, so we got used to it,' says a senior BSkyB executive.)

The final details of Chisholm's departure, when it came, were left until Murdoch made one of his frequent budget review trips to London in June 1997. These visits usually sent shivers through the spines of senior management in News International and at BSkyB. Rarely did a Murdoch trip to London not coincide with management changes, strategic shifts or even abrupt departures. (It was at the end of a similar trip to London in 1995 that two long-time Murdoch lieutenants, John Dux and Gus Fischer, both of News International, found themselves out of a job.) The rumour mill started to work as soon as Murdoch arrived at Wapping, headquarters of News International. Some believed he would dump the editors of his two broadsheet titles, *The Times* and *The Sunday Times*. Others thought he was attempting to woo *The Sunday Telegraph*'s Dominic Lawson to join his NI team. In the end, however, it was to be the future of BSkyB that dominated Murdoch's thinking.

For a harried week in mid June, Murdoch went through the budgets of his UK operations. But in spare moments, he was also negotiating with Chisholm. It had already become clear that Chisholm's preferred outcome, the elevation of David Chance to the chief executive's suite, was not going to happen. The reasons were complicated – indeed far more complicated than the subsequent press coverage suggested. Chance was unwilling to take the job if it meant another round of 80-hour weeks, holidays on the hop, and the prospect of seeing BSkyB's hard-won reputation soured by the unknowable costs of going digital. He was also unsure that he would enjoy the task (or that he was even equal to it) without Sam Chisholm. The two had been the perfect double act, and those who worked with both insist that Chance flourished best when he took direction from Chisholm. 'Sam had the ideas, the strategic vision,' says one senior colleague. 'David was brilliant at carrying it out.'

Even so, Chance may have accepted the job had he been truly wooed by Murdoch. Scores of executives have been on the receiving end of a Murdoch charm offensive. 'He knows how to court, how to make you feel terribly important,' recalls one former Murdoch executive. 'When he wants something, he seems to know just what to say to get it.' (The same had been said of Chisholm.)

BSkyB officially said that Chance had been offered the job but turned it down. Chance himself says Murdoch was taken aback by his decision not to take up Chisholm's mantle. It is more likely that Chance never felt truly wanted. He had also suffered a health scare in April 1997, having to take time off from work due to stomach pains (probably an ulcer). His doctor told him the pains would not go away until he slowed down. Was it worth running a health risk just to stay at BSkyB?

'I have known for some time that Sam was not going to carry on forever,'

Chance says. 'I did go through a period when I wasn't well in March and April [1997], which for me brought things to a head. It gave me a bit of time. It may sound hard to believe, [but] when you are fully at work, at 80 hours a week, it is difficult to focus on something like where you are taking your career, things you want to do with your life. When I did have some time off through my stomach illness, that gave me time to reflect. And the illness itself brought things to a head. I thought, hang on: you have been working like a maniac since you started your career, you've done Sky. I was there when it launched, I went through the competition with BSB, the merger, the turnaround, I have been heavily involved in going from zero subscribers to 6.3 million. Was this something I wanted to keep doing for another four or five years, if I was going to take this job?'

Although he will not say it, Chance, says his close friends, was also worried about Murdoch's eventual plans for his daughter. 'Why should David keep the seat warm for Elisabeth?' one senior BSkyB executive said at the time. 'That would be an intolerable position.' Chance privately conceded that Elisabeth's position at Sky was a 'factor' in his decision to step down.

An intriguing further possibility is suggested by a senior Sky insider. 'The fact is, David [Chance] shocked everybody. My take is: how [could David] escape Sam? He has been dominated by that man for years. And he has done very well, and he is very loyal. But if you want to escape the influence, you don't step into his shoes. He wanted to break away. But Sam would be on the phone every second, and it would be difficult for David to escape. Once he gets his head together, and stops feeling the exhaustion, [he can take decisions]. David hasn't been able to put in place his own structure that would allow him to survive. He is constantly compromised, and he is frustrated that he can't do it.'

Even if Murdoch did not woo Chance sufficiently, it is clear he had hoped to keep him on, in some capacity. 'Chance is a valued employee,' says a source close to the Murdoch family, 'and we want to keep him. We don't want to let him go. That was a surprise. That was not the plan. The plan was to get rid of Sam, and keep David. Sam encouraged David to go, [as] it was too dangerous to show that it was David doing all the work.'

Whatever the mixed motives, it appears that not everyone was against the idea of working at BSkyB even if Elisabeth remained. Murdoch soon had his chosen replacement for Chisholm in mind, and the source was an unexpected one. Just six months before the announcement of Chisholm's departure, American-born Mark Booth, 40, had gone from Australia's

Foxtel to Japan, to become chief operating officer of JSkyB, Murdoch's pay-TV joint venture. Before that, he had spent two and a half years trying to salvage Foxtel, Murdoch's pay-TV system in Australia. Booth knew Chisholm well, particularly from the days when the BSkyB chief executive played a larger role in the Murdoch global TV empire. And he had relevant credentials. As a young man, he had helped develop the pay-TV system in the UK, launching and then running MTV Europe on behalf of its then owners, Robert Maxwell and Viacom, the US entertainment giant. Booth had come to England in 1986, with a three-page business plan for MTV Europe, on behalf of the music channel in the US where he had previously worked. For a time, he ran Maxwell's cable interests, although the two fell out (and Booth sought and won a £3-million pay-off, with which he bought and redesigned a house in California).

Booth then went to Australia and soon realised that 'all roads in television in the UK led to Chisholm'. The two men hit it off, and stayed in touch. It was Chisholm who introduced Booth to Murdoch, who, in 1994, asked him to run Foxtel, his Australian pay-TV network. Booth, say those who have worked with him, was a Murdoch supporter, but had stores of reserve, unlike the average American – a little distance on events, a quotient of cynicism, even irony. He may have hugged people in public, and been infamous for his salutation on the phone – 'Hey Big Guy' ('So American', was the comment of one English colleague). But he was dangerous if underestimated, and – in common with all Murdoch executives – able to stay focused and alert even after hours of negotiations. ('No piss pot', was the rather simple judgement of one former colleague.) He was obviously close to the Murdoch children, particularly Lachlan, and got on well with the father. Friends of Chisholm even pointed this out: this was a man who knew the way to the boss's heart: through the offspring. He was bright, even savvy (another unusually un-American trait) and wore his growing power well. He did not ask people to wait upon him, did not require immediate attention and succor. His most un-American trait of all was his slight impatience in conversation. Lulls did not suit well; and interruptions even less so. But he would prove to represent a sea-change at Isleworth. During the curious inter-regnum in the autumn of 1997, before Chisholm left and before Booth was officially in place, Booth visited parts of the company that hadn't seen Chisholm in months. There had been good relations between Sky News and Chisholm's office, and between Chisholm's office and Sky Sports. The rest of the company barely got a look in. Booth told colleagues that things would change. Not everything would now be done in small circles at the top: there would be more openness, more exhultation. Power, thought Booth, was not about ritual humiliation, management by crisis, put-downs, and public wrath. 'Not my style,' he told Sky executives, when asked whether he, too, would rule by Chisholm's curious mixture of cajoling and censure.

Booth may have been new to BSkyB, but he was already well schooled in the Murdoch way of business. 'Being at News Corporation, I got a taste of the News culture,' Booth says. 'It was interesting being American and being put into Australia, when the News Corporation ethos was to take Australians and put them into America and other markets. It was unusual, to say the least. [Being] exposed to the people who had been in the company for 30 years, I had a real insight into how the company had developed from the start.'

Booth was contacted just two weeks before the announcement that Chisholm would step down, and asked if he wanted the job. By that time, Chance was out of the picture, and Murdoch was keen to put in place a man he trusted (and one who could work with Elisabeth without feeling threatened). Booth said yes.

The final deal, which would see Chisholm step down at the end of 1997, with two years' salary and two years' worth of bonuses, was agreed over dinner at the Dorchester Hotel in London on 13 June 1997, attended by Chisholm, Murdoch and legendary public relations guru Sir Tim Bell.

Murdoch insisted that the announcement be handled by Sir Tim personally. He knew that news of Chisholm's departure was likely to have an effect on the shares of BSkyB, then trading at just under £6. It was agreed that only Chisholm's departure would be revealed publicly the following week. The fact that Chance was stepping down too, becoming a consultant to the company, was to be kept a secret, at least for a few weeks. 'The last thing we wanted was a double whammy,' says one source at Lowe Bell Communications, Sir Tim's PR agency.

At the Dorchester meeting, it was agreed that even Sir Tim's own staff – those who would eventually have to handle the fall-out – were to be kept in the dark over the weekend. 'Tim was afraid the Sunday [newspapers] would get wind of the story, and make it more difficult to control the news flow,' an insider recalls.

In the way of British media, however, the news started to circulate, at least at high levels. By early the following week, at least two chief executives at competing media companies knew about Chisholm's departure. *The Evening Standard*'s media correspondent, Lisa O'Carroll, was told by her own sources on Monday that an announcement would be made the following day. She called Chisholm, who extraordinarily agreed to go on the record. 'I will be here tomorrow, next week, next month,' he said, intimating that the rumour was simply untrue. That story ran in late editions of the Monday paper. The next day, Tuesday, 17 June, at 7:30 am, confirmation of Chisholm's departure flashed on screens throughout the City.

Later, a Lowe Bell source would insist: 'Sam didn't lie [to *The Standard*]. What he said was technically true, because he was staying until the end of the year.'

At first, reaction to the news was muted. After an early sharper drop, BSkyB's shares were down just 11p by mid-morning. Most City analysts (and institutional shareholders) had assumed Chisholm would step down at some time. Indeed, many professionals in the City preferred David Chance and Richard Brooke, the finance director, to Chisholm, who was widely seen as prickly. While institutional investors knew the chief executive had done a good job, they did not believe that BSkyB would sink without him.

But through the course of the morning, it became clear that Sir Tim's efforts to keep Chance's departure a secret were doomed to failure. At least two City investment banks (Henderson Crosthwaite and Rothschilds) knew by early Tuesday that Chance would leave at the same time as Chisholm. 'David [Chance] wouldn't play ball with [Bell],' says an insider. 'It would make it look like he had been passed over if there was no mention at all of what he was going to do.' The share price began to react, as the company and Chance scrambled to come up with an agreed response. By the end of the day, the shares were off 22p, and BSkyB finally confirmed that Chance would step down on 31 December 1997, to become a consultant to the company. Chance agreed to work ten days a month for a year, with an additional year on option. 'I am doing it because Sky has a major initiative coming up in digital, and there are a lot of people I have brought into the business, particularly in marketing, distribution and business development, and I do not want to make this transition more difficult,' Chance says. 'I think I can offer something to the company and to the people I feel responsibility to.'

'You know the definition of a consultant, don't you?' asked a senior ITV executive. 'Someone whose hands you want to tie, to ensure they don't go work for the competition.'

But 22p was manageable. It looked, after all, as if the reaction to Chisholm and Chance's departure might be weathered without too much damage to the share price. That was not to be. 'I have never seen a company suffering from such a long run of bad news,' says one senior fund manager, whose company at one time owned more than ten million BSkyB shares. 'Every day seems to bring news of another problem.' The first surprise came just a day after Chisholm's departure was announced, when *The Financial Times* reported that the ITC had asked the partners of British Digital Broadcasting to rethink their shareholding structure. (It was widely believed in journalist circles that Murdoch himself had leaked the story to Ray Snoddy, the FT's media correspondent.) In a letter dated 4 June 1997, the ITC had told BDB that they would not win the licence for digital terrestrial television unless BSkyB was removed from the consortium. But it was not until 18 June that the news was made public. By that time, Chisholm had announced his departure, and Chance's plans to become a consultant were widely known. The effect was to start a rout on the share price from which the company had not recovered as late as the autumn of 1997.

A few days later, *The Financial Times* again broke a damaging story. The Premier League, it reported, was looking at setting up its own channels for the digital age, without recourse to a broadcasting intermediary like BSkyB. Within a week of Chisholm's announcement, £2.5 billion had been wiped off the company's market capitalisation.

Behind the scenes, the ITC had spent several months looking at the two competing bids for the DTT licences. Although the regulator was pleased to see such interest in what had recently been written off as a 'dead-end' technology, there were immediate concerns about BSkyB's position within the consortium. By the calculations of some City analysts, BSkyB would derive 70 per cent of the benefits from BDB, in exchange for just 33 per cent of the equity. This was due to the nature of pay-TV pricing in the wholesale market. As with its supply to cable, BSkyB would provide its premium channels to DTT at a discount-to-DTH price. The overwhelming bulk of the money spent by consumers on BDB would end up in the pockets of BSkyB.

The ITC looked first at the issue of BSkyB's ownership. 'We sought to see whether BSkyB was controlled by News Corporation,' Peter Rogers, the ITC chief executive, explains. 'And the answer [that came back from senior counsel was], "No, it is not". But you know what everyone thinks about who controls it, including Mr Murdoch. Who decides whether Sam Chisholm will go or stay, and who within 24 hours decides who his replacement will be and where will he come from? Was there a beauty parade, were the other shareholders consulted? It must have been done pretty bloody quickly if they were, and you certainly didn't read much about it.'

The ITC then considered whether it was right to have BSkyB as both a buyer of programming (as equity investor in BDB), and as supplier (through the sale of premium programming). Says Rogers: 'Our position was [that], just because someone has a dominant position, you shouldn't stop them trading, but given [their dominance] it wasn't acceptable to us that they should have a position on both sides of the contract – namely as sellers of the product, and [with] a material interest on the decision to purchase those services.'

The ITC took advice from the Office of Fair Trading, Oftel and even, for the first time ever, the director general of Competition in Brussels (DG4). The result was the same in every case: BSkyB's presence in the consortium posed insuperable competition problems. DG4, which was already looking into BSkyB's position in the marketplace, with particular reference to the BIB interactive joint venture, told the ITC that their work was still at an early stage. Their 'inclination,' however, was to believe that 'the award of the licence to the applicant on the terms envisaged would be in breach of community law,' Rogers says.

Internally, there was considerable support for the BDB bid, which was viewed as strong. The ITC executive decided to ask its lawyers whether there was any way the proposal could be salvaged. 'At this stage, we hadn't come to a decision [as to] who would win,' Rogers says. But he and his colleagues wanted to know: 'Are we in a position, legally, to say we will award the licence to BDB but only if BSkyB surrenders its shareholding and Granada [a large BSkyB shareholder] doesn't control it? And the answer came back [from the lawyers], "yes you can", but at greater length and with a commensurately large bill.' The ITC had attached conditions on licence applicants before, but nothing quite on this scale.

The letter from the ITC was received by the BDB partners on 6 June. Murdoch was furious, and suggested the consortium threaten to sue. Murdoch says: '[Going into BDB] was a very bold move from Sam. I never thought we'd get in or that the thing would get through. When we got that letter from the ITC, I was not surprised, although I was annoyed. I wanted to fight it.'

Carlton's Michael Green counselled patience, and suggested the partners demand a meeting with the ITC to discuss the unprecedented request.

The meeting was held on 11 June at the ITC's offices in Foley Street, London. Rogers and Sheila Cassels, the finance director, represented the ITC, while Green and Nigel Walmsley came from Carlton, Chisholm and Chance from BSkyB, and Steve Morrison and Kate Stross from Granada. Four sets of lawyers helped fill the room. The whole meeting would be recorded, and a transcription given to each of the participants.

The lawyer for BSkyB, Herbert Smith's Dorothy Livingstone, immediately demanded copies of the letter from DG4. Rogers looked at his lawyers, and said: 'I don't see a problem with that. Would this afternoon be alright?' The BSkyB side was taken aback. This appeared to suggest that the ITC was completely comfortable with the decision, and would provide any and all information required. There had been no sense of having been railroaded by outside agencies. In the end, this had been an ITC decision.

Later Rogers would say that, even had the ITC disagreed with the advice offered by the outside regulators, they would have had difficulty going against the advice they had received, awarding the licence to BDB with BSkyB still on board. But there had been no question of disagreement. The ITC itself had concluded that BSkyB had to exit, and the shareholders were given one week, until 18 June, to reach an agreement.

As they left the building after the meeting, Chisholm turned to Green and said: 'Well, there can't be too much doubt about that. We could have stopped the meeting after ten minutes.' Green agreed. The ITC had spoken, and there was no way out.

Privately, Green was not altogether displeased. He had not necessarily wanted partners in the first place. Even better from his point of view, the ITC was insisting that BSkyB provide its premium programming to BDB even after leaving the consortium. The regulator did not wish to see Sky refusing to supply the new platform, to concentrate on its own digital satellite plans. Granada was bemused: it had been a late-comer, and had little involvement in the bid preparations. The ITC had insisted that Granada, as an 11 per cent shareholder in BSkyB, could not control BDB, so any restructured shareholding agreement would have to favour Carlton or be deadlocked 50/50.

But Green was secretly worried that BSkyB might still cause him difficulty if the partners could not agree on adequate compensation for the loss BSkyB was forced to endure. If a deal could not be reached amicably, Green would be in danger of missing out on DTT. (Quite certainly the ITC was prepared to give the licence to DTN if the BDB side failed to meet the ownership conditions.) He subsequently consulted his lawyers, to see whether he could oblige BSkyB to come to an agreement. Recalls Green: 'I did have a jeopardy clause in the shareholders' agreement, which said that if any shareholder put the licence at risk, then the others could buy out the shares and force a sale.' It didn't come to that, and nor did Green want it to. 'Sky had really helped us,' he says. 'As soon as they joined us, they put excellent people on the business plan, and their contribution was very important. We learned all about roll-outs and take-up percentages and pull-throughs and learned about the technology.'

After the meeting at the ITC, the partners returned to Carlton's Knightsbridge offices. 'We sat around a big table, and then someone said: "Who's going to phone Rupert",' Green remembers. 'And Sam said, "Here, why don't you phone him", as if to warn me that everything people say about him is true. And I said, "I don't mind!".' In the end, Chisholm made the call.

'There was then this Mexican stand-off [between BSkyB and Carlton]' Green says. Granada, as a BSkyB shareholder, did not take part in the subsequent negotiations. BSkyB originally asked for an astonishing £500 million for its shares in BDB, and the right to buy £500 million worth of Carlton shares at the then-current price. 'They were so convinced that BDB was going to make money, they wanted to share in its good fortune,' Green says. (Several City analysts had by then produced valuations for BDB, ranging as high as £1.5 billion.)

Green refused to put a figure on the table, but called the opening shot from BSkyB 'completely unacceptable'. As the days went by, the tone of the negotiations became more brittle, with Chisholm insistent that Green make an offer. Within a few days, Chisholm's demand had declined to £200 million. Green told him it might as well have been £2 billion: 'He really wasn't even in the ball-park.' Chisholm had also attached conditions, including the requirement that BDB float within three years. Cheekily, Chisholm also wanted BDB to take space in the old Marcopolo building, headquarters of BSB, the lease to which was still on BSkyB's books. Green finally offered £25 million. Chisholm said, 'Look, you have to put another figure on the table.' Green said, 'Alright, £25 million plus one pound.' Chisholm exploded, and the atmosphere grew tense. Green cleared his diary, as the deadline loomed. Green had managed to get two days' grace from the ITC, and a final answer was due 'by the close of business' on 20 June, a Friday. The negotiations went right to the wire. Green told Chisholm they had to give the ITC an answer by 5:00 pm (although it had been agreed between Green and Peter Rogers that an ITC staff member would wait until at least 6:00 pm, maybe even later). A deal was finally reached shortly before 5:00 pm that Friday. BSkyB would receive £75 million in exchange for its shares (although for tax purposes, some of this would be considered pre-payment on the programming BSkyB was to supply to BDB).

The £75 million proved useful to BSkyB, when it unveiled its results in August 1997 for the 1996–97 financial year. Included in the operating profits was £14 million of the BDB money, enough to push the headline profit figure to £314 million. Without the BDB injection, BSkyB might have disappointed the market with lower than expected earnings.

BSkyB put a brave face on its exit from BDB. And, indeed the departure did not seem all that damaging. Sky continued to have a seven-year programme supply arrangement (provided regulators in Brussels approved), but no longer had to put up its share of the £300 million in peak funding required to get the DTT platform up and running.

On 24 June, the ITC made its formal announcement. BDB had won all three commercial licences for multiplexes B, C and D. BSkyB had agreed to exit, and the award was conditioned on a supply arrangement between BDB and BSkyB. Oftel's regulator, Don Cruickshank, was livid, having advised against giving the award to BDB. He still harboured concerns about the role BSkyB would play in the supply of programming to the new platform. But the ITC had made its decision.

The summer of 1997 saw BSkyB shares float downward, as the market began to realise the blue-sky days could well be over. The regulatory challenges, and the prospect of financially robust rivals in pay-TV, combined to unsettle investors. There was concern that the fresh challenges had come just as BSkyB lost its two key executives. But there was a growing view that the management changes might have been inevitable, and not altogether negative, despite the fact that the transition was likely to be awkward.

The strong growth of BSkyB's start-up phase was now in the past, and a new kind of management was needed for a new set of challenges. BSkyB was no longer the outsider, the outlaw, the upstart, operating at the edge of what was acceptable. The big money always accrues to those who break the rules, and create a fresh market. Eventually, the competition catches up, and the management test shifts. BSkyB was on its way to being a 'normal' company, and Chisholm's style was no longer appropriate.

But Chisholm wanted desperately to be remembered, and to have his accomplishments recognised. Who else had dominated an industry on two continents, as he had done? Who else had seen off rivals, legislators, regulators?

The months over the summer were arguably BSkyB's oddest period in recent memory, with the Murdoch and Chisholm camps both apparently spinning their version of events for the consumption of the British press and the City. This was not what you would expect from a PLC (and certainly not a FTSE-100 company). Newspapers were filled with a wholly British mixture of fact and fiction, leavened by unattributed quotes. The suggestion was of a civil war, with Murdoch and his daughter on one side, and an increasingly bitter Sam Chisholm on the other. *The Sunday Telegraph* of 22 June 1997 was typical. Under the headline *Dynasty: As Sam Chisholm Quits BSkyB and Elisabeth Murdoch Waits in the Wings*, the newspaper's business media correspondent Amanda Hall described a company in near crisis, with tensions building to epic proportions. Most of the coverage was aimed at intimating that Elisabeth Murdoch was a chief reason for the early departure of Sam Chisholm. It did little to dampen such speculation that senior Sky executives (perhaps even Chisholm himself) had been talking to City analysts and journalists in the days after the news of the executive changes. Quote after quote appeared in the newspapers: 'David Chance didn't want to be the meat in the sandwich' (between Murdoch and his daughter); why would David Chance want 'to keep the seat warm for Elisabeth?'.

The effect was to underscore just how much bad blood might have existed between the boss's daughter and the chief executive. Stories of how Chisholm would tell staff not to co-operate with her were told with greater frequency, as the days ticked away to Chisholm's retirement from the chief executive's suite. (He would stay on in London, however, having agreed to take a senior role in the preparations for the Millennium celebrations. He would, it was also assumed, stay on the BSkyB board.)

Even Murdoch himself appeared to weigh in, telling his newspaper, *The Sunday Times*, that BSkyB shares had been grossly overpriced, and that the new management would be every bit as good as the old. A source close to Chisholm was bitter: 'Murdoch hated Sky, he hated its success. He went out of his way to talk the company down. He hated the fact that BSkyB was more successful than News Corporation; he just couldn't stand it.

There ought to have been good news to tell. Although BSkyB had been kicked out of the BDB consortium, it still had a programming supply agreement with the winners of the DTT licence. But concerns over the digital challenge, the issue of succession, and management uncertainty in the wake of the departure of both Chisholm and Chance conspired to ruin any likelihood of a share-price rally. The timing of the stock market rout could not have been worse. Several middle ranking BSkyB executives were about to be able to exercise options over BSkyB shares, only to find that their value had been vastly reduced. Rumours began to fly of a management exodus.

It was, in any event, a defining moment in BSkyB's history. Sam Chisholm was stepping down, and Isleworth would never again be the same. He was leaving, too, just as BSkyB entered a crucial new phase as a major company. It was having to prepare for the critical launch to digital, and it would need to do so in a way that did not jeopardise its core analogue business. It was facing increased pressure from rivals – from BDB, which would launch a competing platform in digital television within a year ('We will break the monopoly,' Michael Green promised in August 1997) and from cable, which vowed to reject the price increases BSkyB had pushed through in September 1997. Cable operators were flexing their muscles, insisting that they would not, any longer, meekly submit to the *diktat* of Isleworth. Rights holders were muttering about retaining more of the value of their franchises: the Premier League, for instance, was holding out for money to allow BDB access to the live matches BSkyB was offering on satellite and cable. Meanwhile, the government announced in late summer of 1997 that it would review the listed events for sports, casting into further doubt the ability of broadcasters such as BSkyB to secure rights to major sporting events in the future. There were pressures from all sides, and the new management had yet to be securely bedded down. Where would Sky go from here? Wherever it was, it would be without Sam Chisholm.

In the end, it was clear that Elisabeth Murdoch would not any time soon take over BSkyB. Equally clear, however, was the fact that Chisholm's reign at BSkyB would not have been extended whatever the circumstances of his health. It was the end of an era, one which Chisholm typified. In the more mature phase toward which BSkyB was moving. Nobody needed a buccaneer.

CONCLUSION

How Sky High?

In the eight years since Sky launched in 1989, British broadcasting had been completely transformed. Consider the evidence: more channels, a commercially minded BBC, a consolidated ITV sector, a new terrestrial channel (Channel 5), a two-million strong cable subscription base, and the prospect of 200 channels of digital TV just around the corner. 'We are living through the last few months of the old world of broadcasting,' said a senior Sky executive in the autumn of 1997. 'Now the adventure begins.'

Throughout it all, BSkyB had been instrumental in creating the conditions for the multi-channel revolution. The early days of struggle, with the launch of two competing satellite services, had been succeeded by a halcyon period of double-digit growth for pay-TV – the prize awarded any pioneer willing to break the rules, recast the agenda, rework the tired formulas. It was only in the very last months of 1997 that the stellar run appeared to be coming to a pause (not to an end, of course: but BSkyB was about to take a breather).

The changes had been wrought, however, and the traditional broadcasting sector would never again be the same. Some even feared that the British industry, inexorably, would go the way of the US, toward declining standards and an erosion of the power of the mainstream broadcasters.

It is a mistake, however, to apply too slavishly the American broadcasting model to Britain. The UK, despite the privatisations of the Thatcher era, had long had a solid commitment to public service broadcasting – a commitment, moreover, that had spilled over into the commercial sector, in the form of strict public service requirements applied to the ITV and Channel 4 franchises, for example. The US experience was influenced, above all, by the competition among network and multi-channel players, in an open advertising environment. In the UK, two of the mainstream channels (BBC1 and BBC2) did not take advertising, and until 1997 there were only two mainstream terrestrial channels vying for the advertising pound, and only one of these, ITV, attracted mass audiences.

All the same, the introduction of multi-channel television had and would have a huge effect on the fortunes of the terrestrial channels. Their share of total audience was poised to decline, as the number of channels rose. It was against this backdrop that the fundamental influence of BSkyB on British broadcasting had to be judged. In the seven years since BSB and Sky merged, the UK broadcasting sector was forced to respond to the competitive threat of multi-channel TV. The BBC restructured itself, in a process that some within called a state of 'permanent revolution'. It cut costs, recast its relationship to the independent production sector, and stepped up efforts to generate revenue from commercial activities. Meanwhile, BBC went through a radical round of consolidation. The wave of mergers since 1996, ignited by the liberalised ownership rules under the new Broadcasting Act, saw Carlton buy Westcountry, Scottish snap up Grampian, Granada swallow Yorkshire–Tyne Tees and United News & Media annexe HTV. By the autumn of 1997, there were just four major ITV groups, controlling virtually the entire Channel 3 system. Carlton had London in the week, Central and Westcountry; United News & Media controlled Meridian, Anglia and HTV; Granada had the North (Granada, Yorkshire and Tyne-Tees), as well as London Weekend Television; and Scottish held both franchises north of the border, and was eyeing Ulster TV. The shareholding register of GMTV, the morning licencee, was already dominated by existing broadcasters. The only independents left in the entire system were Border TV and Channel Television.

The ITV companies had also been offered the opportunity of renewing their licences early, in recognition that the huge taxes paid by the sector might have to be reduced if the competitive pressures proved unexpectedly great. It was a measure of Sky's success that some ITV operators, notably Ward Thomas at Yorkshire–Tyne Tees and Clive Hollick at United News & Media, saw BSkyB's light taxation burden as a chief target in their own campaign to create a 'level playing field' when it came to taxing broadcasters.

The consolidation of ITV came against a backdrop of increasing competition (from cable and satellite and the new Channel 5). ITV's own internal studies suggested the system was heading for decline, with its total commercial audience share dropping to perhaps 54 per cent from 68 per cent between 1996 and 2003. The main ITV players responded, in the main, by buying each other and investing in pay-TV, to secure an additional source of revenue. United News & Media agreed to support one of the licences for digital terrestrial television, in partnership with NTL, the cable and transmission company, and S4C, the Welsh Channel 4. Carlton and Granada, of course, backed British Digital Broadcasting, winners of the main commercial licences for DTT. The BBC's response, in addition to its own internal restructuring, was to form the private-sector venture with Flextech, and to develop new programming strands for digital TV.

The radical changes in Britain were driven, in the main, by technology and consumer demand for greater television choice. But there can be no doubt that the success of BSkyB was the proximate cause for the radical realignment witnessed in the broadcasting sector. So successful had the company been, indeed, that the changes had yet to be fully understood. It seemed likely that the regulatory regime would be altered further to account for the new landscape. At the very least, the strict public-service demands placed on commercial broadcasters looked set to be eroded out of recognition. It was simply no longer possible to run British broadcasting as if we were still in 1985. The mainstream broadcasters themselves, not least the commercially challenged ITV companies, could not hope to compete with Sky while they were saddled with strict programming codes, public service requirements, and sporadic, interventionist meddling from the ITC. Meanwhile, the threat of the Internet, of digital services, of Microsoft and 'PCTVs' was palpable in 1997, and the fear that ITV could not cope was growing.

Still, Sky itself was not immune to the changes. If BSkyB was the undoubted beneficiary of the multi-channel revolution (and indeed was primarily responsible for fomenting it), there was no guarantee the company could retain its grip. The point has been made that BSkyB's success had as much to do with its testing of the boundaries, its willingness to break rules, as with its claim on technology and its programming decisions. BSkyB was, as we have seen, a squatter, occupying space others had barely noticed. But eventually the bailiffs are sent in, when the squat becomes too crowded. The terrestrial broadcasters themselves were poised in 1997 to provide real competition in pay-TV, perhaps for the first time. The Carlton–Granada combine was one source of rivalry. But even the highly fragmented cable industry showed signs, finally, of verve and life. The first sign had come with the consolidation in 1996, when Cable & Wireless subsidiary Mercury was merged with three cable companies – Videotron, Nynex, and Bell Cablemedia to form Cable & Wireless Communications (CWC). But even the other players in the industry, notably Telewest, the former leader, and General Cable, appeared ready to stand up to BSkyB on a number of fronts. (Although Telewest was compromised by its shareholding – including TCI, the US cable operator that, here and there, co-operated with Murdoch. It was not obvious that Telewest would be allowed to threaten Sky if, by doing so, it risked upsetting other, global alliances being forged by the parent companies.)

In late 1997, the cable operators were still working on an aggressive plan to offer a pay-per-view movie service, ideally suited for the digital age. While CWC (and maybe even Telewest, depending on the view of TCI) looked likely to do a deal with BSkyB, to jointly offer Sky Box Office rather than separately back a cable version of pay-per-view, the other companies appeared committed to mounting real competition to Sky on movies in the digital age. Moreover, there was strong resistance to BSkyB's price increase in 1997, and its effort to oblige cable operators to accept the new National Geographic channel. Several cable companies indicated they might even drop Sky News in favour of the BBC's 24-hour rolling news service, in a direct threat to Sky's business – a prospect that frightened the BBC, since it knew that BSkyB would have a clear recourse to competition law if a public-sector broadcaster, using taxpayers' money, upset a commercial operation like Sky News. The cable industry had long been advised by outsiders, including the City, that it ought to take advantage of an ineluctable truth. By 1995, cable was delivering far more subscribers for Sky than satellite. In 1996, the figure had risen to 60 per cent. That meant that for every new Sky subscriber on satellite, cable was delivering two. Cable, not satellite, was the more robust source of growth. This was not great news for BSkyB, as satellite subscribers spent more per household on premium services than did cable homes. But it did mean that Sky needed cable.

Rivals were just one of the two 'R's in BSkyB's way in 1997. The other was regulation. A renewed attack on BSkyB's position looked likely on three fronts: the court action on the Premier League contract (on the grounds it was anti-competitive); the ITC's investigation into the bundling of channels; and the Labour government's threat to extend the number of sporting events that had to run on terrestrial television.

Of the main threats, unbundling looked most likely to cause problems for the pay-TV business. The ITC was looking at the prospect of insisting that retail customers (and the wholesale buyers of programming, like cable operators and, in the future, digital terrestrial television) would be able to take the channels they wanted, without having to take a number of other services. The issue was contentious: cable operators would dearly love the opportunity to supply tailored packages to their customers, dropping unpopular channels and focusing on the obvious winners. Test marketing of small basic tiers in some franchises in 1996 and 1997 showed that penetration soared when more flexible packages were introduced. BSkyB, not surprisingly, was against the unbundling principle. Explains David Chance: 'If you unbundle, you will make the strong channels stronger and the weak channels disappear. [Of] the weak channels, some of them have taken the time – the lifeline through the bundled package – to become reasonably successful channels. UK Living was not much good on day one; now it is better. Nickelodeon is now stronger: if it had had to be unbundled from the start, it may never have made it. The ITC might say, "It should be the survival of the fittest, strong channels shouldn't subsidise weak channels". I'm not sure that's right. One of the things about choice is that you have to give the Nicks and the UK Livings the time to find their feet, which they've done.'

Chance also points out the obvious. If the unbundling exercise was meant to curb BSkyB's dominance in the pay-TV market, it was unlikely to meet its objective. 'From Sky's point of view, it has strong premium channels, and strong basic channels, [like] Sky 1 or Sky News. Unbundling almost strengthens the position of Sky in the marketplace.'

The case in the Restrictive Practices Court was perhaps less of a worry for the main players. It seemed to most industry observers unlikely that the Court would insist that all broadcast rights contracts be negotiated team by team: the implications would be too enormous for the scores of sports that operated in leagues and other associations. There was a real threat, however, that the Labour government would seek to extend the list of protected events, or at the very least to insist that highlight rights be made available on an unbundled basis, separately from the live rights. That could harm BSkyB's lucrative deals with the Premier League, the Ryder Cup of golf, and many boxing organisations.

In the end, there was perhaps little difference between these threats, and those that had always confronted BSkyB. Indeed, Mark Booth did not appear unduly bothered about the regulatory challenges. 'Sky is a lightning rod, and a catalyst for change,' he says. 'Where you are the reason for the change, it raises ire in some and applause in others. It evokes strong emotions. Change in our view is fundamentally good. Instead of having just a few scheduling executives, the creatives in this country will have a huge market. We are approaching the era of the creative revolution.'

As we have seen, regulators and rivals made constant appearances in the history of Sky. But there was to be one crucial difference after 1997: there would be no Sam Chisholm.

Richard Dunn has this to say about the legacy of BSkyB's combative chief executive. 'He was the right person at the right time for the really critical relationships – whether with the authorities, the studios, the cable companies, the rights owners, and even regulators. You needed a tough arrogant bastard who wasn't particularly bothered by detail, who just would go in and with presence bully people or cajole people or even charm people.'

Just as BSkyB was poised to launch its digital service, and confront renewed opposition on the regulatory front, could the new management cope? Booth believed that the digital revolution was far more an opportunity than a challenge. 'If you don't [launch digital], you are in trouble,' he says. 'For us, it's a strategic no-brainer. The alternative would be to risk the whole business. This gives a radical enhancement to the TV experience. It gives you a navigator, and you can take a lot more control. It's a great enhancement of pleasure to the idea of watching television. You are going to see specialised channels, and the economics of delivering that is going to be substantially changed. If you like yachting or home improvement, you are going to get that. The economics of delivering that to everyone are not attractive in analogue. But in the digital world, you can economically deliver the product if it's an idea people want.'

Whether or not the new management succeeds, the departure of Chisholm and Chance was seen by nearly everyone in the media sector to be a watershed. Says Bob Phillis, until November 1997 chief executive of BBC Worldwide: 'Would BSkyB have succeeded without Sam Chisholm and David Chance? I doubt it. It's always a seminal moment when those that have given birth to the baby and taken it up to sort of adolescence, [decide to leave].'

By late 1997, the new team, led by chief executive-designate Booth, had already started to make its own views known. According to Sky insiders, closely identified with Elisabeth Murdoch, there was a clear strategy to follow. BSkyB's excellent profit results in the 1990s were obviously much appreciated by the Murdoch camp. But they came, perhaps, at the expense of future growth. Under Chisholm, BSkyB had concentrated on sport above all, creating a close identification between Sky Television and its excellent coverage of the national game, football. The movie services, Sky

Movies, Sky Movies Gold and the Movie Channel, were left unattended, the Murdoch team believed. No effort had been made to improve the movie scheduling ('tired' said one colleague of Elisabeth Murdoch), and to add features such as highlight shows, interviews, and other original material. 'We should do for movies what we have done for sport,' says another Murdoch confidante.

Says Booth: 'There is scope for improvement in any company. We must build on our great strengths, and accelerate areas where we may not have been as successful. Sky is amazing. [But] the programming, the branding, and the marketing can all be improved. There is a predominant message that consumers have that it is all about sport. Clearly there is a lot of tremendous value there. So is there a big opportunity to expand the message. It is not just a tremendous place to watch sports. We need to look at the movie channels. We don't have every sport. But we have all the key studios.'

At the same time, BSkyB spent very little money on original programming, and did not put huge resources behind its Sky 1 flagship general entertainment channel. That was the natural result, of course, of the entire strategy under Chisholm. By the mid-1990s, the chief aim was not to extend the subscriber base (satellite dish sales were starting to fall away, and cable was still in the early phases of network construction) but to maximise revenues from existing subscribers. From just 24 per cent of British homes, BSkyB was reaping huge profits.

'A yardstick is revenue per home, and Sky has been the world leader on the pay to basic ratios,' says Booth. 'But the critical yardstick is penetration of homes passed. That's the opportunity. If we take the question that it is about taking the 25 per cent of homes to £100 a month, then you'll just get a lot of unsatisfied, angry customers, and the business would shrink. We'd be better off going now to the nonbelievers and turning them into believers. We have to find new ways of touching people. It's undeniable, growth is slowing. It has to be reinvigorated.'

Chisholm's lack of attention to the issue of original programming was one of the sore points between the chief executive and the Murdoch camp. Says one Murdoch insider of the Chisholm years: 'There are a number of challenges that never got done, like we should not be sitting here for ten years without having developed any original programming.'

That is a bit unfair, perhaps, as the managers of BSkyB in the early 1990s were as worried about generating cash as about creating a viable business for the millennium. Booth and his team inherited something of incalculable worth to any manager: cash. What can't you do with cash?

Original programming was considered a priority by Elisabeth Murdoch. 'We need to be rights holders and not just rights leasors. Right now we rent programming and if we make it work, and we usually do because of our talent for marketing, the next time you go back, it's tripled in price. So we very much recognise that we need to participate in the food chain. We actively are looking at all kinds of ways. [We could] take an equity stake in an independent production house. One of the issues is that all broadcaster have to meet the 25 per cent outside source rules, and so we would want to participate in the contracts that a producer might have with other broadcasters. But 25 per cent would probably give us the stature. What you are really buying is talent, not the physical ability to make programmes, the talent is in the writing, producing, directing, not the overhead of the studios. What is compelling is the people who make the production assets.'

Elisabeth Murdoch and her team intended to revamp Sky 1, the general entertainment channel. 'The rescheduling [in 1996] was important yet only one part of a longer term strategy,' she says. 'Which is that we have to have original programming. That obviously takes longer than rescheduling.'

Mark Booth echoes those sentiments. 'Sky 1 is one of the hidden jewels of the company. The value that is going to come from the programming side is going to be significant. There is still a monopoly in the UK with ITV. We take £180 million [in advertising] out of the market now, and that's just a fraction of what we will take out when we have increased distribution, regardless of the platform. Part of our mantra will be "Sky in every home". The next part is that we will get a disproportionate part of the benefit of the distribution. That's a big part of the upside. The analogue message is getting tired. That can be re-energised, and we hope to do that.'

An attempt by BSkyB to turn Sky 1 into a mass-market channel would not have surprised anyone in the industry, although it might have frightened a few. Says John Birt, director-general of the BBC: 'This surprising thing about the British television market is that we only have one mass audience, advertiser supported channel [ITV], which is very unusual. Most other countries have more than one. So, a strategic prize is open to somebody who can create a second major network in the UK and beyond that perhaps a third. And who are the candidates? Well they can only really be Channel 5 and Sky 1. [But] if you really want to match ITV's broad programme strategy, you'd have to make a very major investment indeed in original UK production.'

Until the late 1990s, the fact that Sky 1 was only available in 25 per cent of homes had been a limiting factor. But with the launch of digital terrestrial television, which was meant, within ten years, to replace the analogue system, Sky 1 would potentially address most of the terrestrial audience in the UK.

But the digital revolution would provide far greater tests than the success or failure of Sky 1. The hugely increased capacity of digital provided the chance for broadcasters to give viewers a far greater range of programmes, and a number of innovative, interactive services. Would these find favour? It was not clear, in late 1997, whether British TV consumers had any particular interest in pay-per-view events or in home shopping and home banking. But BSkyB's control of premium programming (sport and film) well into the next century would ensure that the company continued to tower above the competition. It might not be able to retain its near-monopoly (no monopoly can last forever) but BSkyB would be first among equals in pay-TV. A few years of sluggish growth were likely, as the digital investment ate into profits. However, after this 'digital pause', the rise was likely to continue. The time when the company would post its first £1 billion-plus profits was not too many years away.

However well the management in London coped, the future of BSkyB looked likely to be much more closely aligned with Rupert Murdoch's own global view than the more narrow pre-occupations of the UK. The future of BSkyB, post-Chisholm, would have more to do with Murdoch's international strategy than with the expectations and strategy of the British offshoot. It was not clear, in late 1997, whether Murdoch could replicate his UK success anywhere else in the world; the conditions that obtained in the UK weren't present elsewhere. But suddenly the UK, with Elisabeth Murdoch in place and a new chief executive hand-picked by News Corporation, looked central to Murdoch's global TV aspirations.

Digital was at the heart of the Murdoch strategy. He believed that the huge capacity of digital television would drive the marketplace, creating fresh opportunities for programmers, service providers, rights holders and for the broadcaster itself. People would surely be willing to pay for the extra choice, he thought. That is what the experience of BSkyB had proven. Also key to Murdoch's vision was the virtuous circle of making programmes and broadcasting them on one's own networks, both terrestrial and pay. That would mean a commitment to original programming, and close ties among the various TV offshoots in the Murdoch empire – Fox, Foxtel, Star TV, ISkyB, Primestar and BSkyB.

The late 1990s, as the digital revolution took hold, would be uncertain for BSkyB, and it appeared clear that Chisholm and Chance had left on a high tide. Says Bob Phillis, of the BBC, 'Sam and David's retirement marks a turning point. It doesn't mean it's the end, it doesn't mean that it's all downhill from here. Quite the reverse. It'll obviously be for Rupert and Mark Booth and Elisabeth and whoever else goes in there to take it forward to the next stage. But it's changed. It'll never be the same again.'

Booth, who has to step into some large shoes, had this to say: 'Cultures of companies don't change easily. I will pay a lot of attention to that, to taking the best that Sky has done, and change the things it has not done so well.' His face collapses into a large smile, as he concedes the Chisholm legacy: 'One of the first things I am going to have to do is take a two by four and whack somebody, to prove that things aren't going to be so radically different.'

No one is likely again to match Sam Chisholm's mix of bravura, bluff and bluster, nor his uncanny ability to seize the prize. But BSkyB will survive his departure, and is even likely to thrive. The company now awaits as fresh a wind as the one that blew in with Chisholm in 1990. That new approach won't feel like Chisholm's and nor should it. The challenges are altogether different, and require different skills. BSkyB's buccaneering days are over, and a certain maturity is taking hold. The market that Sky itself helped create is a more crowded, competitive place. As Chisholm himself said, about the team he replaced seven years ago: 'You need degrees of management for degrees of company. They [now] need someone to carry the ball the next 100 yards.' Murdoch will not be grieving too long over Sam Chisholm's departure. Elisabeth, too, will be pleased to see him go. But mark it true, British broadcasting will be a less interesting business, and life at Isleworth less exasperatingly vivid, without him, I promise you.

INDEX